IN THE PALACE OF FLOWERS

FLOWERS

Victoria Princewill

Abuja – London

First published in 2021 by Cassava Republic Press

Abuja – London

Copyright © Victoria Princewill

A CIP catalogue record for this book is available from the National Library of Nigeria and the British Library.

ISBN 978-1-911115-75-5

eISBN 978-1-911115-76-2

Editor: Layla Mohamed

Copy editor: Ibukun Omojola

Proof-reader: Uthman Adejumo

Cover design: Alex Kirby

Book design: Folukemi Iyiola

Marketing & Publicity: Niki Igbaroola, Kofo Okunola, Fiona Brownlee

Printed and bound in Great Britain by Bell & Bain Ltd., Glasgow

Distributed in Nigeria by Yellow Danfo

Worldwide distribution by Ingram Publisher Services International

Stay up to date with the latest books, special offers
and exclusive content with our monthly newsletter.
Sign up on our website:
www.cassavarepublic.biz

Twitter: @cassavarepublic
Instagram: @cassavarepublicpress
Facebook: facebook.com/CassavaRepublic
Hashtag: #PalaceofFlowers #ReadCassava

1

We shall be forgotten, Jamīla realised, watching the funeral rites with empty eyes.

She usually enjoyed the funerals. The slaves heard the tragedies first; gossip slid through walls and under doors. Distress seeped into antechambers: the news, like the life itself, unspooled quickly. In the first house where she had served, Jamīla would rise early to hear the recitation of the Qur'an from the roof. Back then, the older slaves would turn a blind eye whilst she darted into an empty bedroom to peer through a window, scanning the roofs of the houses nearby to see where the imam was reciting from. He would stand on the roof that housed the deceased, the sound of his announcement a bell to her mind. She had always enjoyed the sobriety. A life had been lost, and that weight meant something. Precisely what, she remained unsure of.

It was January; almost the end of the year. Death seemed fitting, as an end to a cycle. Still, Jamīla did not want to be there but whilst women were forbidden from the service, any Abyssinian slave who had served him had to be present. And so Jamīla stood amongst them, at the back of the mosque. He had been one of the noblemen free to enter the harem, a physician for the Shāh and his wives. Jamīla, recalling his slithery presence, suspected the slaves' attendance was required to bolster the numbers.

The imam's monotone never wavered. Jamīla was bored. She stared up at the curved dome of the mosque's ceiling: thousands of minuscule sapphire tiles adorned it. Mingled with dazzling glass, the tiles dripped from the walls. She sought to count them, but, glancing around, saw hers was the only upturned face. She stared at the floor. She traced a silk embroidered shoe over the marble, wishing she could stand on the slivers of exposed stone. She looked up. Every slave in the mosque faced forward; there was nary a shuffle nor a sigh. She lowered her shoulders and lifted her chin, trying to practise solemnity. The faces of the nobles were haggard and drawn. The prince – her prince – her old playmate behind closed doors in the harem quarters, who used to sneak smiles at her through crowds – he too was facing forward, his expression indistinguishable from the rest. For a moment, she wondered how he might behave at her funeral.

But, of course, she would not have one. Not long ago, a slave had died. He was thrown into an unmarked spot in one of the gardens where a glut of bodies lay. Jamīla could not help but see them in her mind, jumbled together: anonymous, rotting, mute. Nobody was notified. Wherever his birth family was, they remained ignorant – filled with faint hope, perhaps or muted despair.

With the ceremony completed, the slaves headed back to Golestan Palace at a brisk pace. The snow had arrived late this year, and it was tentative at first; the falling flakes appeared to falter, so much she barely felt them as they trembled onto her cheek. She brushed her face as she walked, the velvety crunch beneath her floral mules a world away from the soft clouds wrapped snugly around a gable of one of the palace roofs. Jamīla had lived there for only four years, yet without question she felt it was home. The sprawling complex of gorgeous buildings formed a medley of colours as indigo arabesque tiles, stone carvings in flaxen gold and emerald muqarnas, undimmed by winter's first frost, captured the eye. Returning here would always give her pause, even as men sighed, stooped over, brows studded with sweat, working on the Shāh's latest renovation. But it was not hers, any more than it was theirs, and as she tramped through the geometric gardens, shivering under her thin čhādor in the crisp evening air, she felt a sudden thrill at the realisation. On darker days, she had called herself fortunate. She would linger by the precision-cut flowerbeds. *This is your home.* She would repeat the words until the pain of her bruises began to fade. This is your home. Now she felt foolish. Was this her home? Did it matter? *The earth is the earth is the earth,* as her mother liked to say. Jamīla's lips trembled. She continued walking.

Jamīla was the last slave to return to the harem from the mosque, and as she hurried through the passageway to her mistress's apartment, she began to feel a touch of unease. The harem was large, built to house and entertain over 80 wives and concubines, with communal entertaining spaces, like the royal coffeehouse and the royal theatre. The wives all had private residences, most in adjoining interior courtyards, and one had to cross the length of the harem, past the various pantries, salons, and harem offices to get to them. Jamīla's mistress, Chehra Khaanoum, like many of the newer poorer and younger wives, had an apartment even further out, far from the communal spaces. As such, Jamīla was always late getting to her, regardless of her intentions or how she tried to be on time. Chehra used to be more forgiving, but in recent months, her patience had worn thin. There was always something that gave Chehra reason to complain. Jamīla would often hear Chehra's plaintive cries as she snapped at Gul, the most senior slave in her retinue, over the size of her room. When Jamīla first arrived, it was Gul who told her that the wives were housed according to their status. They all lived in grand apartments, plush rooms with high ceilings and gilded furniture, adjacent to the main harem. Chehra's five rooms, though a squeeze for her slaves, were more than sufficient to Jamīla. As she pushed open the door to the apartment, she bumped into Gul standing on the other side. 'Jamīla!' she said, sighing and rolling her eyes.

'I am here!' Jamīla was looking past Gul.

'She is in her room,' Gul said, a laugh in her voice. A robust slave, whose wrinkled smiles revealed a warmer woman than her frame would assume, she ran Chehra Khaanoum's household with benign efficiency. She had little patience for Jamīla's tardiness but thought it more prudent to mask it than openly scold her for it. 'You should know, Jamīla, she is angry.'

'Might I ask why?'

'Abimelech requested you.'

'Abimelech?' A smile spread across her face.

'On behalf of the prince,' Gul said. 'Prince Nosrat summoned you.'

'Then I must go!' Jamīla turned back to the door.

Gul shook her head, grimacing. 'Chehra Khaanoum insisted you stay. She became...unhappy, shall we say. She asked, "Is Jamila his concubine or my slave?"'

'Well, if I was the prince's concubine, perhaps I might have some rooms of my own.'

'Be serious, Jamīla. She wants you to draft a letter to someone on the Shāh's council.'

'Gul, all I do is write correspondence.'

'This is different. She would have him stop seeing you. She shall take a sudden interest in "finding Nosrat Mirza a wife".'

Chehra's door was slightly ajar; she was bathed in a chink of light, pacing the room. Jamīla knocked and pushed it open, watching as Chehra glanced at her and continued to pace at a furious, unstable speed. She was soft and plump with a heavy brow that was perpetually furrowed. She would insist on having her face painted on with precision every single morning, but, due to her frequent naps during the day, would have a smeared face and stained pillow by midday. Her make-up today was meticulous: cheeks burnished tulip-pink, rosebud lips shone a cherry red and the faint lines of soft hair that trickled from her nose to the top of her lips looked lightly brushed. Jamīla, noting this, with muted surprise, realised with some foreboding that Chehra Khaanoum had not had her daily rest.

'Shahzadeh Khaanoum,' Jamīla addressed her formally and dipped into a deep bow.

'Are you ready to work?' Chehra demanded in a high-pitched tone.

'Yes, Shahzadeh Khaanoum,' Jamīla answered, and placed herself attentively beside the desk, wondering whether Chehra might stop walking long enough to offer instructions.

'How was the service?' Chehra asked. Without waiting for a response, she burst out, 'We have work here, Jamīla. You have to *be here* to serve me, not everybody else.'

'Yes, Shahzadeh Khaanoum. What should–'

'I have been invited to a dinner this evening!'

'Shall I–'

'I was certain that they loathed me; they strive to make me uncomfortable. They smile, but they do not speak, their politeness merely a mask…Could I have been mistaken? It was Raem, Raem Khaanoum, who invited me. Are you aware of Raem Khaanoum? She lost her son in childbirth last year, but prior to that she was the Shāh's beloved. They say he does not call on her now. You are to assist me here and when I return. Select my attire; I still have to find…'

Jamīla watched Chehra Khaanoum with interest; even her

burbling seemed frenetic. She had taken to drinking during the day, but she was too alert to be drunk already. Usually when Chehra overindulged, she became sloppy and maudlin. Jamīla thought perhaps she should get Gul, but before she could suggest it, Gul appeared at the door.

'Nothing to alarm you, Shahzadeh Khaanoum,' she said, but her face was fraught. 'The chief eunuch is outside. Nosrat Mirza, it appears, is rather insistent. He has requested the company of Jamīla this evening. It transpires that he is...ah...unhappy with the delay...'

Jamīla stared from Chehra to Gul and back again. Her eyes widened. Chehra marched past her and out to the front door, Gul and Jamīla hurrying behind. Chehra stepped outside and pulled the door closed behind her. Jamīla winced as Chehra began to shout and looked to Gul. The chief eunuch sounded obsequious, his words filled with platitudes and promises. When the front door was flung open, Chehra marched past again and slammed her room door shut. The chief eunuch looked at Jamīla, trying for a smile. His lips withdrew as he spoke, baring two sets of teeth. 'The Shāhzadeh has summoned you to his quarters in the kalwat. Proceed with haste.'

2

The first time Jamīla was sent to Prince Nosrat's quarters, she had felt like she was meeting a stranger. Handsome as always, he looked less comfortable than usual. His large hazelnut eyes searched hers as he stood before her and whilst his gentle rounded face held glimmers of his goofy smiles of old, he was fundamentally changed. He towered over her, far taller than she remembered. His neck was thick, his shoulders broad. He looked like a man, not the boy she knew, struggling to fit in his skin. His old awkwardness pushed through, however. The air was strained and he tried to mask it with a new habit of thrusting his chest out forward whenever he was lost for words. Over the course of that evening, it happened with increasing frequency. She tried at points to play with him as they used to, but when she threw a cushion at him, he snatched it from the air, tossing it to one side, and grasped her firmly by the hand.

'I was told they would explain.'

She stuttered and nodded.

His hand was awkward as it fluttered against her throat. 'May I...?'

She did not know what to say. He stood over her, thrusting his chest forward again. 'Must we?'

'You would refuse?' He looked embarrassed.

'Not at all, Shaazdeh,' she said, wondering if she could still use this familiar title. She paused, then asked, 'Might we be friends as well?'

He sighed. 'They did not explain.'

'I am not sure I...understood.'

He swallowed hard. 'It shan't be entirely unpleasant, although, perhaps at first. You shall come to enjoy it, they said.'

'Who said?' she asked, but he did not reply.

She watched him now, turned away from her, as he struggled to undress himself. She thought about how little he had changed. She felt a swell of pity as she watched him; his movements laced with that old blend of anxiety and defiance.

It was an oppressive room, heavy with dark colours and filled with ornate furnishings. The chandelier that hung in the centre, a solid structure overlaid with gilt and crystals, was in perpetual motion. The crystals would clink at every sound: footsteps across the Mashad rug, the aggravated thrusting of Nosrat as he penetrated her in bed. Jamīla would stare at the chandelier, convinced of its impending descent. She would close her eyes and grit her teeth, the image of the chandelier plummeting to the ground, incinerating them both, a welcome distraction.

He flung the offending robe to the floor with a sigh. 'I thought you might be tired at the service. I do not wish for you to be at odds with your mistress – I merely wanted some time... undisturbed.' Jamīla could tell Nosrat was trying not to sound petulant. She kept her back to him as he spoke.

'Indeed. I am grateful, Shaazdeh,' she said, turning around. The words hung in the air.

He coughed. 'You-you must feel free, Jamīla. I wish for you to do as you please.'

Jamīla paused and then said, in something of a rush, 'Might Abimelech join us?'

'Abimelech? Whatever for?'

'Well...' Jamīla could not think of an adequate reason. *I prefer his company* didn't seem ideal. 'He is your favourite, after all. I assumed you would not mind.'

Nosrat shrugged. 'He is three doors down.'

Jamīla paused. 'He sleeps in your quarters, in the ḵalwat?'

'You expect me to live there with only my father and his men, all alone?' He paused, adding ruefully, 'The ḵalwat is a disagreeable place. And Abimelech is my favourite. But for him, I would not return here. I miss staying with my mother, and all the women, in the harem.' His mouth twitched as he looked at her and she stepped closer to him, wanting to put her arms around him. He stopped her midway and gestured with his hand. 'Go. Fetch him.'

'Yes, Shaazdeh.' She left.

When Abimelech arrived, he ignored the cushions, stacked against a wall near the door, walking past them to the centre of the room. He sat down on the floor. Nosrat looked at him, irritated, before joining him. Amused, Abimelech flung an arm around him. Jamīla watched Nosrat betray a smile and lean on Abimelech's shoulder. She placed herself opposite them, also on the floor, wrapping her arms around herself, watching them, with mild apprehension. Topaz and pearl, Nosrat had once said, pressing her cheek against his and staring at both in the mirror. It was truer now than then. Abimelech's skin shone with a gleam that hers could never match. Even for an Abyssinian, of whom beauty was expected, Abimelech surpassed the standard. Beside him, the fat of his cheek nestled in the crook of Abimelech's collarbone, Nosrat's skin was more pale than pearl, dull by mere comparison to Abimelech's unconscious glow.

Jamīla here requested you.' Nosrat prodded Abimelech, his voice petulant.

'I am very flattered,' Abimelech replied.

Nosrat, hearing his words, quickly acquiesced. 'Well, you have always been my favourite. Tell me, how did you find the service?'

'It was a fitting monument to an honourable life,' Abimelech said.

Jamīla looked hard at him but said nothing.

Nosrat chuckled. 'I found it tiresome. The man was unremarkable. He was just another sycophant hovering around my father.'

Looking from one face to the other, he added in a quieter tone, 'I believe I have raised these concerns before. I do not wish to be lied to. Do not refrain from sharing your innermost thoughts. I do not wish to entertain sycophants in my own rooms. Speak with candour, or I insist you leave.'

Abimelech nodded with a smile but said nothing.

'Speak!'

Jamīla sighed. 'The service was beautiful. It is a marvellous thing to be remembered. We, of course, will not be remembered at all. We shall be forgotten. Such were my innermost thoughts.'

Abimelech was looking at her with something approaching horror on his face.

'We?' Nosrat asked.

'Abimelech and I,' she said, as Abimelech shook his head.

Nosrat frowned, looking from one to the other, and asked, 'Is this something you two have been discussing for some time?' He turned to Jamīla. 'Is this why you sought Abimelech?'

'We have never discussed this!' Abimelech interjected, glaring at Jamīla.

'I am the son of a Shāh. I shall be remembered throughout time.' There was a silence. 'Surely, by extension, you two will also be remembered.' He frowned again. 'What does it even mean to be remembered?'

There was a light knock. Nosrat fell silent as the door inched open. Abimelech moved to stand, but Nosrat brushed past and opened the door himself. 'Well?'

'Hazrat-e Aghdass-e Vaalaa,' the eunuch, voice trembling over the honorific, fell into a deep bow. 'I apologise! I thought it was empty!'

'You were mistaken.'

'Please accept my profound regret; I had not intended to—'

'What brings you here?'

The eunuch stood holding a pair of black mules with raised tips. His hand trembled; Jamīla could see the floral motif on the underside of the shoe. 'Hazrat-e Aghdass-e Vaalaa, I was told you wanted these polished again. I am returning them; I attended to them myself. I understand the old polish was not—'

'I did not like it; was it replaced?' The eunuch began to answer, but Nosrat continued to speak, raising his voice. 'Why was this not done in the daytime?'

'Please, Shāhzadeh, I can return in the morning...'

'You do realise you interrupted me when you tried to enter?' Nosrat paused; there were tears running down the eunuch's face. 'Is something the matter?'

'Shāhzadeh, I am f-fine.'

'You do not seem fine.' Nosrat dropped his voice. 'Would you like an apology?'

Jamīla shot a look at Abimelech. In short, quick strides, he crossed the threshold and was outside the room. 'Shāhzadeh,' he said, inclining his head, 'Wahbi is my subordinate. Allow me to sanction him for his error without continuing to interrupt your night.'

Nosrat looked at Abimelech. He nodded. Jamīla exhaled.

As the door closed, Nosrat turned back to her, shaking his head in wonder. 'He is without fault. How does one become so?' Almost to himself he added, 'What would I be without Abimelech?'

Impatient, unenlightened, alone? Jamīla thought. She closed her eyes and fell silent for a moment, steeling herself. She moved closer to Nosrat and nuzzled his arm. 'Well, Shaazdeh,' she began, with a beguiling smile, 'shall we play a game?'

It was another hour before Abimelech returned, his face wan. Nosrat and Jamīla were curled together on the bed. Nosrat jumped up. 'Oh-ho! He returns. I thought they were keeping you from me, in the harem!'

Jamīla and Abimelech exchanged glances. She wore only a quilted waistcoat, the one Nosrat had worn earlier. Abimelech said, 'Shaazdeh, perhaps I should leave.'

'You have only just arrived.'

'I do not wish to interrupt you.' He added with a light smile, 'I know you cannot abide interruptions.'

'Come over here and say that again.' Jamīla couldn't see Nosrat's face, but she could see Abimelech's: he looked relaxed and amused. Nosrat and Abimelech began chuckling together, an insular, jocular laugh. Watching them, she rose from the bed and wriggled onto a chair, taking one of the cushions spread across the floor and placing it on her lap. She had never let Abimelech see her like this; she was unused to being so exposed in the presence of more than one man. Yet they laughed like they could not see her. She felt like another ornament in the room, adorned but anonymous, as invisible as the voluptuous gold curtains that hung in the carefully constructed archways.

'So, was he flogged?' Nosrat asked, his tone languid as he paced the room. He drummed his fingers on a mahogany bureau before clasping one of the gilded metal handles and pulling open the drawer. 'It is French,' he announced, before removing an item and presenting it with a flourish to Abimelech. 'Do you know what these are?' he asked, watching his face. 'These cigarettes are from the imperial court of Russia, but they were made in London. *Sobranies of London.* Do you approve? They are better than ḡalyāns, are they not?'

'They are much better, Shaazdeh.'

Jamīla smirked. She knew full well Abimelech preferred to smoke a pipe.

'Try one.'

'Certainly – but then, Shaazdeh, I should like to retire.'

'No!' Nosrat and Jamīla spoke at the same time. Nosrat peered at her, but continued regardless. 'I wish to resume our previous discussion, about the service.'

'And how you will be remembered?' Jamīla asked.

Nosrat looked at her, as if seeing her for the first time. 'Yes.'

***

Hours slid by. The room was bathed in pungent fumes. Nosrat refused to open the window further. He was pacing, pontificating. Jamīla was facing away from him, lying on her back, holding a goblet upright. Abimelech snorted as he poured more wine into it: Jamīla kept slopping it as she struggled to swallow. Nosrat shook the stem of his goblet. He stared into it. 'It seems absurd that this – *this* should surpass everything.'

He had not paused for breath. Jamīla hoped he would. She had almost forgotten what silence was like. She no longer knew what he was talking about. He continued. Abimelech gulped back his drink and lay on the floor, his head nudging Jamīla's. She turned towards him, their faces mere inches apart. They had never been so close together.

He had no facial hair beyond his brows and lashes. There was nothing on his top lip, not a wisp on his chin. She traced a cheekbone with her finger. It swooped outwards and hollowed out beneath. He was somehow aged, yet with creamy, childlike skin.

She led her hand across his entire face, pausing before his lips. She hesitated and then crumpled her fingers against them. Abimelech, who had been lying almost perfectly still, grasped her hand. He held it against his lips, kissed it and closed his eyes for a moment. Then he pushed it firmly away from him. He rose and walked over to Nosrat, and stroked the back of his head. Jamīla snorted. Abimelech caught her eye for a moment and held her gaze. He tugged Nosrat's chin and watched him dimple in delight and surprise. Soon they were cuffing each other and laughing aloud. Jamīla watched Nosrat yelping as Abimelech tickled him. She rose to leave, but Abimelech reached out and grabbed her ankle.

'Stay.' He was gasping for breath, Nosrat behind him, tugging him and cackling.

She stood for a moment and watched them, a quagmire of interlinked limbs, squealing voices and vibrant fabric. Then she dressed and left with speed before Abimelech could convince her otherwise.

Outside Nosrat's room she paused. It was too late to return to the harem. Chehra Khaanoum would hear her; she would either be angry or take her to bed. Jamīla suppressed a shudder as she wandered around Nosrat's quarters. She idled until she came to a familiar door, and, pushing it open, froze at the sight. It was not just a room built for a prince, it was a room built for a European prince.

This room, like those in the photographs Nosrat had shown her, had gilt-lined wooden panelling, European chairs pressed against the walls and a chaise longue at the foot of the bed. There was not a single cushion. Unlike Nosrat's room, Abimelech's room was pristine. It was empty of personal items but for a tall smooth pillbox hat that she knew to be his. It was part of the eunuch's uniform, mirroring that of a nobleman's. It sat, serene, on a gleaming bureau, as bold and discreet as its owner. The rest of the room was similar: muted colours, without the explosions of gold Jamīla was accustomed to seeing throughout the palace.

She felt guilty about stealing the bed; no slave was worthy of sleeping in such opulence. She was rather surprised that Abimelech dared to sleep here himself; Nosrat could not protect him from the wrath of the Shāh if he were caught. She wondered what would happen if Abimelech saw her in the bed. She envisioned him entering the room, heavy with drink but light-footed with caution, caught by surprise at the sight of her. She would be flagrantly presented, her brown skin sprawled across the royal duvet for all to see. Abimelech, she suspected, would simply settle himself on the floor at her feet. It was the most gallant of the options – even if his carpet woven with rubies was more luxurious than the mattresses in the harem. Or perhaps he would continue drinking with Nosrat tonight. They would pass out in Nosrat's room, and she could slip away, unnoticed, just after dawn.

She clambered onto the bed, squirrelling herself into a corner. Slipping her hand under the pillow, she withdrew a tattered copy of Hafiz's *Divan* and smiled. It was not a warm night; she pushed some of the bedding onto the floor so that if Abimelech returned, he would have something to sleep under. But when she woke, she found he had slipped in beside her.

3

Her dreams at night always ended the same way. Flickering reinventions of *that night* would stalk innocuous worlds before wholly taking them over. They might start as all her dreams had lately: chasing ibex through mosques she had never entered. Trees would poke their twigs through open windows, roots would spread over the mirrored tiles. The Persian mosque would become an Abyssinian forest, and Dinha, panting beside her, would remind her she was playing a chieftain. Jamīla in the dream would sigh because, of course, she knew what was coming. Each night she sought to do something different at that moment. Before she and Dinha fought, before the latter fled, before the figure appeared to drag her far away.

Jamīla turned over as she woke and found Abimelech staring at her. His eyes, almond shaped and dark, with lashes so long and curled she wanted to stroke them, were often opaque. She started to speak, but he spoke over her. 'You should not be here.' She didn't reply and he turned on to his back, away from her.

No matter how terse his tone, she always felt a warmth when they were alone. It was then and only then that he would speak to her in the language of their home. It was important to her; without those four years of secret conversation she would have forgotten more than her tongue, she would have struggled to retain her history. And it would not have grown with her. At best it would exist as a relic, consigned to memory, insufficient as a medium through which to depict her life now.

Nosrat had learned Afaan Oromoo from his nurses, and had spoken it as a baby, but he refused to speak it to her or have the

'Galla nonsense' spoken in his presence. It had taken Jamīla a while to recall it at first. Her last memories of Afaan Oromoo had been the songs her mother used to sing. She couldn't remember on her own, but whenever Abimelech spoke the tongue, the lullabies rose unbidden.

Her mother's voice was voluptuous; it rolled and clicked like a ductile cube. It moved as swiftly as her hand. Jamīla had two memories of her mother: her voice as she sang her to sleep and her fist as it furled when she fumed. Her mother was not one for punching, but whenever she smacked Jamīla, she would clench her fist first, steeling herself. She would spread her fingers out again immediately, flexing them at the tips, before chasing after Jamīla. Jamīla missed it all. She missed the sting of her mother's palm as it curved through the air like a lasso, languid as it stung her skin. Sometimes it burned the tip of her nose, often it cuffed her chin. Jamīla had no other memories of her mother, not the shape of her body as she stood or the arch of her back when they passed strange men, her shoulders proud as she ignored their praise. She had memories of those memories, but she could never recall those moments herself.

Abimelech turned his head slightly, his glance fluttering on Jamīla's mouth, before fixing his eyes to the ceiling once more. With a light cough, he said, 'You really should not be here.'

She scoffed. 'The chief eunuch sent me to Prince Nosrat. He will expect me to stay the night. Chehra Khaanoum knows. I shall say Nosrat kept me late in the morning. Nobody will ask him, and thus, for now, my time is my own.' She leaned towards him and added, 'Once Nosrat gave me a day to myself. He said I had to stay within the palace walls, and should I be questioned later, he would be my excuse.'

Abimelech looked incredulous. 'What did you do?'

'Well, I stayed with him. I did not dare wander by myself. But he did show me,' she lowered her voice to a stage whisper, 'the Shāh's photography studio and he took my picture! There is a photograph, Abimelech. Of me. It is the strangest thing. I look – I look as I do in the mirror. It is...exact.'

'Well. That is generous of him.'

'You sound surprised.' Jamīla laughed.

'I am not surprised. I know Nosrat Mirza is a fair master.' Abimelech sighed, his words wistful. 'He did not grant me a new name when I arrived. He allowed me to remain "Abimelech". I have served kinder men than he, but none who let me keep my identity.'

'It matters little, in the end.'

'As we will all be forgotten...' Abimelech's tone was sober. 'What compelled you to say such a thing? What were you thinking – were you even thinking?'

'It is the truth.'

'What difference does that make?'

'Does it not concern you?'

'That I shan't have 40 days of funeral rites in the bāzār's most beautiful mosque?'

'No,' Jamīla said in a quiet voice. 'I am referring to the reasons why.'

'I am a slave.'

'Thus your life is of no consequence. You are of no consequence!'

'Is this about Aabir?'

'This is about all of us!'

There was a silence.

'It does not bother you?' Without waiting for an answer, she rose from the bed. Abimelech sat up, following her movements warily. 'Last night, Chehra Khaanoum was nervous and anxious because she was invited to a dinner with women she cannot stand. The day before, we were to discuss why, in great depth, they might hate her. Prior to that, she decided to cry because she felt unloved. All the while, I have to write out her inane correspondence, complete her innumerable errands, help her choose her outfits and otherwise follow her around. Do you know how much of my day involves standing against a wall, playing at being invisible?'

'I could not possibly; I am not a eunuch after all. My day is not remotely similar.'

She had been standing over him, jabbing the air with her finger. At his words, she dropped her hand and sat down with a guilty sigh. 'Of course. I know your experience is the same.' She could not bring herself to voice her real complaint.

'It could be worse, Jamīla. We could be domestics.'

'We are Abyssinian,' Jamīla snapped. 'We would never be domestics.'

'Al-ḥamdulillāh for slave hierarchies.'

Jamīla rolled her eyes. 'It is not enough.'

Abimelech shrugged.

'I know–' she paused and smiled. 'Might I suggest this is your fault?'

'How so?'

'You gave me that book! Mulla Sadra's–'

'–Transcendent Theosophy? I have been searching for that. I thought I might teach it to Nosrat Mirza–'

'I keep re-reading it. I wish I had unlimited time to ponder such questions, about essentialism and existentialism. I know, I know, it is impossible, but it seems absurd that this – the petty squabbling and scheming of the harem – should be my only alternative.'

There was a long silence.

'It is not enough, Abimelech. I feel enraged every day. These lives of ours...do they not strike you as strange? You are not truly surprised by the words I spoke to Prince Nosrat. I know you. You are not satisfied with this life. Would you read Mulla Sadra if you were? You cannot cast your thoughts aside.' She leaned closer. 'I do not simply want out. I want...more. Our minds are not mere basins for our memories. The questions of who we are, where we come from, why we live like this, why one society can sell another – I am tormented by them...'

Abimelech sighed. 'I do not know what to tell you.'

Jamīla stared at him, her face a mask. Then she rose without speaking and headed for the door.

'You are upset with me.'

Jamīla shook her head. 'No, Abimelech. I have to go to the bāzār. I have errands to run.'

'Let me come with you.'

'No.'

'Please.'

'Goodbye, Abimelech,' Jamīla said, but she stood at the door.

Abimelech smiled. 'Let me come with you.'

'Why?'

He rose from the bed and followed her. Stopping in front of her, he took her hand. 'I will tell you what you want to know.'

Jamīla looked down at her hand, encased in both of his. She looked back at him, her face doubtful. 'I know you, Abimelech.'

'I will. I promise.'

4

Tehran's grand bāzār was not the most beautiful Jamīla had seen, but parts of it came close. Unlike most that were purely markets, the bāzār in Tehran was a city within a city. Domed buildings were connected to large labyrinth passageways that folded out onto courtyards, docks and open streets. Mosques and schools were not far from bath houses and guest houses. Bakers, apothecaries and confectioners were found throughout; tailors, shoemakers and craftsmen were generally together. The bāzār was a world apart from the harem in Golestan Palace. In the palace, every word was courteous, every action preceded by a bow. Here, words spun fast and loose, questions roared from full-throated men. For Jamīla, it was brilliant but dismal, the long-tunnelled galleries humming with the footfall of the forlorn.

In summer months, on sticky days, she came here to escape. The blast of cool air that greeted her would feel like a reprieve. In winters, when she entered, the smells assailed her first. They were unusual aromas: a slew of mismatched spices from competing sellers together would make her head spin. The recurring blend, she grew to discern, was a burst of sumac and saffron. The tart lemony sharpness of the sumac combined with the honey vanilla of the saffron was often followed by wafts of tobacco smoke, that she could see curling through the air.

Despite the vastness of the place, it felt as familiar as it did complex. Jamīla knew which corridors sold Chehra's favourite spices and where to get writing paper for Nosrat. He never asked her for it and had access to more luxuriant options, but his response to her first, impulsive gesture told her that he liked being cared for – he liked the pretence that they were young lovers. Thus Jamīla, despite her ambivalence, indulged his little dream and got him cheap trinkets from the bāzār whenever she could.

Jamīla walked in silence beside Abimelech, waiting for him to begin. As they entered the bāzār he all but disappeared, turning once to slip her a silent smile before snaking through the heaving hoards, sweeping through the clamour of shouting traders. Finally, he stopped in a quieter corridor and waited for her to catch up. He was smiling, standing still, as she panted in front of him. He began to speak, but the smell of pomegranates from a nearby stall caught her attention. Her favourite thing to do when running Chehra's errands in the bāzār was to stop in an unfamiliar passageway and buy pomegranates for herself. Jamīla liked the sensation of being slightly lost, and in a world of unending routine, she craved the occasional surprise. She lived for those moments when she bit into the pomegranate and found it unexpectedly sweet or soft. It was not supposed to be either and you were supposed to peel them first, but Jamīla did not care. The best ones were firm and tasted more sharp than sweet, but she relished the unexpected, even when it was unpleasant.

'Does anything take your fancy?'

'Yes, but I shall get it.' Jamīla leaned towards the elderly greenseller and then paused as she spotted fresh âlbâloo. She gestured to them and then helped herself.

Abimelech's brows were raised. 'You are not using money Chehra Khaanoum gave you.'

Jamīla looked at him, chomping the shiny fruit with relish.

'Jamīla! I imagine she did not expect you would spend it on

sour cherries.'

Jamīla continued chewing, her eyes closed now, a blissful smile stretching across her face.

'Jamīla, I am being serious.' His voice rose an octave. 'Is this something you do often?'

Swallowing, she reached out and paid for another handful, popping one into her mouth at once. Abimelech twitched as he watched her. 'It is bothersome, is it not?'

'What?'

'Requesting answers...receiving silence.'

Her eyes were still closed, but she could hear his dry laughter. 'Jamīla, you child.' He stepped closer to her and dropped his voice. 'I did not feel comfortable speaking at the palace. You wanted to know if I shared your frustrations. I do not. I was surprised to hear you speak to the prince as you did. All humans will be forgotten eventually, even if slaves shall be forgotten first.'

Jamīla stared at him in horror – his cool placid smile, his innocent blinking eyes. 'You lie!' The words burst out before she could stop them. 'You-you...'

Abimelech watched her, disdain flickering across his face. 'It appears that you lie, Jamīla – either to Chehra or me. You are stealing money from your mistress, are you not? I shall see you back at the palace.' He turned away.

Jamīla felt helpless. 'It is Nosrat!' she called after him, but she was seething as well. He stopped, turned around, but did not speak.

His silence was swallowed by the sounds of the busy bāzār. The greenseller, brandishing a fistful of pomegranates at a nearby customer, knocked several items out of their place. Fruits ran forward; propelled by his enthusiasm, they tumbled into each other before splitting on the ground. The greenseller cursed and rose to tidy the mess. Abimelech and Jamīla stared together at the fleeing fruit for a wordless moment.

Abimelech spoke. 'Nosrat Mirza gives you *money*? You are paid by a Qājār?'

'You lied to me. Of all the things to lie about – because of some fruit?'

'Jamīla, you looked to be stealing from your mistress. You were being open about it. Slaves are *killed* for less.' Abimelech frowned. 'You could have been seen and reported. Both of us would have been killed. Do you not realise that we are familiar faces? We serve in the palace. We are all watched.'

'Of course, I know this. But you...you patronise and belittle me. I am not a child.'

'You are young, Jamīla.' At the corners of his mouth she spied the glimmer of a smile. 'Your earnestness is proof of your youth.'

Jamīla couldn't look at him. She breathed a tentative sigh.

'Let us not forget your errands.'

They left the food halls behind and entered a timcheh, one of many courtyards spread throughout the bāzār, where merchants sold luxury fabrics and works of art in a courtyard surrounded by jewellers and goldsmiths. Here, proud eunuchs and female slaves wandered with authority, scrutinising goods, shopping on behalf of noble or royal masters. The hall itself was huge. Turquoise tiles illuminated the domes, small lattice windows peered serenely from above. Jamīla had always loved it here. As she walked alongside Abimelech, however, the air felt taut.

He did not speak until they headed back to the palace. He reached forward, took her parcels from her and encased her hand in his. She closed her eyes. His palm was supple, smooth and warm. Larger than hers, it felt softer too. Their gait was in unison, but he felt remote and she shivered in the morning frost.

'I was not honest.'

She continued to walk without looking at him.

He tried again. 'This life chafes at me too. But, Jamīla...I do not wish to be remembered this way. There is no value in this life. None to be found, nothing to carve or create. Do I want to be remembered as a slave of the Qājārs? I said you were young. I meant it. You believe in hope, in opportunity, in the future. There are things I can do here, that allow me to keep going, differences I can make in the court. But those questions you speak of...they cannot be answered here, not by us, not in this place. There is no meaning to be found here, not the kind you desire, the sooner you learn that...'

Jamīla stopped walking. 'What are these things in court that you hope to do?'

'I...' He sighed. 'Those goals seem elusive now. I suspected Prince Nosrat would be granted an official role in the Shāh's government. As his former teacher, I would remain as his chamberlain, run his household and advise him on politics. This is not an uncommon trajectory; other eunuchs have pursued similar paths. They worked for a shāh or a prince and they were able to retire; some retired wealthy.'

'It sounds wise,' she admitted, wrestling to keep the envy from her voice.

'You would not be happier, Jamīla, with more acquisitions. You have this income from the prince, do you not? Has it abated your frustrations?'

Jamīla sighed. 'Would you be happier in this...chamberlain role under Nosrat?'

Abimelech's voice was so quiet Jamīla had to strain to hear. 'I cannot even recall what happiness feels like. I would not be bored. I could still read. I could be useful. But this life holds no meaning for me, Jamīla. With the exception of reading and perhaps the company of a few...friends, I can think of little that keeps me here.'

'Here? As in...alive?'

Abimelech did not reply.

Jamīla hesitated. In a brighter tone, she asked, 'But...what of this role?'

'Nosrat is *uninterested* in joining his father's government.'

She stopped walking altogether and turned to face him. 'What will he do instead?'

'I shall tell you. But before I go further,' Abimelech began looking around, 'you have to promise secrecy.'

'Of course. Who would I tell?'

Abimelech paused, momentarily silenced. Then he said, 'I know you, Jamīla. You are earnest, opinionated – this cannot resurface in a discussion with Nosrat.'

'It shan't.'

'You cannot use it to curry favour with the chief eunuch.'

'I would never.'

'You cannot use it to gain an advantage in the harem.'

'I understand.' Jamīla spoke through gritted teeth.

'You cannot use it if you are enraged by Nosrat.'

'Abimelech, I am not the shameless gossip you expect. Tell me.'

He looked at her, frowning. 'If this becomes public, I will lose everything.'

'I promise, Abimelech. Now...?'

'Nosrat Mirza wants to move to Paris.'

'What?'

'I may have to accompany him.'

'To...you could not mean the city in Fr–?'

'Yes. In France.' Abimelech's voice was clipped.

'Will you?' Jamīla's mind was racing.

'Nosrat is too undisciplined to realise such a plan. It remains a fanciful dream.'

'What is it like?'

'The city?'

'Yes.'

'Dirty, I am told. Not as beautiful as Tehran.'

Jamīla shrugged. 'I meant the religion. France is a Christian country, is it not? It shan't have Islamic laws.'

Abimelech began to laugh. 'No, Jamīla. They—'

'Do they have laws on slavery at all?'

She watched the humour slip from his face. 'I...I...Well, no. No.'

'You would choose to enter a city in Europe as Nosrat's property, without even slavery laws to protect you? Suppose there is a disagreement. You shall be in a foreign country, *without a patron*, without even the law to keep you safe.' Jamīla let a satisfactory sneer seep into her tone. 'You cannot actually indulge this fantasy.'

Abimelech was not looking at her. 'We are unlikely to actually get there. Nosrat is just obsessed with Europe. He is irritable and wants to leave. I suspect we will start by travelling through Persia. Even then, we will likely only end up in Isfahan.'

'Ah.'

'I thought you might join us.'

There was a long silence. 'Me?'

'Yes, you,' Abimelech replied, and they both broke into smiles.

5

Jamīla smelt the strain of rotting blood orange whenever she entered Chehra Khaanoum's room. Chehra loved blood oranges and would eat half of one every night. She left them everywhere: on cushions, bureaus, mantelpieces.

When Jamīla had first begun in Chehra's household, she was summoned one late afternoon. As the door groaned open under her hand, a waft of over-sweetened fruit swam out to greet her. It was rich, layered; the tang of putrid orange sank into her skin. Instinct overwhelmed her and she rushed across the floor, her feet fighting through the stiff carpet. Her hands sank into the curtains, catching herself in them as she sought to push them aside. She finally jerked a window open, staring aghast at Chehra, who continued to sleep, fruit rotting by her side. Forgetting their plans, Chehra had not risen for another hour. Jamīla, too timid to rouse her, hovered on a cushion, submerged in the stench of fetid fruit as it slowly swirled towards the open window and flittered out.

It was almost midday when Jamīla returned from the bāzār; Chehra was only just getting dressed. She stood with her back to the slave, fabric rustling as she adjusted her skirt. Although she had a valet, another Abyssinian slave, Chehra requested Jamīla assist her when it came to fitting the šalīta. There was an optimal point just below the hips where Chehra insisted the skirt should sit, and Jamīla alone was able to find this angle. Today, Chehra struggled by herself, her body twisted from Jamīla, who stood behind her, her head bowed. Jamīla wanted to help but did not dare. Chehra Khaanoum, with the air of one resigned, turned to face her. She began to speak, but Jamīla jumped in first.

'Shahzadeh Khaanoum, I humbly apologise.' Her head remained bowed.

'You should not have left, Jamīla.'

'I am sorry, Shahzadeh Khaanoum. The Shāhzadeh—'

'—is not in charge in the harem, nor in my house,' Chehra snapped. 'I need you!' she added, raising her voice over Jamīla's protestations. 'How many eunuchs and slave girls does the Shāhzadeh have attending to him? How many do I? Am I expected to spare one for a Qājār who has everything?'

'Shahzadeh Khaanoum, I am so sorry.'

Chehra raised a shaking hand to silence her. She spoke with a strained calmness. 'You are not to talk until I say you can. I had work for you to complete yesterday. I had letters for you to write. I had fabrics for you to collect. They have languished because of your *romance*. I had the dinner to attend. I required your presence. Had you also forgotten the plans we had made? The dinner I want to hold for the Shāh and his council? I have told you of its import. It is my one chance to speak without the input of the harem.'

Jamīla nodded and bowed her head.

'I said not to talk!' Chehra shouted and smacked Jamīla across the face. 'Look at me!'

Jamīla stumbled backwards, dazed.

Chehra took a deep breath. She cleared her throat and began again. 'You are becoming rebellious, Jamīla. I will not tolerate it. Last night I told Prince Nosrat's eunuch you were unavailable and then, *then*, the chief eunuch came to supplant me. Who summoned him?'

Jamīla stood, immobile, anxiety rising in her throat.

'I know the source of your defiance, Jamīla.' Chehra's voice was soft. 'The reading. I am responsible. I have indulged you. I permitted the eunuch to give you books. I allowed you to read them in your room. You have taken advantage. You have begun to *challenge* me.' She stepped closer to Jamīla, pressing her against the wall. 'I have had them destroyed. All of them.'

Jamīla gasped, horror mounting on her face.

'Yes!' Chehra shouted and smacked her again, her hand lingering on her skin. Jamīla could feel Chehra's breath, thick with citrus, heavy on her neck. Chehra was staring at her, eyes filled with frustration. 'I should be angry with you,' she said. Both hands found their way beneath Jamīla's clothes, searching and grasping, squeezing and clutching with the same desperate rage that would befall Nosrat.

'I am trapped,' Chehra panted, one hand between Jamīla's thighs. Jamīla closed her eyes. Chehra's voice was forlorn yet fevered, brittle but angry. She was speaking, almost to herself, but her fingers were still in Jamīla. 'I am trapped. I cannot leave the harem. My letters are my one link to life outside. When you scurry after Nosrat Mirza, you deprive me of my life. A thoughtful slave would not do this.'

Chehra stepped back from Jamīla and pushed her onto the floor. Chehra began to breathe more slowly, standing over her, her manner calmer. She raised her fingers to her nose with an absent smile, glancing down at Jamīla.

'You can speak,' Chehra huffed, frowning.

Jamīla faltered, unable to stand. 'I...I collected the fabrics you ordered, this morning.'

'Oh.'

'I purchased the ingredients for the dinner party–'

'There is no date–'

'I thought the domestics should practise it first; I thought they might perfect it before the day.'

'That was Gul's idea?'

'No, Shahzadeh Khaanoum, mine.' Jamīla's voice was gaining strength, but her head remained bowed, unable to meet Chehra's eyes.

'The letters—'

'—should be complete. I have asked Laleh to draft them from my notes.'

'Well, go to Gul for additional instructions.'

Jamīla staggered to her feet, imperceptibly soiled. Heading to the bathhouse, she closed her eyes and started to retch.

***

There were two domestic slaves in the kitchen when she approached. She could hear their low yet giddy laughter, the sound of jokes and sharp asides she could not fathom. She had not seen two domestics working together before. It was, as a general rule, discouraged. Jamīla rarely entered the kitchen unless it was empty, rising from her bed to steal snacks after hours when the soft lament of her stomach awoke her. Last night, swaddled as she was in a monarchical bed, she had slept seamlessly throughout. Now bereft of breakfast and a midnight snack, those familiar pangs were sudden and acute.

As she entered the kitchen the ambience changed. The eyes of the domestics flickered away as she walked in, their heads lowering. She walked with mild discomfort; her feet kept sticking to the floor. Jamīla stopped for a moment, contemplating whether to speak. The domestics ceased their work at once. Her eyes ahead, she continued across the floor, scanning the surfaces for an open bowl of fruit. Speaking aloud, yet to nobody in particular, she announced, 'This floor is dirty.' The harried response of the domestic slaves, as they began scrubbing the floor with vigour, prickled Jamīla's skin. One of them was frowning as she cleaned; Jamīla turned and met her gaze. The room teetered; the tension stretched to snap. The domestic retracted her expression, withdrawing her private pain, or public indignation. Her face bore a smooth opacity; she scrubbed with aggressive strokes.

Looking away, Jamīla saw the bowl of fruit she was after and slipped a peach from it into her pocket. She opened a cupboard and stared into it, saying, 'I just do not want Chehra Khaanoum to complain. It is better to hear an instruction from me than from Chehra Khaanoum...' She hoped it sounded more like cajolement than a reprimand. The frowning domestic was inscrutable now. The other domestic spoke. She first looked at Jamīla, so that Jamīla would know she was being addressed, but did not call her by name. Her words were a mixture of broken Fārsi and her own native language. Jamīla didn't know where she came from and couldn't recognise the African tongue. She suspected the slave was Zanzibari. Any slave brought from further south than Abyssinia was relegated to a less pleasant role. When she first joined Chehra's household, it was Laleh, a fellow Habashī, who had chastised her for befriending the Zanzibari slaves. 'Habashī only!' she had whispered. Jamīla had kept her distance and thus could not understand any slave who was not Abyssinian.

Jamīla looked at the chattering slave and tried for a smile. The domestic sighed and turned to her peer. They exchanged a look, loaded with thoughts as unfamiliar as their tongue. Jamīla watched them with irritation. She could see the arrogance seething through their movements, aggression in the rapid jerk of their forearms as the muscles rotated beneath the skin.

She walked out, pockets bulging, a peach crushed in her fist. She had wasted her own time, and it was making her late. *Their* sloppy standards had wasted her time. As she marched on, she heard their voices begin again; a gentle burst of hubristic laughter made her irate. She almost returned to the kitchen, just to make them stop.

6

Jamīla was shaken awake with a ferocity that made her gasp. Her eyes burst open; a hand against her lips choked any sound. The hand was firm but the fingers delicate. Such details kept her calm. As she struggled to focus, her eyes settled on Sanaa.

Willowy and serene with a nonchalant grace, Sanaa was an object of envy in the harem. She was among the Shāh's favourites, with a beatific smile said to fill a room with light. Jamīla had never seen anything beatific in her nature. She was detached in her manner, avoiding her fellow slaves, although, for reasons Jamīla could not fathom, Sanaa liked her. They were both African slaves who maintained the interest of Qājār men; otherwise they had little in common. Sanaa was several years older than Jamīla and had been in the Shāh's circle for some time. Whilst Jamīla was ultimately a lady's maid, Sanaa had real responsibilities. She served alongside the harem secretaries, an elite group of wives who managed the harem's jewels. She was a world away from the other Abyssinian slaves, and Jamīla saw little of her.

Stunned, Jamīla stared at her. 'What are you doing here?'

'Not a morning person, are we?' Sanaa's tone was brisk as she removed her hand from Jamīla's mouth. 'Not a word.' With a vehement grip on Jamīla's arm, she navigated Chehra Khaanoum's residence, slipping past the sleeping bodies Jamīla lay amongst, ducking into hallways to avoid the staff that roused early. They were striding now first through the harem itself, then past the men's quarters, Jamīla hurrying to catch up as Sanaa led the way. There was almost nobody around. Jamīla had never seen the palace look this empty. But then, she was never even up this early. It was sometime after dawn and just before sunrise. Sanaa stopped abruptly, and Jamīla walked into her. Sanaa took her by the shoulders and steered her round, tipping her chin to lift her face upwards.

They were in the Hall of Mirrors.

The ceiling was covered in square mirrored tiles with multiple chandeliers lining the centre. On the walls were mirrors reflecting mirrors; beneath, rose-coloured chairs dotted the room. Carved marble arches housed large ornate windows, covered by deep ruby curtains that ran to the ground. A blush-coloured sunrise burst through the room, but the only thing to see was themselves, replicated a thousand times, their long, brown bodies blinking, twitching, moving in unison against the shifting shades of morning red.

Smiling, Sanaa spoke. 'I heard a rumour. You are restless.'

Jamīla felt wary. 'A little.'

'Well...' Sanaa paused, then her words surged forward in a rush. 'There is a shuffle coming.'

'A shuffle?' Jamīla looked at her, mouth agape. 'You are certain?'

'Do not forget with whom you speak, little one. Would I come this far, this early, based on a possibility?' She did not wait for an answer. 'Anis al-Douleh wants to act as the new Mahd-e 'Olyā, not that there can be a new one. One does not simply bestow the title of a shāh's late mother upon a favoured wife. Regardless,' Sanaa glanced at Jamīla, who looked lost, and sighed before continuing to speak, 'she has since fallen out with a harem secretary. Her name is Raem Khaanoum. You have not met her, but it does not matter. All of Raem's deputies are being removed from their roles. Anis al-Douleh does not believe she can trust them. So, there will be vacancies – many, and soon.'

Jamīla nodded, trying to mask her uncertainty.

'What would you do, if you could do anything? If you could choose any role in the harem?' She watched Jamīla's face as she spoke.

'Well…I would be interested in working in the theatre,' Jamīla lied. 'Laleh, a slave I live with, helps arrange the performances and helps choose which dancers and musicians perform. Rabiah Khaanoum is in charge, I think…'

'Rabiah is leaving.' Sanaa stared hard at Jamīla. 'You could join this Laleh in the theatre. You might even replace Rabiah. The Shāh has long since forgotten her; she is to be given to a minister whose name eludes me. What are your current duties?'

'I…I do not have many, as I serve Nosrat Mirza. I run errands for Chehra Khaanoum, but I do little else.'

Sanaa frowned. 'Are you telling me that you alone serve Nosrat Mirza?'

'Yes.'

'There is no pressure on him to marry?' Sanaa paused, speaking almost to herself. 'I suppose he is a little young. He is still an adolescent like yourself, is he not? Are you with child?'

'With child? Never.'

'Never?' Sanaa shot her a quizzical glance. 'Tell me, what precisely do you seek? Abimelech implied you were restless, hungry, in search of something more. You stand at the centre of court. You have the unwavering affections of a prince with whom you could beget free children. They could inherit from a prince – you would become a concubine. You could even be a sigheh, a temporary wife! Do you understand what that means? You could never be sold again. But this, to you, is insufficient? When I ask what you seek, you say you wish to work in the harem theatre. I am…confused. To be frank, you *sound* confused. Abimelech had such good things to say about you; I cannot say I am impressed.'

Jamīla frowned. 'If Abimelech spoke to you of me then you would know I am uninterested in watching a tea ceremony or running a dance committee or in being somebody's wife. I am restless, yes, but I am not in search of additional responsibilities within the harem.' It was only when Sanaa looked down that Jamīla realised she was clutching her arm.

'I am not hearing what you do want.' Sanaa's voice was quiet. 'All I hear is rage. The harem is an angry place. I see it every day. Trapped women, spoiled women, sour with desire, shrivelled by their dreams. And people like us do not want for enemies. We must seize every opportunity and fast. If you wish for my help, you need to know what you want. *What* do you want?'

Jamīla sighed. There was so much she wanted to say, but Sanaa was the wrong person to tell. 'I was reading books on philosophy and literature,' she said at last. 'Chehra Khaanoum removed them. I am not at all sure I want anything...besides to read.'

Sanaa's eyes flickered. 'Reading. Hm. I could help with that...but you need to ask yourself how serious you are. What kind of rules you are willing to break. Because this would break all of them.'

She broke into one of her brilliant smiles.

Jamīla blinked as she looked back at her; she was seared by the light.

7

Sanaa had told her to wait until she was summoned. It was more than a month before Jamīla heard anything, and she spent the weeks after their talk holding her breath. When, in March, she received the message from a domestic slave that she was wanted, she rushed to find Sanaa first. She was in the harem's royal coffeehouse, and she was not alone.

'Is this it?' Jamīla burst out, as Sanaa sat talking with Parisa, one of the harem's dancers. Sanaa stopped mid-sentence. She stared at Jamīla for a long time. Parisa looked between the two of them, but Sanaa's placid gaze revealed nothing. Realising she had made an irredeemable mistake, Jamīla hurried away, carrying the weight of Sanaa's silence with her.

She had been requested by Ghadiya Khaanoum, a young wife with whom Jamīla was unfamiliar. Standing outside Ghadiya's apartment, Jamīla was unable to knock; the weight of her fears kept her frozen. She had never engaged in any subterfuge in the harem; any deceit she had attempted had been suggested by Nosrat or covered by his status. This would be the first time she broke the rules without a patron to protect her. She hesitated. Jamīla was not quite sure what she had expected when Sanaa said she could help with her education.

Sanaa, it transpired, had not just served in Tehran but had also been raised there. The eldest son in the house where she had served had been training to become a mullah, Sanaa had told her, with the tight-lipped reluctance of someone who loathed revealing themselves. The gatekeeper, who had noticed her reading in the andarūnī, did not scold her or even question how books had entered the women's quarters. He had said with a firm smile that she was not to enter the men's quarters and he would deliver books to her from the bīrūnī himself. In the end, the budding mullah had noticed, but was amused rather than annoyed to find a female slave reading his preparation texts on Islamic theology. He agreed to let her sit in on his lessons with his tutor, and they had maintained a bond ever since. When he left to undertake his training, she asked to be resold and arrived at court.

'You cannot continue your reading inside the court,' Sanaa had warned her, 'but if you are willing, I can help you achieve something of an education outside of it. There is no reason he would not agree to educate you a little, if we ask.'

'You are not certain?' blurted Jamīla.

Sanaa was still but for the elegant raise of a single eyebrow.

Jamīla, her own face growing hot, proceeded to fumble an apology before Sanaa interjected with a smooth reply. 'You are frightened and nervous with good reason. Do not assume that I would take such a risk for no reason.'

'Why are you doing this?'

'Abyssinians should help each other.' Sanaa's smile was discreet. 'I am sure in the future you will find a way to return the favour.' Before Jamīla could respond, Sanaa began speaking again in a clipped, harried tone that Jamīla had to strain to hear. 'The mullah has returned to the family home. He is unmarried and lives there with his brother's family. His brother has a mistress in the harem. She has been given to one of the Shāh's allies and is keen to maintain her relationship and its discretion. Thus, she is changing the slaves who deliver her love letters. You will deliver a message on her behalf, and with it I shall include a note for the mullah. It will be a reference of sorts. He will intercept the letter and things should proceed from there.'

'So he knows of my visit?'

'The qāpči knows—'

'The *gatekeeper* knows?!'

'He is a trusted friend. He shall ensure the letter is given to the mullah.'

Jamīla paused. 'It seems surreal – your mullah's brother keeps a lover in the court.'

'Is it?'

'There must be thousands of...'

'The court has over 80 wives here. There are almost 100 princesses in one place in Tehran. How many noblemen do you suspect are restless in Tehran, in search of a love affair? The unmarried ones are given wives by the Shāh. Is it so surprising that the married ones find women in the same place?'

Outside Ghadiya's room, Jamīla's eventual knock was answered with the coolest of replies. Nobody came to let her in; she was ordered to enter and make her way to the bedroom. Unable to mask her nerves, she distracted herself by taking the measure of the place. Ghadiya's four-room apartment was one of the smaller residences adjoining the harem. The ceilings were painted in intricate detail; narratives Jamīla did not recognise unfolded along the narrow hallways leading to the bedroom. The entire apartment was coloured cream to cultivate the illusion of space. Ghadiya's room was sparsely furnished, but the ceiling hung low, and as Jamīla pushed the door open, it swung into the centre of the room, brushing roughly against the foot of the bed before juddering to a halt. There were two large columns on the right-hand side, and between them, floor-to-ceiling windows. The silver curtains, though still closed, were almost translucent, crumpling as they spilled onto the ground. Despite the full-length windows and elegant walls, Jamīla decided the apartment was rather compact, and as she performed a deep bow for Ghadiya Khaanoum, her first thought was that of pity.

Ghadiya's face was turned away from the door; when Jamīla rose from her bow, she could see little of it. Long dark hair fanned out over the duvet and an ivory cheek revealed a clenched jaw. Ghadiya did not move from her position but looked at an elderly African slave, who Jamīla assumed was a former nanny, slumped in a chair beside the bed. The slave had her eyes closed, yet opened them on Ghadiya's gaze. 'Maadah is unwell,' Ghadiya announced without introduction. Ghadiya began speaking in Fārsi but switched to an Afro-Persian dialect without first checking that Jamīla understood it. Her voice was sharp and fluid, and Jamīla struggled to recognise the tongue. 'Maadah has always delivered messages on my behalf. However, she is ageing, and as I am moving, I shall need someone young and strong to serve me, hence—' She gestured at Jamīla's person. 'Maadah, open the chest.'

Jamīla watched the slave creak out of the chair. The chest was on the floor by the bed, and to open it Maadah had to kneel. Jamīla heard the crunch of bones as she tried to crouch, followed by a dull thud as both knees hit the ground. Ghadiya lay in composed silence until the action was completed. Having opened the chest and retrieved its contents, Maadah began to turn towards Jamīla, a sealed letter in her hand. Jamīla, watching the incremental twist of her waist as she tried to reach her, covered the short distance in a handful of strides and all but snatched the letter from her. As she watched Maadah's pitiful attempts at fluid movement, Jamīla wondered if she was seeing her own future. The older slave pressed a decrepit palm onto Jamīla's skin and raised her head to look into Jamīla's eyes. She attempted to speak before crumbling into a coughing fit. Jamīla, unsure what to do, stepped back and looked to Ghadiya. Ghadiya was examining her fingernails. Once Maadah had stopped coughing, Ghadiya looked at Jamīla. 'I expect you to be discreet.'

**

A tall man stepped forward from the shadows. Jamīla had been given an unfamiliar address to arrive at. Upon doing so, she encountered a gatekeeper who instructed her to walk with her eyes on the ground until they entered a courtyard. He had promptly disappeared. She had stood, alone, it had seemed, until now. 'You are the slave mentioned in this letter.'

Jamīla nodded. She knew who he was. Hajji-Agha Mullah Shapur Kazem Ghaffari, the young mullah Sanaa had grown up with, was taller than she had imagined. He had the imperious shoulders of a soldier and the self-satisfaction of a Qājār. He was dressed, however, like a scholar. He donned a black turban and wore a long silk robe. His voice was flat. 'What kind of education do you hope to achieve here?'

Jamīla stared, mute.

'You cannot go to school, you cannot talk publicly; your life's work is to serve the petty needs of another. You have no use for the education you risk your livelihood to acquire.' He let this pronouncement hang in the air.

Jamīla was listening, but still she couldn't speak.

'Your name is?'

'Hajji-Agha, my name is Jamīla. Jamīla Habashī.'

'I see.' He paused for a moment. 'Return in one week to collect a reply from my brother and spend the hour with me. We shall begin the process of your instruction.'

'Why would you do this?' Jamīla asked, perplexed.

'Why?'

'When I did not even attempt to persuade you.'

'Why did you not?'

Jamīla hesitated.

Shapur Ghaffari smiled. 'You have your answer.'

He pointed at the door. The qāpči materialised. 'The gatekeeper shall let you out.'

8

'Do you remember Aabir?' Jamīla asked, idly stroking Nosrat's chest. It was almost morning, and she lay beside him, watching the sky ease into light.

Two months had passed since the funeral in January. Since her first meeting with Shapur, Jamīla had been speeding through the *Shahnameh*, keen to complete the reading list he had given her. She had never read epic poetry before, and Ferdowsi's book was as dense as it was tragic. She had shivered when Rostam inadvertently slaughtered his son, and yet she had sighed when he sought to honour him with the royal funeral Suhrāb deserved. *Everybody gets a funeral. Everybody gets their honour, their stories told. Who will tell of people like us? Will you?*

Do you remember Aabir? Jamīla did not repeat the words aloud, but she sighed as Nosrat replied.

'I cannot say I do. Should I?'

'He remembered you. He had stories about playing with you as a child.'

Nosrat rubbed his eyes. 'I grew up in the harem. Every slave has "stories" of playing with me as a child, and there are hundreds of them at court. Who ignores a Qājār prince?'

'He had sharp memories, Shaazdeh.'

'Tell me.'

'He recalled a cat. Aabir told of another, black and white with a damaged tail. You asked to keep it. Aabir kept it for you.' She watched the memory return to his face. 'It was quite a risk he took doing that.'

Nosrat grimaced. 'Shelve the sanctimony. I dislike it. I recall this

Aabir. I remember the cat. It smelled, and nobody would feed it for me because it was not allowed. Soon after, it disappeared. I suspect it ran away. Or possibly it died. Why are we so concerned?'

Jamīla sat upright and looked at him. His face was bewildered with sleep, his body curling against hers.

'Aabir himself died not too long ago.'

'He died.' Nosrat too sat upright. 'Why was I not informed of this?'

'Perhaps because you would not have cared. You had already forgotten him, after all.'

'Jamīla. I shan't feel guilty about forgetting the name of a single slave. There are over a thousand in the palace, and I have yet to include my father's staff, the dancers, the concubines and so forth. Did you know Aabir so well?'

'I did.'

'What was his favourite colour?'

There was a silence. Jamīla's face twisted into a hardened frown. 'Nobody has a favourite colour.'

'Yours is silver.'

'Mine is red.'

'Except, of course, that you do not have a favourite.' Without waiting for her reply, he asked, 'Tell me, what did Aabir dream of doing? He must have thought he would retire. Every slave longs for it, or so Abimelech tells me. So what did Aabir intend to do?'

'He...' Jamīla faltered. Then she straightened and said, 'When you have masters to serve, you lack time for idle talk.'

'Except for the time you spend playing with your masters, memories they are to retain until their dying day, lest you disappear without a healthy portion of your dead owner's wealth as is presumed to be your due?'

Jamīla remained silent. Nosrat seldom took a tone with her,

and enjoyed her spirited ribbing. She could not tell if this was an experience she could walk back from. Eventually, adopting a tone of contrition, she said, 'I apologise, Shāhzadeh, if I spoke out of turn.'

'Be honest, Jamīla,' he chided her. 'You did not know Aabir either.' The room appeared to imbibe the heaviness hanging between them; its moroseness coloured the walls. She felt oppressed by his sobriety, irked by his words. He continued, his voice clipped, 'It is worse for you. You worked with him, or rather you saw him every day. Do you think me naive? You want to imply that I lack memory and reverence for life that is not as privileged as my own. Do I not indulge your arrogant tirades with minimal complaint? You should have known him better. You did him a disservice by forgetting him. I promise you, he never expected me to recall who he was. From you, he sought friendship. You dismiss me as absorbed in my own life. But Jamīla, you, you are similarly absorbed. All your talk about your identity and your desires – what woman do you know who thinks of such things, what slave?'

Jamīla couldn't respond. She stared up at the chandelier; frozen in place. Nosrat rose from the bed, put on a robe and walked away.

9

Abimelech was with Nosrat when the latter received a summons from the Shāh. Nosrat had been shouting before a slave came in with the message. The stain on Nosrat's favourite waistcoat had not been removed, but Abimelech had returned it to him without noticing. It was not his job to carry or clean Nosrat's clothing, but Nosrat frequently refused to complete the written tasks Abimelech set him after their lessons. He shunned most tuition, spurned any political engagement, so when not entertaining him, Abimelech had nothing to do. Bored and surrounded by slaves swamped with work, Abimelech often volunteered to lessen their load. And so Abimelech found himself carrying mounds of Nosrat's washing to his rooms almost every week.

Nosrat was still shouting when the summons arrived. The slave looked fretfully at Abimelech. Abimelech nodded at him to leave. He knew what to do. Taking a deep breath, he looked gently at Nosrat and asked, 'Shaazdeh, would you like me to accompany you to see the Shāh?'

Nosrat stared at Abimelech, his eyes moist. His lips, squeezed into their usual petulant frown, softened. His brow, heavy like his father's, relaxed. The chin, spotted with sparse hairs, so quick to quiver, still jutted out. He placed his head, chin first, against Abimelech's chest and closed his eyes. He spoke his gratitude into Abimelech's torso, his lips moving against the angry red weal that had formed when Nosrat had thrown a candle at him earlier. Abimelech tried not to shudder.

Standing back to look Abimelech in the eyes, Nosrat asked, 'Why do you think he has sent for me?'

'He sent for the council. You are on the council, Shaazdeh.'

'I am aware, Abimelech, but this is an unscheduled meeting. D-do you think something is wrong?'

'No, Shaazdeh.' Abimelech replied, simply.

'Well?'

'I could not say, but...I suspect there is more news from Russia.'

'More?'

'On the Tsesarevich.'

Nosrat blanched. 'The...?'

He does not know anything. Abimelech chuckled. 'You are correct, of course, Shaazdeh. I should get used to calling him the Tsar. But yes, I suspect there is more news about Nicholas II.'

'He is the new tsar of...Russia?'

'He has been the Tsar for quite a few months now. I should not have said Tsesarevich. Alexander III died, after all, last November.'

Nosrat nodded. 'Yes, of course.' He gulped. 'This new tsar could be a...problem for us?'

There was a small silence. Abimelech sighed inwardly but stepped closer to him and stroked his hair. He murmured into it in careful tones. 'We must not keep the Shāh waiting. Let us find you something more formal to wear.'

They made their way to the office where the meeting was to take place, hand in hand. Nosrat was shaking, so Abimelech produced a cloth, dabbing at the prince's brow. 'You have little to fear,' he insisted, without breaking his stride as he led Nosrat to the door.

Nosrat stepped in front of him and tapped his fist against the oak panelling. There was a silence, and Abimelech gave him a light push, so he twisted the handle and went in. Too late, Abimelech realised he should have gone first and introduced Nosrat, who was now thrust before the assembled company. Nosrat's three elder brothers, Mass'oud, Mozaffar and Kamran were already there, alongside the Grand Vizier, Ali Asghar. There were two Persian physicians whom Abimelech did not recognise and a European man smoking a ġalyān. The Shāh was spread across multiple chairs, a glass in his hand, scanning the room without a word. Nobody looked up as they entered, caught up in the frenzied chatter that filled the room. Abimelech wished he had heard what the Shāh had said earlier, or what had caused this enduring tension.

Abimelech felt almost comforted by the nervousness of the men. The Shāh's government had multiple councils and department bodies, but Nosrat had avoided politics, so Abimelech knew little about them. Only at his mother's urging had Nosrat agreed to take an interest in this council. It was the most senior but also the most informal; its existence was flatly denied and hard to prove. The Shāh, battling allegations of corruption and collusion, had to appease government officials, the chief mujtahids across Persia and the European ambassadors who expected transparency and access. He could not be seen to have a private coalition of men with untold allegiances who advised his every move.

The first creak of the Shāh's frame as he adjusted his posture drew everyone's attention. The room collapsed into silence, words falling upon themselves, ideas scooped back into their masters' mouths as the Shāh spoke. 'It is not enough. We know too little of this Nicholas. Yes, that speech suggests we have similar values. But he is a boy, still! Will he recognise Nāṣir al-Dīn Shāh Qājār? I will not take orders from a boy. I will not be a pawn to the Russians.'

'You never could be!' insisted the Grand Vizier, proffering a bow as he spoke.

'Russia is a pawn in our affairs,' boomed Mass'oud. He continued, but another man spoke over him.

'You are the Shāh of Shāhs! The highest of all majesty. Allah's greatest creation! No European country can intimidate you!'

Nosrat's three brothers turned to the speaker, frowns on their faces. The speaker, a short physician with spectacles sliding down his nose, took a deep breath and straightened up, as if to visibly stand by his words.

'Are you suggesting something *could* intimidate our Shāh?' the Grand Vizier enquired, in silky tones.

'I-I...of course not–' His face grew crimson, and unformed words speckled the air as he stuttered his response.

'It sounded like you were,' the Grand Vizier persisted, and Mozaffar nodded.

Mass'oud interjected, in peremptory tones, 'Let us return to the matter at hand, shall we? Let us focus not on the words of an individual but the words of a shāh. Father, I believe you had more to say.'

The Shāh looked to Mass'oud with an indulgent smile. 'My dear boy, how generous you are.'

'Yes!' the Grand Vizier said, echoing the Shāh, before reaching out to pat Mass'oud on the arm.

The Shāh coughed. Once again, silence flooded the room. 'I will not be a pawn for the game between Britain and Russia. I will not be the puppet for them. I am...tired. I am tired of being manipulated. I am tired of angering my people. We need to reconsider our relationships.'

The clamour of voices rose again, each determined to stand out with the poignancy of its affirmation. Abimelech watched the Shāh. The Shāh looked at him and then at Nosrat. Abimelech swallowed. He wondered what the Shāh saw. But the Shāh only blinked, realising his younger son was there for the first time.

His face, withered with age, flattened into a smile.

'My little painter! My fellow men, the artist is finally present! Tell me – your deftness that turns art to transcendence, does it grant you any insight into my dilemma here?'

Abimelech suppressed a shudder. He knew that Nosrat did not know what to say. He could taste the anticipation in the air. Fear was etched upon Nosrat's face. Helpless, he turned to Abimelech. *Do not look at me...*

'Do not look to your eunuch!' The Grand Vizier laughed. The dam broke; the men began to cackle.

'This eunuch was his teacher.'

'Not a very good one, it seems!'

Mass'oud smirked. 'Do not blame the eunuch if *baby boy* refuses to learn.'

'Baby boy?' Kamran spluttered, his brows shooting into his hair.

'I did not study much, either...' Mozaffar offered and hiccoughed.

'Yes,' Mass'oud replied, gazing at Mozaffar's food-stained frock coat. 'Yet you have come so far.'

The laughter was mixed with gasps now.

'You would mock an heir?' Kamran feigned shock.

'Not one able to feed themselves.'

'Let us not get distracted.' The Grand Vizier's smooth voice floated over the proceedings.

Mass'oud nodded. 'Indeed. The Shāh is awaiting answers.'

'Which the eunuch is meant to provide.' A smile flickered across Kamran's face.

'Well, every prince needs a mouthpiece.' Mass'oud quipped.

'For speaking *and eating*, it seems.' Kamran shook his head at Mass'oud, who thrust his chest forward and smirked.

'Enlighten us, eunuch. What would Prince Nosrat have said?'

'What *should* Prince Nosrat have said?' The younger physician chuckled, but the Grand Vizier gave a discreet cough, and everyone turned in his direction.

The Grand Vizier, glad of his audience, looked directly at Nosrat and continued, 'What could he possibly say, that you, prince of the Qājārs, son of the Shāh, the Shāh of Shāhs, had not already considered? Let us hear from you.'

The Shāh spoke. 'I hope you are not mocking my boy.' The echoing laughter, like a tangible substance, was snatched from the room. The Grand Vizier bent forward in a bow that functioned as a denial. The Shāh returned his glance to Abimelech. 'Your name?'

'A'laa Hazrat, I am called Abimelech.'

'Abimelech, do you have any insights to proffer?'

Abimelech paused, unsure if he should answer.

The Shāh continued. 'Do not be fearful of these men. They have rank and intellect but lack the grace of maturity. I have asked you. It was sudden – if you are without insight, you will be forgiven.'

'A'laa Hazrat, I might have...insight to offer.'

The air in the room changed once more. Curiosity was overlaid with suspicion. The European sat a little straighter.

'Proceed.'

Abimelech coughed. 'A'laa Hazrat, I agree you should reconsider your Western relationships. I would not encourage anything drastic, however. To my...humble mind, the problem you face is one of perception. Whilst the British may wish for acquiescence – and I cannot claim to have any insight into what they w-w-want–' Abimelech paused. 'Perhaps they may settle for the *a-appearance* of acquiescence whilst you, A'laa Hazrat, delay any decisions you must make. With regards to Russia, having just lost their tsar, I daresay we shall not be their focus for some time. I suspect his son was not ready to succeed his father, thus their focus will be helping him transition. Those preoccupations in St. Petersburg may lessen the pressure here. And there are pressures here! Tehran is angry, A'laa Hazrat. There are radicals and intellectuals who are unhappy with...who would challenge the Qājār dynasty. In the face of pressure from the British – assuming any such pressure should arise – you could convey the need to stabilise the country before considering international duties. We must not forget the Tobacco Protest. The people have yet to forgive the court for the tobacco concession that was given to Great Britain. They are still wary of foreign powers. Your priority must be your people and yourself, A'laa Hazrat.'

Everyone in the room was silent.

Abimelech looked at Nosrat. He could tell Nosrat was seething.

The Grand Vizier looked as annoyed as Nosrat. Meanwhile, Mass'oud and Kamran looked impressed, the physicians suspicious, and Mozaffar was fiddling with his coat. The European spoke first. 'A thoughtful, if brief, analysis.' He nodded at Abimelech but said nothing else.

The Shāh looked from the European to Abimelech. Then he looked at Nosrat. 'You have a wise eunuch, my son. Such wisdom is an invaluable tool. I may have to borrow his mind.'

'A'laa Hazrat, it was all Prince Nosrat – I am just echoing his thoughts.' The words were vacant, empty of any truth. Nosrat glared at him, unable to mask his fury. To have a slave advocate on one's behalf was perhaps the most shameful thing a man could experience. And this was no ordinary man; he was a Qājār. He was the fourth son of the Shāh. Abimelech felt foolish. Unperturbed, the Shāh nodded and then gestured to one of the physicians. The man turned first to Nosrat and dipped into a quick bow.

'Shāhzadeh, we have yet to formally meet. I am Mirza Fatali al-Dawlih. You may call me Fatali. I shall present an informal agenda for the bulk of this meeting...'

Fatali paced with a youthful stride as he called out various political specifics that the Shāh wanted commentary on. He did not call on Nosrat again, and Nosrat, staring at the floor, avoided opportunities to speak.

'Let us conclude,' the Shāh said. It was followed with a flurry of bows and murmurs of adoration. As the men began to exit, the Shāh raised his hand. 'Nosrat, I need your eunuch to stay. Boy, what is your name?'

'Abimelech, A'laa Hazrat.'

'Abimelech, remain here.' He gestured to his son. 'Nosrat, inform one of the other eunuchs that Abimelech shall be with me this evening. As such, his duties should be passed to– well, whomever. Regardless, ensure that the chief eunuch is informed of this.'

Abimelech knew Nosrat would not do this. The Shāh paused. *He knows too.* 'If he is not, he may be very angry with Abimelech. If that should happen...Well, we do not want a mere chief eunuch to feel a shāh's wrath, do we? *Be sure it is done.*' He raised his voice. 'Everybody out.'

He turned to Abimelech. He extended a hand and invited him closer. 'Have a drink, Abimelech.'

10

Nosrat's mood was so sullen Jamīla could smell it when she entered. Watching him, she felt herself deflate. He was twisted away from the entrance, lying prone in his bed. He wouldn't be seduced. She paused, wondering what she might try. He had not spoken when she had entered, had not acknowledged her arrival. She wanted to leave, open the door with the tiniest twist and disappear into the dark. She did not dare.

She tried to lighten the mood. 'I read a new book.' No response. *What would Abimelech say?* Perhaps they would discuss Paris. The Shāh had photographs of Nosrat's little obsession. Abimelech had shown them to Jamīla. The city was grubby, the buildings bland. Those that weren't crumbling were straight and dull, buildings so anonymous Jamīla could not believe Nosrat preferred them to the muqarnas in Tehran.

But she could not ask him about Paris directly. She could not betray Abimelech's secret.

She looked over at the sliver of Nosrat, visible despite the swathes of fabric hiding him in the bed. No movement.

She sighed. 'It's called *Le Père Goriot.*'

Nosrat rose.

Emboldened, she added, 'It is a novel you may wish to consider.' She walked over to the chaise and sat down without looking at him.

'*Le Père Goriot,*' she repeated. She waited.

'Why would it hold my interest?' Nosrat snapped.

'It is set in Paris, Shaazdeh.'

'You have seen me reading, Jamīla?'

'I have not, Shaazdeh.'

'You suggest something in which I have yet to show interest?'

'Have you no interest in Paris, Shaazdeh?'

He slid off the bed and walked over to where she sat. Jamīla felt tense. 'I have little interest in *Balzac*.' His hand found her throat. 'Stop talking.'

His eyes held a challenge within them. She wriggled from his grasp, rose from the chair and walked around him towards the windows. She traced her hand along the silk of the curtain and eased it to one side.

'I find him thoughtful.' She held the curtain aloft. She stepped closer to the window, letting the folds fall behind her. Nosrat caught the curtain as it dropped, pushing her forward until she was pressed into the glass.

'Oh?' His voice was gentle.

'Yes.' The cold of the window seared against her eye. The tip of her nose flattened against it. She couldn't breathe. He was crushing her into the glass. 'For those who have read his work, *Le Père Goriot* is an honest reflection of class in Paris. It is realistic—'

'*Realism*—'

'It is,' Jamīla snapped, 'how one might find themselves in Paris without a patron, without a family.'

'And how is that?' He pulled her back by her hair, shoved her into the window. 'Tell me.' She shuffled sideways, and slid fully from his grasp.

'It is tragic. It is *pathetic*. Balzac is kind towards the poor. He pities them.' She took a step back with each sentence. Nosrat took a step forward. 'The main character,' she continued, 'is a young man, new to Paris, without means. He struggles to find allies. He has only two friends, a criminal and an impoverished man...'

'You have concluded?' Nosrat's smile was thin. He stood still.

'Will you not tell me what happened to this young male emigrant and his unfortunate friends?'

'I shall not. You must read the book, Shaazdeh!'

'I think, Jamīla, it is time you stopped giving me instructions.'

She swallowed. Her shoulders were trembling. Her face had begun to feel tender. 'You are correct, as always, Hazrat-e Aghdass-e Vaalaa,' she offered.

'You shall listen without comment, Jamīla,' he said, his composure crumpling. 'You shall not talk to me about Paris!'

'Why?'

'Why?! You are to obey me, and this is what I request.'

'You have always requested my candour.'

'Today, I *request* your silence.'

'Shāhzadeh,' Jamīla whispered, her voice trembling, 'I think I should leave.'

'I think you should follow instructions!'

'You are angry.'

'You-you—' Nosrat was spluttering now, his face crimson.

'Why must we not talk about Paris?'

'Why must we talk of it at all?'

'It is your favourite city. You talk of it often. I thought I might acquaint myself with that which interests you.'

He faltered. 'I have little interest in these men: Balzac, Zola or any chroniclers of the poor. I am a Qājār prince. Should my Paris not be that of aristocrats and princes, not idealistic men and criminals?'

'The French executed their last king.'

'King Louis-Philippe I's grandson is in exile in England.'

Jamīla let out a breath. 'The real monarchy ended with the First Republic.'

It was Nosrat's turn to smile. 'How often, when you speak,

do you use your own words? Or are you always a vessel for
Abimelech's thoughts?'

'It appears we *both* listen to Abimelech's thoughts.'

He moved too quickly for her. His hands found her throat.
They tangled on the floor. The violence lacked the effort of his
earlier approach. Jamīla pushed him off quickly with a flailing,
frantic foot.

His body slammed into the wall. She gasped.

'Sorry,' he said, to her surprise.

She didn't reply, their heavy breathing the only sound.

'Sorry.' He inched over to her.

Go *away*.

'Sorry.' He kept his eyes averted, but he leaned over her, allowing
his hand to chance upon her stomach.

She shuddered.

Desperate to distract, she said, 'What is your Paris then, if not
that of Balzac and Zola?'

His gaze, as it fell on her, was wary. He turned away from her,
his hand rubbing his face instead, and it was through his fingers
that his muffled voice emerged. 'My Paris is one of art, of the
thoughts that it inspires, of the work such thoughts produce.' In
a different voice he said, 'Have I shown you the work of Gustave
Moreau? He does not paint as his peers do. His work – have you
seen *Salomé*? He draws inspiration from the Renaissance era.
The result is resplendent. Opulent yet eccentric. Revolutionary
yet regressive.' He fell silent before adding, his hurried voice
verging on fretful, 'Would such a man consider tutelage? He-
he would offer his services to none but the most extraordinary.
A visionary artist. Would not a connoisseur count? A talented
artist with a command of its history? With a crown and a history
of his own? How would a Qājār prince look to a French genius?'

She realised later, he had offered her the answers she sought but to questions she hadn't asked. She could have kept him talking – with empathy, with flattery, with indulgence. But Jamīla was irritated. Her throat hurt. Her face hurt. Her body was aflame. She felt the sneer leaping from her throat as she scoffed, 'You intend to meet a talented artist in a country that hates monarchs and brandish your royalty, expecting to command favour? You would arrive as a *penniless* prince, unless you intend to leave court with your father's jewels stitched into your frock coat. I cannot fathom why you would trade royalty in your own country for poverty in another, nor do I recall your spoken French being even as fluid as–'

He slapped her.

She tasted blood. He stared at her, satisfied.

He raised his hand once more. She caught it before it landed. His face was crimson. She leapt to her feet. She thought she should speak. Apologise, maybe. But as she hesitated, he grabbed her foot. She kicked him off. Harder than before. Then she kicked him again.

'Jamīla!' His voice was pained. His hands clutched his face. 'Jamīla!' – this time with rage.

She flew to the door. Flung it open. Didn't look back. Running.

11

'Sit. Lie back.'

Abimelech watched the Shāh gesture to him with an indulgent smile.

Abimelech met his indulgence with an embarrassed smile. 'A'laa Hazrat...' *Your Most High Majesty...*

'I insist, Abimelech. Worry not.' The Shāh rose with difficulty and went over to a marble table. He picked up a decanter and opened it. With a satisfied sniff, he reached for a glass.

It took Abimelech a moment to realise what was being done. 'Please, A'laa Hazrat, allow me!' He jumped up, and in his haste almost wrestled the decanter from the Shāh.

'Fighting with a shāh, are we?'

Abimelech flinched.

The Shāh's crinkled features opened; each furrow was pierced with riotous laughter. Abimelech had never heard the Shāh laugh. The sound rushed forth with a volcanic hiss. He watched with curiosity before allowing himself to join in. 'Sit down, boy. As I said, you worry too much. You worry about irrelevant things. How is my boy? How is Nosrat?'

Lazy, sloppy, sad.

Abimelech returned to his chair and sat upright. 'Tired, I suspect,' he replied.

'Why does he know so little, when you know so much?' The Shāh's tone seemed neutral, but Abimelech felt a strain of menace in his words.

'I think, A'laa Hazrat, that Nosrat knows his own mind most of all. My job is to serve him. Teach him yes, but serve him most of all.'

The Shāh sighed. 'Worry not, Abimelech. I am not blaming you for his ineptitude.' He poured them each a glass and carried them over to Abimelech, offering him one.

'A'laa Hazrat! I cannot permit you to – it is beneath your dignity...'

The Shāh looked at him. 'Is it not further beneath my dignity to have my son's eunuch attempt to control me? Debate with me? Challenge me?'

'Yes, A'laa Hazrat.'

The Shāh sighed. 'The truth, boy, is that I am stifled too much by tradition. It has cost me many things...' He trailed off. 'Have you known loss?'

Abimelech considered the question. He thought of the family he would never see again, the brother whose death he refused to recall, the sister whose name he wouldn't say. He had blocked out the details of the betrayal and the faces of those who had sold him, but his dreams brought echoes of his screams the night his manhood was stripped from him, the botched, messy, violent procedure that killed most of the boys who were with him. He remembered a pretty slave in the first house where he had served, who treated him with affection. He recalled the slurs she murmured under her breath and the affirmative laughs of her peers. He considered his fifteenth night in the Qājār court, when he was raped by a court physician. He could still feel the hands of the man, pushing his buttocks apart, the weight of his urgent breath as it seared against his skin. He thought of Jamīla's garments in a mess on Nosrat's floor. He thought of Nosrat himself and every time he had had to undress him, kneel before him, and taste him. He thought of Nosrat's hands, pressing down on his head, his gasping, guttural moans as he pushed.

'Nothing so deep as yours, A'laa Hazrat.'

'Perhaps. You are still a boy after all. When you have a family...'

The Shāh looked at Abimelech and blushed. He took another slurp of his whisky and tried, with a trembling hand, to pour Abimelech another glass. His hand tipped the decanter; whisky bled onto the floor. Abimelech sat there, looking at the brown liquid pools immersing themselves in the carpet. They slid into the fabric, leaving it fuller, thicker, fetid – then disappeared, forgotten.

'...and her name was Jayran,' the Shāh was saying, the words washing over Abimelech. He attempted to focus, to look up, but his head felt heavy. He was surprised by how much exertion it required. 'With Jayran, I broke all the rules. It is the very definition of love, my boy: the desire to remake the world to fit around her wishes. She was a sigheh. I made her an 'aqdi and tried to make her son my heir! To make a temporary wife, a permanent one? It was madness. It *caused* madness. I had to divorce another 'aqdi to make it happen. Do you know what happened in the end?'

Abimelech knew and did not care. However, it was clear that the Shāh sought an uninformed audience. He shook his head.

'She died, boy. I suspect she was poisoned. One of the physicians at the time was almost certain. Her sons, too, both died. My whole family was killed, my children and my bride. 34 years later, my heart is still broken.'

'I grieve for you, A'laa Hazrat.' Abimelech said, his tone sober.

'You have grief in your eyes, boy.' The Shāh sighed. 'You grieve for yourself. You are a eunuch. I imagine there was some unpleasantness at some point in your life. Tell me of it.'

'A'laa Hazrat, I could not...waste your time on issues such as mine. I was made a eunuch a very long time ago. I recall little, and I am not one to dwell. I would rather look forward.' His voice was flat. He would not recall those moments. He would not feel those memories. Those years spent harbouring ghosts, haunted by death, were behind him. Never again would he fashion with feverish devotion, and lay on his mattress with careful precision, that collection of nooses. Laid out in even lines, less of a list and more of a dirge, each one was an ode to a life he had watched wash out. On the anniversary of one, he would prepare them all. Every birthday and every death day, then every weekend and then... He began to include an extra one, a final noose, formed from the bedclothes that remained. He would stroke it as it sat against his throat. It would feel snug with a sense of rightness. But as he stood on the chair, his legs would tremble. His hands against the chandelier would shake. The dirge of the dead would falter, and a voice would tell him to wait.

Could he live this life once more – and innumerable times? He could hear his memory ringing in his ears.

Those days were behind him.

He would not break himself apart again to amuse an idle shāh. He would not...

The Shāh continued. 'Tell me of your life now – not of your duties, but of your life.'

'Aʼlaa Hazrat, why would you want to know of my life? I have little to tell. I work, I sleep, I rise, I repeat.'

'You are asking me why?' The Shāh sounded incredulous. He chuckled to himself. 'You will never know the tedium of being surrounded by sycophants. I have advisors with an agenda and silly wives with a complaint. Everyone agrees with me. They pester me with their requests, pretending they are my own. They think me too foolish to see through their designs. They do not know I hold a window to their minds. You ask why, eunuch. Well, I confess I am curious. Who else is worthy of your thoughts, but the Shāh of Shāhs?'

The Shāh stopped and stared at him.

Abimelech paused, then took a deep breath and said, 'I wait under the arches in the Khalvat-i Karim-khani until the gardens are empty. When I can be sure nobody is near, I step out into them. There is something about being in the presence of nature that rejuvenates my mind in a way I cannot fully explain. In the natural world we are all men, we are all equals, we are humbled by those unshakeable details. The sun, the moon, the sky – they remain unchanged by our existence. As vibrant or diaphanous as they appear, they are not dictated by us, our petty whims, our endless wars, our great loves, our unquenchable grief. They are within our sight, but we are not within theirs. We are separated by invisible fault lines. I am made reverent by this notion. It gives me life.'

'Whereas the harem takes life away?'

'Not at all, A'laa Hazrat. Not at all.'

12

'Something must be done about Colonel Kosagoskij,' the Grand Vizier intoned. 'His behaviour has been an affront to the Shāh of Shāhs! Ever since we brought in that colonel, he has sought to keep the Cossack Brigade under control...'

It had not taken Abimelech long to realise that he hated these meetings. They were slow, petty, and increasingly frequent – this was the second in a month.

'But they are the Shāh's men! We cannot let the colonel have his way,' an advisor piped.

Mass'oud looked irritated by this interruption. 'We know this, thank you. The colonel–'

The Grand Vizier continued, 'The Cossack Brigade has too much power, and we should–'

There was a light cough. The Grand Vizier, who had spoken over Mass'oud, stopped at once, but his face bore displeasure. He turned to Kamran Mirza, his face expectant.

'We would be fools to disband the Cossack Brigade.' Kamran looked at his father. 'We cannot destroy the only protection this court has. The Russians are not an imminent threat; the Persian public is. We cannot be rash.'

'We are not being rash!' Mass'oud burst out. 'They take orders from St Petersburg!'

'Even the Persian soldiers in the brigade follow them,' the Grand Vizier added. 'We need to maintain control.'

'I had not finished speaking,' Kamran replied. The Grand Vizier frowned but bowed his head in deference. 'You are not being strategic. You are being impetuous and proud. I expect that from a brother but not a Grand Vizier. If I may be frank, Ali Asghar, strategy is what we need, and this has never been your strength. You cannot be reactive or seek short-term responses. We cannot attack at the first sign of an affront. We cannot appear to endorse the insubordination of a cavalry unit, even when it serves us. It would damage our relationship with the Russians – and we need them. We even need Colonel Kosagoskij, and what we do not need is their wrath.'

Nobody quite dared say anything after he spoke. Abimelech watched the advisors beside him. The silence remained, but one of them sank into a slow frown. Another whispered to Mass'oud Mirza. He coughed and then cleared his throat, but before he could speak, the Shāh opened his mouth. He had been pacing with a tired restlessness that dragged his feet across the floor. He was standing apart from his advisors, with papers clamped in his hand. There was a bottle of wine on a broad, oak-panelled table in front of him. The Shāh sighed. He stopped pacing, and every face was wiped blank in anticipation. His eyes fell upon the youngest in the room.

'Nosrat?' He poured wine into a crystal tumbler. 'Will you not drink with me?'

Nosrat blinked and looked at Abimelech. Abimelech dared not move, with so many eyes in the room. Nosrat turned back towards his father. He inclined his head before moving towards the Shāh and taking the glass from him.

'Tell me something,' the Shāh watched him drink, fixing him with a hardened smile, 'do you agree with the opinion of the premier?'

Nosrat looked again at Abimelech, his eyes widening. Abimelech winced. He took another gulp of his drink as he prepared himself to think of something to say.

'What does the eunuch think?' Kamran's words cut through the room. 'We have little time, Father. Perhaps we should not stall this meeting by drawing words from those with little to say. Abu...?' The Shāh nodded.

'Abimelech, Shāhzadeh.' Abimelech, turning to Kamran, fell into a deep bow. 'I...agree with your words, Shāhzadeh.' *Why speak at all?* His face felt hot.

There was a light snicker from the Grand Vizier. Nosrat permitted himself a light cough. *Nosrat is so petty.* Abimelech looked at Kamran.

Kamran's face was inscrutable. 'If you have more to say, eunuch, proceed.'

'I do...Shāhzadeh.' *Think first. Try not to squander it a second time.* He straightened his shoulders. 'I believe the bigger issue is the state of the country. The people are angry with us, with our relationship to these foreign powers. They want to build railways. They want the prominence of their local goods. They are perturbed by the dominance of the Europeans. We have no Persian national banks; we have already closed many of the new factories. The people believe we are in the pockets of the Europeans, and that angers them; it also impoverishes them. Their anger puts the court at risk. We seek protection from the Russians, which legitimises their point and increases their anger. We need the Russians because the Shāh is at risk for his life – but we also need to wean ourselves off the support of the European powers. They mean to plunder us, both Qājār and country.'

'Us?' the Grand Vizier asked.

Abimelech looked at him, confused, trying not to frown.

'You said, "us". You consider *yourself* a Persian? You consider this your country?'

'I...' Abimelech bowed his head. 'I was speaking about the

Persian people.'

'Of which you are not one.'

'I serve the Persian people.'

'You serve the Persian king. You are too bold, eunuch.'

'He is not to blame,' Mass'oud interjected. 'It is Kamran goading him out of his place.'

There were murmurs of agreement amongst the other advisors.

'You are right,' Kamran agreed, to Abimelech's horror. Abimelech dropped his gaze, frozen to the spot. He tasted bile in his throat. Kamran, indifferent or oblivious, continued smoothly. 'The eunuch went beyond his station. But in the absence of sound advice from politicians, what choice does a dutiful son have? I will bring smart advice to my father from any direction – provided it is sound. And whether you like the eunuch or not, he thinks more strategically than you.'

Do not smile. Do not smile.

The Grand Vizier looked apoplectic.

Mass'oud shook his head.

The other advisors were murmuring, but none dared speak aloud. Mozaffar and Nosrat were distracted. Abimelech watched the latter pour his elder brother a drink, both their heads bowed.

The Grand Vizier took a deep breath and began to speak. 'If I may—'

'The eunuch spoke well, Father,' Kamran Mirza interrupted. 'And he has no vested interest in the outcomes. He does not speak with his eye to the throne.'

As if sensing an outburst, Mass'oud quickly spoke. 'Yes, the eunuch is candid, and perhaps candour is what Father needs, but we have yet to hear a resolution to the very real problem that was raised. The Cossack Brigade is beyond the control of the Qājārs. The lone faction that is loyal to us is under threat from the colonel in charge. How do we proceed?'

'It is very simple,' Kamran said. 'We empathise with the colonel, and we fund the brigade. We ask them to keep our support discreet, and we let things unfold. The key is to play *both* sides. Then regardless of the outcome, we are guaranteed to win.'

13

'Were you intending to tell me?' Jamīla asked.

The sun had slipped away, but the air was still humid. Jamīla sat outside on the ayvān, looking out over the courtyard. In the distance, a cluster of čenār trees rubbed their heads together, their large palmate leaves freckling the darkening sky. Shapur, beside her on the veranda, appeared to listen to her words, but his gaze, as always, hovered somewhere just beyond. He did not answer.

She repeated her question.

In the three months since he had agreed to instruct her, an action he deemed 'futile, dangerous and self-indulgent,' he had seldom looked her in the eye, drawn instead to the natural world by a lure Jamīla failed to see.

Shapur maintained his silence. Jamīla, her eyes on the garden, felt undercurrents of frustration. Much like Shapur's face – which mirrored that of any Persian noble, with its smooth ivory skin, heavy, puckered brow and effortless froideur – his private hayāt was every inch the garden she expected. An elongated rectangle cut into pristine pathways with glazed stone, each square holding a motionless pool lined with potted trees eight metres apart. She knew that if she visited every other house on the street, she would find the same garden within.

She had been slipping away in the daytime to have her secret sessions with Shapur, under the guise of performing errands. Chehra was chirpy; though she disapproved of Jamīla's daytime sojourns, she was pleased that Jamīla was now available to share her bed. Gul appeared not to believe her excuse but had thanked her nevertheless for 'using her wisdom' and 'seeing Nosrat during the day'. It took Jamīla a moment to realise what was being assumed. She decided to bask in the approval, in the 'improvement' Gul insisted she was making.

It was not a belief, unfortunately, that Shapur seemed to share. Her time with him was strange; she could never articulate why when Sanaa asked her. He had collated a list of classic Persian literature and philosophy books that she was to consume, and they were proceeding through Aṭṭār's Manṭiq-uṭ-Ṭayr. But Shapur did not teach her in a chronological or historical fashion, and his assessments of her progress were discouraging and arbitrary. He was rarely warm; indeed, his manner was that of distant didacticism.

Nevertheless, their sessions together had been a useful distraction. Jamīla had not heard from Nosrat. He had not summoned her or sent for her; it had been three months since she had seen him. She had spent the days after their fight riddled with anxiety. *How severe would the beating be*, she had wondered, the one that would inevitably take place the next time he summoned her. She had steeled herself as she waited. *Would there be broken bones? What if Chehra asked questions?* She had let herself feel a small jolt of relief every day she was not called. Eventually that relief turned back into anxiety. He no longer wanted her. She could not, would not, process this. Shapur's dense and varied reading list, inadvertently, brought her ease.

Jamīla and Shapur continued to sit in silence until, frustrated, she burst out, 'I know you are a radical.'

Shapur was still but for one hand, which ran unconsciously along the silver brocade of his waistcoat.

She continued, 'I have your copy of *Gulistan*.' Pause. 'You have forgotten what you had hidden there, tucked into the back pages?'

The hand on his waistcoat was feverish.

'Were you recruiting me?' She repeated the words, as if to prevent his escaping them.

He turned at last to face her. 'I would not recruit a slave.'

The words stung.

'You claim to have read my writings. You should know then how little use I have for slaves, less for a female slave. A free man might be of use. A free man might find work as a labourer or study to become a mullah. There would be opportunities for such a man. A free woman could not live: she could not do unskilled work, could not be educated and could not serve in a household. Freedom thus offers you nothing. It offers me nothing. You should not wish for freedom, Jamīla. You should hope to die enslaved at court. So, no, I am not trying to recruit you.'

'You are comfortable with slavery. You care only for men you can use?'

'I am not unconcerned with slavery. However, slavery is not the only kind of bondage.' Shapur sighed, looking past her again. 'Do you know about the famine of 1870? Millions of Persians were killed. Why? The ineptitude of the Shāh and his men. People ate grass. They ate dung. They abducted children. They ate the corpses of Jewish people. You did not exist. But we did, and we- we lost everything. Our families, our livelihood...'

Jamīla did not care. She was unmoved by his narrative of luxury and loss. Was she not an abducted child? Had she not seen worse than the eating of corpses and the starving of men? What did he think she endured on the boats that dragged her here? More famine, death and desperation than he could imagine. *He was weak.* She gritted her teeth, waiting for his lament to conclude.

He carried on. 'My father restored our fortunes, only for the

Shāh to bring another colossal failing on his people. Another event you will know nothing about: the Tobacco Protest. Do you know of its cause? The Shāh promised the British a monopoly on our tobacco, on the production, sale and export of our tobacco, for fifty years. This time, it was the Muslim leaders – the mujtahids, the imams, and the ulumā – who opposed him, publicly. A fatwa was issued, protests took place *within the Qājār court*. And I...I had been asleep to the politics of Persia until that time. I listened to the clergy, to the scholars, to the learned Muslim men who came out against it, to the women, like Zainab Pasha, who marched in protest. I realised that the Persia I lived in did not serve the Persian people. I cannot abide this court's ineptitude and greed. That does not make me a radical. It makes me Iranian.'

'And I am not worthy of joining your mission.' Jamīla's smile was bitter.

'You are not unworthy. You are simply not relevant.' Shapur's eyes lingered on the pool before them. 'You are not Persian. You will not benefit from the gains that Persians will make. It is not useful to you, and we would have no use for you.'

Jamīla stared into her lap, mulling over his words. 'We?'

There was a silence.

She stared hard at him until he looked at her, frustrated to feel tears forming in her eyes. Once she held his gaze, she closed her eyes and recited,

'The smallest mountain on earth is Jur; nevertheless
It is great with Allah in dignity and station.'

'From *Gulistan*, first chapter, third story.' Shapur's tone was brisk. 'Tell me, Jamīla, did you read all eight chapters, or did you stop there?' But he was smiling.

Jamīla had never seen him smile. He would smirk instead, a boyish curl appearing at both corners, shrinking his lips and shrivelling his eyes. *Ugliness is aging,* her mother had always told her, but then her mother had been filled with aphoristic lectures.

Shapur's smile today was open. He even held her gaze as he did it. 'You are not unlike Sanaa when you speak.'

'How?' Jamīla asked, straightening her shoulders.

'She too was insistent on becoming part of this...*community,* if you will, of Persian intellectuals. She too was undeterred by my dissuasion.'

'Sanaa is a radical?'

'She has proved useful, as of late.' Shapur said. 'Rejecting you is not personal. If an African slave is required, we shall summon Sanaa.'

'How...how is she useful?'

'Well, she is a concubine. She has begun to serve a son of the Shāh. He is said to be infatuated with her. All men are...' His smile was rueful, nostalgic.

'A son, which son?'

'The fourth son. Prince...'

'Nosrat?' Jamīla gasped.

'Yes, him.'

She could not breathe.

Shapur continued, 'She can provide us with inside knowledge. Well, Sanaa can convince anyone to do anything...' He was still talking; Jamīla could not hear him.

14

It burned a cardinal red. Abimelech spoke, half-turned to the Shāh, his eyes still fixed on the smouldering sky. 'I have never seen it quite so bright.'

He was kneeling on a velvet cushion, his eyes pressed against a lattice window. They were in the royal library, of which the Shāh had exclusive use. Since their first encounter, the Shāh had taken to summoning him there twice a week to talk privately. But for the royal librarian and the curator, nobody else was permitted to use the room. Abimelech had enjoyed visiting with the Shāh when it was empty during the day. Perhaps the presence of the curator and the librarian, austere, silent men, who looked askance at the brown eunuch trailing the Shāh, had lent the library its chilly air. The Shāh, having sensed his unease, had begun seeking Abimelech more often at the breaking of the day.

'So bright or so dark?' the Shāh asked as, rattling a small tea glass, he poured himself a drink. 'These are the best of the morning skies. The look before the dawn rises. I live for it.' Abimelech watched the sky change its mind, inviting dappled flecks of softer cherry to lighten the blanket of incensed red that first held his attention. 'You are transfixed, boy!' the Shāh said, and Abimelech spun around in a bow.

'A'laa Hazrat, I apologise.' Abimelech flushed, his heart racing.

The Shāh flapped a careless hand. 'Rise. It is not a crime to appreciate beauty. It looks rather like a painting, does it not?'

'It does.'

'What do you see?'

'The robes in *The Inspiration of St Matthew*.'

'Ah, Caravaggio.'

'Prince Nosrat is enamoured.'

The Shāh chuckled. 'Yes, he is obsessed with art.' He gestured to the walls of the room. 'You have seen my rooms? Lined with his pieces. Works from his childhood adorn my office walls. His mother, silly woman, insists I do it.'

'Do...A'laa Hazrat?'

'"Hang these! Not that!" She meddles, that woman. Not that I blame her. She is sad. The councils hate her. They refuse to hear her advice, so she decorates my rooms. It gives her something to do. She gives me his nonsense to look at...' His voice drifted.

Boldly, Abimelech said, 'I would love to have my room adorned with art.'

The Shāh's glance was wistful. 'You are not unlike a man I once loved. He was my chief tutor and first premier when I was a young shāh. We called him A...' The Shāh struggled for a moment, his mouth grasping at the air. 'Amir Kabir,' he burst out finally. 'You must know of him. He built the Majma'-e Dar-al-Sanayeh. I trust you are aware of it?'

'The Polytechnic School of Arts and Crafts! The first of its kind. In *your* reign the first art schools arrived...!' Checking his enthusiasm, Abimelech bowed his head. 'I am unsurprised at such an achievement, A'laa Hazrat. That is a legacy.'

'It is not my legacy. That honour is his. He founded the Dar-al-Fonoun as well. The Dar-al-Fonoun taught traditional art. The Majma'-e Dar-al-Sanayeh had artists from a range of fields training new, young talent. Amir Kabir was a visionary. An extraordinary man. A dear friend.'

'He has died?'

'By my hand, if you can believe it, boy. I gave the order.'

Abimelech faltered, his breath caught in his chest. He could not look up at the Shāh. He kept his head bowed and sat very still.

'That disgusted, are we, boy? It was a different time. I had no advisors such as you.' He placed a hand on Abimelech's shoulder. 'The most precarious position in a royal court is that of a monarch's favourite advisor. Shall I tell you why? The favourite is usually the smartest man in the court. His plans work, the Shāh gives him more responsibility, and the country thrives. But there is never just one advisor in a court. There are many, and every man who is slighted by the Shāh's preference of the one makes an enemy of the advisor and vows to take him down. In the end, the advisor is just one voice. If you have eight voices calling him dangerous and one man pleading for his life, then the die has already been cast. I regret my disloyalty. I regret my foolishness, and as this country crumbles – yes, boy, crumbling it is – I wonder what Amir Kabir would have done, and I lament.'

'I offer my condolences, A'laa Hazrat. You have lost many people.'

'I have had a long life, boy. A long life is not to be envied: seeing your loved ones march to their death is the lone guarantee. I regret only his loss of life, but not my actions. It is a shāh's prerogative to execute his subjects if he sees fit. It so happens that in this case, to do so was a mistake. Yet it also sent a message to my other advisors. They knew their own positions were precarious. They could not get too comfortable, too bold, too ambitious. They had their dreams, but they knew their place. When a shāh executes his former tutor, it is no small thing. Imagine if Alexander the Great had executed Aristotle, would not the whole world be afraid? So, no, I do not regret it at all.' The Shāh straightened up, his voice firm. 'Nevertheless, he would have liked you, and you him. You would have been his favourite.'

The istkan in the Shāh's hand trembled, the liquid inside it sloshed, and fell onto the floor.

15

'Is that new?' Jamīla asked, pointing to Abimelech's head.

He had sent a eunuch to Chehra's apartment, summoning her to his room. It felt strange to request her like this. He had previously sought her on behalf of Nosrat. If they planned to meet privately, they would make plans in person, usually after entertaining Nosrat. When she turned up at his door, she looked petrified.

Jamīla was thin. Her face, full but not soft, like muskmelon, was flat. Gone was the subtle glow, just beneath her skin, like sultry red cherries at the start of spring. Instead her whole body, shrunken and hunched, appeared to sag.

She walked into the room slowly and looked around. He wondered what she saw. It always had been sparse, tidy. But her shoulders seemed to sink with a kind of relief, although he didn't know why.

'Well,' she repeated, her voice determinedly jovial, 'is it new?'

'The...my hat? Our uniform?' He feigned ignorance. 'We all... wear this, Jamīla.'

He was still standing in the entryway to his room. She strode over to him but then seemed to lose her nerve, looking past him into the passageway. *It had to be about Nosrat.* He let her pull him into the room. He took pity on her, noticing the wary look in her eyes.

'Yes, the diamond aigrette is new,' he said, touching the plume that was pinned to his new black pillbox hat.

She reached behind him and pushed the door shut.

'I have not seen him, today, Jamīla. If you were hoping to see

Nosrat Mirza,' he said, keeping his tone rueful, deliberately oblivious to her discomfort, 'I have disappointed you.'

'I suspect I shall survive that disappointment, Abimelech.' She laughed; it was a hollow sound.

I should just ask you, he thought, but couldn't.

'Who gave you the aigrette? Has another sigheh wife fallen for your charms?'

'*For my charms?*' Now it was Abimelech's turn to laugh. His too was empty. 'I do not seduce! What rumours are you hearing, or *starting*?'

Her smile seemed real at last. 'Well, tell the truth then,' Jamīla said. 'Who gave you the aigrette?'

He wanted to say Nosrat's name, just to see the look on her face. Or rather, to get her talking about whatever had happened. Instead he returned her smile and said, 'The Shāh.'

'The Shāh?' Jamīla looked confused. 'The Shāh of Shāhs? You have met him?'

'Yes.'

'Alone?'

'Yes.' He felt a glimmer of pride.

'You?'

'Why is that surprising?' Abimelech fought to keep his tone neutral.

She busied herself with clambering onto his bed and arranging herself in a sitting position.

'Well?' he asked. His chest felt tight.

'You said Nosrat was not interested in politics. I did not think there were other ways to access the Shāh.'

'There are for women.'

Unexpectedly, Jamīla snapped, 'Are you going to tell me what took place, or do I have to beg you to answer every question?'

Abimelech felt certain she had just refused to answer one of his. But he knew raising that was unwise. 'Honestly?' Abimelech paused. 'Nosrat Mirza embarrassed himself before his father twice. It was at these council meetings that we attend. Nosrat refuses to learn world history or pay attention to current affairs. When the Shāh had political questions, Nosrat failed to answer, and I spoke up in his stead. My words–' Abimelech paused. 'I am grateful that my words appeared to resonate with both the Shāh and one of his older sons, Kamran Mirza. The Shāh sought me out after that and continues to do so regularly. He likes to "borrow my mind".' Abimelech, who had been leaning against the door, straightened up.

Jamīla said nothing for a while. Then she spoke. 'You are his advisor, now?'

'Yes!' It came out more forcefully than intended.

'What is he like?'

Abimelech hesitated. 'Wistful, clever...thoughtful. He is as remarkable as they say.'

Jamīla looked unimpressed. 'What does Nosrat Mirza think of this?'

'Why?' Abimelech bristled.

'Why?'

Abimelech sighed. 'I...do not think he is aware of the extent of our friendship.'

'How could he not know?'

'Well, he was present when his father... the Shāh asked to "borrow my mind" in front of him – and many senior men at court. I do not know if he is aware we have continued to meet. Nosrat hardly schedules me any work. He does not read the books I set, so–'

'So you...Well, how does this work? Do you see Nosrat regularly?

Do you have a set schedule for the Shāh?'

'I have seen Nosrat Mirza, but it has been infrequent. I saw him twice in the past month–'

'Twice?'

'Yes.'

'And before you captured the Shāh's attention, how often did you–?'

'Jamīla. I know what you are implying: I am neglecting Nosrat Mirza. Believe me when I say he would rather be neglected. He does not do the–'

'Nosrat is jealous. Possessive. Entitled. He will not take kindly to your preference for his father. He will feel used.'

Used? One has to be a utility for that to take place! 'How could I possibly have used Nosrat?'

'To gain access to his father!'

Abimelech frowned and walked over to the bed. He sat on the edge of it and leaned towards her. His voice was low. 'Jamīla, I feel chastised. You and I have talked at length about the kind of lives we seek, the type of lives we want to live. I have been blessed with this extraordinary opportunity – to be of use. To be useful, not merely to my peers, but to the Shāh of Shāhs. He is...Jamīla, he is my friend. He is kind to me. He is not violent.' As he spoke, the memory of their previous conversation swam to the front of his mind. 'This is a good opportunity for me,' he continued, firmly. 'I know you are struggling at Chehra's and without Nosrat, but that is no reason for you to–'

'I am not struggling,' Jamīla snapped. 'Sanaa had solved my troubles – at your behest, if I am not mistaken–'

'What did Sanaa do?' Abimelech demanded.

Jamīla smiled. 'I have a tutor outside of the court.'

'Jamīla!' Abimelech pulled off his hat and ran a hand through his hair. 'This is not what I had intended. I thought you should have a-a-a distraction, a function at court to—'

'I do not need a distraction. I do not need baubles to entertain me. I need—' Jamīla sighed. 'I am not bitter as you have implied. My tutor is a nobleman and a mullah. He is also a radical. So I am busy, I am excited, I am...'

Abimelech wondered if she felt any of the words she said. *Are you lonely?* 'Do you miss Nosrat?'

Jamīla flinched. 'Do *you* miss Nosrat?'

Abimelech shook his head. 'I asked you first,' he said, with the kind of smile one gives to a child.

'No.' Her voice was flat. 'You?'

'No.' His was empty.

'No,' Jamīla said as she clambered off the bed. 'I suspect you do not. But always remember, he might miss you, and he may not take so kindly to being cast aside.'

Abimelech looked hard at her. He looked at her tired, wan face – discomfort etched in every line, the furrow of her brow, the crack along her lips – and felt an inexplicable wave of guilt. 'Nosrat will be fine. You, however, sound like you need to give up this business with the tutor. A radical mullah? He sounds dangerous.'

'Abimelech, you are not listening to me!'

'We are not listening to each other, it seems,' he replied, but he smiled.

He put his hands on her shoulder blades as he gave her a playful push to the exit. She pulled a shabby niqāb from her skirt pocket and hooked it over her face. Then she sped off with her eyes down, and Abimelech wondered what Nosrat must have done to make her so afraid.

16

Jamīla watched Chehra squirm in her seat. They had been ushered into the royal coffeehouse with 20 other wives, all of whom had requested time with the Shāh that week. Prior to confirming their request, each wife was to be interrogated by Kohinoor Khaanoum, the wife who handled the Shāh's harem diary.

Even within the confines of the palace, the royal coffeehouse was intimidating. It was set in a grand hall with ancient folk tales painted on the ceiling; a marble fountain sat in the centre of the room whilst ornate lamps adorned with crystals illuminated the mirror work along the walls. It had taken Jamīla some time to realise it was the women who made her uncomfortable, not the architecture itself.

Today, as on other days, the wives sat in groups. The women had entered in a flurry, the heady mix of their perfumes, ambergris, saffron and camphor, filling the air and following them behind. Kohinoor had the chairs rearranged to resemble an audience; the new and young huddled at the back, the older women spread out along the front. The front row housed a medley of women, with faces so varied they could have hailed from different eras. Chehra would request that Jamīla note the different looks: gold paillettes adorning foreheads, or sprinkled on uncovered hair, a bold beauty spot just below a ruby lip, maybe a dark line of wasma contouring the eyes... Jamīla could never recall their looks exactly and Chehra never tried to emulate them. Despite her requests she always kept to convention like the newer wives at the back. Each face half hidden behind a luscious wedded brow. Each brow darker than their natural raven hair. Each darkened by a thick coating of wasma painted over the top. As Jamīla trailed Chehra, in search of a seat, and the clutch of new harem wives grew closer, little distinctions began to appear. Adherence to expectations could be measured by anxieties. In some crooked brows, she spied the unsteady hand of a nervous slave unused to the wasma spoon. Of all the hunched and wary women, the fiddlers all had fingertips heavily hennaed. Their cheeks blazed red like ripened cherries. Jamīla suspected, like with Chehra, the flush was partly fear. Chehra's brow was smooth: a single line with a delicate arch she forgot to feel proud of. Her hennaed hands hesitated before selecting a seat in the middle, smiling at an older woman she knew. The woman returned the smile and made a light gesture with her hand. Another elderly woman, who had spurned the uniform of a šalīta over white tights in favour of trousers, caught the interaction and swatted the hand away.

Chehra frowned; her cheeks went from pink to red as she looked down at her lap. Jamīla didn't know how to help her. She looked at the younger wives, whose awkward gazes sought to avoid Chehra, at the older wives and at the eunuchs against the walls, as each group talked amongst themselves.

One young wife, Yasmin Khaanoum, had become the talk of the harem. The Shāh, known for his preference for poor village girls, had plucked this educated noblewoman from the home of a cousin and married her. She had been betrothed to another man but, without consulting her parents, had left with the Shāh and his men after they caught sight of her resting on the ayvān. She had visited the Shāh at least once every week for the past few months. Given his predilection for girls of a lower class, his sustained interest made her an object of curiosity within the harem. Initially she was accused of being a widow and thus sexually experienced already. Recent rumours declared her to have practised with the family eunuchs and developed skills the Shāh could not resist. For her part, the woman was haughty and proud; she wore the rumours about her like a badge of honour, making daring asides in private conversations. In public, she bore the air of a noblewoman. She was alienating all but the 'aqdi wives, who, at the behest of the Shāh, took her under their wing.

Kohinoor entered the coffeehouse at a brisk and confident pace, the chief eunuch and a cluster of slave girls and eunuchs hurrying behind her. She marched into the centre of the room, smiling as it fell silent. The chief eunuch handed her a piece of paper and turned to the other eunuchs with a glower. At once three eunuchs left the room and reappeared with a chair. Kohinoor looked at the stiff four-legged seat and shook her head. 'I must stand for these proceedings.' The chief eunuch flushed. One of the other eunuchs moved the chair to the side.

'Thank you for coming. This meeting is, as always, the most important of the week; I appreciate you coming on time. I have already received a number of requests, and we will proceed in chronological order, beginning with the earliest.' Kohinoor looked around the room once more and smiled. 'If any of you have any requests you would like to submit today, please consider this your notice: the practice of making requests *at the meeting* is hereby forbidden. This meeting is for assessments only. The only questions that shall be answered are those that have already been asked.'

There were a series of murmurs. Kohinoor spoke over them in a soft voice, 'I have never found it helpful for people to speak simultaneously. Whilst I am speaking, you would do well to refrain.' The room fell silent, as though a hand had flattened the people within it. A restless tension remained; Jamīla could almost hear the outrage bubbling below the surface. Finally,

Yasmin stood up.

'It is customary for participants of the meeting to raise their hand if they have questions, not rise from their seats, Yasmin Khaanoum.'

'You are, as ever, correct, Kohinoor Khaanoum,' Yasmin said, in a voice even silkier than Kohinoor's. 'I do not have a question. I am leaving.'

There was an uproar. People began to shout, several women gasped whilst others cheered. A couple of older women stamped their feet and ordered their eunuchs to bang empty chairs on the floor. Jamīla stared at Kohinoor, her eyes wide.

'What is this?!' Kohinoor shouted over the din. She glared at Yasmin. 'Why?' She turned, raging, to the chief eunuch. He gestured to three others, and they moved almost imperceptibly towards Yasmin. The room quietened, the shouting reducing to murmurs.

'I had a question I have not had time to submit. I expected I could ask it here. Since I cannot, remaining here is a waste of my time.'

'Well, why were you so tardy?' Kohinoor spluttered. Her face was an intriguing contradiction of expressions. Her eyes were wide and stunned, her lips drawn together in a frown, her formidable brow arched comically upwards. It was as though her body could not decide how to proceed.

'I was prescribed bed rest.' The murmurs grew louder. Everybody knew what 'bed rest' was for. 'The physician's orders. My slaves were too busy attending to me to concern themselves with filing notes.'

Kohinoor's face coalesced into a scowl. She said nothing.

Finally, the elderly wife wearing trousers stood up. 'Let us honour Yasmin with a round of applause – and please, do not leave. We know why you are feeling fragile. You must make your request first and then return to your bed and sleep.' She broke into a hearty applause, but she was not looking at Yasmin as she did so. Her eyes were on Kohinoor. The room continued her enthusiastic support. Kohinoor slouched as she brought her hands together to honour Yasmin. Yasmin placed both hands over her stomach and stared round the room with a radiant expression.

'Yasmin. What do you require?' Kohinoor asked as the applause died down. She was not looking at Yasmin. She turned instead to the chief eunuch who handed her two heavy appointment books. She placed one on the chair beside her and lifted the other into her arms. There was a table before her, but she continued to hold it aloft, staring down at it as she waited for Yasmin to speak.

'It is rather a small request. I require the Shāh of Shāhs to join me on two evenings each week instead of one.'

'And why is that?' Kohinoor asked in a careless tone.

'For personal reasons,' Yasmin said, allowing her hands to return to her stomach.

Kohinoor gave Yasmin's stomach a thin smile. 'I must have the specifics for the appointment book. The Shāh of Shāhs runs a country and has powerful negotiations to get through every day. He has diplomats to entertain at night. If he is being *compelled* to set two nights aside for you, then pregnancy is not enough – the Shāh has had many children.'

'I understand, Kohinoor. Allow me to explain. The Shāh, as you know, is an extraordinary poet, a divine being accomplished at many things. His paintings and photography will be spoken of for centuries to come.' There were fond whispers of agreement and admiration from the audience and even the eunuchs. 'It would be an honour for me to bear a son that had even a fifth of his ability. As such, the Shāh and I intend to introduce our son to his great works, right away. The Shāh himself volunteered to devote two evenings a week to his new family. He will be reading his works to our unborn child, that he may know his father, the Shāh of Shāhs, before he is born. Those are the specifics.'

Kohinoor's face was almost purple. 'Fine. Right. Yes. The chief eunuch will sort out the dates. Go to him.' She thrust the book back into his arms and, looking over Yasmin's head, called out another name. 'Anahita Khaanoum, you wanted...'

Jamīla stopped paying attention. She slumped against Chehra's chair, her head bent down beside the sigheh's ear. She was tired. Her eyes had barely closed before she was jerked alert by the sound of Kohinoor barking out Chehra's name. She could hear light snickering from the women and slaves in the coffeehouse. Kohinoor, looking straight at her, sneered, 'You are overworking your slave, Chehra Khaanoum? Or is she poor at her job?' The room collapsed into outright laughter, and Chehra struggled to find something to say.

Jamīla wished she could dissolve. She dared not look in Chehra's eyes, dared not spy the promise of punishments her gaze would proffer. She clenched her fists.

'You have a request?'

'I...I...yes, Kohinoor Khanoom. I-I intend to host a dinner at my apartment. I have tried to hold dinners before, but the chief eunuch would tell me they had been rescheduled. I...Well, I understand that there may be certain rearrangements from time to time, but it has happened many times.'

'Yes? What do you want, Chehra?' There were more snorts from the women.

'Well, this dinner is...next week,' Chehra continued, stumbling over her words. 'The Shāh is attending. I would like for you to – I do not want it to-to be rearranged.'

Kohinoor snickered. 'I cannot make such promises. If you have sloppy slaves, that is not the fault of the harem. Perhaps if they did their jobs and made appointment requests with adequate notice, this would not happen.' The laughter returned and Kohinoor paused, looking round the room with her thin smile. Emboldened, she continued. 'We all know the use you put your slaves to. Let them do their real jobs, and maybe things will change.' The chief eunuch, frowning, quickly called out the next name, and Kohinoor shot him a withering glare. Another woman rose to her feet, but she herself was laughing, and her eyes were on Chehra.

Jamīla was overcome with a hot flush of shame. She did not have to look at Chehra to know that she was bright red. She looked around the room, over the heads of the women, gazing at the eunuchs to find some common ground. Most looked away, but her eyes fell on one she recognised. Abimelech. This was not the way she wanted Abimelech to see her, standing behind her predatory mistress, mocked for being inept by a bully in front of an audience. When the meeting closed, she hurried past Abimelech, her head bowed. She could see him watching her as she went, smiling a fathomless smile.

***

Chehra hurried ahead of Jamīla into her room and threw herself face down on the four-poster bed. She was screaming into her pillow. Jamīla hovered by the door, uncertain if she should enter. But before she could, Gul appeared and tugged her back by the arm.

'You were with her,' Gul whispered, swatting away Jamīla's attempts at an explanation. 'She will blame you. Let her...exhaust herself first.' Gul went in, instead, ordering Jamīla to their room. Jamīla sat by the door and listened to Chehra shriek and hurl things around the room. Gul seemed to be murmuring to a gentle rhythm. Finally, there was quiet. Gul exited and Jamīla rushed out to meet her. She felt heavy with trepidation.

'Gul?' she asked.

'She is sleeping. When she rises, I suspect she will−'

'−seek me? Blame me?'

Gul sighed. 'Chehra is proud. She has expended her rage. She will not want to relive whatever took place there.'

Jamīla was sceptical. 'What am I to do?'

'She will call you. Be even more deferential than usual. Be obedient, be reticent.'

Jamīla sat outside the door, waiting for Chehra to wake. She wanted to believe Gul, but every day that passed without word from Nosrat, without retribution for her violence, made her ever so slightly more hopeful that the day was not coming. She could not believe that Chehra, even more sullen and violent than Nosrat, would also let a humiliation go unpunished. Jamīla was not that fortunate, surely.

'Jamīla,' Chehra eventually called out.

'Yes, Shahzadeh Khaanoum.'

'I have a serious question.'

'I am here, Shahzadeh Khaanoum, f-for all that you need.' Jamīla scuttled into the room and dropped to her knees beside the bed.

Chehra raised her head and looked over at Jamīla. 'Are you?' Her voice wobbled.

'Always, Shahzadeh Khaanoum. How might I be of service?'

Chehra rolled onto her back and looked up. 'I am thinking of having a baby.'

Jamīla was surprised. She couldn't think of anything to say. 'Yes, Shahzadeh Khaanoum,' she said with a gulp, feeling foolish. Her thoughts were racing: she wondered if this was why Chehra had been so persistent in her plans for the Shāh to visit. Chehra had never expressed an interest in children before and was altogether too petulant and delicate for Jamīla to picture her nurturing a child. On the other hand, if Chehra had a son, then Jamīla might have some real work to do, setting out an agenda that assigned him a tutor and gave him access to the Shāh. They would see the Shāh much more, which would give Jamīla the opportunity to catch his eye. Suddenly Jamīla saw an array of possibilities lying before her: chamberlain, concubine, advisor.

'I need to know if I should,' Chehra said, her tone a touch irritable. 'Make a list.'

'Of...Shahzadeh Khaanoum?' Jamīla said, gulping.

'Arguments. Produce a list of arguments supporting the decision!' Chehra snapped, but her voice was fearful. 'I need to know what they are.'

'Yes, Shahzadeh Khaanoum.' Jamīla swallowed. 'F-first, you would have s-someone to love, a family member you need not share. Second, it could be a boy, which would make the Shāh happy.'

'Wait, *wait!*' Chehra snapped, with real anger now. 'Slow down. Jamīla, this is not a game – this is real. It is my life I am talking about. I have to think through each argument.'

Jamīla nodded. She closed her eyes briefly. 'Why do you want a baby?'

'Why do I want a baby?' Chehra repeated and then shrugged, with an embarrassed smile. 'It might be nice, I think. Everyone was so nice to Yasmin. So, they might be nice to me.'

17

Jamīla's arms were full when she spotted Abimelech in the garden. He began to laugh, watching her as she stood sagging under the weight of her shopping. Annoyed, she placed her bags on the ground. 'Are you not going to assist me?' she demanded as she stumbled and knocked several of them over. All manner of fruits and vegetables rolled out across the garden. Onions and tomatoes began to race, speeding down the clean-cut fault lines of the meticulous flowerbeds. Others rolled onto their backs, proffering their bellies to the baking sun, preferring to be roasted among the fragrant flowers than boiled to their deaths with terse precision in a dark, unknown kitchen. Jamīla was torn between wailing and laughing. Abimelech did not share her dilemma – he burst into laughter as Jamīla had never seen. His eyes crinkled and gleamed, his mouth broadened, his body grew weak. She could not describe the sensation that rose through her chest, but she knew that all she wanted was to freeze the moment and live in it forever.

He followed her into the kitchen, unpacking the bags and placing them on the counter. Jamīla looked at him in surprise. 'You can go now,' she said.

'It is the Ta'ziyeh, tonight. You will be busy. I told Gul I would help.'

'You are always doing this, and the other slaves take advantage. You are not to do so. It is beneath you, beneath any senior eunuch to help in a kitchen.'

'Nobody is too senior to help another person.' He smiled and walked over to a domestic and offered to assist.

There were several domestics in the kitchen. It was crowded and cramped. Gul was watching them with mild impatience as they chopped fish. Spotting Jamīla, Gul bellowed out an order, 'Gather Chehra Khaanoum's favourite ensembles. Prepare several outfits and clean her room. She was eating blood oranges again earlier.' Gul frowned at Jamīla. 'I hope you did not purchase more.'

'I had to – she insisted—'

'Well, now I insist. Find a physician who says they are bad for pregnancy and bring him here.'

Jamīla glanced at the domestic slaves.

'Oh, ignore them. Who will they tell? They know nothing and understand less. They *do* know that they are replaceable,' Gul said, chuckling, 'so they shall not speak.'

Jamīla glanced again at the domestics. One of them held her gaze. She froze for a moment, then turned to Gul. 'Should I find a physician first or prepare the princess's clothes?'

'Prepare the clothes and clean her rooms first. Borrow the domestic attire for yourself. Their uniform is kept in a closet in the sleeping quarters.'

'What – why?!'

Gul fiddled with her sleeve as she walked over to Jamīla. She gave her a brief pat on the arm. Then turning away, she said, 'Chehra Khaanoum insisted.'

'But why?'

'I...would not give it much thought.' Gul's smile was uneasy.

The explanation did little to tackle Jamīla's annoyance. She took a deep breath before turning back to Gul, who was in full flow.

'...only her third encounter with the Shāh in all the years she has been here. It cannot go wrong.'

'Yes, of course.'

'Worry not, Jamīla,' Gul added, drawing Jamīla to her. Gul's mouth tilted down as she spoke. Her breath, fluttering as it hovered above Jamīla's face, caused the latter to look up at her with confusion that shifted into alarm.

Gul looked around. The kitchen seemed to sway under the weight of its people. Dark-skinned women with withered arms stood at various stoves, boiling vivid meats. Whilst these elderly women were still, younger domestics rushed around them, faces eager and animated – gone was their usual downcast step. Today, they polished with flourish and marched through the pantry, arms stacked with metal kitchenware waiting to be filled. This would be their first opportunity to see the Shāh up close.

'You are handling this well.'

Gul's quivering breath dripped into the double curve of Jamīla's top lip. She wondered if she might get that close to the Shāh, if his breath might dribble onto her skin, as he sought her advice, or, more plausibly, as she was given instructions.

'Thank you.' Jamīla couldn't help but sense she had reason to be concerned. But Gul stepped back and patted Jamīla on the arm with a regretful sigh.

'Back to work,' was all she said.

Jamīla entered Chehra's dressing room, wondering what to dress Chehra in. As she opened a lesser-used wardrobe and pulled out a dress, an unusual envelope fluttered to the floor. It was a love letter, addressed to another princess in the harem. But Jamīla had not written it for Chehra. The handwriting was Gul's.

If Nosrat's interest had made her less available to work, his silence left her free to run errands. Gul sent her back outside, collecting packages, posting letters and ordering fabrics in the bāzār, which she balanced with seeing Shapur when he remembered their sessions. So Jamīla was surprised to discover

Gul was writing letters on Chehra's behalf. She wondered why Chehra had not asked her. She felt a wave of, more than mild, resentment that the one interesting thing in Chehra's life, the one possibly positive thing, a secret lover within the harem, was the one thing she was kept away from. Jamīla was not sure why she imbued the love letter and its intended in such a flattering light. It was likely due to Gul herself, who was the only one Jamīla had seen have a real relationship with another woman in the harem.

Jamīla had suspected many relationships between female slaves, and the Shāh, too busy to attend to all his women, was rumoured to encourage his wives to take pleasure in their slaves and bring them along when they saw him. Gul was always very discreet, but Jamīla had suspected something. She began to acquire a steady stream of modest trinkets that she kept beside her pillow. It was then that Jamīla realised that this was not the story of two slaves, but that Gul was with a royal wife within the court. Elaheh was, like most sighehs, a local woman, born to poverty and plucked by the Shāh whilst lying prostrate outside her house as his *droshky* travelled through an impoverished village. This was not unusual, but despite attracting the Shāh's favour with her quiet, mollifying temperament, Elaheh did not seem to relish it nor maximise the opportunities given to her.

Jamīla discovered their relationship when, slipping away for a moment of peace, she caught sight of the two women in the royal coffeehouse. Elaheh's hair hung loose; Gul held a thick strand pressed to her lips. Elaheh lay gently against Gul's chest, and her eyes were closed. Jamīla held that image in her mind for a long time. Every interaction she had witnessed in the court was a form of exchange, a transferral or assertion of dominance, of fearful or resigned acquiescence. Gul and Elaheh didn't just look like equals; they looked like women in a world where hierarchies did not exist. Jamīla could not imagine a love that might render her speechless, but she found she wanted to try.

When evening fell, Jamīla enlisted one of the domestics to help her put on the uniform. It was a white two-piece, comprising long, loose trousers and a flat white shirt. Jamīla wasn't sure what the fabric was; it resembled the gabi her mother wore, but it chafed against her skin. Jamīla could not help but think a domestic might enjoy fitting her in one of their outfits. The domestic slave finished dressing her with a smile. The smile was brief, and as she walked into the bedroom where the other domestics had gathered to watch, she said something Jamīla could not grasp. Her tone was indignant. Jamīla waited for the others to laugh or sneer, but instead they patted the complaining domestic with empathy and headed back to the kitchen, passing Jamīla with averted eyes. She rolled her own, took a deep breath and began to follow them behind.

'Jamīla, take more sherbet,' Gul said, taking a large china bowl from one of the domestics. 'There is wine on the sofreh. Stand at the back. You are to linger.' She turned to the domestics and switched into Zanzibari. Then she spotted Abimelech, still helping the domestics fill the bowls. 'This is why they call you the kindest man in the harem.'

Abimelech gave her a smile sweeter than any Jamīla had ever received. 'I doubt anyone calls me a man, Gul,' he said, with laughter in his voice.

'You are more of a man than any of them,' Gul pronounced, a catch in her voice. 'We all know it.'

There was a silence. Jamīla looked from one to the other, wondering but not daring to speak.

'Now, go! Enjoy the rest of your evening. You really deserve it.'

Abimelech bowed to her and disappeared. Gul stared after him for a moment, a look of admiration on her face.

Gul had chosen a green, bejewelled sofreh to spread on the floor for the dinner. Jamīla looked at it, smooth and flat, a vivid jade peeking out from under the bowls. The centre of the sofreh was laden with sherbet bowls, and Jamīla, hugging hers to her chest, wondered if she might hide it in the kitchen for later. Chehra had never served a formal dinner before. The domestics served the princess's meals, and, with the exception of Nowruz, the Persian New Year, Jamīla had rarely seen banquets at all.

Despite the occasion, the last Nowruz she remembered had felt less formal than this. The Shāh had spoken from the Ivān-e Takht-e Marmar. A towering building, walled on all sides except the front, where it stood open, it housed the magnificent marble throne beneath its vaulted roof. The court had unrolled a vibrant set of entertainers to keep the public enthused. The usual animals were brought out to entertain: fighting rams and the chattering monkey, and most thrilling of all, the bears. The Shāh and his favourites stood at the pishtaq, a rectangular gateway lining the arched opening, laughing along with the public. And there, standing in a place of honour beside him, had been Sanaa.

As she approached the sofreh to place her sherbet bowl, Jamīla looked regretfully at the laden fabric, wishing she could slip something into her pocket. It was filled with food – boiled meats, salt fish and turnips, radishes and wild aubergines – but her gaze returned to the chelō kabāb and the gleaming gold of the circular raw egg yolk placed carefully on top of the steaming white rice. She had tasted it once; Nosrat had organised a miniature banquet in his rooms after he realised she had tried neither lamb nor antelope. They had sat with Abimelech, kneeling before a

sofreh, merry with wine, presented with a bevy of mysterious
foods, and Nosrat shouted, 'Bismillah' before each of them had
swallowed their first mouthful. Jamīla, who had been inclined
to eat with both hands, was tacitly encouraged to use just two
fingers and the thumb of her right hand. She continued to do
that later, as she and the other slaves consumed their dinners
of acorn bread, cheese and fruit on a shabby sofreh before
resuming the errands of the day.

There were more eunuchs lining the walls of Chehra's salon
than Jamīla had seen in the apartment before. She wondered who
they belonged to. Jamīla felt them watching her as she lingered
over the food. She returned their stare defiantly, as they slowly
averted their eyes, facing forward as they stood holding bowls of
fresh water, waiting for the men to arrive and wash their hands.
The front door burst open. Jamīla heard the thrust of the wood
slamming into the opposite wall and jumped. Gul hurried into
the salon and grasped Jamīla's elbow.

'Go and fetch Chehra Khaanoum, *now.*'

Jamīla, rubbing her arm with mild indignation, resisted the
urge to ask why Gul couldn't do it. She was aware of the eunuchs
gazing once more at her. 'What has happened?' she asked instead,
and Gul's eyes flashed.

'I should be asking you. Fetch the princess and take her out into
the hallway. I would warn her; she must know what she has done.'

Chehra was pacing in her bedroom when Jamīla pushed it open.
Her eyes were panicked. 'What was that sound?'

'You are wanted, Shahzadeh Khaanoum.'

Chehra stopped. She shrank visibly. 'By whom?'

'I know not.'

'You shall accompany me!' Chehra commanded, but her voice
was weak and her lips trembled. Jamīla looked around the room.

The clothes she had selected were tossed across every surface; the room a dazzling rainbow of colours, vivid and multi-layered fabrics crumpled with neglect.

Chehra's eyes followed Jamīla's gaze. 'This was you, I suspect? Should I be surprised? You cannot dress me without guidance? How can you not know what I like? Do you know anything about who I am? Does anyone?' Her voice took on a slightly desperate tone, but Jamīla was indifferent.

'Shahzadeh Khaanoum,' she began, 'there is a large commotion outside. It seems you are the cause. Even Gul is concerned. I suggest you accompany me now and do not delay.'

Jamīla's bow was deep, and her eyes fell on Chehra's feet as she walked out. Chehra's legs quivered.

'You.'

Kohinoor was at the door.

It took Jamīla a moment to realise she was talking to *her*. Chehra stood between them, and at Kohinoor's words, she turned with fresh-faced relief to Jamīla, as though she had escaped a verdict.

'Kohinoor Khaanoum.' Jamīla dropped hastily into a bow.

'Do not address me by name.'

Jamīla bowed again and said nothing.

As Kohinoor stepped into the hallway, Jamīla became aware of the crowd of women standing behind her. It was a mixture of slaves and princesses, and whilst they remained silent, their gaze was singular and accusatory.

'It was you. You placed the request for the Shāh to join your mistress for dinner?'

It hadn't been Jamīla, but she suspected that such a reply would be unhelpful. She remained silent. She could taste the rise of panic in her throat. There had been many reasons she could be caught or called out; she couldn't fathom *why* in this case.

Chehra was nodding emphatically, and Jamīla heard rather than saw Kohinoor's snicker. 'Rise, girl,' she sneered, 'I daresay you were given your orders.' Jamīla stood up, fixing her gaze just below Kohinoor's chin. Kohinoor stepped over to Chehra, placing a hand on her shoulder.

'It was very discreet. Smart, one could say. With all the women so excited to attend the Ta'ziyeh themselves, nobody focused on the Shāh. You would have had dinner with him, which was permitted, and then go to the Ta'ziyeh with him, which was not. You would have returned to the kalwat with him, to the Shāh of Shāh's quarters. You would have risen with him and had breakfast with him. You would have spent such time alone with the Shāh, with extended time for you to…air your thoughts, list your grievances – time for which you had not sought permission. Tell me, am I inaccurate, Chehra?'

Jamīla could see Chehra wincing; she couldn't tell if Kohinoor's grip had broken her skin or if Chehra was simply afraid.

'Am I inaccurate?'

'No, never, Kohinoor.'

'So this was your secret plan?' There were murmurs from Kohinoor's entourage. Kohinoor stepped back to look at them, her brows raised.

'I was–'

'Tell me Chehra, do you see us, women and wives of the great Shāh, as fools?'

'No, I–'

'Puppets, perhaps?'

'Never–'

'Yet you violate the rules, act treacherously to secure your own agenda, leaving the women who abide by the system to lose out. Perhaps you believe those rules do not apply to you? In any case,' Kohinoor added, speaking over Chehra's harried protests, 'it matters not. The Shāh is unable to attend your dinner tonight. I have spoken to him. He asked me to deliver the message. You may want to attend the Ta'ziyeh tonight, but...I would not, were I you. I would remain here.'

Chehra was silent; the wives and slaves behind Kohinoor were not. Their voices were a chorus of schadenfreude, mutters and whispers ranging from pity to disdain.

Kohinoor turned to leave. As she headed to the door, she turned back and added, 'Do not call on the Shāh again. Not until you have been forgiven. I shall tell you when that is.'

***

'Have all the domestics tidy the salon, throw away the food and wash the sofreh. There is some acorn bread for Chehra's slaves. Send the others back to their princesses.' Gul spoke with composure, and Jamīla, still trying to process what happened, felt slow.

'I would prefer you lead this, Gul.'

Gul's eyes flashed again. 'I am uninterested in what you want. You are so naive. The two of you are so naive.' Gul pushed past Jamīla and headed to the slave's quarters. She began to undress.

'You are...leaving?'

'I am going to watch the Ta'ziyeh.'

'How? Kohinoor Khaanoum—'

'—did not banish Elaheh Khaanoum, just Chehra. I shall accompany Elaheh, and I am *trusting* you to manage the household. I need time to dress. I cannot be shepherding domestics too.'

'Is this what makes me naive? Being oblivious to the contours of your personal life?'

Gul glared at her. 'You could have asked Nosrat for a schedule, possibly even Abimelech, then found yourself in the same wing of the palace, in a garden, and she would have had the access to the Shāh, and that would be it.'

'I did not think I needed to.' Jamīla felt indignant. *Do I not do enough for her?*

'You should have,' Gul snarled.

Jamīla watched Gul turn and leave. Her feet slid flatly along the floor; her body drooping until she had slumped to the ground.

She felt the isolation peeling away at her, eroding layers of syrupy skin, her reddish-pink underbelly whimpering to the surface. The hallway was empty; in the apartment, the mistress and chamberlain aloof, slaves without orders gathered in the salon, and yet there was a complete absence of sound. To Jamīla, the silence felt stifling; for the first time, her loneliness felt like a fortress. The walls that had risen to protect her suffocated her whole. She could not hear her intake of breath, could not feel the thick slop of tears hissing down her cheeks.

'We should take her along.' It wasn't until Elaheh dropped into a crouch and slipped a delicate hand under her chin that Jamīla felt a sensation that didn't promise harm. 'Jamīla?' Elaheh continued, repeating her name until she allowed her eyelids to unfold. 'Come with us. Come to the Tekyeh Dowlat.'

'She cannot come like that,' Gul said hurriedly. Jamīla did not look at her.

'Of course, she can.' Elaheh's voice was gentle. 'It's the Ta'ziyeh. All are permitted to come; none are to complain.' Without waiting for Jamīla or Gul to respond, she withdrew her hand from Jamīla's chin and placed it under an arm. She lifted her onto her feet and clasped her by the hand. As Elaheh steered Jamīla to the door, Gul shuffled behind, seeming to hold back. 'Come now.' Elaheh's voice was soft but firm. 'We are *all* going to the Tekyeh.'

18

At night, in the summer months, the air never seemed to cool. Jamīla stood before the Tekyeh Dowlat, feeling stiff and sticky, as she tried to recall when she had last gone inside. She hated the month of Moḥarram; each year it felt like the whole world was in collective mourning. The streets were flooded with processions, with performances, actors indistinguishable from spectators; people flung themselves to the ground as they sought to relay, on the requisite days, the different stages of mourning. It was always impossible to avoid, but Jamīla had navigated the desolate public with dispassion. The air in the harem was, conversely, one of excitement; for once, the women were allowed to participate in something. Ta'ziyehs were held in the harem, but the interest was minimal. The women wanted to attend the Tekyeh Dowlat, and many dressed in full regalia under their black chadors to venture forth every day to honour the women who suffered after Ḥosayn was killed.

'Who will check on Chehra?' Jamīla heard Gul whispering to Elaheh.

'Jamīla is not going back,' Elaheh snapped.

'I can,' Jamīla announced, her tone flat. 'I can do that.'

'No. And,' Elaheh glowered at Gul, 'you should be more compassionate.'

Gul blushed. 'I am sorry.'

Jamīla frowned. 'Why?'

Gul looked reproachful but didn't reply.

Elaheh spoke. 'Chehra's request for the Shāh concerned you. She would have him forbid you from seeing Nosrat whilst she found him a wife.'

Jamīla couldn't bring herself to speak. They walked on in silence.

'Do you know the story?' Elaheh smiled as they stood outside the Tekyeh Dowlat. They were being buffeted by attendees. Many looked at them with irritation; noblemen, who would not dare touch a woman in public, shoved past Elaheh, her stationary position adjacent to the door an affront to the spectacle.

Jamīla felt a smile grace her lips and thought of Shapur. She knew of the story and of its parallels to one told in the *Shahnameh*. She preferred that tale but knew never to say that. 'I know it is a martyrdom, but of whom...? I know the Moḥarram is mourning Ḥosayn, but do they not mourn different men every day?'

'Yes! Tonight they mourn Ḥosayn. Each day prior they honour those who died before him, who supported him at the Battle of Karbala.' Elaheh's eyes lit up as she launched into an explanation.

The words drifted over Jamīla as she traipsed behind them into the Tekyeh Dowlat, the contours of it causing her to catch her breath. It was, like most buildings in Tehran, ornately domed, but it stood close to a hundred feet high and twice as wide. Inside, it resembled an amphitheatre; thousands of women were already present, pressed together, gathered on the ground. The walls, lined with azure blue tiles, surrounded Jamīla on all sides. They burned preternaturally bright, glowing in vivid harmony alongside glittering glasswork that stretched from the tip of the dome itself to the earthen ground. She was reminded of the vivid mosques she had seen on her one trip out of Tehran, to Isfahan, and thought back to her first trip away from home.

The world outside her compound looked nothing like Jamīla had imagined. She kept her eyes on the ground in front of her, engaged in a futile dance with the sharpened stones that sought to scratch and spike her feet. Whenever she raised her gaze for a moment, her eyes caught the groaning buttocks of the man chained in front, or fell on the procession of indifferent limbs, further ahead, tramping forward in forlorn unison. She preferred to keep her head bowed. She had imagined the outside world was passive; smooth and yielding, like the plants in their compound, easily cut and plucked for food. Out here the world was hostile: the sun spread its ire, frying her skin with its wrathful rays, branding them all with shiny puckered weals, with radiated skin. The ground felt like grains, coloured in the shade of crushed teff; her feet crunched on dry roads, pricked and pockmarked by brittle stones. Around them it was mostly flat, save for the mountainous peaks that rose in the distance. Rugged like braised charcoal, littered with a thousand green dimples, they seemed from afar to nuzzle each other.

Elaheh was holding her hand. 'Look, Jamīla! See how the stage is elevated above the audience.'

Jamīla shifted out of her grasp, but all she saw through a sea of black chadors was a smooth, vast ring, raised to eye level, speckled with dirt and grain. She said as much, her tone offhand, but inside she began to seethe. Perhaps it was the glittering glass, the marble tiles and the blinding lustre of a thousand gleaming candles, but Jamīla felt at turns dizzy and irate. The theatre appeared to drown her, and as everyone rose, applauding the Shāh's entrance, she felt the crush of bodies might swallow her whole.

Kohinoor stood beside the Shāh on one side and Abimelech on the other. Jamīla stared at Kohinoor, thinking of her own mother, toiling, aged and alone, spurning her fellow pastoralists. She wondered who might mourn her or honour her after her death; she wondered if they would have reasons why.

19

The alabaster horse sniffed as he stamped, his sleek mane rippling, his smooth nostrils fluttering. Abimelech could not see the face of the man seated atop the horse, only the vivid fur of his emerald *astrakhan* hat and the tip of the white egret feather that was pinned to it. Abimelech had watched *The Martyrdom of Ḥosayn* every year since he had arrived in Tehran. He would sit beside Nosrat, who would whisper feverishly in his ear. Today, it was the Shāh beside him, and as Abimelech watched the actor playing Ḥosayn, sitting broad and still, one hand cajoling his nervous mount, he realised the actor wore the same garments as the Shāh himself.

Everyone saw themselves in Ḥosayn. Nosrat used to mumble when inebriated that Ḥosayn and he were alike. Nosrat, too, was true to his principles, resisting his father's orders and remaining an artist as he desired. The Shāh would claim the imperialists – either the Russians or British, depending on his mood – were men like Yazid, demanding loyalty, offering wealth, but ultimately corrupt. Abimelech often felt that, if the men were like Yazid, whose agents killed Ḥosayn for standing up to him, then the Shāh could not possibly be like Ḥosayn, as he acquiesced every time. Yet, here the actor stood, wearing a tunic identical to the Shāh's, woven with the same boteh motif, but with brilliant green piping. He donned a white shroud and gazed for a moment on the bodies of his comrades, which lay strewn across the stage. Abimelech, who knew the routine by heart, still had to look away from the man readying himself to die.

'You want us to leave?' Abimelech asked. He was standing barefoot in the compound, the mud melting against his feet. The ground turned viscid, slithering around his ankles, as though to permeate his skin. The rain fell as if ejected from the sky.

'You have been kind to host us these past weeks.'

His aunt looked defensive. 'You have suffered undue tragedy, I know this. There is a man coming here in two days.' She raised her voice to pre-empt and silence any replies. 'His name is Tolfamee. He is a good man. Abeba is small, we can keep her. But you and Abel will go with him.'

'Why would you send us to strangers?'

'I...I...Tolfamee is a good man.'

'Must we do this?'

'Yes.'

'Why?' Abimelech cried.

'We need the money.'

'How...how will this make you money?'

'Tolfamee will pay us, for the two of you.' Her voice was choked.

'You intend to sell us?'

She didn't answer.

The arena, raised high above the heads of the audience, was poised in expectation. Ḥosayn raised his head, and suddenly Abimelech found himself gazing at him. The actor was always handsome, with a strong, pale jaw and knitted heavy brow, but this man's face was haunted, hollowed out.

Abimelech wondered if Kamran Mirza ever considered himself to be like Ḥosayn. The accusation had been levied multiple times. The Grand Vizier's eunuchs would whisper it: Kamran moved through the palace with the righteous, muted posture of Prophet Mohammad's real heir, surrounded by a swathe of corrupt officials attempting to make their move. The parallel had never quite sat with Abimelech. Kamran was too confident to be deemed a modest, humble, Ḥosayn-like figure, and at no point had he appeared to make any claims to be the rightful heir. Abimelech refused to give the succession much thought; he knew if he envisioned living under Mozaffar's inept reign, he would hang himself on the day of the Shāh's death. But each day of this year's Moḥarram had found the Shāh coughing rather more heavily, each step taken more slowly, his hand grasping Abimelech's shoulder for support.

Today Abimelech could not help but reflect on his empty experiences, compared with those of Ḥosayn, who fought for his principles, who had principles to fight for. He thought back to the wars that had shattered his home, cost him his parents and siblings. He could see the smoke from his mother's charred flesh rising as his hands covered Abel's eyes. He had watched her crawl away from her children and then run upright from a blackened hut, slowly, so that she would be caught, but from far enough away that they would not be found. He would not forget the wild cackles of sweating soldiers, stamping and cheering around the pile of burned bodies, oblivious to the three children hiding naked behind a nearby bush. He could no longer picture Abeba's face...

He watched the genies appear, men clothed in an array of vivid colours, the blue mood of the Tekyeh Dowlat transformed into a multicoloured vision, with radiant reds, peaches, whites and blacks and a series of men in deeper shades of green; he envied Ḥosayn both his allies and his cause. As Ḥosayn spurned the genies' help on the grounds that he 'must die to keep the purity of the faith', Abimelech felt a strange sense of grief rise like blood in his throat. Ḥosayn's death was brutal and swift, and Abimelech once again had to look away. He thought of the actual story, the real Ḥosayn who led 72 men and their families through Karbala, refusing to bow to the corrupt Yazid or his men. He thought of Ḥosayn, telling his men to flee with their families, as the soldiers surrounded them. He thought of his mother and the sacrifices she made when the soldiers came for their village. Where Ḥosayn asked, she acted, and both paid for their principles with their lives.

'Your face is wet,' Kohinoor said with a slight chuckle, leaning past the Shāh to look at Abimelech.

'I am hot,' he replied, and as he helped the Shāh to his feet, he saw that his eyes too were streaming.

20

Jamīla was early. She had been rereading the *Shahnameh* as Shapur instructed, unsure as to what the general aim would be, but she had underlined a few passages and was keen to get his attention. As she arrived at his house, the qāpči opened the door at once.

'I watched from the window,' he said. He looked embarrassed.

'Oh? Should I be flattered?' Jamīla asked, trying to smile.

He shook his head. 'I apologise, but—'

'He is out.'

'Yes.' The qāpči was blushing now.

'When will he return?'

'He did not say.'

'The session is cancelled, then?' Jamīla demanded. Her skin grew hot with frustration.

The gatekeeper looked alarmed, but his answer was non-committal. 'I suspect so...'

'Should I wait for him?'

'No.'

'What did he tell you, precisely?'

'He told me to send you home.'

Jamīla turned on her heel and left. She could hear the gatekeeper shouting his apologies after her. *How indiscreet*, she thought, fuming to herself. How indiscreet of both of them. She did not want to return to the apartment. She couldn't recall what errand she told Gul she was on. She sighed. She swore she would not go when Shapur rescheduled their meeting.

And yet, the moment, not even three weeks later, when she held the note in her hands, crisp and slim with his brief instructions setting an appointment for the next session, she began counting down the days. She gabbled excuses at Gul, not caring if they were believed, and hurried down to the house an hour ahead of schedule. She was panting as she banged her fist on the front door.

The gatekeeper gasped. 'Jamīla! You are taking a big risk.'

'Is he in?' she demanded as she was ushered inside. She was led into the andarūnī to wait in one of the pantries. Jamīla had never entered the women's quarters in Shapur's house before. She suspected neither of them should be there, given how the qāpči kept shaking his head.

'Keep silent!' he ordered as she sat on a cushion. He ordered the domestic out of the room but caught her arm at the door. He looked at Jamīla and back at the slave. He squeezed her wrist and hissed in her ear. The domestic whimpered. He shook her arm. She nodded. He pushed her and she left.

Jamīla frowned, horrified. 'You did not need to hurt her!'

'Did I not?' the gatekeeper snarled. 'And if she mentioned your presence or asked why you came?'

Frustrated, and unable to come up with a response, Jamīla sighed.

'Who would be hurt then?' he continued.

'Is he here?'

The gatekeeper rolled his eyes. 'You are an arrogant—'

'He *always* leaves! I wanted to arrive before he cancelled—'

'I know why you came early, Jamīla.' He raised a hand to silence her. 'He is here. But he is not happy.'

'Then he should keep his appointments!' she insisted.

'Jamīla!'

'He has cancelled four times!' She gestured for emphasis, her hand flying close to the gatekeeper's face.

He stopped and gave her a hard look. 'You know he is taking a huge risk.'

'You know he takes bigger ones.'

The gatekeeper's eyes were wary. 'I am a humble doorman. I know little.'

'You know...Zainab P—?'

'I know you shall remain here in silence until the mullah comes to collect you. I know you shall not leave this room, and nobody but he shall enter. I know you do not wish me to repeat this conversation to him or anyone else.' He glared at her. 'I know that if I have to return here today there will be trouble for you.'

She sat in the corner by the storage cupboard, far from the door, too scared to move. Perhaps she had been reckless in arriving early. She had thought it was tactical, to catch Shapur as he left. She had only visited when the house was empty; she had forgotten he didn't live alone. As she sat in the silent pantry, she heard noises all around her. Soft steps she assumed were slaves pottering in nearby rooms. She was never brought to the andarūnī; she would always be taken to the men's quarters, and thus, though this was a home, she often forgot. To her it had been a slew of anonymous rooms with world maps and full-length bookshelves. There was never any food or water to drink. It was less like the bīrūnī in a family home and more like a library. She wondered what the gatekeeper must have told the slaves to ensure they kept away.

The door burst open. Jamīla jumped as Shapur strode over. He looked angrier than she expected. He pinched her arm and pulled her to her feet. 'Not a word,' he said, and then, to her horror, he picked her up. He carried her out of the women's quarters. He marched into the bīrūnī. Her face was inches from his. She kept her eyes closed as they headed up the stairs. Each step caused her to jolt against his chest. Her nose pressed against his chin. She didn't dare move.

When he finally placed her down, they were in a bedroom. She staggered back and walked towards the window. She wondered if it would open, if she could climb out if necessary, but he crossed the room to stop her before she reached it.

'You fool.'

'I...apologise.'

'You apologise?' He slapped her across the face. Then he stepped back and looked away.

Jamīla felt stunned, and a little relieved; it did not seem like worse was coming. 'Your family is here. I should not have come.'

He faltered, expecting defiance. 'I told you to come today. I did not say come this early. We must be careful. Little deviations can cost lives!'

Jamīla was sullen. 'You kept cancelling.'

'I-I...yes, well—'

'Without notice.' Straightening, she said, 'I would walk all this way. Is a cancellation not a *deviation*?'

'Yes, it...'

'Why risk it? Why cost lives, Shapur?'

He blushed.

Jamīla stared at him in shock. *His cheeks were actually red.*

He frowned and muttered, 'You are right. You behaved poorly, but I am also responsible. I am sorry.'

'You are...?'

'I am. Very. Does your face hurt? Not too much, I hope?'

Jamīla gazed at him in surprise.

'I suppose they hit you harder in the harem. You must be fine.'

Jamīla arched an eyebrow, but he wasn't looking. 'Where do

you go?'

'Where do I go when?'

'When you cancel our appointments.'

'Ah.'

'Where?'

'Jamīla. You have questioned me on my *associations* before. These are the groups with which I spend my time.'

'With Zainab Pasha?'

He gave a tight nod.

'Your group seems very disorganised.'

'Disorganised?'

'Yes.' Jamīla suppressed a smile.

Shapur drew himself up. 'It is not *disorganisation* you are seeing, Jamīla. It is the difficulty that arises when multiple factions of the same group need to be managed. When plans are based upon expectations one is privy to but not in control of, when inadvertent mishaps happen. Last week, for instance, we—' He stopped and looked at her. 'You are here for a specific reason, for your *instruction*. Let us begin with where we meant to start last time.'

'Last time when you left to...'

'Jamīla, focus.'

'I am focused,' Jamīla retorted.

'Focus on why you are here.'

'That is why I am here.'

'What is?'

'Your...other life. I want to know more.' Jamīla gave him a pointed look.

He looked away from her and said in a voice devoid of inflection, 'Did I not tell you we have no use for an Abyssinian slave?'

'You told me you had Sanaa.'

'Sanaa insisted.'

'As do I.'

'You are not Sanaa,' Shapur said, and he snickered.

Jamīla wanted to kick him. Instead she said, 'No, Sanaa is more of a Sūdābeh than I am.'

'You know nothing of Sūdābeh.'

'The wife of a Shāh who sought the affections of his son as well?'

Shapur stared at her. 'You completed the *Shahnameh*?!'

It was Jamīla's turn to smirk. 'I did. Tell me what I want to know.'

He looked at her, standing in the middle of the room, with new admiration. 'There are cushions in the cupboard,' he said, gesturing to the painted wooden wardrobe. 'Place them on the floor beside the bed and we can talk.'

Jamīla did as he said as quickly as she could, lest he change his mind.

Shapur, sitting beside her, glanced at her face once before looking out through the window before them. 'The last time I cancelled, I met with Zainab. Often when I have had to cancel, that is the reason why.'

'What do you do there?'

'We...discuss proposals, plans.'

'Plans for?'

'How we might articulate the changes we seek. How we would... implement them.'

'Where do you meet?' Jamīla demanded.

'The location can vary.'

'Where are the headquarters?'

'Jamīla,' Shapur said with a sigh, 'you cannot simply turn up. You must be invited.'

'Invite me.'

A door slammed in the distance. Shapur jumped up, grabbed

Jamīla by the arm and pushed her into the wardrobe. 'I am leaving now. When the qāpči comes, he will let you out and send you home. Do not refuse.'

His voice was muffled as he spoke through the door. Jamīla did not dare open it or protest. She seethed silently, slumped against the plush fabrics that hung behind her.

A week later, Jamīla stood outside Sanaa's apartment, waiting for her to return, dread and outrage flaring under her skin. It had been a month since she had seen her, gliding through the main harem quarters just before the end of the Moḥarram.

As she drew close, Sanaa gestured for Jamīla to follow her and walked inside, holding the door ajar. 'What a pleasant surprise, Jamīla. What brings you here?'

Jamīla paused. 'I was going to ask a favour.'

'Ah.'

Jamīla had never been inside Sanaa's apartment, nor that of any concubine. As she followed Sanaa through the hallway, her shoulders brushed against both walls. There were two rooms; the door that opened onto Sanaa's bedroom was ajar. Her stroll became hurried as she moved to pull it shut. She guided Jamīla to a chair in the salon. It was tall and wooden, the flat seat smooth and dark.

'I can stand.'

'Let me fetch you an istkan,' Sanaa insisted, hurrying out of the flat. As Jamīla looked around the room, she realised there was nothing personal about it. The chandelier, small and gold, adorned with five candles, was kin to those Jamīla had seen in the harem. The walls were bare. Where others were painted with ancient Persian stories, or cut with mirror work and arabesque tiles, Sanaa's were bland. The walls and ceiling were the same shade of cream, and the curtains, full-length and diaphanous, were pale gold. She wanted to venture into the bedroom but settled for pacing the salon.

Sanaa re-entered. 'My apologies,' she said, as she placed the small tea glass in Jamīla's hand. 'We – the concubines – share a pantry. Not-not all of us. But a small number. We share a pantry, we share a bathhouse. As such, sometimes…Well, I apologise for the delay. We have not spoken for some time; I have thought about you. How-How is Chehra Khaanoum? And-and Shapur. Do you call him Hajji-Agha? He is not always so formal…'

Jamīla had never seen Sanaa this talkative before. She stayed silent, watching her. She looked at the istkan Sanaa had given her and placed it on the floor.

'You can put a cushion on the floor.' Sanaa chuckled, a high, false note. 'I am just trying to…familiarise myself with these *Western* customs the Shāh seems so enthralled by.'

'Why?'

'Why?'

'Well, according to Shapur, you have a very different agenda.'

'What did Shapur tell you?' Sanaa's tone bore the hallmarks of shock: a raised pitch, an uncommon swiftness, but her face was cool and watchful.

About your affair with Nosrat. Jamīla couldn't coax the words onto her tongue. It was old news now, and yet, with Sanaa sitting coolly before her, the wound reopened again, as though made fresh. 'He had plenty to say. He is not…talkative, as you well know, but once he does talk, he can get excited.'

'That is true.'

'He seems to think I am similar to you,' Jamīla lied.

Sanaa snorted. 'Similar how?'

Our men. 'Our interests, I think.' Jamīla glanced behind her, at the hallway.

'We are alone.' Sanaa's voice was light.

'It matters not.' Jamīla's was swift, thick with guilt.

'Ah.'

There was a silence.

'Zainab Pasha,' Jamīla said, watching Sanaa's face.

'We are never...quite...that alone, dear.'

'We have similar interests, Sanaa. Maybe even similar goals.'

Sanaa smiled. 'Well, I am happy to share some of my interests with you.'

As I have shared mine. Jamīla resisted the urge to frown.

'I look forward to it.'

'Shapur will make certain of it.'

'Shapur?'

'He will do whatever I ask.' Sanaa's smile was confident, and Jamīla felt herself bristle, wondering how many other men would do *whatever she asked.*

'You are generous.' Jamīla nodded as she rose to leave.

Sanaa's mouth twitched. 'Visit me again, Jamīla. This was fun.'

21

As the speaker raised her hand, the room fell silent.

Jamīla watched as the small, cracked palm crunched into a fist that punched the air with an angry velocity. 'We are done.' The owner of the fist, a slight, pale-faced woman, drowned in a printed chador, looked almost identical to the other women curled on cushions throughout the room. In one fluid moment, however, the speaker shook off her chador and untied her hair. The audience began to gasp and then applaud as her loose dark hair slithered over her shoulders to spread down her back.

'We are done with the old ways. With the old rules, with the old men.' Zainab Pasha allowed herself a wry smile. 'What we are doing here will be different.'

Jamīla had arrived late to the meeting, and the qāpči had glowered as he let her in. Shapur had written down the route and the address and handed it to her with gritted teeth. She took it without a word and decided to end the lesson at once. As she rose to leave, she knew it would be her last one. She needed nothing more from Shapur – nor Sanaa, if she could help it.

'Let me tell you all something. Men, women, slaves – we are more Iranian than them! The cowardly Qājārs declare themselves royalty, sell off our possessions, barter away our achievements...,' Zainab Pasha hissed. 'They – who spurn their history to line their pockets – they are not the true Iranians. This is not their country. And we shall take it from them.'

The room seemed to swell. Jamīla rose to her feet, her hands coming together in angry, ardent applause. Here she could enjoy the release of being able to shout, to complain, to rail against something, anything, especially the things that controlled her. As she looked around the room, every face bore the same expression: a release of tension, an emphatic freedom – and Zainab Pasha had given it to them.

But Zainab Pasha was not finished. She raised that small, cracked palm once more and within moments had quelled the crowd. 'I have one last thing to say. The Qājār cowards who shiver and bow before the so-called Western visitors, mediocre men with money, who cannot build, only *take* – those Qājārs are *Persian*. They take that Western title and they wear it like a crown. Well,' her voice dropped ominously, 'I am not a *Persian*. No foreigner will give me my name – not the Greeks, nor the French, nor the British. I am from Iran. I am *Iranian*. I will use the name my people gave me, the words our people built, and I will not have a shāh who bows to a purse!'

The applause was thunderous. No event at the harem had ever caused Jamīla to think that women could make so much noise. Even the men were emphatic and empowered. Zainab looked pleased with herself as she tucked her hair back into her chador and threaded her way through the audience, taking a seat on a cushion along the back wall.

A voice called out, 'I hear the Shāh is unwell.'

'Indeed,' Zainab replied, dismissive. Somebody else stood up to speak, but Jamīla knew she wouldn't listen. Amidst the noise and applause, Sanaa had disappeared. Jamīla spotted her beside Zainab Pasha, whispering in her ear. She had hoped Sanaa might introduce her; now she saw that was impossible. Without a speaker, the audience settled back onto their cushions and back into their groups. Looking round, Jamīla found it less of a collective and more like an awkward gathering of different tribes. The room felt smaller and shabbier than when she first entered. The walls were peeling, and people were pressed against each other but for thin, empty lines between the different social groups that had naturally formed.

The chatter was vibrant but with the self-conscious braggadocio that Jamīla had often heard in the ḳalwat. It was not just the men, either: the room was filled with people gripped by the increasing fear of their own irrelevance. Only by asserting themselves, defining their stance and redefining it in light of another presentation, were they able to retain some semblance of an identity they could take pride in. Once Zainab Pasha had stepped off the stage, the unity she sought to bring was fractured. Nobody quite dared to speak to the room as a whole. The speaker who had followed Zainab sat down without forming a sound.

Jamīla finally spotted Shapur, the loudest voice in his group of men. She caught his eye, smiling, and began to head over, but he broke eye contact and turned away. She could not help but feel disgusted at the sham of their collective, as segregated by title and status as the very people they sought to attack.

'This is a farce!' Jamīla shouted.

There was a moment of stunned silence, as heads turned trying to find the speaker. Jamīla felt herself cringe as the stern frowns of noblemen fell heavily upon her. The weight of their judgement propelled her to her feet.

'This is a farce,' she said again.

She waited for someone to challenge her, but there was nothing, just an unyielding oasis of silence.

Zainab Pasha was leaning against a wall. She glanced at Jamīla without much interest, then looked away. Jamīla felt galled.

They were the only two people standing upright in the room. Both women. Standing over a sea of men. A slim slave in a niqāb and a small woman whose chador exposed her uncombed hair and the defiance of one who had fought greater odds.

Jamīla wanted her to engage. She longed for it. She wanted to catch her eye. She called her out by name.

'This is a farce, Zainab,' she said and decided to leave.

Zainab Pasha did not reply.

It was fine, Jamīla realised. She did not need this leader's authority, her proverbial blessing. She had seen through an environment that had intimidated her. Its hypocritical nature was as hollow as the world outside. She turned to go.

'What could possibly make you say that?' Shapur demanded in a tone that admonished more than it asked.

'Can you not see yourselves?' Jamīla snapped back. 'You sit, according to your class, according to the codes of Persian culture. Do you fail to see the hypocrisy? Slaves with slaves, Africans with Africans, the noblemen together. Are we not fighting against the Qājārs, who have built their legacy on their lust for money and stature? How will we move forward if we do not unite as one?' She looked back at Zainab and found her energy drain away. Her hands, which had moments earlier gesticulated with confidence, fell to her sides.

'Was there more?' a woman sitting at Zainab's feet asked, her formal Farsi betraying her class as much as her clothing.

'I...Well, I am leaving. This is not what I...this is not...' Jamīla found herself stuttering when she sought to sound smooth. A grand, articulate finish was required, before she slid back to her life in the court and gathered her courage to grovel before Nosrat. Her shoulders slumped.

'Stand still.' She heard Zainab Pasha command and froze, unsure whether to obey. Of course, freezing was what Zainab had ordered and thus resembled the obedience she required. Jamīla watched Zainab scan the room, wondering what she was thinking. Zainab looked tired. 'You are not wrong.' With that, she shook off any weariness she had betrayed. She stood straight, her chin raised. Jamīla could not bring herself to look in Zainab's eyes; her peremptory manner absorbed all the defiance Jamīla bore. 'But you are being dramatic. We should unite, but, naturally, we have differences. What matters is whether we have a shared agenda.'

There were rustlings within the group. One of the men who had been talking with Shapur stood up too. 'And if we do not?' He too was small, but taller than Zainab and rather rotund. His portliness suggested an affability that neither his eyes nor his tone shared.

'Do you have a different agenda?' Zainab's voice held an implicit warning, unmoved by the man's tone. 'Where was your voice when I was speaking earlier? What kept you from presenting an agenda of your own?'

One of the other men beside him stood up too. 'Other people have thoughts too,' was all he said, careful to avoid incurring Zainab's wrath whilst not alienating the men with whom he stood united.

'People have thoughts?' Zainab's voice was scornful now. 'Oh yes, men have thoughts. We have seen the reluctance of men to do more than think. We have seen even today men retract from thought, content to let the women think for them, only to deny it when that narrative is exposed!'

The murmurs grew louder; looks of outrage flashed across the faces of those congregated. Jamīla could see the group beginning to splinter along gendered lines. Shapur interjected. 'It is not a matter of man and woman. It is a matter of–'

'–slave and nobleman, concubine and heir, scribe and scholar!' Another man from his collective jumped up. He clutched at his beard when he spoke, almost bouncing on the balls of his feet. 'We are different. We are not meant to join together as one. Are we expected to march with *women*? *With slaves?* This girl complaining about the lack of unity – what does a slave from Africa care about Iran? What does a slave like her know? People want different things. It would be amiss to pretend otherwise.'

Jamīla sighed. She was more used to being ignored by noblemen than being spoken about and spoken for, but it seemed to amount to the same thing. *Endless inaccurate presumptions.*

'No!' Zainab snarled. 'We share the same premise. We seek to remove the Qājārs. We want an Iran that serves the people, not one that enriches aristocrats and greedy shāhs. We *all* want that freedom.'

'Yes,' the agitated man returned, swift and unrepentant. 'Iran for Iranians.'

'Yes,' Zainab repeated, as though he were a slow child. 'Iran for Iranians.'

'But she is not an Iranian.' It was the pudgy man who interjected now. 'She is an African.'

'She is not even an African. She is a slave.'

'Your point?' It was Sanaa who was on her feet now, her slippery voice cutting through the air like acid, corroding all immediate replies.

The men hesitated for a moment. This time it was Shapur who replied. 'Your agenda may well be different from that of the Iranians.'

'That is what you believe?' The words were thrust forward, a challenge.

'It is not what I–'

'It is true!' Various voices insisted, one atop the other, a collision of anger and anxiety from assertive men unused to so many women speaking at once in their presence.

Aghast, Jamīla turned to Zainab Pasha. She wanted to apologise, to retreat, to retract her words. But the situation had spun faster and further than she could have conceived. Zainab was not looking at her.

'You want to thrust out the slaves? Is that it?' Zainab asked. A quarter of the room was filled with slaves. They looked at the small group of wealthy men who were now on their feet. Nobody answered. 'As always, your cowardice inhibits you. You can bluster, you can bemoan – but can you outright admit what you want? No, never. You follow behind a woman, and then you dare to denounce her when you have no thoughts, no plans, no ambition, no desire.' They stood, still silent, but the faces of the men reddened in unison as they bristled under her gaze. 'Leave, if you must. This movement does not require men like you. We require–'

'There is another option.' Shapur spoke over her. Jamīla watched as Zainab stared at him. Her face was sober, but a muscle was pulsing in her jaw. Shapur spoke with an urgency in his voice that Jamīla had not yet heard. He was, she surmised, afraid. 'We do not ignore the wishes of the individuals. But a general meeting is not the place to air one's grievances. We are all committed to serving an agenda that benefits the people – all the people. If you are concerned that you are being ignored, then let us listen. But we must speak at a more appropriate time. Ego will get us nowhere. Listening will.'

Jamīla watched as the pudgy-faced man and the agitator allowed themselves to be calmed down by Shapur's words. He turned to Zainab and spoke, but his voice was raised to address the room at large. 'This was productive. We shall have a similar meeting at another point, to reconvene on these issues.'

As he left the room behind the men, he tapped Jamīla on the shoulder. 'Well done,' he said, with grim satisfaction. 'Consider this your last meeting.'

22

Jamīla was stunned. Her modest hope had been that Zainab Pasha might listen to her, that she might have a chance at some oratory herself and that she could be noticed. Naive as it was, she wanted the opportunity to prove her relevance and the insights she thought were useful. She wanted to wait until the men had left and discussions had returned to the groups before taking leave, but their anxiety was inflammatory, and even after they left it continued to fester. Groups began raging against others, declaring their right to be there or their right to dominate. Jamīla was not prone to tears, but she felt she had wandered up to the Shāh's throne and, in trying to burnish it, had set it alight. She began to leave and saw Zainab Pasha staring at her. She could not fathom the content of the glance, and did not care to. She started to hurry, zigzagging her way through people so she could get to the door, but as she rushed towards it, Zainab appeared in front of her, standing with her arms crossed.

Jamīla did not know what to say. She couldn't meet her eyes. The noise of the room slid away; they had been swept into a vacuum where only Zainab and her opinion mattered. Jamīla would not apologise. She would not be humbled even when she was wrong. Her life had been withered by unquestioning humility and the only moments when she felt alive were when she defied it. She looked up into Zainab's haughty eyes. She would not apologise.

'Do not be sorry,' Zainab said, startling Jamīla.

'I...you?'

'You are new, are you not? I am sure that discussion was alarming. This is a very disparate group, and disagreements are common. You may have sparked this one, but we were due a fiery debate.'

'Why—'

'—do we stay? Ultimately, we all want the same things. It is not uncommon to seek it in different ways, or prioritise one's own needs and impulses. To disagree is human. We live in a world with too little humanity. Noblemen fighting with slaves, slaves who can respond and challenge them, is itself a victory. This community, its existence, is its own success. To that end, you should stay. This is your home, as much as it is mine, as much as it belongs to any of those men who left. I am sorry if they made you feel like it was not. Stay, please. People like you, the owned, the Africans, the women – you need this more than they. When the Qājārs sell to wealthy foreigners, it is the poorest that suffer the most. So stay.'

'Thank you…' Jamīla felt compelled to say more, to legitimise the trust Zainab had shown her. Given her blunder, she wanted to say something that would render her important, lest Zainab remember only her insolence and not her abilities. 'I agree with you…about the Qājārs. I work in their court, and I see first-hand—'

'You live in the Qājār court?' Zainab's expression took on new curiosity, and she placed a hand on Jamīla's arm, drawing her closer. 'What do you do?'

'I am…the concubine of Prince Nosrat.' Jamīla's voice shook as she spoke.

'Oh really?' Zainab looked at her. 'We have another slave here, Sanaa Habashī, who is the concubine of Prince Nosrat. I was under the impression she was his only woman. The Qājār men make loyal youths it seems.' She smiled. 'But you are too?'

'I have been for years…but also,' Jamīla added, 'I am close with the Shāh's favourite eunuch. I mean, very close. The Shāh consults on every matter with this eunuch.'

Zainab looked at her with renewed interest. 'That is interesting. Do you know Sanaa? She is one of the most loyal and diligent members. She had never mentioned someone so close to the Qājārs before.'

'I...well...' Jamīla gritted her teeth. 'Sanaa actually introduced me to Shapur. He-he is the reason I joined.'

'How unsurprising. She is always recruiting people to the movement. This friend of yours, the eunuch, how does he feel about the Qājārs?'

'Abimelech?' Jamīla said, laughing. 'He loves the Shāh. He spends all his time with him.'

'Ah.' Zainab frowned for a moment. 'That is rather unfortunate...'

Jamīla, cursing her forgetfulness, added, 'But he wants to leave, actually.'

Zainab's frown deepened. 'Which is it? Does he love the Qājārs or not?'

'Oh well, I-I am unsure.' Jamīla watched Zainab as her eyes moved from Jamīla's face to others in the group. 'Look, he-he told me something. I am not supposed to tell anyone.'

'What?' Zainab asked, but she was mouthing something to somebody across the room, and a few people, Sanaa included, were making their way over. She turned back to Jamīla. 'Can this wait?'

'Prince Nosrat wants to move to Paris. He wants to take Abimelech and me.'

'The prince wants to move to Paris?' Zainab turned fully to Jamīla, making a dismissive gesture towards the people across the room. 'Sanaa never said!'

'Well,' Jamīla said, trying to suppress the satisfaction she felt, 'only his innermost circle knows this.'

'And you are that?'

'I have been the prince's concubine for years now.' She paused and added for effect, 'He has taken photographs of me.' There was a hint of pride in her voice.

'That Qājār vanity,' Zainab replied. Then she fell silent. 'He has taken photographs of you? He is quite smitten, I assume.'

'Very,' Jamīla insisted, watching her face.

Zainab's voice dropped. 'Would you like to work for us?'

Jamīla stared at her, mouth agape.

'You are right.' Zainab's tone was empathetic. 'I should not have asked.'

'No I—'

'Let us...talk more on the subject.'

'Now?'

'No, not now.' Zainab chuckled. 'I shall send you a message, through Sanaa. She has privileges that allow her to travel more than most. Henceforth, should you wish to speak to me, do not contact Shapur,' she said, her lip curling. 'Seek Sanaa.'

23

'They are stupid,' the Shāh muttered, pacing back and forth. Abimelech offered a non-committal 'ah' that had the Shāh turn to face him with a frown. They were in the Shāh's personal quarters, in a salon Abimelech had been in before. Today it was rather unkempt, and the Shāh, who was known for being fastidious, was oblivious to the tunics in a heap on the floor, the empty bottles nuzzling overturned shoes. 'You are not listening!'

'I am!' Abimelech replied, wondering if he should adopt a formal tone. The Shāh loathed it, but under his accusatory gaze, Abimelech felt unsure how else to mollify him.

'Are you?'

Abimelech nodded. 'You are annoyed because your physicians have forbidden you from travel.'

'Because my wives – who *hate* each other – united to pressure the physicians into it!'

'Yes.'

The Shāh glared at him. 'They are stupid.'

'Yes.'

'You are not listening!'

Abimelech had, in fact, stopped listening the third time the Shāh had repeated this routine. He wondered whether the Shāh was in fact too ill to travel, whether this repetition of empty narratives was an indicator of something more serious. 'Why do you want to travel?' he asked.

The Shāh's glare was triumphant. 'I *knew* you were not listening, Abimelech!'

'I was. I have forgotten.'

The Shāh frowned. 'They are...It is for Tchaikovsky.'

Abimelech sighed. Was the Shāh making up words?

'His...Are you uninterested in ballet?'

Abimelech sat up and smiled. 'I am, yes.'

'You say with a smile!'

'Not at all.' He adopted a neutral expression. 'Please tell me about this ballet, about this Tchaikovsky.'

The Shāh continued to frown for a moment. 'You must have seen a ballet once. Do the dancers in the harem not perform from time to time?'

Abimelech shook his head. I *avoid* them.

'They are stupid,' the Shāh muttered and resumed his pacing.

'Please, tell me about this Tchai...'

'Tchaikovsky!' The Shāh turned to stare at Abimelech, who was on his feet. 'I shall. Sit, boy! In two days, his *Swan Lake* will debut in St Petersburg. I should be attending. The men on the council do not want me going to Russia without them. My women in the harem do not want me to go at all. I will not go and do business with the premier or those sycophants. I want to go and watch Tchaikovsky's beauty realised...They have formed an alliance and are stopping me. They claim I am unwell. They are stupid.'

Abimelech swallowed hard, then said, 'I remember you telling me about *Swan Lake*. It debuted on January 15. That was ten months ago. It is Octo–'

Before he could finish his sentence, the Shāh was face down on the floor.

'NO!'

He was screaming over the Shāh's warm body, his hands trembling as he struggled to know what to do. The Shāh was dead. He was not dead; he could not be dead. He was warm. He must be alive. Could dead bodies be warm? He must not touch

him. He did not want to touch him. He had to touch him. He
might not be dead, just dying.

He had to find a physician. He hurried out of the room, but
headed instead to the Divan Khana to find the Grand Vizier.

The Grand Vizier's face bore a perpetual smirk, and when he
saw Abimelech, his face dazed and haggard, his expression did
not flicker. He followed Abimelech without a word and sent a
eunuch to collect his private physician.

The Grand Vizier crouched over the Shāh's body without
speaking for a moment. He blinked a few times and stroked
his face. Then he straightened up. 'You are right not to find a
physician first. We need to control the narrative. Find the brothers
– well, find the eldest three, bring them here and then return
to your quarters. You are the eunuch of that irascible boy, are
you not? Say nothing to him. Distract him, if you will, and do
not return here. There will be an official announcement later,
updating everyone on the status of the Shāh.'

Abimelech wanted to protest. He looked at the Shāh's body,
prone and immobile on the bare floor. To Abimelech, the Shāh
was an imposing figure, tall and upright. Dominating every space.
Lying here, sprawled and still, he became small, real. Finite.
'Perhaps you should place a cushion underneath his head,' was
all he said in the end, and walked away.

Kamran proved easiest to find. He was sitting outside on
an ayvān, surrounded by soldiers, reading a book. Abimelech
approached with trepidation. Before he could get the words
out, Kamran nodded. 'Father. Is he dead?'

'I...The Grand Vizier is in there. He is sending for his private
physician. They will tell us, I suspect.'

Kamran frowned. 'The Grand Vizier loathes you. Why would
he send you to tell me?'

'No...' Abimelech hesitated. 'I found the Shāh—'

'You sent for the Grand Vizier first? Ahead of his *children*?'

Abimelech could feel the eyes of the soldiers boring into his back as he struggled to stand his ground. 'I had limited time. The Divan Khana was closest, and I did not know where any of you were. I did not have much time – I had to focus on saving the Shāh's life.'

'Which the Grand Vizier can do with his abundant medical skills?'

'The Grand Vizier can be discreet—'

'And we cannot?'

'Would you keep this from your mother? From your siblings?' He added hastily, 'Shaazdeh!'

Kamran sighed. 'Just tell me where they are.'

Abimelech searched for Mass'oud next. His chest felt heavy. Mass'oud was assertive and bullying at the best of times; Abimelech dreaded an interrogation that made Kamran's resemble gratitude. He wished he could return to the Shāh. He would feel more useful, sitting by his side. Hunting the Shāh's sons was a useful distraction, until he had to explain why he was there, and the fear came rushing back to gnaw at the pit of his stomach.

In Mass'oud's quarters he was directed by a eunuch, who pointed at a room in the far distance from which screams and squeals could be heard. Then he ducked and disappeared, leaving Abimelech on his own. Abimelech recognised the dancer who opened the door. She cocked her head, arched an eyebrow. She asked, 'Are you here to join us?'

Abimelech felt his face grow hot. 'I need to speak to the prince.'

'A pity.' She placed an ivory hand on his cheek. Abimelech trembled. 'Think about it.'

'It concerns his father.' Abimelech coughed.

'You are one of the pretty ones.' She stepped closer to him. 'Mass'oud would like you. Or I could have you all on my own.'

'He might be dying.'

She paused. 'Mass'oud?'

'His father.'

'Ah.' She turned to call to Mass'oud and then said, 'I could make you enjoy it. I know you still feel things.'

He felt his mouth drop open, and then hers was on his, and she had pressed him against the door, her hands slipping beneath his frock coat. He could hear her heart beating, pounding against his, but the panting in his ear was all him. She continued to kiss him for a moment, taking his hand and placing it over her breast. He didn't know what to do. It felt so warm and soft, but he was panicking, *panicking*. They were standing in a doorway with an amorous prince nearby, and whilst he had seen innumerable naked women, slaves with bodies bared against their will, he had never so seen an ardent woman, felt a bare breast with a crisp and pointed nipple, nor smelled a neck as erotic and desirous as this...

She stopped, stepped back and smiled. 'You know how to find me,' she whispered, and then, adjusting her clothing, added in a louder voice, 'Mass'oud Mirza is through there,' and pushed him forward.

Abimelech, already tense and flustered, found Mass'oud spread out on the mattress, completely naked and open as if he thought Abimelech would climb on top of him. The two other women on the bed Abimelech recognised as slaves from the harem – a domestic with striking eyes, whose tongue was tickling Mass'oud's ear and an Abyssinian, whose large breasts Mass'oud was stroking with the proprietary grasp of a merchant at a market stall. Abimelech didn't know where to look. His eyes kept finding

Mass'oud's long, thick penis, which Mass'oud presented with a particular pride. Abimelech's gaze flickered away to Mass'oud's eyes, large and long lashed, to his lips, twisted into a pout, back to the women, hovering around their breasts before shooting back to Mass'oud. He felt like a starving man staring at a feast. He forgot why he came. He just stood, his body throbbing, surprised at this desire for Mass'oud when he had cringed before Nosrat and every other man who had slept with him since he arrived.

'Do you want to touch it?' Mass'oud ran his hand along his penis with the smile of a man in complete control.

'Yes.' Abimelech couldn't believe he'd spoken. He waited for Mass'oud to laugh. But instead he rose and leaned over.

'You are...very beautiful.' Mass'oud straightened up, until he was on his knees facing Abimelech who stood at the foot of the bed. 'We are all very jealous that Father gets to play with you.'

The word 'Father' made Abimelech flinch. He remembered why he was there. 'Shaazdeh, your father collapsed a few hours ago.'

The women gasped. Mass'oud asked, 'Is he dead?'

'He was not moving – the Grand Vizier went to fetch a physician.'

Mass'oud sighed. 'Well, if he is dead, he will still be dead in an hour. If he is alive, then I have no reason to leave.'

'I must. I have to tell the others.'

'Have you told Kamran?'

'Yes.'

'Well, Mozaffar can wait. He is probably drunk anyway.' The door behind them closed, and Abimelech realised the dancer had rejoined them. Mass'oud looked around Abimelech at her. 'You – go and find a eunuch and make him find Mozaffar. Tell him father is dead. Or not dead. Mozaffar shan't remember. Tell him something grave. Then return here.'

Abimelech was frozen. He felt all the established rules were being rolled away. The two slaves lying on the bed rose to kneel beside Mass'oud. The domestic continued to nibble on his ear. The Abyssinian leaned over to lick Abimelech's face. Mass'oud slapped her lightly. 'I get first touch,' he said.

Abimelech gulped. He found, for the first time, he was being seduced, not overpowered. 'I am sorry...Shaazdeh,' he said. 'I am a eunuch. I cannot–'

'What can you feel?'

Abimelech was stunned by the boldness of the question. He felt ashamed. He wanted to cry. He wanted to run. He wanted to pin Mass'oud down and have sex with all three of them. 'Nothing. Everything–'

'Has been done to you.' Mass'oud nodded, pulled his face towards him and kissed him, a slow, tender kiss. Abimelech grabbed his face and kissed him harder; the Abyssinian slave joined in, slipping her tongue into his mouth whilst pulling his hand from Mass'oud's face to between her legs. The domestic reached underneath and began peeling off his clothes. 'Get onto the bed,' Mass'oud insisted, his voice gentle. 'We shall find out what you like.'

24

Abimelech lay awake the following morning, unable to rise from his bed. A young eunuch had already been in and pulled the curtains apart, placed correspondence on his table. They knew better, by now, than to give Nosrat his letters; he never read them, and Abimelech would be blamed for failing to get him to where he should be. But as Abimelech felt the sun streak in through the open windows and watched the shadows dance like greetings along the walls, he felt crippled by intense sorrow, of the kind he could never fully explain.

The numbness he had felt after his brother's death had engulfed him for so long that when the first piercing prongs of a new feeling emerged, he couldn't recognise it for what it was. He had bumped into Jamīla leaving Nosrat's room a few years ago. She had been dishevelled and unhappy. She was wearing Nosrat's frock coat and clutching her own garments, but the coat kept slipping off her shoulder, and he could see, curling along her collarbone, a bruise that was beginning to form. He had stopped her and tried to question her, but she was uninterested in replying; indeed, when she tried to speak, her voice was muffled; she had a welt on her lip.

He had recoiled in shock at her voice, and she had left before he could compose himself. He found Nosrat in his room, stretching like a cat, a smirk upon his face as he bent his fingers back. Abimelech felt a burst of emotion bubbling in his throat, but it wasn't outrage on Jamīla's behalf, nor sympathy at her vulnerable state. It wasn't until later that he'd realised: it had been lust, plain and simple. When Abimelech had faced Nosrat, he realised to his dismay, all he felt was envy.

He would wait for the feeling to abate; there was no longer anything he could do. He could not masturbate. He could not even understand why he felt this way; for years, he had not felt anything. Now, he was overwhelmed with spasms of desire. He excused himself from Nosrat's presence, headed into the room he slept in, jumped onto the bed and bit down on a pillow, but the silenced scream was no respite. He lay there, churning with lust, unable to relieve himself or distract himself as he waited for the feeling to go away.

In Mass'oud's room, he had wondered if things might be different. Would touching a body help release the overwhelming tension? He found kissing torturous. It managed to sate his desire whilst reigniting it, so he oscillated between a moment of release and the unending fire of need. It was arduous; he was enjoying his own pain, but whilst they were eventually sated, smiling and rolling in a pool of languor, he was still aroused. He couldn't bring himself to tell them, or touch them; he could not even speak lest he scream. Instead, he rose and bowed to their tired faces, wishing he could lie between them, peeling off his own skin.

It was moments like these where he questioned his own existence. What kind of life could he possibly strive towards? There was no world where he and happiness would meet, no world where he stopped serving others, none where his body might actually serve him. He could not recreate the family he had lost, and those he had considered family – Nosrat, Jamīla, the Shāh – were distant or dying.

For months, in the face of each male slave, he saw his brother, moments after his death. He was not cold yet, even as the blood scrambled to escape, flushing from his wound as through a crack in a river dam. His body still retained the vibrancy Abimelech envied and had taken for granted. His eyes, however, were empty, so absent they were hollowed out. Never until that moment had life seemed tangible to Abimelech. For it was as though a joiner had stepped forward and carved it from his brother's eyes. Abimelech had begun to scream then, rousing the others who lay in that cramped room. Like him, they were would-be eunuchs, bodies desecrated by incompetent men, their wounds ineptly dressed as they waited out the night. His brother had not been the first to die: not the first boy of their group, nor the first boy that night. As the men who had performed the castration hurried back in, Abimelech was struck by the sleeping bodies of the young boys who survived. How had they slept in this funereal room, shaped to swallow its every inhabitant, unstirred by the cries of fleeing life that seemed to start almost every hour?

The memory propelled him from the bed. He plucked the correspondence from the table and went through it, looking for anything about the Shāh. There was a letter addressed directly to Abimelech. There was no announcement about the Shāh, only this letter in unfamiliar writing. It was an invitation to a confidential council meeting, a polite, decorous note signed with an F. The request looked innocuous enough, but Abimelech knew it meant much more. All was not well, but all was not lost. *The Shāh must still be alive. The Shāh was still alive. The Shāh was alive.*

For now.

25

He arrived at the meeting place ahead of time. Despite his punctuality, he was the last to appear. They were in the Divan Khana, in an unfamiliar room. The whole hallway was abandoned. This room in particular had been one of the Shāh's favourites. A solemn space with a dusk-coloured ceiling and stripped, grey walls, it had been marked for one of the Shāh's renovations and then forgotten about. Abimelech had heard of it but never entered before. It stood – with the original furnishings pulled out – a hollow majesty, with an air of tragic sobriety that made Abimelech feel small. Three men Abimelech recognised at once sat on cushions on the ground. Behind them, against the wall, stood their eunuchs. The Grand Vizier rose first and greeted Abimelech with an ominous flash of his teeth. 'Welcome,' he said, and Abimelech started. As Nosrat's eunuch, he either followed behind or led the way. Abimelech was unsure who told the Grand Vizier to treat him as a man, but he saw how much the effort cost him, and he began to feel wary.

He dipped his head in reply.

'You know Mirza Fatali al-Dawlih and Mirza Firouz Farman Farmaian.' The men nodded. The Grand Vizier did not bother to introduce the eunuchs. Knowing he was not to join the eunuchs lined against the wall but unsure of what to do next, Abimelech hovered before them all, trying to mute his nerves.

Fatali gestured to a cushion beside him with an affable smile. 'Sit, boy!' he ordered, and Abimelech, glancing at the eunuchs behind, settled down.

'Now,' the Grand Vizier began, 'I trust we all understand what is at stake this evening.'

Abimelech stared at the faces sitting around the circle. He did not wish to interrupt. They looked sombre, and even Fatali wore a frown.

'Are we ready to present our arguments?'

Abimelech had to interject. 'If I may, Amin al-Soltan?'

'Already?' The Grand Vizier looked amused. 'You are quite the chatterbox, eunuch.'

'I humbly...' Abimelech stopped and began again. 'I have not been informed of the discussions we are due to have at this meeting.'

The Grand Vizier frowned and looked to the men on either side, waiting for them to explain. Fatali did. He turned, with an earnest smile, to Abimelech and grasped his arm. 'It is quite serious. It is regarding the Shāh's recent collapse.'

'I know of nothing that followed,' Abimelech mumbled. Fatali nodded.

Firouz leaned over. 'Perhaps you should let Fatali explain, hmm?'

Abimelech looked down. He could see the Grand Vizier was smiling.

Fatali began again. 'Last week, the Shāh, our great Shāh of Shāhs, collapsed. He has yet to recover. We are all quite concerned. We have a single priority, and that is to find an interim ruler. It should be the crown prince, the Valiṇahd, but...well...' Fatali paused, then said, 'What I am telling you now is confidential. Mass'oud Mirza sent a slave to inform Mozaffar of his father's decline. Now, Mass'oud told us that his slave told him that Mozaffar was inebriated when they found him. Worse, he had been—'

'It looked rather like he had died, so we are told,' Firouz said, raising an eyebrow. 'He was lying in a pool of all possible bodily fluids. The slave confirmed they were his own.'

The Grand Vizier snickered, as did one of the eunuchs.

Fatali rolled his eyes at the men. 'The point is, that whilst the Shāh will recover, it could take some time. The Shāh has had a more than 50-year reign, a hitherto unfathomable idea. We cannot let that be disrupted by insufficient leadership, certainly not in this time of turmoil. As such, today—'

'As such, today,' Firouz interjected, 'we are discussing our choice should such a man seem necessary. You obviously are unaware, but several of the European advisors roaming around the court are aware of the situation and wish to offer their suggestions. Now, we are expected to indulge them and obey them. We are not going to do that, as you can imagine.'

The Grand Vizier let out a dark chuckle.

Firouz continued, as if oblivious. 'We have thus convened this meeting so that we can have a debate, shall we say. We need to decide who will be the optimal candidate and *all agree*. We shall meet with the British only when it becomes necessary, and we must be discreet prior. Nobody can be made aware of the severity of the Shāh's illness. Provided they think it a mere trifle, they will not take the time to plan and decide on who their favourite is. Should the moment arise when an interim leader becomes necessary, they shall be divided over whom to choose, and thus our choice will take precedence. Now, the other men on the political strategy council will obey whatever we decide, so it is important that we three agree on one name. You, Abimelech, are here in an advisory capacity only. You are here to please the Shāh, because he is fond of you. Do not feel you have to argue for any candidate and do not speak unless you wish to add something hitherto unsaid. You are clear?'

'Yes.'

'Good.'

Fatali shot Firouz a reproachful glance. He turned to Abimelech.

'If you have not had time to formulate an opinion, then you can say so. Perhaps you might agree with one of us?' He gave him a rather firm smile. 'We all know,' he continued, now speaking to the room at large, 'how much the Shāh trusts the advice of his son's favoured eunuch.' Firouz and the Grand Vizier both frowned, but neither said anything else. The Grand Vizier shot a look at Abimelech, but Firouz maintained his opaque expression, staring straight ahead.

The Grand Vizier gestured to one of the eunuchs standing behind them. He left and returned with a glass of water. Sipping it, the Grand Vizier turned to the three. 'Who would like to begin?'

'I shall,' Firouz said and rose. He glanced around the room for a moment and added, 'Amin al-Soltan, I must chastise you. This is a rather poor presentation. There is no food and, as your eunuch has reminded us all, no water. Send all the eunuchs out at once to remedy the situation. Insist they cannot return unless they have multiple dishes, their arms stacked high with food.'

If the Grand Vizier was annoyed, he hid it well. 'You heard him, boys. Go!' He turned to Abimelech and said jovially, 'Not you, of course. Tonight you are one of us!'

Abimelech did not know how to respond. The Grand Vizier turned away, and Fatali whispered to Abimelech. 'You know Firouz is not hungry. He just did not want the eunuchs to hear his argument. Gossip spreads, even amongst the loyal, at the right price.' Abimelech found it easier to smile at Fatali, who beamed back at him. 'Impressive, I know. He is sharp.'

'When you are quite finished,' Firouz said. Fatali wore a cheeky expression and proffered an elaborate bow.

'There is no real debate here. It can either be Mozaffar or Kamran Mirza. I would insist on the latter. Yes, he is younger and yes, the succession is Mozaffar's birthright, but Mozaffar has proven himself inept in every possible way. Kamran, on the contrary, has proved himself competent. He too lacks the appropriate lineage, but the circumstances are different. He has more experience, he is his father's favourite and he is younger than Mozaffar. When I argue for Kamran Mirza, as I shall, one might suggest I am just accelerating a natural progression and seeking to do it seamlessly. Have him rule as an interim leader now, and when the great Shāh does pass, it will seem natural to have him resume his role. We all know Mozaffar Mirza – his lusts would shock a dancing girl. Can we really attempt to secure a glutton, a man who, on top of that, is ignorant of politics and the people, for the most powerful role in the land? How will he negotiate with the Europeans? He cannot fight for the rights of this court against the Russians when he knows nothing of them. Most of all, he does not even want the job. Now or later. To choose Mozaffar Mirza would be to gamble away the precious, impressive legacy of the current shāh, Shāh of Shāhs. As such, I propose Kamran Mirza.' Here, Firouz paused. Right on time, the eunuchs re-entered the room, arms laden with food. Without looking at them, Firouz took a slightly self-mocking bow and sat back down.

Abimelech was awed. He looked at the other two men. If they were nervous, they did not show it, though neither hurried to follow Firouz's speech. The eunuchs stepped between the men. Two unrolled a grey sofreh and the third unloaded the food onto it. Abimelech had shared meals with Nosrat or other slaves only and couldn't permit himself to take a *dolma* from the same bowl as the Grand Vizier. He looked at the food – antelope kabābs, lamb stuffed with chestnuts and raisins, doves and partridges roasted whole – and sighed. He sat still as everybody began to indulge, the sound masking the silence.

Abimelech whispered to Fatali, 'We should consider Mass'oud Mirza.'

Fatali stared at him in surprise. After a moment, his face relaxed. 'You are new to the Shāh's circle, of course. I forget that; your rise was so sudden, so recent. You may not be privy to old conversations when the matter seems to be settled.'

Abimelech said nothing. The words unsettled him. As if sensing this, Fatali smiled.

'To return to your suggestion, we could not; it would be too radical.'

'I disagree,' Abimelech murmured. 'The Shāh of Shāhs himself was a radical choice.'

Fatali said with a tight smile and shook his head. 'It is not an equivalent situation. The Shāh of Shāhs--,'

'Was not the intended heir. He was the younger son--,'

'Like Kamran Mirza--,'

'The Shāh of Shāhs is less rigid than your assertions imply. He is fond of Mass'oud Mirza; his fondness is not tempered by the humble background of Mass'oud Mirza's mother.'

'You were not even an idea in 1860, Abimelech,' Firouz, joined the conversation, his voice clipped, 'but we were men and advisors in this court. You may not know what took place here, but we do. We remember it well. I shall spare you the needless details, but suffice to say one of the Shāh's wives was killed by the others. She too was of humble origins, and he had promoted her and made her sons his heirs. They all died. Lineage is important. Mass'oud is not a contender.'

In a break between mouthfuls, the Grand Vizier said, 'I was going to advocate giving Mass'oud Mirza a chance, but I agree with Firouz. We cannot flout tradition.' He darted a look at Firouz and hesitated before continuing to speak. 'However, that argument compels me to support Mozaffar Mirza and insist that we all do. Kamran Mirza might be admired – by some – but he is not the Valiʿahd; it is not his birthright.'

'This is an interim role. It is nobody's right,' Firouz snapped.

'Please. It is an audition. Whoever is chosen will be seen as the successor. Kamran was never meant to be the Valiʿahd.'

'Neither was Mozaffar. How many of his brothers had to die before the role was open to him?'

The Grand Vizier sighed before speaking. 'Mozaffar Mirza is not dead yet. We cannot...'

Firouz spoke over him, 'We cannot...be wise? Be bold...?'

'I cannot just change my mind according to *your will*,' the Grand Vizier said in a dangerous tone.

Firouz laughed. 'Did you not admit to doing just that? I understand that you struggle to be objective here. We all know you and Kamran Mirza are not...close.'

The Grand Vizier blushed. 'I will not indulge ḵalwat gossip! Fatali, Firouz and I have spoken long enough. Who do you endorse?'

Fatali looked at the Grand Vizier, and then for reasons Abimelech could not fathom, turned to him and smiled. 'I support Mozaffar Mirza.'

'What?' Firouz sneered.

Even the Grand Vizier looked surprised. 'Please,' he said, with polite condescension, 'elaborate.'

'You should be pleased!' Firouz turned to the Grand Vizier, a fulsome smile on his face. 'You have an ally!'

'Well...I...Well, I think that Mozaffar Mirza could do a good job,' Fatali stammered. Firouz scoffed. The Grand Vizier was silent. Abimelech felt embarrassed for Fatali. 'Look,' Fatali continued, 'he should be given the chance to try. This could be a test of how he would actually lead. I think, I believe, that...well...that...

well, with the right advisors—'

'Assuming he chose us. He might dismiss us, the councils, the entire government,' Firouz muttered.

'Well, he would have some advisors. I think that, well...dismissing him before he has the chance to prove himself is unfair. And he is the Vali'ahd – it would be unreasonable to do so without... without grounds!' Fatali straightened up on his last point; some of his confidence had been restored.

Abimelech kept his head bowed as he rolled his eyes. He liked Fatali, but that was a poor defence.

'No grounds? How about decades of indifference? He is a child. He would be toppled by radicals or bullied by the British—'

'Or by the Marj' al-Taqlid. We can't have another Tobacco Protest. Or another famine.' Fatali's tone was wry, and the eunuchs gasped.

'Do not compare the son to the Shāh's worst moments—,' the Grand Vizier began.

'I suspect,' Firouz raised his voice, 'that is exactly what we should do.' Abimelech wanted to nod, but didn't.

'It would be an insult to—'

'Were you not endorsing him?'

'Yes, Firouz, but that need not mean—'

'—that he should behave like his father? Or that he be as wise as his father? Were you encouraging ineptitude? Well, that does explain plenty.'

'You!' The Grand Vizier's face was apoplectic. But Firouz began to laugh, and Fatali joined in. The Grand Vizier, glancing at Abimelech, twisted his face into a defiant smile, forcing a laugh through his clenched teeth.

'Do you support anyone?' Fatali asked, turning to Abimelech. The laughter in the room stopped at once. Firouz watched

Abimelech with nonchalant curiosity; the Grand Vizier's gaze was one of studied indifference.

Abimelech was torn. To his mind, there was only really Kamran Mirza. He would have said as much, but knew he needed to be careful. He was reluctant to support Firouz over his lone ally, Fatali. He wondered if he should trust Fatali's open warmth. He couldn't be certain that Kamran replacing his brother was smart. Were there to be a civil war because of this decision, advisors, courtiers and future historians would ascribe that colossal mistake to him. The other men would hurry to disavow their role in the decision. But he knew that Mozaffar would make a terrible shāh.

As he sat and pondered, he realised that the men were somewhat afraid of him. He could not be bribed or bargained with, much less demeaned or belittled. They had no power over him; he already had the friendship of the Shāh. There was no access or prestige they could now offer. To an extent, the speeches and the debate were for his benefit. He needed to be swayed, and they only had their words.

He wouldn't hurry.

After a long silence, he spoke, looking at Fatali.

'I have not come to any firm conclusions, yet.'

Firouz snickered, 'Do you need more time?'

'I need more information. All I see here are hypotheticals.' Ignoring Firouz's interruptions, he proceeded without even raising his voice. He knew, after all, that they would listen. 'There are good reasons to support Kamran Mirza, but there are reasons to suspect that rejecting the Vali'ahd could create a fractious court. If Mozaffar Mirza felt his legacy was being taken from him and the military stood behind him, what might happen?'

'It is a temporary position, and Kamran Mirza is the minister for war. He is very popular with the military. They would not abandon him,' said Firouz.

'More hypotheticals,' Abimelech shot back, and the other two men looked at him in surprise.

'What do you propose?' the Grand Vizier asked, looking at Abimelech with new apprehension.

'Interview the candidates. Find out what they want, what they like, what they will do. Include the Shāh's closest advisors, have them assess both sons, ask a series of questions, and see how they might manage the transition and how they would govern.'

Firouz, his voice low, said, 'It is not an absurd idea...in principle. But both men will just say what they think we wish to hear. They know our alliances, and they will manipulate us.'

'Well, how do we get around that?' the Grand Vizier asked.

It was Fatali who answered. 'The boy will interview them – Abimelech.'

There was a silence. Abimelech froze. He felt the malevolence in the room deepen, but nobody spoke up to disagree.

26

Jamīla was alerted to Abimelech's presence by Gul's beaming voice in the passageway.

'To what do we owe this surprise?' she exclaimed. Jamīla could hear the sound of her smile.

It could only be him. The harem's martyr. The harem's king. But despite her scorn, she felt her heart pound with excitement.

Abimelech walked through Chehra's apartment into the pantry, his voice low and thoughtful. 'Well, it was perhaps a fruitless journey rather...,' he began.

'But how?' Gul asked.

'Well, I do not wish to waste your time...'

'Nonsense,' Gul pronounced. Jamīla heard the opening of cupboards. 'I shall ask Jamīla to join us. I know you two are close friends.' She walked across to the slaves' sleeping quarters, and Jamīla moved away from the door. Gul pulled a face when she saw her. 'Stop pretending you were not listening and come along.'

She gathered them both into the salon, and Jamīla stared at Gul in surprise. 'Well, Chehra is sleeping,' she said, by way of explanation. 'And Abimelech came especially.'

Jamīla was rarely in the salon. Chehra had few friends and had not dared to entertain since that disastrous attempt with the Shāh. As the three of them stood awkwardly in the centre, Jamīla realised that, as the lowest-order slave, she had to attend to the other two. She pulled three cushions from the corner and placed them in a circle behind the others. She took the drinks Gul had brought from the pantry, only two, and placed them in front of the cushions.

'Well,' Abimelech said with a cough, sounding uneasy. 'Let us not presume...' He settled onto a cushion and offered his doogh to Jamīla. She wanted to take it. She didn't. Dimpling, he continued, 'I had a message from Nosrat Mirza to give to Jamīla, but I thought, rather than send a note, or a eunuch with a message, I might pay you all a visit. I thought I ought to speak to you in person about the state of the Shāh. I have a free afternoon, so I decided to spend it visiting all the wives, speaking with their chamberlains. I know one can feel quite removed from the action here in the harem, and I wanted everyone to know that their concerns, fears and prayers were heard.'

Gul looked stunned. She held a hand to her chest. 'Is there any news?'

'There have been no changes to his health, I am afraid.'

Jamīla scoffed.

Gul, sitting opposite her, glared and shook her head.

'No, Jamīla is quite right. It is as I feared – an unnecessary exercise, that inconvenienced you both–'

'No!' Gul almost shouted, and then looked behind at the wall. Chehra's bedroom was on the other side. She lowered her voice. 'No. You are thoughtful. You came here and have gone around the whole harem, reminding the wives at a time like this that they matter. You knew they would be afraid and not just for him.'

Jamīla looked from one to the other. 'What else would make them fearful?'

Gul looked at Abimelech. She sipped her drink.

'What do you think will happen to them when the Shāh dies, Jamīla?'

Jamīla shook her head. 'I do not know, Abimelech.'

'Think, Jamīla,' he said, in a voice just below a whisper.

'They would stay here, would they not?'

'You mean the son would inherit his father's wives? Concubines perhaps, but wives? Jamīla, this is not the *Shahnameh*. And even then, Sūdābeh failed to seduce both father and son. Wives are not passed between the two in real life. No, any new shāh will want his own things, his own advisors, his own wives—'

'His own slaves,' Gul interjected.

'Yes, and the slaves can be resold.'

'And the wives remarried?' Jamīla asked.

'No.' Abimelech's smile was wan. 'The women are just...expelled from court.'

Jamīla was speechless. Horror slithered down her spine.

'So Abimelech was very kind to reassure all the wives,' Gul said with a smile.

'You flatter me.' Abimelech's mouth twitched as he looked into his drink. 'I am returning to the harem pantries, after I talk with Jamīla. The domestics are washing cushion covers from the coffeehouse. I thought, if you had some dirty ones, I could collect them and take them down. I would return them to you myself, worry not. I can even take anything from the slaves' sleeping quarters—'

'This court does not deserve you!' Gul exclaimed. 'I will bring them to you when you leave.'

Oh please. Jamīla put her hands in her lap. She sat waiting.

'Oh, I should let you talk with Jamīla,' Gul added, rising to her feet. 'She is probably eager to hear about Nosrat.'

Jamīla almost jumped. How had she forgotten he had a message from Nosrat?

'Thank you for visiting!' Gul trilled as she left, her joyous voice interrupting Jamīla's thoughts.

'This is a gorgeous room,' Abimelech offered. Jamīla scoffed, looking around the sparse room. To her, the bland cream walls spelled monotony.

'Gorgeous? Gorgeous? When were you last in a sigheh's salon? These walls are all one colour. There are no painted stories...some wives have muqarnas and arches. Kohinoor Khaanoum forbade Chehra from getting a bigger chandelier. She cries all the time about this room!' *Why were they talking about this? Gul had left!*

He looked at her like he was reading her thoughts. Yes, she conceded without speaking, *Gul could be listening outside the door, at least for a moment. She was human after all; she could be curious.*

He looked at her like he was reading her thoughts. *Yes, she conceded without speaking, Gul could be listening outside the door, at least for a moment. She was human after all; she could be curious.*

Jamīla took the cushion Gul had vacated, seating herself next to Abimelech. *He smelled nice.* Composing herself, she asked, 'W-what did Nosrat want?'

Abimelech turned to face her. They were inches apart. 'He did not want anything. I lied.'

Jamīla stared at him, willing herself not to smile. She looked away, then rose to her feet. Finally, she asked, 'Well, *why are you here?*'

If Abimelech felt insulted, he masked it. 'I took your advice. When I told Nosrat about his father's collapse, I told him how close we were. I told him I had been there. I apologised for my absence.'

'Oh.' Jamīla felt deflated. This could not be why he came to visit.

Abimelech nodded. He stood up too.

Sighing, she asked, 'What did he say?'

'He said he had replaced me as his chamberlain.' Abimelech

had spoken in a matter-of-fact tone, but there was a fury behind his words.

Jamīla was surprised. 'You...you are angry.' She felt a small buzz of excitement.

'Me?'

'You are...insulted?'

'Jamīla, do you think I wish to be teaching Nosrat subjects he refuses to learn? Indulging his endless temper tantrums? I am *surprised*, Jamīla, not insulted. Nosrat has no need of any staff besides domestic slaves...and perhaps concubines.'

'So he is still seeing Sanaa?'

'No.'

'No?' Jamīla gasped.

Abimelech frowned. 'I meant, yes.'

'You said no, but you meant yes. Why did you say no?' Jamīla's eyes glittered.

'Well, are you hoping to...do you think that...I do not encourage–'

'You sound flustered.' Jamīla smiled with feline grace. *Do not be mean.* She straightened her shoulders. 'Is he seeing Sanaa?'

Abimelech stepped closer to her. 'Are you still seeing Sanaa?'

'I–'

'Are you still seeing Sanaa – and the radical tutor, who is also a nobleman *and* a mullah?'

He makes it sound ridiculous. 'Why?'

'Well, Jamīla,' he said, putting an avuncular arm around her shoulder, 'I think I underestimated Sanaa. She seems a little... She could be dangerous.'

Really? 'Really?' She blinked up at him. 'Should we be scared for Nosrat too?'

'Jamīla, be serious.'

'I am being serious.'

'I do not think you are.'

'No?' she countered, and stretched up towards him. 'Well, I am. Sanaa and Shapur are serious, and so am I. They have introduced me to Zainab Pasha. I attended a meeting where she spoke.'

He looked at her, unimpressed. In a single, swift movement, he clutched her jaw between his fingertips. 'When we last spoke about Nosrat, you were scared to pass him in the passageway. When I last spoke to Nosrat he...Now you are running around with Iranian radicals. And you want to return to Nosrat. Do you just oscillate between bad and worse decisions?'

Jamīla twisted out of his grasp. She pushed him away. 'You hurt me.'

Abimelech sighed. 'Jamīla, I am concerned for you. My words may be harsh—'

'No, you hurt me. My face. I thought...I thought I could trust you not to hurt me like all the others.' Jamīla blinked back tears, turned and started to leave.

'No. Wait.' He grabbed her hand. Dropped to his knees. Kissed it.

She spun round and stared at him, unable to speak.

'Forgive me and let me make peaceful amends.'

Jamīla suppressed her sigh. *Hafiz.* Of course.

'Ah, Abimelech, you are not the only man who promised penitence and broke down after.' *See, I can recite Hafiz too.*

He did not blink. He was still on his knees, still holding her hand.

'Rise, please,' she said, her voice tired. 'Let us not make slaves of each other.'

27

Abimelech sat in one of the Shāh's offices, waiting for Kamran to arrive. He had spent several nights researching Persian history and collecting contemporary papers, trying to tie the information together into a relevant set of questions. The men, having decided Abimelech would conduct interviews, had left the work to him and remained unreachable, unless one counted the eunuchs that they had following him, which Abimelech didn't. Abimelech had had his eunuchs send requests to the princes' eunuchs, only to have his letter to Mozaffar returned to him without comment; Kamran's returned with a time and date written over it.

He brought boxes of his research with him, suspecting that Kamran and Mozaffar would find this process beneath their dignity. An abundance of notes, of paper, of research, would convey seriousness on his part, perhaps even respect. Now as he sat with these boxes stuffed with paper, he felt silly. He flicked through the papers on the table. The first set of questions was not amongst them. Trying not to panic, he looked in horror at the eight boxes piled with paper he would now have to search. He turned to the younger eunuch, who was sitting on a cushion behind him. He couldn't make him do the work. He sighed.

As he slid off the chair, and bent over the boxes, the door burst open and Kamran entered. Abimelech turned, crouching to gaze at Kamran as the latter stood over him.

'You are not going to interview me,' Kamran said, a smile tickling his lips. The eunuch on the cushion began to write.

Abimelech, hearing the scratching of a qalam, snapped, 'Do not write this down.'

Kamran took a seat. Even as he relaxed, he dominated the space. Abimelech half-suspected that Kamran could sit with ease wholly unsupported, floating on a raft of his own self-confidence. He gazed around the room. 'I presume the council is nearby?'

'There is always somebody close. They have taken, as of late, to having me followed.'

'*You?*'

'I suspect they want to know what you shall say.'

Kamran leaned back in his chair. 'Well, Mozaffar will say nothing – that I have been told to tell you. You are not worthy of his time.'

Abimelech shrank in his seat. 'His...?'

'Or his presence, as I recall.'

'Ah.'

'Mass'oud, it appears, is unhappy. He felt eligible, as he is a governor. He also expected you to have been to see him.'

'Ah,' Abimelech said again. His face grew warm.

'You two are friends, then?' Kamran's mouth twitched. 'I was not aware.'

Abimelech dropped his gaze. 'Hmm.'

'You're close with everyone in the family, it seems. Well,' Kamran permitted himself a chuckle, 'with the exception of Mozaffar.'

'Wh-what did he say?' Abimelech asked, hastily.

Kamran stared at him for a moment. 'His precise words were, "You may be questioned by a common slave to sanction the theft of my birthright, but I shall refrain from joining this spectacle".'

'Do you agree?'

Kamran straightened up. 'It is not a matter of opinion. This is his birthright; I would be taking it from him.'

'I would not...characterise it thus.'

'He is not wrong.'

'An interim is not a successor. We are seeking a...replacement whilst his father recovers.'

Kamran rolled his eyes. 'We all know the interim would be the successor.'

'So why agree to it?'

'Father is still alive. We still honour his wishes. And thus, those of his favourite eunuch.'

'So, you are agreeing to be interviewed, Hazrat-e Aghdass-e Vaalaa?'

'No...Mozaffar was right.'

'I am a "common slave"?' The words slipped out.

Kamran's smile grew as Abimelech's face tightened. 'No, do not withdraw. I liked that bite, that ego, that hubris. You keep that hidden, I assume?'

'No, Hazrat-e Aghdass-e Vaalaa, I spoke out of turn. I apologise...'

Kamran looked bored. 'I should leave.'

'Why did you come?'

'A certain curiosity. Perhaps a little vanity. I wanted to see what this was. I have seen. I am leaving.'

'Well–'

'I told you, you are not going to interview me.' He stood and walked the length of the room towards the door. As he opened it, he collided with a group of eunuchs who were standing outside. He chuckled at their alarm and walked on, scattering them like mist. Abimelech sat frozen to his seat. The eunuch beside him folded the paper he had been writing on. Without a word, Abimelech reached forward and snatched it from the young boy's hand. He crumpled it and gestured for the eunuch to leave. Then he sat there, pondering what to do.

28

He woke, sodden and convulsing, as he tried to focus his eyes. They were no longer infrequent, the carnal dreams that haunted him late at night. He couldn't shake the sense of shame, along with the unquenched thirst and frustration. It had followed the usual pattern: a darkened street, a purple sky, the object of his desire facing elsewhere, shrouded in black. Usually it was a woman – he could tell from the fingers that traced the length of the wall. They were light, delicate and soft nut brown. He would wake and find himself thinking of Jamīla, his skin aflame, tears searing his eyes. He would roll out of bed clutching a pillow, his teeth piercing it to silence his shriek. This time the figure was a man. He backed Abimelech as they all did, wholly covered as they all were, but his fingers were pale. Abimelech pushed through the thicket of the night, chasing the man as he walked further away, as slow as Abimelech sped, yet he could not close the gulf. His hand reached out to touch those fingers, the lone visible glimmer of flesh, but the body shifted into a shorter one, female, brown – and still elusive.

He rose, in abject agony, his horror compounded by the sudden unplanned presence of a prince in his room.

It was Kamran.

'You like your sleep,' he said, surprised. 'I rather expected you to rise early.'

Abimelech didn't know what to say. His door was flung open; Kamran leaned against the frame. For a fleeting moment, Abimelech wondered how he looked. Was the sweat visible from there? He glanced down at his arms, noting with relief that he had not scratched them hard enough to draw blood. Some nights he rose to find rivulets of red adorning the sheets. He was often too frantic to notice until dawn had broken and the day had begun. He wiped his face with a clammy hand, blinked to clear any final tears, and sat upright, his gaze hovering around Kamran's midriff.

'I should apologise,' Kamran said, but didn't. 'I have entered your room without your consent.'

Kamran paused. Abimelech knew he was expected to reply. But he was still aroused, as he was after such dreams. Aroused and unable to expel his desire. He settled for biting his lip, pressing his fingers into his thighs and staring hard at the buttons on Kamran's frock coat, waiting for him to continue.

'The last time we spoke, I was unfair. I was hard on you,' Kamran said with an easy smile. 'I know you were bullied into holding those "interviews" by Father's senior advisors.'

I am one of your father's senior advisors. Abimelech gulped, realising he wasn't certain it was true. Instead of speaking, he nodded with the gratitude he knew Kamran would expect. Kamran smiled.

'This is serious. Mozaffar is right; it *is* disgraceful to steal his birthright. But this is about more than him, or even I. It is about Iran. The council needs to know there is somebody competent who can follow Father. I need to convince you–'

'You have–'

Kamran ignored him and continued, 'That I am that man. Still, I will not interview. It seems farcical, somehow. Instead, you and I will have discussions. We will talk about anything you choose, but through that, through seeing my temperament, you will arrive at the answers you seek.'

'I-I...of course.'

'You will need to put on clothes for this conversation.'

'Yes-yes...I—'

'We are beginning right now,' Kamran insisted, before breaking into laughter at the look on Abimelech's face.

***

Abimelech struggled to match Kamran's strides. After their talk in his room, Kamran had left and given him an hour to prepare himself. Abimelech felt frazzled. He retreated at once to Nosrat's bathhouse, suddenly grateful for Nosrat's refusal to form political alliances in the palace as it guaranteed that his hammam, unlike any other, would always be empty. It often felt like a sacred space, with its grand octagonal dome, segmented into sections by tiled stone pillars. It offered miniature rooms for undressing, most of which were unused, and had a long marble passageway that led to a secondary dome, octagonal like the first, but with a shimmering pool at the centre. The walls were a vivid blend of colours, adorned with floral motifs and Abimelech liked to take his time studying each pattern, even though he had seen them so many times before. Today as he entered, he stumbled up the spiral staircase and hurried through the passageway, only remembering moments before entering the water that he still wore his trousers. He pulled it off and flung them onto the neighbouring tiles. Then submerging himself in the unheated pool, eyes closed, fingers shredding his arms, he waited for his yearnings to subside. He tried to deny the questions that fluttered like butterflies across the water. *Could he live this life once more and innumerable times? Could he live this life at all?*

They were striding through parts of the palace Abimelech had not seen before. These halls were more than empty. As Kamran strode with speed, the solid heels of his mules clicking on the marble tiles, the echoing sound it made struck Abimelech as forlorn. They stopped at a tall, barren room with bare walls and long-locked windows, which Kamran went and opened, allowing the entrance of light. There was a stack of cushions in a corner. Kamran gestured to Abimelech, who hurried over to choose from the stack, finding each heavy with the mottled scent of aged perfume. He carried them over to Kamran, cursing his choice of dress. An audience with a prince required the smartest of clothes. As such, the frock coat he wore was one of Nosrat's; the prince had thrown it at him whilst being fitted for another. The fabric was thicker than any Abimelech had seen, and the brocade to this day still inspired wonder. The coat was too ornate for so sombre a room, and Abimelech, expecting they would sit on chairs, was wearing, not his usual loose zirjameh but the European trousers the Shāh preferred. The trousers were too tight to stretch in. He watched Kamran slip with grace onto a cushion, only to chafe as the stitching scratched when he sought to do the same. He found he could not cross his legs, so he settled for kneeling, hoping Kamran wouldn't comment on it.

'This is one of the few places where we shan't be overheard,' Kamran said, his voice flat. He paused, looking round the room. 'To be more precise, this is one of the few places nobody would dare to come.'

'Why? What is this place?'

'What is this place?' Kamran repeated in an incredulous tone. 'Are there not grand bedrooms and pantries? Did you not spy the structure of a coffeehouse? Did you fail to note the great hall? *What* is not the question you should be asking.'

'Ah.' Abimelech nodded and half-smiled. 'To *whom* did it belong?'

'Her name was Jayran. Jayran Forough al-Saltaneh.'

'I have heard of her.'

'I was four when she died, so I do not remember her. I do recall these quarters being forbidden, however.'

'She had quarters outside of the harem?'

Kamran looked at him. 'You must know Father's favoured wives have several houses.'

'Yes, but those are outside the court. These are...'

'Yes, she was not confined to the harem as most women were. But from what I understand, she did not live as most women did, nor as most royal wives.' Kamran, sounding irritable for the first time, added, 'I did not draw you out to talk about Father's wives.'

'One can hardly help it. These rooms seem to carry her.' Looking around, Abimelech added, 'I cannot tell if they mourn her or honour her.'

'Can they not do both?'

'Certainly, but—'

'I must say, Abimelech,' Kamran announced, 'you do not speak to me as a slave to a prince.'

Abimelech felt cold. He wasn't sure whether it was more prudent to speak more or stay silent. He bent his head in a profuse bow, as apologies and titles spilled over each other in their haste to exit his mouth.

'Worry not,' Kamran said with a smile. 'I prefer it.'

Abimelech stared at him.

'I do. I merely expected that I would have to raise it. But you are...quite familiar already, it seems!' Kamran gave a careless laugh and then, spotting the look on Abimelech's face, broke into heavier chuckles.

'You said you wished for us to have actual discussions. Have you had a forthright discussion with anyone who called you by a title?'

Kamran stopped smiling. 'I suppose I have not.' Then, 'I was not aware we were having those conversations just yet.'

It was Abimelech's turn to smile. 'Such discussions do not tend to have a formal beginning. I believe it to be the mark of a good conversation when one cannot tell how it began.'

'Where do you find the time for such conversations?'

'I have been fortunate.' Abimelech paused, shaking off the memories of days past that had come to mind, unbidden. 'Nevertheless, such moments are infrequent.'

'Perhaps this will change that.'

'Yes.'

'Well...'

They both smiled at each other. Abimelech asked, with a shy laugh, 'What was your childhood like?'

Kamran rolled his eyes, but he was smiling. He stretched out his legs as he thought about it. His gaze fell on the colourless walls. 'Happy. Father was attentive. His own father had not been, and he himself had lost many sons. To some, these might be reasons to assume a lack of interest in a son like me, one lacking the lineage to become the Vali'ahd. On the contrary, he indulged me. He adored me. I was always intellectual, curious, clever. I was restless. He threw me into the heaving pit of politics when I was a boy. I was six when he made me governor of Tehran, 20 when he made me Amir Kabir and 22 when I started to govern several cities, finally without a steward.'

'Do you enjoy it?'

'I would enjoy it far more with less global interference.'

'Why?'

'Why?' Kamran sighed. His glance fell on Abimelech's trousers. 'See how you perch; you cannot sit properly in their clothes. European clothes were not made for Persian use...I am not like those radicals. I do not loathe the Russians or the British. I just know that they are different. They make things to suit their needs. What could Iranians make? What might we need?'

Abimelech's eyes grew wide. 'Is this how you would run the court?'

Kamran threw back his head, the laughter in his throat both warm and dismissive. 'Not if I want to live. I would be killed in the first month. No, this is, as you call it, conversation.'

Abimelech began to look forward to these conversations the way he had envisioned he might the arrival of a lover, back when he dreamed he would one day know such things. He didn't long for Kamran the way Nosrat longed for him, or even the way Abimelech himself longed for Jamīla. No, his desire for Kamran was a different animal. He waited for him, every day. Kamran, who teased him like an elder brother might, ribbing and jibing, exploiting his superiority, also led him down the path of intellectual enquiry.

Kamran would turn up at his room unannounced; Abimelech would hear him sweeping past Nosrat's door, accompanied by a string of broad-shouldered men. Nosrat, if he was there, would hurry out and look on, but Kamran wouldn't blink. He never knew what day or time Kamran would appear, but he favoured afternoons. Abimelech would be waiting by the door.

'How can you not support protests?' Abimelech asked Kamran one evening as they talked into the night.

'I find chaos to be the enemy of stability. In my experience, protests tend to present the illusion of a cohesive group, but one tends to find protesters are just united in negation. They dislike *this person or that new policy*, and one can adhere to this, one can put a halt to *that*, or encourage a person to change their behaviour or leadership patterns. But things do not change simply to change – a government is rarely trying to fix the unbroken. Why would they, when it takes money, and planning creates opportunities for discord? Thus, when there is a change, a significant upheaval, there is a corresponding reason – there is a problem which needs to be fixed. Our earnest protesters, out there in agreement about that which they do not want, are not so united with regards to what they do want. Thus, we can halt a solution to an existing problem, adhere to the collective will of the people, but we are then left with the problem and no means to solve it. Protests are not constructive. They are not useful tools one might call upon to build or rebuild a country. They can dismantle, but they cannot create. They destroy, but they do not grow. So, yes, I am underwhelmed by them. I might even concede that I find them harmful. They are the opposite of helpful, at least for long-term use.'

Abimelech paused. He didn't like Kamran's argument, but found he couldn't refute it either. He sighed, then said, 'But what of the Tobacco Protest? You opposed it?'

'Abimelech, this is not a simple question. I have been a vocal critic of Iran's international alliances at the expense of its people.'

'Then which protests do you believe hold people "united in negation" whilst not being constructive?'

'The very same is a key example. The court needed money. The tobacco deal was misguided, but those who sought to end it should have at least considered what might replace it. Those are the hard decisions of a leader. Not having to think about the consequences are the easy benefits of being a critic.'

Abimelech paused again. 'Well, yes...,' he began, looking around. 'When before the Tobacco Protest were women allowed to vocally critique society?'

'When?' Kamran scoffed. 'Every day in the harem. Who do you think holds the real power in the court?'

29

It was November. In the month since the Shāh's collapse, Abimelech had made himself familiar to the men within the Divan Khana, eventually arranging for them to hand him policy reports away from the court. As he was shut out of the committee meetings he used to attend with the Shāh, Abimelech would be completely in the dark without these measures. He did not complain, however, and resolved not to inform the Shāh when he recovered. The men in the Divan Khana, unaware of the concerted effort by the Shāh's advisors to keep him out, handed Abimelech the documents with an air of bemusement as to why he might want them. They were 'dry' or 'unread by the Shāh.'

'He never acts on our assessments,' one of the younger men had told him before being shushed by a peer. He was the second son of a general, with the kind of burnt, pimpled skin Abimelech had come to associate with the children of the European physicians he had seen around court. This young man was Iranian, however, and Abimelech, to his great shame, could never recall his name. Still, Abimelech would arrive at the Divan Khana with a ready smile and a stream of harmless personal questions, to allow the man to feel as though he mattered amongst the crush of generals' sons trying to curry favour or attain some visibility. Abimelech was still the trusted ear that three Qājār royals had so far clustered around. Thus, despite Abimelech being more in need of the men in government than they were him, they were obsequious, fluttering under his attentions, perhaps daring to wish that he might raise their name or their thoughts in the presence of Kamran or the convalescing Shāh, and they might be summoned for their insights, rising to a new level of visibility and meaningfulness, to a life that mattered.

'Have they ever had anything profound to say?' Kamran asked, when Abimelech outlined his observations to him.

'Well...'

'There is no room for pity in this world, Abimelech, especially towards the incompetent. Remember you are an African slave. By all accounts they should be pitying you. If they are unable to rouse themselves into lives of prominence with all the advantages they have been given, then they are mediocre and so thoroughly steeped in their mediocrity that it is impossible to surpass.'

Kamran, slumped against a cedar tree to avoid the blistering sun, was approached by one of his broad-shouldered men, who was carrying a fan. There was a flurry of shuffling and ordering before a small eunuch, with the full cheeks of a child, was brought forward to stand in front of Kamran and cool him down. With his eyes closed, Kamran nodded and gestured for the men to move away. They went and stood in the sunlight, patches of sweat starting to appear across the entirety of their uniform. Abimelech kept looking away, unable to meet their eyes. Kamran had his closed.

'You should be less glib,' Abimelech said in a light but uncertain tone. 'You will have to choose from them when forming your own government.'

'I would not.'

'No?'

'Why would I choose my father's men? I would have my own.'

'Well, the Shāh's men are hardly all bad. After all, I would count as the Shāh's "man".'

Kamran chuckled. 'Yes, you are Father's man through and

through. Poor Nosrat.' He paused and added, 'But again, just because the Shāh's men are not all *bad* does not mean I would include them in my council.'

Abimelech was confused. Kamran was still laughing. They walked back into the palace; silence filled the space between them but for the gasps of Kamran's sweating lieutenants. They returned to Jayran's quarters. Kamran strode forward without a word, peering into rooms until he settled on one facing the light. He made a brief inscrutable gesture, and the two youngest men hurried forward to unlock the luminous windows. Their ragged breath and obvious hurt caught Abimelech's eye for only a moment. His mind had latched onto a troubling thought. He felt his world transforming beneath his feet, from a firm foundation to a muddy morass.

He hadn't realised he had spoken aloud until he heard his own voice declaring, 'So I will not be an advisor in your court.'

Kamran stopped laughing, but looked unabashed. 'I would not equate you with the men from the Divan Khana. But, no – come now, Abimelech, you cannot expect to be a senior advisor in my proverbial court.'

'Wh-Wh-'

Kamran watched him with pity as he spluttered. Three men were hurrying around him, laying cushions on the floor for him to sit. He sat down and sighed. 'Abimelech, I enjoy these discussions. And I trust you are loyal. But I do not think it would be bold of me to say that you consider me a mentor, that you look to me for advice, perhaps even with admiration.'

'Of course!'

'I cannot be advising my advisors. I need to learn from them, not them from me.'

The air was pregnant with all that Abimelech dared not say.

Kamran looked at him, an unreadable expression on his face. He was aware that the situation had changed, but Abimelech could not tell how he felt about that. They sat in tepid silence, facing outwards, staring at the floor-length windows before them. Lightly closed, they creaked open, and the air forcing its way into the room was cold.

30

He followed Jamīla to the grand bāzār, in silence, at a distance. Later he would buy all the pomegranates at the greensellers for her, and she would laugh and then frown in surprise when he confessed to have trailed her from the palace. But he knew he was being followed by the Grand Vizier's men, and if they thought Jamīla knew something, they would trail her too. Jamīla was still friends with radicals. How legitimate her boast was about knowing Zainab Pasha, Abimelech had yet to verify. But were it only partly true, if she knew someone in that circle, and that news flew back to the court – Abimelech could not bear to contemplate it. He kept his face a mask, as he approached her, holding his breath, as hers swept through emotions. He watched as delight, distrust and alarm captured her expression again and again. *'Why have you followed me?'* she asked in Afaan Oromoo. He turned to the other people lingering at the market stall, their eyes on the fruit, their mouths shouting loud. They were not listening. But of those small children playing on the ground, two were African; one looked like he could be Abyssinian. Abimelech looked back into Jamīla's sceptical face and tried to think of something innocuous to say, a truth she would find plausible, that spies would not question.

'I missed you. I always miss you.' Abimelech watched his words gratify her with a guilt he could not shake. 'Let us talk.' He added, 'Tonight?'

He let her quickly into his room. Her eyes had a contentment he had never seen before. She stood before him, watching him as he took both her hands in his, and he wondered how much his next words would sear her or come as a reprieve. 'Disregard all I told you earlier,' he said. His gaze dropped to her hands, which she jerked from his. He staggered backwards but continued without pause. 'I was being followed – and needed to speak to you alone. Had I been forthright, you would have been in danger,' he looked up at her, 'because of the company you keep.'

There was a long pause.

Her voice was cool as she asked, 'Why did you summon me?'

'The Shāh is unwell.'

'We are all aware.'

'Yes, well, the council is trying to choose the right successor.'

'That news has also spread.'

'Did you know that I am to decide?'

A scornful sound escaped from her mouth. 'Why? You are the favourite of the Shāh, surely with his death you lose your value.'

'I-I...I did not mean "successor." I should have said "interim" Shāh, whilst he is still alive but recovering.'

'I see. Well, that is a tidy promotion.'

'A precarious one, rather.'

'Well, with the ear of the Shāh, why do you need me?'

It dawned on Abimelech that she would not help him. He had insulted her, manipulated her and failed to anticipate her reaction. Her arms were crossed and her back was straight. She was resolute. He needed her to be herself. He did not know what to say – or rather, he did but didn't want to say it. He couldn't anticipate her response. Any response would distract from the central issue and push them down a tangent he did not want to pursue.

'I did mean those words I said earlier.'

'You told me to disregard them.'

'So you should.' He felt an inexplicable urge to laugh. Instead he began, 'I am a eunuch.' He sighed. 'All I have to offer is my own unending frustration. Do you want me to yearn and yearn into eternity?'

She looked stricken.

'Jamīla...'

He let the word hang in the air. 'I need someone to talk to. I cannot seek anyone else.' His smile crumbled at the corners. He felt himself beginning to shake.

Jamīla was silent for a long time. Her eyes looked past him. When she finally spoke, her frown had dissipated. 'I will help you.'

Abimelech sighed, relieved.

Jamīla raised her eyes to his. As their eyes met, her expression began to waver, and a smile began to form at the corners of her mouth. Creases quivered in her cheeks, crinkles by her eyes. She started to look away, but Abimelech reached out and took her hand, pulling her closer as he did.

They stood still, their eyes a cornucopia of nervous glee, as they smiled wordlessly at each other.

His hands found her face, cupping it in his palms; up close, her skin was like butterscotch and pillowy to the touch. Her breathing was rapid, racing – he could not understand why she was so nervous. Only later did he realise it was he who was trembling, even to have his fingers against her skin, to hold her face inches from his, to smell her lips from here, to wonder about...

'You should kiss me,' she said, and Abimelech almost jumped. He stepped back, lifting his hands from her face, letting them fall against his sides. He shook his head twice, but he couldn't find the words to disagree.

'I...'

'Do you not want to?'

He realised at once that despite knowing so many eunuchs, she did not understand what he was, what it meant, what kissing her would do to him. He also knew he could never tell her; the idea of her pity, of the paralysing truth rising to fill the air between them made him shudder in his skin. He gulped. What could he tell her? He wondered if she would ever forgive him for the lies he placed between them. 'I am...the eunuch of Prince Nosrat. I could never—'

'I am not his!'

'You were.'

Jamīla frowned. 'Do you consider me *owned*?'

'We are all owned.'

'I seem to be owned by multiple figures. Not just the court, but the prince, my history with the prince. You have been spared such...*ownership*.'

'You are certain of this?' Abimelech spat, and she looked at him in horrified surprise.

He turned away, and the room seemed to sag between them with the weight of all that was unsaid.

When she spoke again, it was in a choked voice, but Abimelech could not bring himself to turn around.

'You requested my help. Let us...discuss that.'

'Yes.'

'I have a requirement.'

'Oh?'

'Yes.'

'Well?'

'You will tell me the outcome.'

He turned to her. 'Why?'

Jamīla did not speak.

'Will you tell your radical friends?'

Again, Jamīla did not speak.

'Ah. You are their puppet – their eyes in the court.'

'Not everyone considers me property, Abimelech.' He flinched. 'This has nothing to do with them. Do you find me so utterly incurious that I would not wish to know the outcome for myself? You expect to use me but not inform me as to what happens? I wish to know, and I want to know that you will tell me. It has nothing to do with them. What do they care who wins? They hate all the Qājārs. So having the third brother from the fourth wife, as opposed to the first son of the late whomever...really, it matters not.'

There was a long silence.

'I will tell you the outcome.' He paused and added, 'I...I am sorry.'

'What for?'

'Everything.'

'Well. What must you do?'

Abimelech hesitated. 'I was to assess them – but Mozaffar Mirza refuses to be interviewed. Kamran prefers conversations, and I am meant to deduce his fitness based on those.'

'Hardly any work, really.'

Abimelech gave a hollow laugh. 'Very little, indeed.'

When Jamīla next spoke, she sounded puzzled. 'These conversations sound intense but...also what you thrive at.'

'Well, they are.'

'So...why do you need me?'

'Well,' Abimelech said, trying not to sound as sheepish as he felt, 'I already know whom I should select.'

'But of course. If the current Valiʿahd was the ideal choice, there would be no question at all.'

'Precisely.'

'So what is the problem?'

Abimelech hesitated before answering. 'My own future would be uncertain.'

'Under Kamran Mirza?'

Abimelech nodded.

Jamīla began to laugh. 'Your hero is not loyal.'

'Well–,' he tried to continue, but she spoke over him.

'How humiliating!' she said with a laugh.

'How kind,' he snapped, clenching his jaw.

'I am sorry...but that is shameful.'

'I...'

'He seeks your endorsement but shan't return the support.' He watched her repeat the words and wander through the room, picturing it. 'I would die.'

'I have options.'

'The drunk crown prince. Supporting him for security?' She clutched her stomach, horrified, and then turned to him, amused. He wondered whether she found this funny at all. 'How important is your input?'

'I...Well, the Shāh listens to me.'

'Yes, Abimelech, but your word will not be that upon which the future of the monarchy lies.'

'I did not imply it was.'

'You did, rather emphatically, as I recall.'

Abimelech was irritated. 'It will be taken into consideration...I suspect it would serve to bolster the words of his other advisors. In any case, I would not turn to Mozaffar Mirza because I was spurned by Kamran. That would be vengeful. I was referring to Nosrat.'

'The *other* drunk prince.' Jamīla chuckled. 'Yes, Abimelech, that sounds very wise. There is a third option you have yet to consider.'

'Oh?'

'Convince Kamran Mirza he is wrong.'

Abimelech felt his cheeks grow warm. 'I am not sure he is,' he admitted, his eyes on his feet.

'He is.' She paused, then asked, 'What did he actually say?'

'He considers himself my mentor, and is looking for men to mentor *him*.'

Jamīla rolled her eyes. 'Abimelech, that is not a tough perspective to change. You just need to prepare harder ahead of these... conversations.'

Abimelech sighed. 'Jamīla, this is not a knowledge game. He is smarter than me. He *is* my mentor. He is right.'

'Persians always think they are right. They are smarter, they know best. They just expect that to be the case. He is a man, a Persian, a royal. He would not expect a young African slave to be more intelligent than him. You may be guilty of the same. You do not expect an African slave to be smarter than him...'

His skin prickled. 'I diminish myself. Is this...is this what your radical friends tell you?'

'You never believe I could have an idea of my own, do you?'

'I sought you out for your very ideas, did I not? I rather thought you would not be so foolish as to mistake insight for humility. I do not suspect Kamran Mirza is smarter because he is a Qājār. Was I not advising the very Shāh of Shāhs? Do we not dismiss the Vali'ahd for his ineptitude? I suspect Kamran is smarter because he is. I am not so consumed by hubris that I cannot recognise that sometimes the rich royal son is the smarter one, even if I despise the system.'

'You love the system. You want me to help you rise within it.'

'I want to survive.'

'Survive? Will Kamran Mirza banish you from the palace?' Jamīla sneered. 'Let us be frank. You stand to lose the power and pleasures you have accrued serving the Shāh, or rather *the Shāh of Shāhs*. Under Kamran Mirza, you would be a eunuch, perhaps the chief eunuch, but not a political force. You want power.'

'Everyone does.' Abimelech rolled his eyes. 'Your radicals too–'

'You do not know what they want–'

'And you must not tell me.'

'Oh?'

'Oh? Is this not treason? You are talking to people who want to assassinate the Shāh.'

'They are not like that! They want freedom. They want an Iran that serves the people–'

'Please. The Qājārs will not listen to them. You know this! They will try and remove the Qājārs and replace them with people who will. How are they removed? Murder.'

'It will not–'

'How can you be so naive? How can you pretend?'

'You wanted to leave! I am trying to find a way–'

'Do you think that *Africans* will get to share in this new *Iranian* freedom? Will slaves?' Abimelech watched her, knowing she had no answers for this. It had probably never been raised. Typical Jamīla, overwhelmed by the cerebral discourse, had forgone the difficult conversations in favour of the transcendent narrative. He smirked at the irony. 'Tell me what the new world looks like, the new Iran where the Qājārs have stepped down, their lives and luxuries intact. What happens to the slaves who work there? Do they carry on as slaves? What if they want freedom for themselves? Will they be granted the same rights as Iranians? Have you answers to these questions?'

'Was there more?' she asked.

'Oh, I have plenty.'

She shook her head.

He sighed. 'Jamīla. You could be killed for treason. There would be no question. If someone suspected you...Has nobody noticed your absences?'

'I...' Tonelessly, she said, 'They think I have rekindled things with Prince Nosrat.'

'So you have to hope Sanaa keeps your secret.'

'Sanaa is not one for pyrrhic victories. She would not do something so stupid.'

'You are heedless, Jamīla! Secrets travel – how are you not being more cautious?'

'I am.' Jamīla sighed. 'You always underestimate me. Always. I leave the harem in a niqāb. Nobody can identify me. When I enter the harem, the chief eunuch assumes I am returning from Prince Nosrat's quarters. He does not even ask.'

'And what of the slaves? What do your radical friends think of liberating slaves?'

Jamīla hesitated. 'There is...division over the subject of slaves.'

'Some of your friends are against your freedom?' Satisfaction seeped into his smile, but it flickered when he thought of Kamran.

'They question our right to be part of the movement.'

'And yet you stay?'

'Some are leaving.'

'Leaving to what?'

'Form their own group,' Jamīla said, unthinkingly.

'What is this group called?' Abimelech's words were a bit too hurried, and Jamīla's askance gaze gave him pause.

'I am not your informant.'

'Maybe you should be.'

'Why?'

'You spy on us for them?'

'I...'

'Consider this an act of...balance. Keeping your indiscretions even.'

'Even?' Jamīla spluttered. 'Are things even on both sides? Is it even to help the oppressors if one is part of the resistance?'

'Are you, though? You said the resistance does not want you.'

Her face hardened into something remote and contemptuous. 'How sad you are, Abimelech,' she said, 'fighting to remain enslaved. You, who once sought a life of purpose, have arrived here. What a fall.'

31

It had been agreed that Jamīla would work for Šahrvandān, an offshoot of the radical organisation to which Shapur belonged, Mellat-e Irān. With the Shāh unwell and out of sight for almost two months, there was a new sense of urgency. Jamīla, too, felt a need to act and this appointment had filled her with excitement. The Šahrvandān was run by Zainab Pasha and dominated by noblewomen; Jamīla had been keen to assist such women in their endeavours. Yet, despite the appointment, and her vocal enthusiasm, she had not been called upon to do anything. She suspected Sanaa's hand in this. Jamīla had been attending the meetings, watching as the people squabbled over whose voice and whose ideas took centre stage after Zainab's. Zainab, she knew, was planning something, and when she was finally summoned one evening, the message relayed with coolness from Sanaa, she felt for the first time that she might be involved in something potent.

She slipped out, using Nosrat as her excuse, and hurried in the dark to Zainab's house. There had been no men that evening. Only four women were present, including Zainab, and they sat with chadors unravelled, bodies outstretched, languid and earnest at the same time. As they unfurled languorously, heads propped against cushions, Jamīla could not believe these were noblewomen by day, unable to leave their households without an explicit purpose. Unlike the women in the harem, who, on the most quiescent of days were impervious to serenity, the women here, despite their dangerous undertaking, were serene and calm.

'Our husbands are friends,' Yagana said somewhat drily, gesturing to the other women, who laughed dark chuckles. She was not as pale as they were but far more striking to look at, with high cheekbones and thick lips upon which sat the light sprinklings of a burgeoning moustache. 'I suggested they take a hunting trip. Wardiyyah's husband genuinely likes her – she made the plan.'

Wardiyyah rolled her eyes and gave an indulgent chuckle. 'He "genuinely likes" Aadila too, hence his inviting the women to join.'

'He would have scuppered our plans,' Aadila interrupted, her gentle, almost childlike frame at odds with her sharp tone.

'What are they hunting?' Jamīla asked, unsure whether to sit. Together, these women formed an impenetrable wall of confidence, their inclusivity making her feel unwelcome.

'Ibex, I suspect.' Yagana turned to the women and they chuckled again. 'They are obsessed, for reasons I can never quite fathom.'

'But am grateful for,' Wardiyyah added, and they spluttered. 'Eight days of absence…We should have planned this sooner.'

Zainab coughed with a smile. 'We should focus now, ladies. It is less easy for Jamīla to join us, and we have work to do.'

The women nodded in unison and sat upright. Wardiyyah began. 'Jamīla, Zainab tells me you have access to the Shāh on two fronts, through his son and through his favoured eunuch. We were hoping you could tell us how close the Shāh is to this son and this eunuch. What information are they privy to – do they sit on his councils? Do they sit in on meetings?'

Jamīla looked into Wardiyyah's round, fleshy face, soft and open with steely eyes. She knew that they were assessing her usefulness, but in truth she couldn't recall which councils or meetings Nosrat attended. She had always stopped listening when Abimelech began to tell her. 'Well…' She paused and then coughed to give herself time. Yagana and Aadila exchanged the briefest of glances. 'I know that Abimelech – that is the eunuch

– has access to very h-high-level meetings.'

'High level?' Zainab repeated.

'He...' Jamīla took a deep breath. She saw Wardiyyah glance at Zainab with something mirroring disbelief. 'The Shāh is unwell.'

'Yes.'

'We are aware.'

'If this is the level of intelligence you can gather–'

'One of the councils – I do not know which – is deciding which son will serve as an interim Shāh if it is necessary.'

'Mozaffar Mirza is not definite?' Zainab was looking at Jamīla like she had transformed into the Prophet Mohammad himself.

'Mozaffar Mirza might not even be likely. The-the eunuch I mentioned, he was scheduling interviews on behalf of one of the councils. They were to measure eligibility.'

'Who else could be eligible?'

'Kamran Mirza.'

'No, that is not possible...'

'I helped him – the eunuch – with...it. He confided in me.'

'Jamīla.' Zainab sat upright, staring at her. 'This is incredible. You are very close to this eunuch?'

'Can you influence this eunuch?' Aadila asked, speaking over Zainab.

'It will not matter,' Wardiyyah said. 'Assuming this is true – and I believe the slave,' she added, darting a thick smile at Jamīla, 'anyone other than Mozaffar Mirza would spark a civil war. That could be worse for us. The Shāh's advisors know this. They will not let anyone take the throne unless Mozaffar dies.'

'Then this information is useless,' Aadila interjected, frowning at Wardiyyah.

'Well...' Wardiyyah hesitated, looking at Jamīla. Jamīla felt the pity emanating from her eyes.

'Aadila!' Yagana gave her a soft yet stern glance. 'Not everyone is comfortable with your brazenness. Do not be so rude. The slave is so young.' She turned to Jamīla and asked in a gentle voice, the kind one might use when stroking a cat, 'How old are you? You cannot be much older than 15.'

Jamīla felt herself mumbling, hoping they would leave it at that.

'How old?' Aadila narrowed her eyes as she tried to read Jamīla's lips.

'I-I could only guess,' Jamīla said, unable to meet her eyes.

'She is unaware!' Yagana gasped, her hand clutching her chest. 'You poor little girl!' And the other women began to make sympathetic noises too.

'The lives of slaves—' Wardiyyah began, but Zainab spoke over her.

'Women, please. The information is useful. It tells us how close Jamīla is to the eunuch and how close the eunuch is to the Shāh. Clearly he is valuable, and either he is indiscreet or Jamīla is privileged. Either conclusion is favourable. Let us tell Jamīla of the task we would have her do.'

The women nodded. Finally, Wardiyyah spoke. 'We need to know who the silent figures are in court and how much influence they wield. Who, aside from your eunuch, is involved in selecting the interim shāh – those people will have influence in a number of departments. Find us a list of the departments focused on international trade and commerce; find us the names of these powerful silent figures or a transcript of one of the meetings.'

Jamīla was staring. 'The eunuch is loyal to the Shāh. He will not share such information.'

'Why so?'

Jamīla did not speak.

'You have not told him about us, have you?'

'Of course not,' Jamīla lied, her heart racing.

'Then it is settled.'

Yagana straightened. 'It is dark. Perhaps we can have a droshky drop Jamīla home?'

'Not...not to the court, to the bāzār. I can walk from there.'

Jamīla ran across the gardens with her head bowed. She had waited until she knew the chief eunuch would be taking his dinner, confident that she could bribe a young eunuch or proffer Abimelech's name and expect favour. As she hurried through a side entrance, she stumbled into the chief eunuch himself.

32

'Jamīla,' he said, with a smile that revealed both sets of his teeth.

She dipped her head in acknowledgement but said nothing. She raised her foot to take a step, and he clenched her shaking arm in his narrow fist. 'Where were you tonight?'

'With Nosrat Mirza,' she replied, as his hand tightened on her arm.

'Why enter from outside?' the chief eunuch asked. 'You can reach the harem from the ḵalwat without having to leave the premises. Do you usually walk out of the palace before returning to the harem?'

'I...' Jamīla stumbled. 'I wished to look outside.'

The chief eunuch smacked her with the length of his forearm. She fell backwards, gasping. He yanked her back up and threw her into the wall. She was crying. He watched her, his expression greedy.

'I do not like liars, Jamīla. You have not been with Nosrat Mirza for quite some time. So. Where have you been? Where have you been going?'

The chief eunuch grew irritable at Jamīla's silence. He crushed his fist into her face. 'You are lucky,' he said, standing over her as she lay choking on the ground. 'Chehra Khaanoum wishes to see you.' He added, a smile in his voice, 'Expect to bleed.' Then he drew her up with one arm and pushed her forward. 'Go.'

The walk to Chehra's room was unusually long. Jamīla struggled to walk upright. She kept her eyes on the ground until she entered Chehra's apartment. The hall was deserted; the rooms soundless.

She pressed her ear to every door that preceded Chehra's. She hoped to find Gul. She needed a mediator, preventing Chehra from doing her worst.

Her hand hovered before Chehra's door. Each time she curled her fist, it quivered. She stood clutching the door frame, trying to catch her breath.

The silence was shortened by the sound of Gul's voice coming from inside Chehra's room.

'She's here.'

The door burst open, and Chehra was before her. Jamīla closed her eyes, steadying herself for what she knew was to come.

'Wait.'

Jamīla glanced upwards in surprise and for a moment met Chehra's forbidding eyes. Chehra turned away towards Gul and added, 'Bring the used sheets and place them on the floor.' Then, 'Instruct the slave.'

Chehra walked backwards into the room and sat on a cushion facing the door. She sipped carelessly from a goblet beside her. Jamīla, who dared not look up again, saw clear liquid slop down her front.

Gul was looking at the ground. She walked towards Jamīla and spread the sheets in front of her. In a low voice, she said, 'Lie face down.' She hurried away and stood behind Chehra.

Jamīla started. The sheets were stained and smelled like a woman's monthly cycle. She stared at Gul without speaking, but Gul averted her eyes. Chehra smiled. Jamīla lowered herself onto the sheet, her feet stretching into the corridor. It was ludicrous. If someone were to wander through the hallway, what would they think, seeing this African slave with her face on a sheet in her mistress's room and her legs obstructing the passage? She wanted to ask if she should move further in. The thought made her chuckle, and though she made no sound, her heaving shoulders alerted Chehra, and she stood up at once.

She dragged Jamīla by her hair along the sheet until her face made contact with the dried blood. She pushed Jamīla's face into it and stamped on one of her hands.

'You are too timid, Gul,' Chehra called over her shoulder. 'I have little use for a craven slave. Can you master yourself?'

Chehra raised her foot from Jamīla's hand and kicked it to the side. She walked away, and Jamīla heard the sound of a bureau being opened.

'Tell the slave to rise, Gul.'

Jamīla rolled over, cradling her hand. The crunch of Chehra's boot had crushed bones. She wanted to scream. She closed her eyes and bit harder on her lip, fresh blood dribbling against her teeth.

'You know what to do, Gul.'

Chehra sat and watched until Jamīla confessed to having attended a 'meeting'. As her back continued to bleed, Jamīla screamed it was for noblewomen to talk freely. Why was she there, when she was a mere slave? She thought Chehra Khaanoum might find it useful. Presuming Chehra's thoughts got her the sharpest whip of them all. 'Harder!' Chehra snapped at this indignity. Gul, her hand trembling, struggled to send the metal end towards the accused. In the end, it was Chehra who wrought red ribbons across Jamīla's back as she wrangled with the whip, swinging it like a lasso. As Jamīla lay wailing in a heap on the ground and Gul left, crying tears Jamīla could not bring herself to shed, Chehra sat still, munching on a blood orange. 'You are permitted to return.' She paused, sucking out the juice. 'I shall accompany you.'

33

Nosrat's quarters were empty. His bedroom was as messy as Jamīla remembered. There was a chair sprawled on its side, cushions spread in disarray and pungent food peeking out from an upturned dish that sat in the centre of the bed. The room looked gaudy and messy, its occupant small and showy, not unlike her mistress Chehra Khaanoum. They spent their petulance, arrogance and violence on the backs of their obedient slaves, whilst publicly they trembled before their obvious superiors.

As she glanced around this room, recalling the moments he had held her by the throat, his fists clenched beneath her chin, watching with a half-moon smile as she gasped and flailed, she felt pity for the girl who ever thought his world might have something to offer her mind. She was young then, she remembered, as she set about with opening his bureaus, in search of papers. She found almost nothing, a sheaf of unfinished love letters, some written to her, others to Sanaa, jumbled together. A cursory glance told her his letters to either said the same things. They were angry, myopic and melancholic. They read like the works of a diarist; their names were simply placeholders at the top of the paper. There were sketches too of Sanaa's face. In each image she looked almost desolate. Jamīla, who knew her to be resolute and cool, shuddered at the pictures. She pushed them back into the bureau, leaving it open, and then proceeded to Abimelech's room.

She wondered why she had bothered with Nosrat; he had a longstanding ignorance of politics and, if Abimelech was to be believed, a sloppy laziness that suggested he would never have kept notes, be they his own or his eunuch's. Abimelech's room was spotless, of course. The room did smell fragrant, recalling the scent that Jamīla herself wore. Curious, she pulled bureaus open and closed them again. There was nothing anywhere. *Where did Abimelech tutor Nosrat? Where was his own private office?* It had never occurred to her to ask; she did not think he would have one. But of course he did. Wherever he kept his important things, it did not seem to be here. She looked at the perfectly angled duvet, with the chunk of air between it and the ground, and slipped her hand into that gap. She moved it as little as she could, determined not to disturb anything. Her hand felt a smooth, carved box made of simple wood, its edges sanded inelegantly, the work of a sharp-eyed amateur. Could this be something? She withdrew her hand and held the box in the light. It resembled a chest of sorts; her fingers ran over the keyhole with a frustrated sigh.

Jamīla returned for the box the day she and Chehra were to attend Zainab Pasha's next meeting. She pre-empted Chehra's suspicions by announcing it was to be a record of sorts, a place to store notes from the meeting. Chehra Khaanoum looked with apathy at it as Jamīla spoke. 'It is ugly,' was all she said at first. Then, after a pause, when the droshky struggled over a dip in the road, 'Why do you talk so much? I have indulged this nonsense too often. Do not talk like this and embarrass me when we arrive. Keep silent.'

When Jamīla arrived, her hand was heavily bandaged and clenched in Chehra's. If Zainab Pasha wondered why Jamīla had not contacted her earlier, to deliver privately what was asked, she kept such thoughts to herself. Chehra proceeded ahead, her eyes seeking out a leader. Jamīla walked slowly behind. She felt ashamed, humiliated, bloody and broken and visible to all.

She stood behind Chehra as often as she could, not that Chehra noticed. Underwhelmed as the evening unfolded, Chehra stood with a frown, tapping her foot, her face flickering for a moment upon spying Yagana. Chehra was not the only person staring at Yagana. Jamīla, watching Yagana purse her full lips in a brief pout as she looked carelessly around, realised why.

'Is she familiar, Shahzadeh Khaanoum?' Jamīla whispered, feigning ignorance.

'I told you not to speak,' Chehra snapped, her hand twisting Jamīla's good wrist as they stood against a far wall, watching the event.

Jamīla, wincing, continued, 'I have met her before. I can introduce you.'

'I told you not to speak!' Chehra snarled, but she was blushing now. Yagana heard the exchange and looked across at them. A bevy of emotions rippled across her face as she stared at Jamīla's. Haughty beauty made way for shock, anger and finally concern. Averting her eyes, Jamīla suspected the bruises the chief eunuch had bestowed had yet to fully fade. As Yagana proceeded towards them, Jamīla thrust the box forward. Chehra wasn't looking. She was staring at Yagana, her face a painful shade of crimson.

'You must be Jamīla's mistress. A princess, I believe,' Yagana said, dipping her head as she stood before Chehra.

Chehra mumbled and nodded as Jamīla slipped the box into Yagana's hand.

'Jamīla is a smart girl. We have great respect for her.'

'Oh?' Chehra turned to look at Jamīla with an accusatory gaze. 'How has she earned such respect? Does she do things for you?'

It was Yagana's turn to flush. 'Jamīla has helped us to settle disputes during the meetings. She is good at assuaging concerns and maintaining peace.'

'How enlightening. Jamīla refrains from such a role at court.'

'Well, I—'

'You have been having disputes?' Chehra asked in a pointed tone, avoiding Yagana's gaze.

'No more than any large group of individuals. I am sure the harem must have its share of discord.'

'Well, actually,' Chehra began. She met Yagana's eyes and blushed all over again, her words turning to mumbles.

When Yagana made her excuses, she shot a worried glance at Jamīla, and by the end of the evening, Wardiyyah had sought Chehra out and distracted her whilst Aadila approached Jamīla.

'The box was unhelpful,' Aadila said, cornering Jamīla by a window.

'What...what did it contain?'

'Personal items. They were irrelevant to our mission.'

'Well...perhaps—'

'I suppose you stole this from your eunuch friend?'

'Yes. What was in the box?'

Aadila stared at her. 'I think he should be allowed to retain his privacy, Jamīla. You are not entitled to his secrets.'

Jamīla said nothing.

'I have spoken with Zainab, Yagana and Wardiyyah, and we all agree. This should be your final mission.'

'No!' The word burst out. 'I can find the information you require. I can—'

'It is too dangerous.'

'No, it is not—'

'It is too dangerous for you. We can see your face, your back is hunched and you are walking with a limp. We know you were beaten and flogged. Perhaps if your information was helpful, it might have been a worthy sacrifice. But the information was useless – you cannot spy. Whether that is because you have a vigilant mistress or because you yourself are inept remains unclear. Nevertheless, this is not worth your life. You are not even Iranian. You cannot die for another person's cause.'

Jamīla's voice was fragile. 'Are you...are you banning me from...'

'Listen to my words, Jamīla. I told you, you are welcome here, but as a participant only. You can no longer do private work for us.'

34

The next meeting Jamīla and Chehra attended concerned the preparations for a demonstration that was to take place outside the Shāh's favourite mosque in the bāzār. Different groups would find themselves marching from different locations, and Jamīla and Chehra were part of a small woman-only faction being told how the events would unfold. Jamīla could tell Chehra resented the man who was giving them orders. He spoke through his nasal passage, in a dry, high-pitched tone. He flattened the map, smoothing it repeatedly over the table. Chehra, who was no longer listening, fiddled with the ends of the map.

'Please remove your hands.'

'You are giving me an order? If you are to speak to me, you may address me as *Shahzadeh Khaanoum*.'

'Oh, a princess, are we?' His voice was mocking. By now their murmuring faction had fallen silent, and everyone was watching as the exchange unfolded. 'Well, we are not your subjects here. We are all Iranians, all citizens. Hence our name: Šahrvandān. Your title is irrelevant here.'

Jamīla interjected. 'Please, I have a question about our location on the day.'

Without looking at her, he said, 'The location should not concern you. You are an African. Slaves will not be present, only Iranians.'

Jamīla felt the atmosphere change. The silence held an anticipatory quality; it knew it would be broken and was waiting to see by whom.

Chehra straightened up and said, glancing somewhere over the man's head, 'My slave does not go where you tell her to. She shall go where I tell her to. I expect her to accompany me to the march. I may not be a princess in here, but I am certainly one outside. Would you have princesses left vulnerable, without attendants?'

'I thought, *Shahzadeh Khaanoum*, you would wish to be discreet, lest the Qājār court discover you are allied with radicals. The presence of a slave would mark you out as a wife of the monarch, would it not?'

Chehra scoffed. 'You know nothing of court. The Shāh has over 80 wives; each has a number of personal slaves. Noblewomen, too, have a set of slaves. Marching with my slave will not reveal my identity. I shall march in a burqa'. My slave will attend with me. There shall be no discussion–'

'Iranians are not the only people affected by the policies of the court,' Sanaa interjected smoothly. Jamīla had not seen her walk over.

'Slaves are not people,' the man said, his smile thin. Their discussion had gathered an audience from the different groups scattered across the rooms, and his words caused an outburst. Voices crowded each other out as they sought to argue with the man.

'If they won't consider us people, then why should we stay?' one voice called out, and across the room, the brown figures gathered there assented. Jamīla watched as Iranian women looked away from their own slaves. Some fell silent, others were shaking their heads.

'Slaves are not people,' Chehra agreed. The room fell silent to listen to the sigheh. 'But they serve people, some even serve the highest people – and if such people want them to march, then they shall march. You do not own my slave, do you...'

'Mirza Mohammad Rafiqdoost,' the man finished, a little

perturbed. He took a deep breath and replied, 'I agree with you, Shahzadeh Khaanoum, the march should present a united front of Iranian women and men, joined together against–'

'Slaves may not be people to you, but not all Africans are slaves. I am African. I am a concubine to the Shāh. Am I to be excluded from the protest too?' At Sanaa's words, someone applauded. Chehra looked at Sanaa with surprise. She turned to Mohammad.

'The concubine makes a good point.'

Sanaa's face remained impassive, and Mohammad appeared a little lost for words. Jamīla, bristling, found herself countering Chehra. Here, at least, they could speak like equals. 'Her point is selfish. Who will support the slaves' right to protest? Why are we here, if we cannot expect to be heard?' She did not look at Chehra. The dissent resumed with a vengeance as the noblemen and slaves talked past each other. Jamīla looked across the room and saw Shapur hurrying over, looking disconcerted.

Sanaa turned to him and said, 'Mohammad, here, forbids the slaves from going. African concubines may also be prevented. Had you supported this plan?'

Shapur looked stunned, his gaze moving from Mohammad and Chehra back to Sanaa. Jamīla moved closer to Sanaa, who reached over and took her hand. 'Well,' he said, 'these are... unprecedented demands.' At the smattering of voices, he added, 'Not-not unreasonable demands. On-on both sides.'

'There are more than two sides,' Sanaa countered, rolling her eyes.

'C-correct, but that makes it even more complex!' Shapur spoke with the triumph of one proposing a solution. 'We – Zainab, Mohammad, myself – shall discuss, with a few others, the current conflict and find a resolution. Following which we shall resume outlining the logistics of the demonstration and prepare to march.' He glanced across the room at Zainab Pasha before turning and saying, 'Perhaps we should close early today, in order to manage this, ah, conflict.'

The room began to empty as people dispersed. Jamīla watched nervous noblewomen give tentative orders to truculent slaves. Shapur sat on a cushion and Sanaa stood over him, speaking into his ear. Jamīla could not hear what was said but noted with some surprise that Shapur looked almost cowed, and Sanaa more defiant than Jamīla had ever seen her. Shapur caught sight of Jamīla and flushed a little. Sanaa, following his gaze, looked at Jamīla and smiled. Jamīla walked over. Sanaa said, 'We are in agreement, Ja   mīla. I want slaves to march at the protests too, I promise.'

Jamīla gritted her teeth. With Chehra beside her and her failed attempt at spying, the movement no longer felt like the place for her. Nevertheless, Sanaa's words had galled her; she wanted to tell her so. Yet, as she looked at Sanaa's face, her courage melted away. 'I know,' she mumbled.

'Good.' Sanaa glanced back at Shapur. 'A few of us shall remain behind to talk this through. Join us.'

Jamīla sighed. Chehra was readjusting her chador. 'I would, but...'

'Chehra Khaanoum.' Sanaa spoke over her. 'We are continuing our discussion with the organisers of the protest. Would you like to remain? A royal voice would prove insightful. Would you and Jamīla care to stay?'

Chehra shook her head. 'Jamīla and I have to return to the harem. I would have thought you had duties as well. As for my position, I have made myself very clear, and my slave is not going to contradict me. As such, we shall leave and allow the organisers to decide.'

Jamīla knew with certainty that when they returned to the

harem she would once more be whipped.

***

The royal coffeehouse was empty. As Jamīla nursed her glass of doogh she wondered, resentfully, why she had to miss the *Shahnameh*. The harem dancers were performing it that day, and Chehra, who had banned Jamīla from entertainment since she was caught, had allowed her to attend. But Sanaa had insisted on meeting 'whilst everyone was distracted', and Jamīla couldn't see how to refuse.

She didn't hear Sanaa arrive, but caught her slender frame standing before her as she glanced up from her drink.

'Did you add pennyroyal?' Sanaa asked with a slight smile.

'Peppermint.'

There was a small pause.

'You deserve an apology,' Sanaa said, as she took a seat opposite Jamīla. 'I took advantage. I should have looked after you, not just myself.'

Jamīla wondered whether this promised apology would materialise. She inclined her head and waited for her to carry on.

Sanaa too waited.

Jamīla attempted a smile. 'This is...unexpected,' she said, trying to remain honest.

Sanaa exhaled. 'Well, it is true. You and I work together, and I believe we are stronger as a team.' She gave Jamīla an expectant look.

'Yes, yes, we...would be.'

'Great.' Sanaa smiled and, caught in its glow, Jamīla felt lighter and closer to her, against her own will.

'You have a beautiful smile – you must have heard that before.'

Sanaa laughed. 'Not as much as you may think, but I have always been aware.'

'What is it – your smile – what is it filled with?'

Sanaa stopped smiling, her face remote. 'Rage,' she said, almost idly, spinning her tea glass.

'Rage?'

'Rage.'

'It feels so...light.'

'Yes. Well...when I smile, I feel most myself.'

'You are mostly enraged?'

'You are not?'

'Well...I–'

'Of course, you are. Why else are you here?'

'Yes.' Jamīla nodded, relieved.

'Right. So let us be frank. This is not the first clash between the Abyssinians and the Iranians. Šahrvandān will not protect our interests. Zainab is an Iranian nationalist. She will put her own concerns first.'

Jamīla stared at her. She would never have expected Sanaa to criticise Zainab and could not quite decide how she felt upon hearing it. Her chin dropped a little, and she sipped her drink, her head bowed.

'I do not mean to say Zainab is bad,' Sanaa spoke in slow and careful tones, as if trying to prevent the words reaching back to the woman in question. 'I am trying to explain that...everyone puts their own interests first. The Qājārs do it, Zainab does it, we do it when we complain about slavery in meetings on nationalism. We should not expect nationalists to cater to us. Their fight is not ours – we have our own.' She put her hand under Jamīla's chin, cupping and lifting it upwards, until their eyes met. 'Do you agree?'

'I suppose. But I would not know where to begin – how would we form such a community, how would we even recruit, who would we trust?'

Sanaa smiled a different smile now, a beam with the wattage turned down. It livened her face; she was simply pleasing herself. 'You ask the right questions, Jamīla. However, you have no need for these concerns. Such a group already exists. All I want to know is—'

'—do I want to join?'

35

Jamīla felt more nervous attending a meeting of slaves than she did attending that of radical Persians. It was a warm night. Sanaa had told Chehra Khaanoum that Jamīla had taken ill in her apartment. The chief eunuch had been invited to see her but had demurred. Sanaa was an exemplary concubine; if Jamīla was with her, then he believed her. Jamīla never understood how Sanaa had maintained such goodwill, had suppressed her desires without ever forgetting them. She felt so callow beside her; Sanaa was the optimal version of herself, more beautiful, more driven and much more discreet. She watched out of the corner of her eye as Sanaa strode ahead of her under the darkened sky, her chador billowing in the cool wind.

Jamīla reached for Sanaa's hand as the qāpči let them into the room. The proprietors of the house were away for the week, and their slaves had offered the largest room in the andarūnī. There was, Sanaa had explained, no fixed location, each meeting depended on where there was an empty house. Jamīla glanced around the long, narrow room, paint peeling off the ceiling. Every single face was brown, but of varying shades. There were the light brown 'red' Abyssinians, like herself, sitting in the centre of the room, long limbs stretched or curled in jocular postures, and there were darker-skinned slaves, clustered in huddles, pressed against the walls. There were more of them and they were louder, yet many were anxious; some shot nervous glances at the Abyssinians. As Sanaa and Jamīla entered, Jamīla saw a cluster of faces turn to stare, whilst a number of darker-skinned slaves turned away. She chose to bask in the admiring gazes – with their chadors removed, she was certain they fell on her as much as on Sanaa. She darted a glance at Sanaa, trying to mimic the haughty opacity that illuminated her face. They strode towards the centre of the room without a break in their pace, causing gathered slaves to scramble out of the way. With growing dread, Jamīla watched as Abyssinians looked askance at the other African slaves who were moving closer to them.

She turned to Sanaa and whispered, 'We have to avoid the issues we had at Šahrvandān.' She spoke in a low tone but felt a little pleased with herself at pre-empting such natural contention. Whenever people gathered, there was hierarchy, but Jamīla felt determined that the hierarchy that arose here should not be based on cultural status and skin colour. She looked at Sanaa, trying to gauge her response, but Sanaa was glancing past her at a group of Africans sitting behind them.

'Where do you suppose they are from? Mombasa? Zanzibar?'

Jamīla, confused but determined not to appear so, blinked for a moment. 'Yes,' she said. And then, 'Exactly. We need to make sure they feel welcome.'

Sanaa didn't reply but instead turned to a few of the Abyssinians sitting in the centre. Catching her eye, one of the men broke into a smile; several others rose from their cushions. 'Salâm, Sanaa...and you have brought another from the court. Always recruiting, I see.'

'Salâm, Tawqir,' she said, returning his greeting with a nod, before turning to the only Abyssinian in the group who had not risen. He was smaller than the others, his head bowed over a sheaf of notes. 'Barahim,' Sanaa said, her tone almost forceful. 'Do we have a common language between us? We have not had so many people before. I see domestic slaves here. How well do they understand Farsi?'

Barahim looked up. 'I tried to say as much to the other men, but...'

'We speak Afaan Oromoo, and Barahim translates it into Farsi,' Tawqir said emphatically. 'Everyone understands.' Bristling a little under the strength of her gaze, he added, 'Everyone who wants to understand. Most of them just want action. They will follow through when we give out orders.'

Jamīla was stunned. It had not occurred to her that they might not all speak the same language. She tugged on Sanaa's arm. 'How can I help?'

'Go to each group, to each...nationality even. Find someone who speaks Farsi who can translate. Ask the Abyssinians if anyone knows a Zanzibari dialect. Collect as many languages as you can, then bring those people over so they can help us lead today's discussion.'

As Jamīla turned, one of the other men reached out and put his hand on her arm. 'Stay here. I will do it.' He turned to Sanaa. 'Barahim has written out an agenda for this meeting. Go to him and let him tell you how he wants it to unfold.' Jamīla wanted to reply, but Sanaa looked at her and shook her head. Jamīla stayed where she was and watched as this man made his way round the groups.

Once they had gathered a number of men together from the different countries and provinces present, Tawqir hushed everyone and then stepped forward. He was a tall Abyssinian, a handsome eunuch with a svelte frame and round face. He had the confidence of a man used to being listened to. With his luxuriant frock coat and arrogant demeanour, he resembled any number of smug eunuchs in the court who had the favour of a few wives in the harem.

Tawqir gestured to Barahim to step forward and looked around at the translators who were gathered at the front. 'Are we all ready?' he asked in Farsi. His voice was loud and slow, and one of the Zanzibari men gritted his teeth. 'We have a few things to discuss today. Many of us are new, so I shall provide an overview of who we are, how we came to unite and what our purpose is.' At this point he broke off and looked to Barahim.

Barahim blushed. 'Yes-sorry-I...' He glanced down at his notes and took a deep breath, squinting at the crowd. 'We were joined with the nationalist movement Šahrvandān, which was unhappy with a number of the Shāh's policies. However, our needs were not aligned so we sought to–'

Tawqir was staring at him in disbelief. He snatched the papers from Barahim's hand and gave him a pointed frown.

'Let us try that properly, shall we? I am Tawqir. I wanted to talk about why we are here today. I believe...' He stopped to look at the pages. He squinted. He frowned. Jamīla could not tell if he was simply a poor reader or unfamiliar with the text. *Why try and lead if you do not know what to say?* She wanted to get Sanaa's attention. But before she could, Tawqir began again, saying aloud, 'Some mishandling from the others. Forgive them. We began as a nationalist movement, joined with Šahrvandān. Most of us were following our masters. Now Šahrvandān was one faction of a larger protest movement, but the movement was focused on amplifying the voices of the people of Persia. Our plan is...' He hesitated and trailed off as he glanced down at the papers in his hands. He gritted his teeth. Holding the papers close to his face, he shuffled them. 'We...' He stopped and smiled, ignoring the papers and looking up. 'Before discussing the plan, let me talk about how we were...ah...feeling. Yes, we felt that we were neglected by the nationalists – a movement that managed to bring even women into the fold – in Šahrvandān, here in Tehran, a woman was at the helm. Yet, whilst the rights of Persian women were indulged, the voices of African slaves were not.' He paused for a moment, swallowed and smiled. Jamīla suspected he was replaying his words in his mind. 'We thus decided that in the absence of Persian support, we would organise a movement for ourselves. We shall have our own protest. We shall ensure that we are heard!' He was shouting by the last word, bouncing on the balls of his feet. Everyone else was silent, motionless.

Tawqir's zeal seemed at odds with the passivity of the room. Jamīla, feeling embarrassed, stopped listening as Tawqir reeled off a list of objectives. Instead she glanced at Sanaa. She looked almost aghast, and the moment Tawqir stopped speaking, she began.

Two other voices collided with hers. A hefty man, with tired skin and a jutting jaw, had leapt to his feet. He began speaking in a language Jamīla did not recognise but was followed by a man at the centre, who was translating his words into Farsi. The hefty man was irate; he spat out his words with disgust. The translator, by contrast, was repeating his words calmly. Jamīla, who had been watching the hefty man, only caught the end of the translator's speech. '...never listen to us or pay attention! How is giving us orders hearing our voices?'

Tawqir, nodding solemnly, his face twisted by the effort, stepped closer to the translator and asked, 'What could we do to ensure you felt heard?'

The translator turned to the heavyset man. 'Yussuf?'

Yussuf spoke, but the translator chose not to relay it. By this point, Tawqir and his men had gathered round the translator, urging him to speak.

Tawqir offered the translator a gentle smile. 'Speak to *me*.'

The translator looked uncomfortable and turned to Yussuf again.

Sanaa snapped, 'I would imagine that Yussuf might appreciate being looked at or spoken to, given he just complained about being ignored.'

Some of the Abyssinians bristled. Yussuf, hearing his name, looked at Sanaa. The translator had not translated the Abyssinians' comments to Yussuf; he was too busy being spoken to by Tawqir and his men.

Sanaa pushed through the Abyssinians who had gathered and grabbed the translator by the arm. 'Tell Yussuf what I said!' she demanded before turning to the rest of the crowd. 'Listen!' she began. 'I know you are tired of being dictated to. We are sorry. Let each group form a list of concerns or wishes, and we – as a movement – will decide which ones to tackle and how. Does that sound fair?' She turned to the other translators. 'Tell them what I said,' she insisted.

Tawqir turned to her, stunned, but the ambience in the room began to change. Jamīla looked at Sanaa, standing proud and satisfied, her expression not unlike Tawqir's from earlier. As the groups worked, Tawqir glared at Sanaa whilst the Abyssinians around him sat muttering to each other, no longer stretching in the centre of the room but huddled together, their faces defiant, expecting persecution.

As Jamīla listened to the groups of slaves outline their specific requests, her appetite for rebellion began to cool.

'Each night he forces me, pulls off my clothes, throws me onto the floor when he is finished. His wife drags me out by my hair, prodding me towards the bathhouse. She is crying. I am crying. She will not let me dress myself. I stand naked and shivering. She spits at me and walks away.' The woman wasn't speaking to Jamīla, but their eyes met across the hubbub of people. The nearest translator, a slim Abyssinian, spoke in flat tones as a younger, darker slave wrote it down.

'She does not feed me when they fight.'

'I just want more hours to sleep.'

'He has his way with me and lets the eunuchs watch.'

The words, which at first appeared to float over the room, now seemed to fall, and Jamīla felt coated in these tersely toned horrors.

'No,' a translator close to Jamīla said, looking at a scribe. 'He penetrated her with a poker, she said, not his hand.'

Jamīla swallowed.

She looked for Sanaa. She was moving between the groups, checking what was being written. Hurrying over, Jamīla said, 'I'm hearing a plethora of...grievances but no requests, no solutions, no demands. We should change the focus of the conversation.'

Sanaa shook her head. 'I suspect they have never said these words aloud before. Let them. We are not controlling them. Should they offer a list of—'

'I agree with...Jamīla.' Tawqir appeared and smiled. 'Let us be practical. They can cry in their own time.'

Jamīla felt a wave of relief and a shiver of guilt rise at the same time. She looked away from Sanaa as Tawqir raised his voice once more.

'Everybody! Everybody!' He marshalled the translators into repeating after him. 'Let us focus now on *solutions*.'

***

'And how effective were these plans?' Abimelech asked idly, and Jamīla looked at her feet.

'They are naive.'

'How so?'

Jamīla couldn't recall how it had happened, but the slaves had dispensed with the note-taking altogether and began shouting out the kinds of resolutions they sought to see.

'Better food!' shouted a domestic.

'Celibacy!' a young Abyssinian girl whispered, but the translator shouted it, and all the men laughed.

'I want to rest—'

'I want to go home!'

'Yes.' Tawqir spoke over the others. 'How about the option to return home after a decade of duty?'

'How would we request such things?' Sanaa interrupted, her voice as slippery as stained silk. 'And to whom?'

'Someone suggested a petition.' Jamīla tried to keep the scorn from her voice. They were seated once more in Chehra's salon. Chehra had taken the other slaves to watch the harem dancers rehearse. Jamīla had taken advantage of the empty apartment to bring Abimelech round.

'Perhaps they are not so naive.'

'Oh?'

'Why did Shapur's movement plan a march?'

Jamīla shrugged. 'Precedence? They have worked before. The Tobacco Protest...I am sure there were others.'

'Who marched?'

'Noblemen and w... Ah.'

'What do you think will happen if the slaves did more than petition?'

Jamīla was silent.

'They will be executed. What do you think will happen if they even petition?'

'They...really?'

'Yes. They will be executed.' Abimelech sighed. 'The Shāh has killed people for less. A collective of angry slaves rising above their station? That will look like civil war, like unrest, like terror.

He will put them down, and he will not think very hard about it. They may purge the palace, not knowing who was involved.'

'No...'

'Yes.'

'And you support this man?'

'In his shoes, I would do the same.'

'No!'

'Of course.' Jamīla stared at him, eyes widening. He continued, his tone matter-of-fact. 'If you keep people downtrodden and they unite to defy you, you cannot expect mercy, not if you had not shown them any. So you have to kill them, lest they kill you.'

'But you would not...'

'I would not keep slaves. But if I did, I would not have a choice.'

Her words curdled on her tongue. They sat in silence. Then, 'Somebody thought the British consulate might emancipate them.'

'Yes,' Abimelech replied without much enthusiasm. After a pause, he added, 'The British have been vocal, if not sincere, about their opposition to slavery. I have heard stories of slaves going to the consulate.'

'How many slaves have been freed as a result?'

'I confess I only know of rumours, but...'

'Were they returned to their homes?'

'To their families you mean? In Zanzibar or Abyssinia? No, Jamīla, I doubt that.'

'Then that is as naive a suggestion as the others.'

'The British would make for a powerful ally—'

'Ally or patron?'

'They would not offer patronage to former slaves.'

'Then what is gained? Why leave a noble household, where food and shelter are provided, to toil and fight for it on the streets? Assuming one would hire a former African slave. A woman. A rebel.' Jamīla sighed. 'Our lives are not so hard. Run errands, manage correspondence–'

'"Our lives are not hard"? You have lost your appetite for revolution?'

'I...I never sought revolution.'

'You were never content with your station. How many times have you been whipped or beaten?'

'By Nosrat Mirza or Chehra Khaanoum?'

'Exactly!'

'Well, I could have avoided Chehra Khaanoum's. I chose to be rebellious.'

'And Nosrat?'

'Well...'

'How do you think the Shāh or his men treat the women in the harem? The concubines, the dancers, the slaves?'

'Well,' Jamīla sniffed, 'most of the people pleading for emancipation were domestic, some even worked outdoors. I doubt the Shāh, his men or any noblemen were paying them any attention.'

Abimelech rolled his eyes. 'You wonder why they want to be free? Could you work as a domestic? Outdoors? Getting calloused hands, doing back-breaking work under the burning sun?'

'So you think their demands are legitimate?'

'Yes!'

'But they shan't be listened to.'

Abimelech sighed.

'They will be executed, their lives and their wishes forgotten.'

Abimelech was silent.

'So they are naive then!' She felt a second conversation had taken place, secreted within the first, permeating every defiant question and every scornful retort. Yet, as certain as she was, she could not discern what had been said by whom or who had won, if someone had. 'So, Paris then,' she said, to change the subject.

Abimelech looked alarmed. 'You want to leave? With Nosrat Mirza?'

'I thought you were going. You think rebellions are futile but emancipation is not. Is this not the only option left available?'

'I might...stay behind.'

'Oh? Why?'

Abimelech didn't reply.

'The Shāh. Of course.'

'Well...'

'Worry not, Abimelech. I have other methods. I suppose I shall have to return to the prince's bed.' A tight pragmatic smile flickered across her face.

Abimelech said nothing, but his alarmed expression resurfaced.

'Well?'

Abimelech was silent before stuttering a few words. 'It...he...'

'What?'

'You...you cannot accompany him,' Abimelech snapped.

'Why?'

'Ah...because, well, he may not be going alone.'

'How do you know?'

'S-Sanaa,' Abimelech said. He sounded increasingly flustered. 'She—'

'She told you?' Jamīla paused. 'Or have you spoken to Nosrat again? I thought—'

Abimelech took a deep breath and, speaking over her, said, 'He is taking Sanaa to Paris.'

36

Fatali arrived last, holding a candle aloft. His handsome face had a curious smile on it, and he glanced at the other three men. The Grand Vizier stood in a corner, his chin almost pressed to the wall. Firouz had his arms folded, his eyes on Abimelech.

'This is very discreet of you, Abimelech!' Fatali spoke with a nervous laugh in his voice. 'It is almost midnight, after all.'

'I did not wish to be overheard, and I understood you were waiting for my assessment.'

'We have been waiting for quite some time.' The Grand Vizier's careful voice oozed out of a crevice. 'We sought you in October. It is January.'

Abimelech had returned them to the room where they had all first gathered. He recalled their last meeting. The three of them, three of the Shāh's most powerful men, armed with their own collection of eunuchs and titles, had sought to intimidate him with their imperial superiority and remind him of his station. As he summoned them, using his loyal eunuchs to request they arrive alone, he wondered what his own motivations were, for he could not quite decide.

'I wanted to inform you all,' Abimelech said after a pause, 'that I have spoken with Kamran Mirza, and though he is able, I do not think it prudent to defy history and tradition.'

'You are endorsing Mozaffar Mirza, then?' Fatali asked.

'No!' Abimelech burst out, and grimaced. He saw a flash of white and realised the Grand Vizier was smiling at his response. 'I cannot support either brother. I withhold my assessment. I believe we should not interfere; let things unfold as they will.'

Nobody spoke for a little while. Abimelech was not sure what to expect; he knew the Grand Vizier and Fatali were in favour of Mozaffar's ascension, and yet they were as silent as Firouz. Firouz broke the silence with a light cough. He turned to Abimelech and asked, 'Will that be all?'

'Uh...yes.'

'Good evening to you, then.' Firouz began to walk away.

'Firouz.' Fatali's hurried call echoed off the walls. 'You cannot leave just yet.'

Firouz turned, and in the darkness Abimelech could not see his expression. He was looking at Fatali, and when he spoke, his voice held the lightness of mockery. 'Can I not?'

'Please!' Fatali cried.

Abimelech heard the rustle of fabric; the Grand Vizier had moved forward for a closer look at the scene unfolding in the darkened hall.

Perhaps Firouz pitied Fatali, perhaps he actually liked him – or perhaps he loathed Abimelech that much more.

'Eunuch. Your name again is...'

Abimelech rolled his eyes, protected by the darkness. 'Abimelech.'

'Yes, Abimelech. Well. You spent a number of weeks closeted away in silence after promising to grant interviews to Mozaffar Mirza and Kamran Mirza.'

'Yes.'

'Did they prove fruitful?'

'They did.'

'Both interviews?'

'...Yes.'

'How funny. Kamran Mirza told me Mozaffar Mirza forbade you from interviewing and that he too was not to be interviewed.'

Abimelech felt his face grow hot.

'Really?' The words were Fatali's, touched with disappointment and hyperbolic shock. 'You have not spoken to either prince—'

'I have spoken to Kamran at length! He—'

'Kamran *Mirza*, eunuch.'

'He did not like formalities.'

'Did he like the interview? The one you say was "fruitful"?'

'We did not have interviews—'

'You are dishonest, eunuch—'

'We had conversations—'

'Fruitful ones?'

'Firouz.' It was Fatali again, but the Grand Vizier spoke over them both.

'How disloyal.' The words chastised, but his tone rang with triumph. 'Kamran Mirza let you talk with him, and Mozaffar Mirza forbade you. Nevertheless, you refused to nominate Kamran Mirza after he gave you his time. The prince and I have our differences, but he is a loyal man. You are not.'

'That is...inaccurate!' He had to keep still. He had to keep calm.

'He is not loyal?' came the silky reply.

'I was not *disloyal*. I am loyal to the Shāh and the rules of lineage. I decided stability was more important than—'

'Kamran Mirza would not promise you a plum role in his court. Is that not why you abandoned him?' Firouz's icy tones inspired gasps from Fatali and the Grand Vizier.

'I did not...that did not...'

'Kamran is responsible; he would not fill his court with flatterers.' The Grand Vizier's tone was disdainful. 'You were bitter.'

'No, I...'

'This is irrelevant.' Firouz turned to Fatali. 'Can I leave now? Perhaps we all should.'

'Well,' Fatali said and paused. 'We should tell him.'

The Grand Vizier demurred, 'Let him find out with everyone else,' and walked to the door. Firouz also turned to exit, but Fatali stood still.

He watched Abimelech with something like pity in his expression. 'The Shāh was walking around today. He is believed to have made a full recovery. He is expected to resume his duties from tomorrow. There is no longer any need for an interim shāh.' He too headed for the exit.

Firouz, who had been watching Fatali as he spoke, added, 'This did prove insightful. We know what kind of slave you are, eunuch. Disloyal, deceitful, ambitious...I daresay I shall bear that in mind. Until next time.'

***

For weeks, Abimelech saw neither the advisors nor the Shāh himself. He felt certain the Shāh must have asked for him and shuddered to think what he had been told. He couldn't decide on a next course of action; he couldn't turn up before the Shāh without being summoned, and there was no chance to speak to him alone. The only recourse was an option so painful he didn't want to consider it.

He had to speak to Nosrat.

He was unsure when Nosrat was to be in his room. He no longer knew his schedule, and despite still sleeping in Nosrat's quarters, living mere rooms down, Abimelech had not even seen him since Nosrat told him he had been replaced. As he raised his hand to knock on the door, it swung open, and he came face to face with Sanaa.

'Abimelech!' she said, her voice an octave higher than usual.

'Did I startle you?'

'You did, rather.'

Her face was back to its placid mask, but she was concealing her hands. 'What have you there?' he asked, as pleasantly as he could manage.

She cocked her head, as if confused, and then displayed her trademark smile. Abimelech let it wash over him. He was still curious, but did not want her to stop smiling. Perhaps it was the bleakness of the recent weeks; he needed to bask in the joyous warmth of her smile. 'Nosrat is not in at the moment, but I think you can expect him soon. He should be returning from the mosque.' She walked past him, her hands holding what looked like folded documents. He watched her go, with a realisation gnawing at his stomach. Something felt very wrong. He had discussed her with Jamīla before. Why..? Sanaa was one of the radicals! He froze for a moment. He felt a rush of horror. He turned to call after her, but she had already disappeared.

As he waited for Nosrat, his anxiety grew. He felt a desperate desire to tell someone what he had seen. He could not confide in anyone from the court. The Qājārs would have her executed on the suspicions alone, and any slave would use it to render her their slave. They might also give her up to the chief eunuch in exchange for some kind of promotion. He thought of the only person he could tell and decided that he would. He could confront Nosrat another day, but he could not risk speaking to Nosrat now with the suspicions of Sanaa's treachery written across his face. He paused for a moment, wondering whether to leave Nosrat a note. It felt like a futile effort, having drawn up the courage to face Nosrat, to then postpone it without so much as a word. He pulled a piece of paper from his pocket before realising he had no pen. He headed back to his room to select one and found the door ajar.

For a moment, he thought of Sanaa, striking whilst she knew he was out. After all, he had information that could be of use to the Qājār's enemies. He pushed the door open with a creak and saw a Persian man bent over a bureau, riffling through it. At the sound of the door, the man turned around. It was Nosrat.

He looked unabashed at having been caught going through Abimelech's things. No master would ever feel such shame, but Nosrat had spent years insisting they were equals. He gave Abimelech a beautiful room in his quarters and arbitrary expensive gifts. He did not enforce any of the official duties a eunuch was supposed to carry out and had let Abimelech abandon them altogether. As such, to find Nosrat searching through Abimelech's scant possessions when he presumed the latter to be out was something of a shock.

He stood staring at the prince, his expression neutral.

'Well?' Nosrat demanded. 'Do you not bow before your prince?'

Abimelech fell into a deep and long bow.

'Enough.'

'Allow me to apologise, Hazrat-e Aghdass-e Vaalaa.'

'For what, exactly?'

Abimelech looked up. 'Well, I should have bowed, of course. You are the Shāhzadeh. I am deeply sorry.'

'Ah. You are sorry for that.'

'Hazrat-e Aghdass-e Vaalaa,' Abimelech began, 'allow me to apologise for all I have done. My life is to provide service to the Qājārs. If I have somehow failed, then I have failed at life.'

Nosrat's laugh was bitter. 'The Qājārs. I thought you were my eunuch.'

'I am.'

'Yet you left me to serve my father.'

'I am always...I am always loyal to you.'

'WHEN?'

Abimelech stopped, taken aback. He wanted to cry. He wanted Sanaa to return and smile her rapturous smile.

'I have a new tutor, a new – I had to replace you because you left me and then you never spoke to me again. You left for the most powerful, the most pliable and you did not turn back once. So if you wish to apologise...'

Abimelech knew better than to plead with Nosrat, to assuage his truculent mood. Quietly, he said, 'Is that why you are here? Are you collecting my things, casting me out?'

'No. I would never...' He took a deep breath. 'If I tell you something, will you keep it to yourself?'

'Of course.'

'I think Sanaa is plotting something. Things have gone missing from my room. Either she or you took them – and you have little need for anything I have, what with your access to the Shāh, so that leaves her.'

Abimelech tried not to frown at being considered a suspect. 'Something has been taken from my room.'

'Your diary. Yes, I noticed.'

'Ah.' Abimelech's tone was calm, meditative even, but his body began to tense.

'Yes. I am...unaware of the contents, Abimelech,' Nosrat said in a somewhat louder voice. 'But I knew you kept a book of your private thoughts in a chest beneath your bed. When I came to check your room, I saw it had been taken. I happened to think you had hidden it.'

'Ah.' Abiemlech repeated. 'Thus, you are now...in here,' he said with a cough and tried not to sigh. He kept his head bowed, trying to slow his heartbeat, wanting to refrain from reacting to this new assault on his dignity. *Could you live this life once more and innumerable times?* The words hovered in the air before him.

'Well, I know you are privy to,' Nosrat coughed, 'policy and governance...I thought I might hide anything I found, so that she would not target your room next.'

'Right.' Abimelech did not know what to say. 'Thank you, Hazrat-e Aghdass-e Vaalaa.'

Nosrat shrugged.

'You know what Sanaa is up to?'

'Spying, I presume.'

'Will you…tell anyone about her?'

'Who could I tell? If she is spying for the Grand Vizier or the British or whomever, I risk telling the wrong person that I know. Besides, I have little worth stealing.'

'And she could be executed.'

'She would deserve it.' Nosrat sighed.

'Forgive me, Nosrat, but you do not seem…'

'Sad? Outraged? I am tired of Iran. Tired of people I cannot trust. I have known she has been spying for some time. I just want to leave for Paris and never return.'

'So then, why are you here? Hazrat-e Aghdass-e Vaalaa, why are you protecting me? If you do not care and you are angry with me, I do not deserve such attentive loyalty. My behaviour has proved I am unworthy.'

'Do not pretend, Abimelech,' Nosrat muttered, bitterly. 'You do not see yourself that way.'

'I am a slave. My self-worth is all I have. So no, I do not. I cannot. But you can and you do – as is your right as a prince.'

'I…'

'You are not alone,' Abimelech continued, taking great pains to hide the urgency in his voice. 'The Shāh thinks the same – his advisors have told him so.'

Nosrat did not look surprised. 'Father is stubborn,' he said, climbing onto Abimelech's bed.

'But not steadfast. He believes these lies.'

'Tell him otherwise.'

'He will not summon me!' Abimelech's voice cracked, and he turned away from Nosrat's prying gaze.

'You are truly upset. I know,' he added, 'how much you value your friendship with the Shāh—'

'I value my honour! It is all that I have, and they are taking it from me!'

There was a long silence.

'I should go,' Nosrat said in a strange voice, and Abimelech realised that it was always he who was dismissed from Nosrat's presence, never the other way around.

'Thank you, Hazrat-e Aghdass-e Vaalaa.' Abimelech bowed again.

'Thank you?'

'You tried to...protect my notes from Sanaa.'

'Ah, yes. Well,' standing up, he looked back at Abimelech, 'I wish I could help you with your other problem.'

Abimelech looked at him.

'W-with my father, I mean.'

'Well,' Abimelech said, suddenly eager, 'perhaps you can.'

'Oh?'

'Ask him to meet with me, join me in his library. Or-or...I could go to him. You could send me to him to run an errand on your behalf. Maybe I could even—'

'You had this all planned out.' Nosrat's face contorted into a frown. Disgust, surprise and a shadow of shame fought to craft the final expression.

'No, I did not!'

'I find that hard to believe.' Nosrat was seething.

'Hazrat-e Aghdass-e Vaalaa, you are in my room – and you offered to help. What could I have arranged?'

Nosrat frowned, but his face held a wariness it lacked before. 'I shall want something in return,' he said. Then he left without another word.

37

They met at sunrise. Abimelech arrived early and stood under the arches of the Khalvat-i Karim-khani staring out at the garden before him. It looked as it often did, with the smooth veneer of winter spreading like a setting sun low over the plotted land. The identical flowerbeds buttressed by shrubs were newly coated in a layer of ice crystals. The air itself felt brittle with morning frost. But the ablution pools retained their liquid form, their gentle motion visible within the smooth square lines. Abimelech's gaze kept landing on silent pools he hitherto hadn't seen; he could lose himself in the neutral tremors. Beneath the waters in the nearest one, the geometric floral tiles blinked in vivid peacock blue. He could only see the surface of the others. Benign shimmers that held the promise of infinity. He wondered what might happen if he wandered into one, disappeared into the tranquil immersion. He might cease to exist. The thought gave him an unexpected jolt of hope.

The Shāh appeared. The steps he took were firm and forthright, but he walked with a stoop. Almost four months had passed since Abimelech had seen the Shāh and as he drew closer to Abimelech, the latter could see his face was drawn and tired. He was not sure which was the best moment to bow. Usually, as with Nosrat, he was summoned to their presence and thus, upon seeing them, would immediately sink into a bow. Here, however, he was forced to watch the Shāh make his way across the ayvān, standing as though they were equals. Abimelech, who was taller than the Shāh, had been standing as he always did when alone – shoulders broadened to their full capacity, legs apart, chest thrust forwards – a stark contrast to his posture when surrounded. An imperceptible stoop drew his shoulders in and lowered his soft chin, proffering an expression of subservience that hovered somewhere between meekness and placidity. As the Shāh grew closer, Abimelech bent further into a comprehensive bow, his eyes fixed on the ground beneath him.

He could see the hem of the Shāh's robe as it swung into view. The Shāh was standing so close his clothing brushed the top of Abimelech's bowed head – a gesture that, to the eunuch, felt more intimate than a kiss. 'My boy,' the elder man said, and Abimelech watched a tear drip from his own eye and disappear before it hit the ground. 'Raise your head, boy. Rise up.'

Abimelech rose with difficulty. He could not speak.

'Are you well, boy?'

'A'laa Hazrat,' Abimelech began, his words surging forward in a rush, 'I am so glad that you are well.'

'Nothing can kill me, boy. I know that.' He sighed. 'Nosrat is concerned.'

Abimelech did not know what to say. He wanted to look at the Shāh, but the Shāh himself was avoiding his gaze. The Shāh looked out at the garden, his eyes falling on the pool Abimelech thought to disappear into. He wondered what the Shāh saw in that water, what memories might have resurfaced as he sank his gaze into it.

'I am concerned,' the Shāh said, speaking a little louder to overcompensate for Abimelech's silence, 'that you have been lied about by my men.'

Coughing, he added, 'How is my son? I was not aware the two of you were still so tightly bonded.'

'My loyalty does not waver.'

The Shāh looked at Abimelech, who felt a nervous thrill at

the weight that lay behind those eyes. 'I have another son who may not agree.'

Abimelech closed his eyes. 'What men want for themselves and what men want for the Qājār court, the Qājār subjects and the Qājār legacy – sometimes these things diverge. According to my duty, I chose to protect the Qājār reign over the ambitions of a single man.'

The Shāh sighed. 'You are right – but it is a shame. Kamran was born for such a role, and Mozaffar...I do not even know what Mozaffar is good for. If the boy did not resemble me as closely as a nightmare, I might suspect he was not mine. How could this unkempt drunkard be my heir? But I cannot upend the system to serve my will. Not after Jayran. I learned my lesson.'

Abimelech, relieved by the Shāh's tone, ventured, 'They hate me now.'

'Yes...yes, you should be careful.'

'I...' Abimelech didn't want to ask, but he didn't know what else to say. 'Is...am I safe?'

'Kamran would never hurt you. He never expected the throne.'

'I have more than one enemy.'

'As do I, boy...'

Abimelech was silent.

'You need not fear.' The Shāh put his hands on Abimelech's shoulders. 'You need not fear.'

'A'laa Hazrat, I think I have to.'

'Why?'

'Something has been taken from my room.'

'What?' the Shāh asked as, steering Abimelech with his hand, they began to walk.

'My diaries. I kept them secure, and Nosrat—'

'Nosrat would not take your things—'

'No, he tried to hide my notes because he suspected—'

'Suspected who?'

Abimelech froze. 'It was too late; my diaries had already been taken when he came to my aid.'

'Suspected who?'

'He did not know. I think his eunuchs had seen unfamiliar faces around.'

The Shāh sighed. 'There are always unfamiliar faces. This palace holds thousands of people.'

'Yes...but someone has found my private thoughts.'

'What do they say?'

Abimelech was silent.

'Have you said treasonous things?'

'Is it treason to speak against the Shāh's men?'

The Shāh stopped walking and looked at him. 'If they are family.'

'If they are not?'

'Then it is not treason...but it could be dangerous.'

'I do not know who has my diaries.'

'Who do you suspect?'

'I do not know enough to say.' Abimelech bit his lip.

'You suspect someone.'

'I—'

'Out with it, boy.'

'It is just an instinct.'

'Instincts can be wise. They are like gods to men. What does your instinct tell you?'

Abimelech paused. Then, as that face slithered to the forefront of his mind, he spat, shaking the word from his tongue, 'It was the Grand Vizier.'

The Shāh looked at him, his eyes seeming to gaze on the words he had spoken. 'If you suspect the Grand Vizier, you ought to prove it. First, however, you need somewhere you can hide.'

'Must I hide?' Abimelech demanded.

'Perhaps not yet, but soon. I may not be shāh for much longer. It is then you must hide.'

'How? How can I hide when I have nobody to trust?'

The Shāh paused. 'There may be a way. I can assign you some property of your own that will become yours upon my death. With it, I will attach some money. Live as a modest man and you should be fine. It would be far from Tehran. When I die, you must leave at once. We need not think about this yet. But once I grow frail, I shall consult my lawyers, and we shall make provisions for you.'

The Shāh waved away Abimelech's heartfelt words of thanks. 'You may not know your enemy, but it is the Grand Vizier you should fear. He suggests I do nothing in the face of public outcry. He seeks to spend every last tomān in the treasury coffers and let the people starve. We cannot risk another famine. He has an agenda; I am certain of it. I cannot agree with him, but I cannot comply with the people. I cannot support the nationalists, not when we need the Europeans.'

It took Abimelech a moment to realise that the Shāh was once again asking for his advice. He felt the sharp sting of relief as he took a deep breath and began to speak.

***

The crack whistled through the air, and the tall, pale eunuch crumpled to the ground. Abimelech, watching, realised that until then he had never seen a person executed right in front of him. The body fell with an inelegant thud, and for a moment, the stillness of terror seemed to drift along the air. The Shāh's body twisted in fright as he stared – not at the men before him, petitioners with rifles at the foot of the mountain – but at his own men, who, at his own request, had granted him a wide berth to march his horse forward alone.

In that single moment when the bullets fried the air, hitting the wrong man and then the right man's horse, the Shāh turning in helpless panic, the horse rearing with its dying breath, Abimelech realised he was unarmed. Before he could process much else, the sound came flushing back as a stampede of horses flew past him, pounding the ground. The soldiers fired at the group of protesting men, and within minutes, after a sleek volley of bullets sped towards the armed protestors, a small massacre had taken place. Eight bodies lay bloodied and writhing inches from death as a handful of the other protestors took their chances on the mountain.

Abimelech couldn't watch as the horses cut them down, overtaking and trampling and then dragging their bodies back. His mind was consumed by that awful horror, the sense that this was a terrible way to die. But his body had snapped into action and had raced towards the Shāh and pulled him out from beneath his dying horse as it flailed with piteous cries. Abimelech was alone with the corpses and the trembling Shāh. Every other man had chased after the attackers. The horse's desperate whinnies rang with eerie familiarity. They sounded like the cries that the animals had made when they, along with his parents and their entire town, were burned alive by restless soldiers who happened to be passing through. He knew the kind response was to take one of the guns lying beside the petitioners and send the horse more swiftly to his inevitable sleep, but Abimelech, sitting beside the sobbing Shāh, couldn't bring himself to move.

38

Jamīla had been sitting on Abimelech's bed, hoping to surprise him, when he staggered in. Blood spattered his coat, speckled his face. His eyes did not flicker as they caught her, back straight, mouth agape, taking in his appearance.

'I had him back for just a day. A day and...'

'He is not dead?'

Abimelech shook his head.

'Then who?' Her voice, faint as shed flowers, seemed to reach him at the end of an echo.

His smile was stretched, thin and wan. His brow drew together with the effort. Blood rolled along the furrow. It was fresh. 'It was not the Shāh.'

Jamīla nodded. 'Ah. He was the target.'

'Indeed.'

'The actual victim...'

'Already forgotten.'

'Of course.'

***

Jamīla took a deep breath. She opened the door and Chehra flew out, throwing herself into Jamīla's arms. Before Jamīla could ask why she was summoned, Chehra said, 'Did he survive? Did he survive the attack?'

'Shahzadeh Khaanoum,' she asked, thinking of Abimelech, 'you do not mean...the Shāh?'

'He is well?'

'Yes.'

Chehra breathed a sigh of relief.

'He survived yesterday's attack.'

'B-but he is well?'

'Yes. The attackers were thwarted.'

'They say it is a gift...,' Chehra said mournfully, staggering backwards into the room. She leaned against the wall, and Jamīla, gritting her teeth, had to lift Chehra off it and return her to the bed. 'I lay there for hours – did you know that, Jamīla?'

Jamīla suppressed a sigh. She suspected she was to hear about the sexual activities of the Shāh. She tried not to shudder, easing Chehra into the bed, her gaze turned from hers to discourage further discussion.

'We were told it was a gift.' Chehra's voice soared for a moment. Curious, Jamīla turned back and caught Chehra's eye. The latter sat upright and stared at Jamīla without blinking. 'Have you lain prostate in the dust for hours awaiting the arrival of a king?'

'I...'

Chehra laughed, a high, untethered sound. 'I said arrival. He was not coming for us. It was not a visit! He was rumoured, *rumoured* to be passing through. Do you know how many hours I lay there? Do you how many days I did it for? They said he liked village girls, so I wore my shabbiest clothes. My nose, touching the dust. I still think about that nose.' Out came that frightening sound: wild, high, rabid. Both a laugh and a shriek for help. 'I do not remember what he said to me. I cannot recall his droshky stopping. But I remember the haste with which my parents pushed me towards him. It was a great honour.' Her tone grew darker. 'If they could see me now...'

Jamīla suspected they would be thrilled to see where Chehra had landed, in her padded room, served by slaves in a household of her own, but she held her tongue. Chehra's moods had become erratic once more. Before evening fell, Gul, her eyes on the floor, told Jamīla to return to Chehra's room, and as the door slid open, Chehra reached and grabbed her with both arms, pulling her inside.

Chehra cried, 'I cannot bear it!'

Jamīla was confused. 'Bear—'

'He was attacked. My shāh!'

'He is well—'

'Yes,' Chehra said, sighing. Then, 'I am ridiculous!'

'No...your concern is admirable. You are a devoted wife.'

Chehra smiled at her, the wan smile of a tired woman. 'Perhaps I could be, Jamīla. With...your help?'

But her hope did not last long.

A climate of fear spread through the harem; rumours of repeated assassination attempts put everyone, not just Chehra, on edge. Jamīla felt stifled in the apartment. She could not stand to be near Gul, and Gul was determined to avoid her. She had nobody to talk to in the harem. Under her pillow, someone had left an old copy of the Balzac book she had used to taunt Nosrat. It must have been Gul. Jamīla would not think of her. She thought about Abimelech. Had he recovered from the shock of the attack? She had not heard from him. She remembered that afternoon the three of them spent in the salon and sighed. She would not think of Gul. She wondered instead when Nosrat would leave for Paris. She thought about Abimelech. Did any part of him wish they could leave as well?

Chehra began to deteriorate. Her fears became anxieties. She grew paranoid and angry. Each attack strengthened her loyalty to the Shāh, and she refused to return to Zainab Pasha's house and forbade Jamīla from doing the same. Soon, Chehra began to rise before Jamīla, who would enter the sigheh's bedroom and find her up and pacing. Her hair would stand on end, fragile and flattened, like a hand having been driven into a wall. Her lover had concluded their relationship; none of Chehra's messages had received a reply.

It was coming to the end of March, and Chehra's unravelling had no end in sight. It reached its apex after the twentieth; she had been spurned again, this time during Nowruz. Nowruz had been stressful; the harem was always breathless over whom the Shāh would choose to celebrate salām-e sar-e dar, the third day of ceremonies. The first two days did not involve the harem. The Shāh would join them on the second day after the celebrations but, as many of the 'aqdi wives had said with a sniff, it left them feeling like an afterthought. The third day felt special. Not only did the Shāh include a select group of women alongside his favourite advisors at court, but the public was invited, and entertainment provided especially for them. The Shāh would stand on the royal balcony of the Marble Throne and address the Persian people. The women who joined him on the balcony were seen by the whole of Tehran. The weeks prior to Nowruz were tense. Frenzied chatter about who was or would be chosen reigned supreme. Favour was sought from powerful wives; favours were called in from them too. The 'aqdi wives moved about smoothly, trailed by an entourage of sighehs, eunuchs and slaves. This year, the fears of sudden attack had dimmed some wives' enthusiasm, heightening the drive of others. Either way, tension underscored the event. The Shāh had insisted that he would participate, and, as Abimelech later told Jamīla, it was publicity he could not afford to miss. Chehra had hoped to be included in the list of wives chosen to join the Shāh.

It was a sign, she had insisted later, grasping at Jamīla's face: not only had the Shāh lost interest, but she would never regain it again. But Jamīla had never known Chehra to find anything personally in the Shāh. She was surprised at this consequent devastation. At best, Jamīla felt Chehra found him a useful means to carry out her plans. In all the years she had spent serving Chehra, those plans had not deviated from three central themes: alleviating boredom, commanding respect, and keeping Jamīla away from Nosrat. As such, Jamīla struggled to respond. Each morning, she observed Chehra's pacing with mild curiosity, listening to her fret as she adjusted her skirt, nodding as she wrote Chehra's grievances in her diary and waiting for the moment to pass.

It didn't. Chehra had stopped eating and refrained from leaving the apartment. Jamīla, whose day had been distilled down to following her mistress around, would sit on a cushion in Chehra's hot, sticky room, the windows sealed shut and the smell of putrid blood orange a faint ode to days past. As Chehra lay still and silent, Jamīla wished she could compose her thoughts in her own diary. She had retreated from the politics outside. She would ricochet from Abimelech to Sanaa, each more compelling than the other. Other times, she thought longingly of Nosrat's escape to Paris, of wandering long and winding streets where nobody knew her name. She thought of Sanaa taking her place, in his heart, in her getaway. She wanted to confront Sanaa, to at least ask her about it, but when granted the opportunity, her courage would always slink away.

39

'You cannot leave.' Sanaa stared at Jamīla. They were in Sanaa's apartment; a performance was taking place in the harem. Jamīla had been summoned – a fact that still amused her – by an irate but quiet Sanaa, enquiring about her absence.

'Can I not?' Jamīla rolled her eyes.

Sanaa faltered. 'You know we value agency above everything. You do not need permission to leave. I am just surprised. You were so keen to join.'

'I was.'

'You were? What has happened?'

Jamīla sighed.

'Are you no longer interested in radical change?'

'Are you?'

'Why ask such a question?'

Jamīla hesitated.

Sanaa watched her as the silence stretched and made itself comfortable. 'I often thought of you as a younger sibling, Jamīla. Well, not a sibling; siblings have their own characters. You were, at heart, like me...'

Jamīla stared at her. She blinked and took a deep breath. Trying to keep her tone casual, she asked, 'Who will listen to slaves?'

Sanaa frowned. 'Nobody will listen if we do not speak.'

'They may execute us if we speak.'

Sanaa cocked an eyebrow. 'Will they? Is that what Abimelech told you? He is the Shāh's favourite pet.'

'You were too...once,' Jamīla shot back, and Sanaa stared at her.

'The difference,' Sanaa said, her voice shaking, 'is that I was doing my job. I did not pray at the altar as Abimelech does.'

'He does not.'

'Is that what he told you? What else has he said?'

Jamīla stuttered for a moment. 'He is not wrong, is he? They will execute us.'

'Hundreds of slaves? You think the Shāh will kill hundreds of the slaves? That would draw too much attention and widespread condemnation.'

Jamīla was speechless as Sanaa broke into a smug version of her trademark smile.

'Abimelech is wrong. They will not kill that many slaves.'

Jamīla frowned. 'They would not need to. They would just kill a few.'

'The leaders,' Sanaa said, her eyes bright. 'They would expect it to frighten the others. To make them cower. This country knows nothing of its people – and yes, we are its people.'

Jamīla sighed. Here was the radical Sanaa, who spied on the royals, plotted against them, but there was also the practical Sanaa, who slept with the royals, planned escapes with them. Then there was the Sanaa who formed secret groups inside secret groups, the Sanaa with a smile full of rage. What would she do? What wouldn't she do? Jamīla could not even begin to discern her true agenda, certain only that it differed from almost everything she said. Sanaa's last words drifted back to her; malevolence dipped in honey. Shaken, Jamīla asked, 'Are you not one of the leaders?'

Sanaa pulled a modest face. 'Well...'

'Are you not one of the people they would kill?'

'I would happily die–'

'This soon? With so little achieved?' Jamīla snapped. 'This was why I left! They wanted to be martyrs. They wanted to die for the cause. Nobody wanted to do the hard work of trying, or living day to day with failures, or small victories that could be eroded. They wanted to preach, die, or complain. Nobody wanted to live.'

Sanaa paused and then broke into a vibrant smile. 'How fascinating, Jamīla, I do not recall that at all. I remember slaves talking about their daily lives. I recall you wanting to silence them.'

'I was talking about the leaders.'

'The leaders. Is that how you see me?' Sanaa asked, and then, with ice in her voice, 'Is this how Abimelech sees me?'

'I think for myself. A movement with dead leaders will not go anywhere.' Jamīla took a deep breath. Now was the moment to challenge her, but at the last moment, she lost her nerve. She shook her head and backed away. She might not be able to speak, but she could, at least, leave.

She sought out Gul. 'We have to take it in turns,' she said. Gul had been avoiding her since the end of last year. Their relationship and the burgeoning intimacy had been tarnished, punctured by the red weals Gul had drawn on her body, coloured by the convulsed sound of Jamīla's cries. Since then, Gul made sure to be asleep when the other slaves retired and ate her meals outside when she went on errands. In order to find her, Jamīla rose earlier than she used to, following Gul to the kitchen and grasping her by the arm. Gul spun around in shock; the domestic scrubbing the floor shot them an anxious glance and left. 'We have to take it in turns,' Jamīla repeated. 'I cannot spend every day in that room with Chehra Khaanoum. One day I will smother her – that will be bad for us all.'

Gul nodded, averting her eyes. 'Of-of course. How is she?'

Jamīla wanted to roll her eyes. 'She feels forgotten by the Shāh. I suspect she wants her malaise to reach him. I cannot convey it if I am seated at her bedside.'

'I can,' Gul said, with a quick nervous smile. It met Jamīla's closed expression and retreated; Gul once more averted her eyes.

'Thus keeping me by her side. How kind.'

'No! I...' She took a deep breath. 'One of his newer wives is getting married.'

'Great.'

'Yes, to a young physician at court.'

'Fascinating.'

'I mention it because it could be a solution for Chehra Khaanoum. She could be married to one of the Shāh's advisors too.'

'Right. How would that happen?'

'Well—'

'The Shāh cannot remember to pick her as part of a group, but you expect him to single her out as a gift to one of his men?'

'No, I—'

'This is a good plan, Gul.'

'If you would let me finish!' Gul snapped, and Jamīla stopped. They looked at each other for a moment, exasperated. Jamīla, leaning against the countertop, took a deep breath. Gul, however, remained irate. 'Can I continue to speak now? Or do you have a few remaining retorts?'

Jamīla nodded.

'It would not be a great stretch of the imagination to consider that the upcoming bride might recommend Chehra to her husband for one of his friends. All that is required is the how.'

'Do you not think the wives are too competitive to help each other?'

Gul looked at her, her nostrils flaring. 'She has no reason to compete. She has achieved the best a woman of her stature could. She might be open to help. It will cost or cause her nothing.'

'Right. Sounds...like a good plan.' Jamīla was quiet. Then she asked, 'Do you not think Chehra Khaanoum will be bored there too, even if she is not forgotten?'

'When are women's lives not boring? What is excitement but the offspring of choice? What can women choose?'

'Zainab Pasha's life is exciting!' Jamīla said, without thinking.

'The infamous radical?' Gul chuckled. 'I doubt it. She shouts, she stamps her foot, pulls off her chador – and little changes. Perhaps she is energised. But it is a pointless exercise that I have little patience for.'

'You think nothing will change?'

'For whom? Us? Her ilk? They might be offered a trinket, if they are not ignored. For those who consider that progress, then there will be progress.' Gul took a deep breath. Then she added, 'For those of us who loathe the world of men, who see so much greed and so little heart, becoming more like that is no victory. And, of course, for us, for slaves, it is not a right we will ever attain. So I am indifferent.'

'So women will attain false meaning and slaves nothing at all?' Jamīla sighed and turned away. 'Well, I am glad I spoke to you this morning.'

Gul's laugh was more open now. 'You have to be realistic. You cannot pretend that tomorrow we will not rise and serve Iranians. Or that if tomorrow we rise and Tehran is burning, that will be better for us all.'

'So why do anything at all?'

'There is always a myriad of reasons. The one you choose is for you to decide.'

40

The challenge lay in actually convincing Chehra to consider marriage as an option. Gul had ordered Laleh Habashī to partner with Jamīla on this task. Laleh, once a favourite of the sigheh's, had been ignored when Chehra and Jamīla began their secret excursions. With Chehra's rapid and prolonged return to bed, Laleh had seen her even less than before. Of those who muttered bleak thoughts against Jamīla and tried to curry favour with Gul, Laleh was the most adept and the most prolific. But Laleh, with a gaze of pure serenity, was the kind of girl who would smile and smile at those she hated most. When Jamīla had cornered her and asked her to join, she had beamed and reached for her hand. They entered Chehra's room together, Laleh standing in front, despite not knowing what they were about to say.

Chehra looked worse than Jamīla had ever seen her. Her skin was broken and inflamed where she had scraped it; swollen sores seemed to smart her cheeks. Her hair was stringy, unwashed and overgrown, but the dark bristles that sprouted from her chin, speckled her top lip and spread over her cheek looked fresh and bright, vibrant like the clear buds that opened in spring.

Laleh looked horrified. She turned to Jamīla with a neutral expression before hurrying over to Chehra, reaching out to touch her and recoiling, as though standing before someone with leprosy. 'Shahzadeh Khaanoum,' she said and bowed, placing her hand on a shoulder through the duvet. 'Let me bring you a razor. I shall clean you up and dress you, and we can proceed with the day.' She closed her eyes for a moment, taking careful breaths. Jamīla knew she was trying not to inhale the stench in the room. Jamīla noticed too; it smelled rather more putrid than usual. She cast her eyes about, trying to locate the source, wondering if a rodent had found Chehra's rotting fruit and chosen to die right beside it. She missed what happened next, but she heard the scream.

Laleh was on the floor and Chehra had risen from bed. 'Jamīla!' she called. She knelt on top of her duvet, flailing arms outstretched, her body spread like scaffolding, the nightgown dripping from her brittle limbs, the diaphanous dress of a poltergeist. The posture was menacing but the tone plaintive. 'Get her out of here!'

Jamīla trudged over to the bed. Laleh had scuttled out of the way, sitting on the floor by the window, out of Chehra's immediate sight. 'Shahzadeh Khaanoum,' Jamīla began, wondering once again why she alone could calm such an unpleasant woman, 'I thought of a way to solve your problem.' She shot half a glance at Laleh, who was smiling again. 'We found a way.'

'What problem? What...what?'

Jamīla stepped closer to her and pressed Chehra back into the bed. 'Rest. You are not appreciated here. But I know a way to change that...'

'I am not appreciated...,' Chehra mumbled, turning away.

'She is drunk,' Jamīla announced. 'She is drunk, and,' lifting the duvet, she shook her head, 'she has soiled herself. Who did this? Who gave her alcohol?'

Laleh rose and said, her tone arch, 'It was not me.'

'But you know who. Find them, bring them here now!'

'Is that your place?'

'Excuse me?'

'Surely, this is Gul's responsibility.'

'Ask her.'

'I shall,' Laleh said, meeting Jamīla's stern gaze with a tight smile. 'In the meantime, I shall approach the chief eunuch.'

There was a silence.

'What do you want, Jamīla?'

'A name.'

Laleh gritted her teeth. 'It was me.'

***

Gul refused to tell Jamīla how she had cajoled Chehra out of bed, but Laleh wasted no time in mocking Jamīla because of it. 'You are not too disappointed?' she hissed with a smile as they bent their heads together, tidying their sleeping quarters.

'Girls,' Gul announced. 'Rather than accompany Jamīla tonight, I think that Laleh should. Both of you can keep an eye on Chehra and help steer the conversation towards her future if need be.' She crouched beside them and let her voice drop. 'Consider it an evening of fun for you two. Yekta is nice and guileless. It will be relaxed.'

The run-up to the event was anything but. Chehra wouldn't get into her dress, then she had a tantrum about her shoes. She cried for an hour about the Shāh and asked Jamīla to tuck her into bed. She then threw a shoe at Laleh, accusing her of sleeping with the Shāh. Jamīla could not recall how they convinced her out of her room.

'Her apartment is much bigger than mine!' Chehra said with a sniff as they arrived. Jamīla agreed. Yekta's apartment was lighter too. Each elongated room they were led through had four floor-to-ceiling windows. A eunuch ushered them into a meticulously painted room where a long, crimson sofreh lay heaving with food. There were about twenty other wives gathered about and a smattering of slaves pressed into the walls, practicing, as ever, invisibility. Jamīla and Laleh walked in behind Chehra, and as the eunuch pointed, they helped her onto a cushion.

'Chehra brought a cortège?' one of the women spoke with a chuckle. Jamīla recognised Raem Khaanoum, a former harem secretary who had fallen from grace. Several of the women turned to look at Chehra, who appeared not to have heard them and was staring into her glass. A eunuch stepped forward, a bottle in his hand. Laleh prodded Jamīla, who intercepted the bottle with a shake of her head.

'Yekta, Chehra's slaves think they can run your dinner!' Raem laughed again, and Jamīla stared at her for a moment, puzzled as to why she was being so cruel. She averted her eyes, casting them down towards Chehra, who was frowning now, but still at her glass. Laleh stepped away, leaning against one of the far walls, but Jamīla did not feel comfortable leaving Chehra unaccompanied.

Yekta, a slender woman with a youthful, jolly face, leaned across the sofreh to Raem. 'You are being unkind today,' she said. Raem smiled at her as Yekta continued. 'We have not seen Chehra for quite some time. I do not wish to scare her!'

Jamīla was unsure whether to push Chehra to engage. It was a general rule that dinners were for eating, and conversation was to take place after. This usually applied to formal dinners, but Jamīla couldn't be sure if it was expected here. Yekta's tone was open, and she was smiling across at Chehra's forehead. Chehra was still gazing into her glass, indifferent even to the sofreh beneath it. Jamīla glanced at the remaining guests. Beside Yekta was Yasmin Khaanoum, who had given birth to a son in February. Jamīla was surprised she would deign to attend a sigheh wife's remarriage but, fêted as she was, it was easy to see why. Most of the remaining women were far older, and as Jamīla watched them, she saw the easy camaraderie she had witnessed at Zainab's house when Yagana, Aadila and Wardiyyah had lounged and laughed with the uncomplicated joy of familiarity.

There were a handful of women, including Raem, who leaned in and cooed at Yasmin, nodding at her every word, laughing at each cruel aside and smiling at her airy mien. It was the older ones, however, who laughed the loudest. With wrinkled chins and heaving chests, they banged their glasses and made jokes. Jamīla watched in wonder as the genuine friendship between these ladies caught the attention of Yasmin's admirers and they began to look with a mixture of guilt and envy at the carefree older women chuckling away.

Yekta, somewhere between the two groups, rose from her place to join her elders. She crouched behind them with her welcome smile as one of them, with a wrinkled lip, whispered tartly in her ear.

'Oh, I do not concern myself with such things!' Yekta said, giggling, and the older woman stared at her in disbelief.

'You are not serious.'

'I am.' Yekta smiled, but her tone was firm. 'You may think me silly, but it does not excite me. "Running my own household" sounds like pressure. He has young sons, and I think as long as they are happy, I am happy.'

'Well—'

But Yasmin leaned across the table to intervene. 'A child's happiness is paramount. My life is that of my son. What is power when those who wield it cannot bring joy to those they love?' Her coterie of admirers made noises of assent. The elderly woman who had whispered looked at her with mild interest. Yasmin straightened up and added, 'The most powerful woman, after all, is the one who does not need power but finds it granted to her.'

'Which is what you have!' Raem intervened and Yasmin smiled, until she realised Raem was looking at Yekta.

'Well, yes,' Yekta said with her guileless grin. 'But I spurn power for joy.'

Jamīla was bored. She looked down at Chehra to see how she was faring, but Chehra was gazing at Yekta with yearning in her eyes.

Yasmin stood up. 'Let us offer a toast to the marvellous Yekta on her exciting new marriage and to all women who are brave and bold and achieve what they desire. To women who wield power but know that mothering, that raising sons, that loving one's husband is more important. To all such women who rise and thrive, I salute you. It is not an easy world in which to do so.'

'To Yekta,' said the woman with the wrinkled lip, on the heels of Yasmin's speech. 'To Yekta. I would rise, but my bones are too stiff!' She snorted and the room broke into chuckles. Her lip and all its crevices wriggled as she smiled and carried on. 'Yekta, this is your evening alone. Have a marvellous night.' As the woman led the applause, Jamīla felt apprehension flood the room. Yasmin was looking at her with an unfathomable expression; Jamīla knew she never wanted to receive that gaze.

'How did it happen?' Chehra suddenly asked, her voice croaking through the cheers. Every face snapped towards hers.

Yasmin, now seated, with a feline smile, asked in a careful voice. 'How did what happen, dear Chehra?'

'How-how did that...How did Yekta find a husband?'

'Oh!' Yekta said, and she blushed, looking around at everyone. 'I could not say. I was chosen. It was a gift.'

'The Shāh is very generous,' Yasmin interjected.

'Is that something you wish for?' The wrinkled lip quivered again as the older woman asked.

Chehra nodded and looked down at her glass.

'Well, there must be a way.' Yekta looked at the wrinkled lip. The elderly woman and her friends fell silent.

'From what I understand, the Shāh grants women he admires to noblemen he admires even more. Either the Shāh cannot bear to let you leave his side or he bestows you as a gift on the worthy. You just have to be noticed, Chehra.' Yasmin's smile grew creamier as her glance moved from Yekta to Chehra.

'Well,' Yekta began in an uncertain voice. 'I could ask my husband after the wedding if he—'

'No!' More than three women interrupted at once.

Yasmin rose again and the other three fell silent. 'Do not sully your marriage bed by making such demands. You are a gift from the Shāh. Your husband will always be on his best behaviour. That is difficult enough to maintain. Let us not make your marriage more difficult before it has even begun. Chehra does not need such help, does she?' Her eyes fixed on Chehra, but it was another woman who answered.

'No.' The wrinkled lip jutted forward, each dimple shaking hard. 'Chehra Khaanoum shall be fine.'

41

Jamīla snickered as she read Abimelech's note. She sent his eunuch away without a reply. This was not a request, not a reflection of desire, but a command, an expression of will. She waited a week before responding. A small part of her had expected – hoped for – a second letter reiterating the original request. It would have been better somehow, she had thought, if there were no pretence involved, no appearance of choice. She was a slave obeying a command. But the week had passed in silence. When she returned to his room, she felt a strange mix of trepidation and excitement as she stood outside Nosrat's door; she was not sure what to expect.

Nosrat opened the door and stood before her, his face a mask of surprise. She realised, as his eyes examined her body thoroughly, that it had been about a year since they had seen each other.

'Would you...would you like a drink?' he asked her. His voice had changed. She couldn't explain how; perhaps she was just unused to hearing it. But his tone was careful, considered, even as the words he chose were not.

'No,' she said and began to bow before stopping and looking up at him, confused. 'Hazrat-e Aghdass-e Vaalaa,' she added but stood up straight.

'Thank you,' he replied and then blushed.

She walked past him into the room.

'Would you like a cigarette?'

She didn't answer but turned towards him, her hand reaching behind him to push the door closed. He glanced at the door and nodded. She walked further into the room. He remained behind her, keeping still, but she heard his neck crick as his head turned to follow her movements. His bedroom smelled familiar: the musky, dirty smell of boy, of rich boy, that had always made her think of copulation, hung heavily in the air. She couldn't tell if his room actually smelled of intercourse – whether he had had it recently or whether she simply associated it with him, with the oscillation between his indolent need and aggressive want, that manifested as–

'I have food.'

She walked over to the bed, suppressing a sigh.

'I can have the windows closed, if you have a chill.'

She let her clothes fall onto the floor, then she turned to face him.

He was different from when they used to be lovers. This new Nosrat was perpetually melancholic. She wondered whether Sanaa had done this to him somehow, had brought him a new perspective, a depth that sharpened his outlook on life and pushed him from petulant to pensive. In bed he did not try anything new per se, nor take an interest in what she might enjoy but instead would ask repeatedly how much she liked what he was doing. He wanted to be pleased by her pleasure. He wanted her to be pleased with what he offered.

A month after her return to Nosrat, Jamīla had yet to glimpse Abimelech. Their last contact had been the note he had sent – his elegant, fluid cursive conveying an ardent desire on the part of the young prince for his first love to return. She felt frustrated. It struck her as absurd that their re-acquaintance in the Persian royal court, having met as slaves for hire in Abyssinia, was to be without significance, a mere inadvertence in the grand scheme of their lives.

Abimelech had caught her eye only because he kept so still, untouched by the whirl of noise around him. He stood apart from the others, restless young men whose rangy bodies cut through the air like swimmers, eyes as antennae, seeking out the girls. The customers, performing a pantomime, would raise their hands to prod and pluck at the bodies they wanted. Jamīla watched them all, certain she was trapped in a dream. The seams of this world were vivid and exposed. And that one boy kept so still. His eyes had a brittle expression, and they held her gaze for more than a moment. Jamīla knew from the way everyone stared at her that her face was still bloodied. Pity fell like peppered raindrops as they approached her with their unease. His was the face that didn't change. It drank in her bruises with no response, looked on at the lesions that were starting to form. There was still blood in her mouth when she opened it, and it was then that he started to smile. He walked away without warning, and Jamīla sought him out every day. But he disappeared amongst the others, and the surprise she felt held a chilly note of sadness.

When they met again at court, Jamīla at first hadn't noticed Abimelech, one of five eunuchs the chief had summoned. The incoming slaves were ushered into groups, headed by each of these eunuchs. Until they had mistresses, they would report to these eunuchs, learning the rules of the harem and the scope of their roles. The chief eunuch weaved his way through the crowd of kanīz, pushing the slave girls to form lines behind a specific eunuch. Jamīla was standing between two Georgian girls, each of whom gave her an unfavourable glance. She felt uncomfortable sandwiched between them and tried to extricate herself by stepping out of the line. The chief eunuch misread this as defiance and marched over to discipline her for it. In the ensuing commotion, Jamīla cast around for an ally who might protect her from this unexpected assault. It was then that she spied that boy from Abyssinia walking over to defuse the situation. She stared at him, a jolt of recognition causing her to smile. When he looked at her, it was without familiarity but with compassion. 'Let her join my group,' he had insisted, and the chief eunuch had responded with an uninterested nod. She had forgotten that he hadn't recognised her, but as she recalled it now, she wondered whether it served to illustrate the meaningless nature of the original encounter.

The bed was still damp. As she lay beside Nosrat, feeling the chill of his semen against her thighs, she wondered how much had changed. Had Nosrat ordered Abimelech to return Jamīla to him? Was she a parcel to be passed between princes and their slaves, donated like a set of old robes, only to be requested by their former owner once he spied them worn so well? As she watched him lying still beside her, she was unsettled by a myriad of questions.

'Sanaa,' she said now in an absent tone.

Nosrat sounded startled. 'What made you mention her?'

'Oh,' Jamīla said. In the darkened room, with heavy curtains holding back the light, she couldn't quite see his expression. 'I did not realise I spoke aloud.'

'You did. Why?'

Jamīla paused. Nosrat reached over and tried to grab her face. It was clear that the darkness enveloped hers, because the top of his palm slammed against the edge of her chin, his fingers catching her ear and flailing through her hair. She flinched and withdrew. She was no longer used to having to accommodate his aggression. 'Hazrat-e Aghdass-e Vaalaa, I cannot speak if you are holding my face.'

He let go and turned away.

'I have to ask Sanaa something.'

'Tell me.'

'Hazrat-e Aghdass-e Vaalaa, I am not at liberty to do so.'

When he turned back this time, his voice was shaking. 'Why not?'

'Chehra Khaanoum gave me an order, and she is counting on my discretion.'

Jamīla heard the tension escape him, despite his silence.

'*Do you still see her?*' She wanted to ask the question aloud. Instead, she lay back, counting the minutes until she could leave.

42

When she sent a message to Sanaa, she suggested they meet in the Hall of Mirrors. Jamīla, whilst she refrained from saying so, felt certain that this should be their last meeting. They met at dawn, not unlike the first time, the light trembling through the room, reflecting off the endless glass, refracting in sharp tremors that flickered across Sanaa's face.

'It has been some time,' Jamīla said, unsure how to begin. 'Chehra Khaanoum has been unwell. However, she has asked that I seek your counsel. She is looking to be given in marriage to one of the Shāh's men. She thought you might know who could influence the Shāh to grant such a favour on her behalf.'

'Is that why I was summoned?'

Jamīla faltered.

Sanaa looked at her, her face animated now. 'You chose this place – the place where we first discussed how best to,' she gestured with one hand, forming an ornate yet dismissive twirl, 'utilise the machinations of the harem. But if you recall, Jamīla, it evolved into a more productive conversation. Let us skip these banalities and speak with candour.'

Jamīla was stunned. Unsure of how to respond, she said, 'Here?'

'Not here. Tell Chehra Khaanoum I wish to discuss this outside the court. Then meet me tomorrow in the bāzār.' She dropped her voice. 'Shapur and I are working together again. We could use you.'

They were standing in the centre of a room that glimmered on all sides. Jamīla glanced behind her and watched as a thousand Jamīlas did the same. Their faces looked apprehensive and unhappy. The numerous Sanaas reached out and pressed their hands on the Jamīlas' shoulders. The Jamīlas shrank back. 'Sorry,' she muttered, and her doppelgängers mouthed the words. 'I have had too many hands...'

'Oh,' Sanaa said, her face returning to its impassive pose. 'You have returned to Prince Nosrat. Good!'

'It is?'

'It could prove useful.' Sanaa leaned forward, her hand hovering above Jamīla's shoulder, her words coming swiftly. 'I know the slaves' gatherings did not amount to much. They splintered, fractured, and I left them too. But you should not, must not, cannot give up on the notion of genuine resistance. Do not think this is it. Do not return to Prince Nosrat and his fantasies about Paris. That is not the change we need. The change is here.'

Sanaa's words became harder and louder, her hand made that gesture again, and Jamīla wondered whether Nosrat had changed his mind about taking Sanaa with him to Paris. Jamīla no longer felt jealous or even excited that Sanaa had lost out. She could not muster the excitement to think about an escape. She wasn't sure what to expect regarding Chehra's future house. Maybe she could settle into a comfortable routine, living in an andarūnī, beyond the reach of predatory men. But she would never see Abimelech again. She would never go home. None of these changes would work in her favour; she would attain nothing she actually wanted. She pushed the thoughts aside. 'Were you not going to Paris with Prince Nosrat?' The words marched out before Jamīla had time to process them.

Sanaa looked uncomfortable for a moment before saying, 'No. Why would the prince take his concubine?'

Jamīla didn't answer.

'Did he tell you he would take you to Paris?' Sanaa shook her head, but her brilliant smile burst forth like the advent of spring. 'Oh, he was never going to take you or anyone. I did not realise you hoped to join him yourself.'

'I heard he was taking you.'

Sanaa's face became watchful. 'Heard where?'

'He was to take you, and then something changed his mind.'

'*Changed his mind?*'

'It was not long after that he sought me to be his concubine again.'

'What are you suggesting?'

Jamīla kept silent.

Sanaa's expression grew frantic. 'I need to leave.' She all but ran for the door.

'Wait.' Jamīla grasped her arm. 'Do not run. How would that look?'

Sanaa stopped. She closed her eyes. Jamīla watched her regain her composure with reluctant marvel. 'You wanted me to help Chehra Khaanoum find...'

'A husband.'

'Right. I know who she should speak to. I will visit you at Chehra Khaanoum's apartment and inform you of my progress there.'

'Thank you, Sanaa.'

'One last question.'

Jamīla looked warily at her.

'Who told you?'

She paused. Then, sighing, she said, 'Abimelech.'

'Abimelech?' she muttered, her brow furrowed. 'He would not say something so...strange. Thank you, Jamīla.'

Before she could ask what Sanaa meant, the latter had slipped out the door.

Jamīla stood alone in the room, gazing back at the echoes of her face, every single one forlorn.

43

A week later, Jamīla entered the apartment to find Chehra entertaining guests. Whilst she was still loath to leave the apartment, Chehra now allowed Jamīla to open the windows, and she entertained guests, no more than three at a time, on the ayvān. Such gatherings had often devolved into rows. Chehra would order people out or else orchestrate a screaming match, which she always won. Usually the other participants would give up, a pitying gaze on their faces as they backed out of her apartment. Chehra was always pleased that the liars knew better than to challenge her, but Jamīla suspected these victories were actually quite pyrrhic. After all, she once reminded Chehra, she would do well to retain allies rather than make enemies. Chehra disliked such a line of critique, and Jamīla was whipped once more.

Jamīla was thus surprised when she saw cushions laid out on the ayvān. 'Who let Chehra receive guests?' she hissed when she found Gul in the kitchen. Gul stared at her for a moment, her mouth agape. Then, in silence, they hurried to Chehra's bedroom and stared at the veranda outside. There was Chehra, surrounded by cushions, laughing away with Raem Khaanoum, who was drinking a doogh, and Mahin, a new young wife, who was sitting stiffly.

'We need to find who let them in!' Gul said emphatically and Jamīla agreed. Neither of them moved from the window as they watched the conversation unfold.

'I heard he is angry with her,' Raem was saying, and her eyes glittered as she gazed at Chehra.

'Well, good—,' Chehra rushed, and Mahin interrupted with a

question, 'Where did you hear this?'

'I could not say.' Raem lifted her chin. 'I do not gossip. I–'

'Why is he angry?' Chehra demanded.

'Her son – well, their son was sick on one of his paintings.'

'A valuable one?' Chehra gasped.

'One he painted. So…invaluable, because it was the great Shāh of Shāhs.'

'It would have been cleaned,' Mahin said. 'There are some great domestics – they can clean anything.'

'Well,' Raem frowned and sipped her doogh, 'he has not seen her or his son since.'

'Oh?' Chehra sighed and shook her head.

'How long is "since"?'

'A long while,' Raem snapped.

'A month?'

'Mahin, why must you doubt what I say?'

'I am not doubting, Raem.' A smile flickered across Mahin's face. 'I am adding clarity.'

'She does not lie, Mahin,' Chehra said suddenly; the other women were still.

Raem sipped her doogh. Mahin lit a cigarette.

'Do you think she lies?'

Neither woman replied.

'Raem, she has called you a liar!'

Mahin offered Raem her cigarette. Raem handed her the doogh.

'I think you lie, Mahin,' Chehra said.

Raem looked up at Chehra, her eyes alight. 'Does she?'

Mahin stared at Raem in what looked like shock, but morphed into recognition.

Gul and Jamīla looked at each other.

'Yes. I trust you, Raem,' Chehra asserted, looking behind the cushions for her drink.

'Your eunuch can make you another, Chehra,' Mahin said with a smile. Raem glimmered back, amused.

'Mahin, you are new,' Chehra said, replacing the cushions and facing her. 'You know very little. Raem has been here a long time – Raem has been a favourite of the Shāh. She has also been,' Chehra continued, oblivious to the other women's smirks, 'rejected by the Shāh, never to gain his favour again. So she does know, better than you, what is happening to Yasmin.'

Raem's smile slid from her face. Mahin looked at Raem, but her expression was unclear. Something twitched about her lips, a thought perhaps, a realisation.

'Raem was rejected?' Mahin smiled, stretching on a cushion.

'Yes – it was about her son too, was it not, Raem?'

Raem's face grew gaunt. She staggered to her feet. 'My son was dead at birth. He was dead in my arms.'

Mahin looked horrified. She stared at Chehra, then Raem, and glanced towards the windows, seeking help. Jamīla and Gul had their faces pressed against it. Mahin's expression paralysed them. Jamīla wanted to flee, but Mahin's face twisted as they started to leave.

Chehra stared at Raem. 'Yes. This angered the Shāh, did it not?'

Jamīla dragged Chehra in as Raem began screaming. She left Gul to see the two princesses out.

Sanaa turned up shortly after. Gul, alarmed at the slew of guests turning up uninvited, stood blocking the entry. Wives she could not bar, but a concubine could at least be questioned.

'Gul.' Jamīla hurried over. 'Sanaa is here to help with Chehra Khaanoum's request.'

'Right...'

'Perhaps you were not informed.' Sanaa turned to Gul as she

entered the hallway. 'You do run this household, do you not?'
And she broke into her luminous smile.

Chehra, hearing the arrival of a new guest, hurried out of
her room. She spotted Sanaa and clapped her hands together.
'Marvellous, marvellous, what a delight! Jamīla, bring our guest
a drink!'

Jamīla was stunned. But she gritted her teeth and headed to
the kitchen.

'Sanaa has solved my problem,' Chehra all but yelped, taking
the drinks and handing one to Sanaa. They were seated on the
veranda, on the very cushions the two princesses had vacated.
Sanaa smiled with empty-eyed brevity and, as she raised her
glass to her face, she inched away from Chehra. 'The physician
who attended to the Shāh is said to be in need of a wife. He
is obviously the Shāh's favourite, and Sanaa here will put in a
good word!'

'With the physician?' Gul asked, surprised.

'No,' Sanaa replied. 'I will speak with Omid Khaanoum, who
recommended Yekta to the Shāh.'

'Everything is resolved!' Chehra looked like she might burst
with joy.

'Well...' Sanaa paused and then sipped her drink.

'Speak.' Gul's eyes were narrowed.

'From what I understand, this physician is quite young.'

'So...?'

'So, he has...modest means.'

'Chehra Khaanoum is not after a fortune.' Gul's tone was
haughty. Her mouth twitched. 'She would stay here if she was.'

Chehra was not listening. She was staring at Sanaa, her eyes
following the slave's every movement – her arm's fluidity as she
raised her glass, her shoulders jostling as she leaned forward,

the slight curl of her tongue as she spoke.

Sanaa ignored Gul. 'His modest means will not accommodate all the slaves who live in this apartment.'

Gul turned to Chehra but did not speak.

Chehra did not quite answer. Instead she leaned closer to Sanaa and asked, 'What would happen to my slaves?'

'Most would be left behind, assuming there was work available here. You could, of course, ask your husband to accommodate them.'

'Hmmm,' Chehra demurred. 'I think I would want to begin again.'

'Yes, that sounds smart,' Sanaa agreed, breaking into one of her beatific smiles. Chehra smiled back, elated. Jamīla watched on in horror as Sanaa added, 'You do not want to risk angering a future spouse by bringing an army of individuals to be fed and maintained.'

'Well,' Chehra said, glancing at Laleh before basking in Sanaa's brilliant smile. 'Perhaps one or two. A lady must be attended to, after all.'

Jamīla felt a burst of panic. She was being excised from her own household. They were erasing her. It was as if she did not exist.

Sanaa followed Chehra's gaze and looked at Laleh too. 'Well, yes, a little girl to grow up with you. And perhaps an older one to show her the ropes.'

Chehra ordered Jamīla to walk Sanaa out. Sanaa strode beside Jamīla, unperturbed by the silence. Once out of Chehra's sight, Jamīla stopped. Sanaa turned back to look at her, and Jamīla knew she should speak. She couldn't. Without a word, Sanaa faced forward and continued her unflappable glide. Jamīla felt that, for the first time, she had experienced a true betrayal.

44

Despite the Shāh's reassurances, Abimelech could not shake a sense of disquiet. He returned to the council meetings, attending with the Shāh, standing discreetly behind him, facing the Grand Vizier and Kamran without saying so much as a word. The Grand Vizier controlled the treasury; Kamran determined military policy. Thus, both were present at almost every meeting – everything from international trade to domestic policy was determined by the government's purse and touched by the threat of war, external and, increasingly, civil.

Kamran treated Abimelech as any other eunuch in the room – he ignored him. Abimelech knew better than to speak; the Shāh would seek his thoughts in private. The Grand Vizier, however, sought to exploit the chill between Abimelech and Kamran. He challenged the former whenever he could, and Abimelech couldn't see what could be done. For the first time, he felt helpless. He recalled the Shāh's promise to grant him property after he died. The prospect of being sent away to a remote location to hide from vengeful courtiers did not inspire excitement. The Shāh noticed his discontent and would prod him about it, but it wasn't until his room was ransacked a second time that Abimelech allowed himself to confide his fears.

'I am concerned, A'laa Hazrat,' he admitted one evening, sitting on a cushion in the royal library and facing the Shāh. 'My room was searched, items were taken, I am followed everywhere. I have an enemy. Someone is trying to discredit me. They might try to have me killed.' He thought about, but didn't mention, the Shāh's former advisor, Amir Kabir. The Shāh thought his loyalties were firm. Abimelech knew their foundations were weak; the right voice at the right time could convince the Shāh to turn against him, and without power of his own or another advocate, Abimelech would find himself adrift. He was terrified – nothing was proceeding as planned. He had made powerful enemies where he had hoped to make allies; his lone ally, the most powerful man in the country, was an ageing lion surrounded by upstarts, punctured and heaving towards an inevitable demise.

The Shāh gave him a tired chuckle. 'This is what power looks like, my boy.'

'A'laa Hazrat, I do not yet have any power.'

'Having the ear of the Shāh of Shāhs is not power enough for you?'

Abimelech averted his gaze. After a pause, he spoke. 'I do not trust the Grand Vizier. I think we should know his movements at all times. I have a small number of eunuchs at my disposal, but I cannot keep them from their duties without evoking the ire of the chief eunuch.'

'Why do you need to follow the Grand Vizier?'

Abimelech looked at him but did not answer.

'You think he is behind the assassination attempts?' The Shāh chuckled. 'It is the radicals – they want a nationalist court. It is not the Grand Vizier.'

Abimelech said nothing. The Shāh looked troubled for a moment. There was silence, in which the Shāh gulped his drink, slopping it down his chin in a manner that reminded Abimelech of Mozaffar.

'You suspect the Grand Vizier, boy?'

'Yes, A'laa Hazrat.'

'Of what?'

'Of...something. I shan't know until he is followed.'

'You cannot have him followed because...?'

'The chief eunuch would not let me put so many eunuchs to personal use. He would grow suspicious. He might even alert men in the ḵalwat, the Divan Khana or on your council.'

'So we need to circumvent the chief eunuch.'

'Yes. Unfortunately, I do not know how. He is very powerful. He could—'

'—be replaced.'

'Oh. Oh! I...well, yes, he...But we would have to—'

'By you.'

'I...? Me?'

'Does this not solve our problem?'

'Well, yes, yes...But we would have to—'

'Then there is no concern—'

'A'laa Hazrat!'

'Did you just interrupt me, boy?'

Abimelech was tired. He was tired of talking to people who did not listen. 'Forgive me, A'laa Hazrat, but replacing the chief eunuch will cause tension in the harem. He has a number of powerful allies.'

The Shāh frowned at him. 'You told me it could be done and would solve your problem. Now you are changing your mind?'

'No, A'laa Hazrat, not at all, no!' Abimelech took a deep breath. 'We need...to mitigate the surrounding issues. We need to avoid fighting in the harem. We could reinstate him as a deputy eunuch. Or...I could be appointed "head eunuch", meanwhile his position does not change as chief, but I will have the power to recruit as many eunuchs as I need to follow through on my agenda.'

'Boy, this does not concern me. I have no interest in how you appease the squabbling factions of the harem. Usurp the chief eunuch, hire the chief eunuch, kill the chief eunuch.' He gave a chuckle. 'I have spent decades battling against the confluence of power and thwarted ambition that resides there in febrile form. Do not concern me. You have my blessing – resolve the issue on your own.'

Abimelech left, relieved, before realising he had no idea how to implement such advice. Without allies he could trust, he was unsure where to turn. He thought about asking Jamīla for help, but the gulf between the two of them felt so broad he couldn't begin to cross it. By writing his note to Jamīla, delivering her into Nosrat's hands, imploring her to do things he wished she wouldn't, he felt he was taking away the very thing he had thought they might someday achieve. But now she was with Nosrat, and she would either escape with him to Paris or join the angry mob that brayed beyond the palace walls. Either way, they were no longer on the same side. Even if they were, it occurred to him that she too would not know how to proceed. There were over a hundred eunuchs in the harem, whose regular duties were overseen by the chief. Neither he nor Jamīla had marshalled a team of men or slaves spanning a hundred; neither had plotted a coup to overthrow an existing superior. The more he considered it, the more he realised that the person he needed was Kamran Mirza. Kamran, however, had not spoken to him since last year. In the council meetings, Kamran addressed the Shāh and ignored everyone else. Abimelech could not bring himself to look Kamran in the eye. He waited two days and then sent a eunuch to deliver a message to Kamran Mirza asking them to meet.

The message he received back was delivered by a bashful eunuch. The letter was not sealed; the eunuch handed it to him with the eagerness of someone relinquishing a grenade. He hurried away without a backward glance, leaving Abimelech to finger the letter with hesitancy.

Abimelech,

*I could not conceive of any reason that you and I should have
to meet. Let us not waste each other's time. Mine is valuable,
and I shall do you the courtesy of assuming yours at least
matters to you. Therefore, I suggest we refrain from contacting
each other further.*

Abimelech spent the rest of the day following the Shāh around.
He spoke little, certain that if he opened his mouth, he would
cry. When he returned to Nosrat's quarters at the end of the day,
he caught sight of Jamīla heading to Nosrat's room. She stood
outside the door, running a hand through her hair. Her chador
was pulled down, gathered in a loose bundle around her neck.
Even from that distance, he could see her throat was taut, her
whole body tense. Abimelech had to turn away. He could not
bring himself to think of this other mess that he had created.

He entered his room and saw that once more it had been
ransacked. The perpetrators were not looking for anything in
particular. The bed was slashed, the bedding shredded, pillows
were cut open and the feathers were singed – they had been
set alight. The bureau was dented in various places – someone
had taken great pains to inflict damage on the wood.

The legs were snapped off the chairs, and the floor was covered
in burn marks. He stood on scorched earth. The curtains had
disappeared, the windows were locked and the keys had been
removed. The smell of burning remained, along with other smells
he could not identify, but which left a fetid air.

Abimelech was not sure if this was the Grand Vizier's doing, or if
someone had told the chief eunuch about his plans. A small part
of him suspected Kamran Mirza was not as superior as everyone
believed and had ordered this petty attack – a punishment

for Abimelech's apparent entitlement. Abimelech knew that he had to ask Kamran again. Assuming he was not so ignoble, he was the only person mature enough to give Abimelech the appropriate advice. Even if he was responsible, the only way to deflect blame from himself would be to assist Abimelech when the latter called for help.

Abimelech lay down on the floor, his back pressed into the scorched ground, looking at the mound of ash that might once have been letters, books or poems. If before, Abimelech felt embarrassed by Kamran's rejection, the Shāh's fickleness and Jamīla's silence, the night he spent in his decrepit room allowed those emotions to coalesce into anger.

The next day, Abimelech stood through a political stalemate, a council meeting populated with British diplomats in which the obsequious Grand Vizier and watchful Kamran tiptoed around inflammatory topics in careful tones. The tension in the room was elastic. It would stretch, but only until a certain point before it snapped, and voices began to shout. It occurred to Abimelech that after a lifetime of tact and tentativeness, he had arrived nowhere, and as the meeting concluded and the men began to file out, he found it was he who was shouting.

'Kamran Mirza!' Abimelech bent into a long low bow as various voices speculated at the audacity of this slave to raise his voice to the son of a shāh.

Kamran smiled his confident smile, brushing off the outrage, and turned to Abimelech. 'Can I help you...Abimelech?'

'A few days ago, I sought your wisdom, Kamran Mirza.'

'Yes.' Kamran's smile became more indulgent, and he continued to speak.

But Abimelech, the blood rushing to his face, spoke over him.

'After you warned me not to contact you again, my room was set on fire. Now, I am far beneath the dignity and the attention of a prince, a son of the Shāh of Shāhs, but despite that – or because of that – I would not expect my plea for help to be met with the destruction of the one room I called my home.'

There was silence now, and Kamran Mirza's face was a horrified mask.

The Shāh stared at him. 'Someone set a fire – in this palace? In my palace?'

'They were not trying to disrespect you, A'laa Hazrat. They sought to harm me – and they succeeded.'

The British looked uncomfortable.

Kamran snapped, 'I am not responsible for this!' His face was white, his expression horrified.

Abimelech believed him; the prince's expression was stunned – he even looked a little sad. Nevertheless, Abimelech continued to speak. He straightened up, and a sober expression clouded his face. 'Last year, whilst the Shāh was unwell, I was given the weightiest task. I was to assess the sons of the Shāh of Shāhs, to choose one to serve as an interim leader whilst the Shāh took the time to recover. I did not choose Kamran. I thought I must protect the legacy of the Shāh, respect the lineage of the Qājārs, and so I abstained. I realise that my behaviour has invoked the ire of many. I realise Kamran Mirza begrudges me for not insisting he be given his brother's birthright. Nevertheless, I did not suspect that such offence would be taken at my request for help that the place where I slept and the little I had would be destroyed. I am a slave. I should not even be speaking this much in the presence of such illustrious men. But I have learned what happens when I try to address matters privately.' He did not look at Kamran.

The Shāh turned to his son. He looked almost apoplectic. The Grand Vizier, his eyes bright with excitement, ferried the advisors, British and Persian, out of the room with discreet speed. He then returned himself and lingered by the door, watching as the Shāh stared at Kamran, enraged but also surprised.

'Some people long for power,' the Grand Vizier said, stepping into the centre of the room. 'Betrayals can be hard to forgive. I am sure Kamran Mirza will not repeat his behaviour. The slave, it appears, received the message.'

'Is that correct?' the Shāh asked, his eyes bulging. 'What message does burning my palace send?'

The Grand Vizier gulped. 'Perhaps we should ask Kamran Mirza.'

'How dare—'

'Are you accusing my son?' The words were spat from the Shāh's mouth. 'You are very bold to accuse my son after he has denied his involvement.'

'The slave – the slave – he accused Kamran Mirza!' the Grand Vizier shouted.

'Yes.' The Shāh turned to look at Abimelech, nostrils flaring. 'He did.'

'The real question,' came a voice from behind him, 'is why the Grand Vizier is still here at all.' It was Kamran who spoke, and the Grand Vizier responded with a series of stuttered incoherent sentences. 'What is your connection? If you have none, why are you meddling?'

'I-I am not meddling!' The Grand Vizier looked furious.

'So you are connected, then?' Kamran shot back.

'He-he has enemies,' the Grand Vizier spluttered, thrusting a finger towards Abimelech's chest. 'The chief eunuch is worried about his station. Perhaps...'

The Shāh gave a loud sigh and turned away.

'Are you blaming the chief eunuch?' Kamran's smile was broad now, and the Grand Vizier, now that the Shāh's back was turned, gave him such a venomous glower that Abimelech wished he could leave. 'Be ready to explain that when I summon him before the Shāh.'

'I am not blaming him!' the Grand Vizier all but shrieked. 'I am explaining that Abimelech, here, has a pattern of disloyalty that has created an abundance of enemies.'

Kamran frowned. 'What is his disloyalty against the chief eunuch?'

'He is trying to take his role. Once again, this slave's ambition is the root of all his problems.'

'It was my plan,' the Shāh said, turning back around. 'So, according to you, I have caused the slave's problems? Am I also to blame for the destruction of the room?'

Calmly, Kamran interjected, 'How did the chief eunuch learn of this plan?'

'He was given formal notice relieving him of his duties.'

'Was this given by Abimelech?'

'It was granted by the private secretary of the Shāh. There is only one eunuch who would dare...who is powerful enough—'

'Did he verify this claim? Did he...ask Abimelech or the private secretary?'

'I—' The Grand Vizier flapped his hands. 'I cannot say.'

'But you heard this from him?'

'Yes! Well...I—'

'So if I summon the chief eunuch right now, will he say that he told you this information?'

'I cannot speak to what—'

'Or that you told him?'

The Grand Vizier fell silent. Kamran opened his mouth again, but the Shāh raised his hand. 'Have you been sowing discord in my court, Ali Asghar? Have you knowingly thwarted the plans of the Shāh?'

The Grand Vizier fell into a deep bow. Kamran slipped past him and grabbed Abimelech by the arm. 'Time to leave,' he said.

**

They stood under the arches of the Khalvat-i Karim-khani. The sky was a dull blue startled by a flare of peach hovering just above the palace gates. Abimelech, unable to look at Kamran, fixed his gaze on the twisted marble column behind him. The resplendent mix of jade and viridian polygonic tiles was a familiar one. 'You are either the most foolish slave I know, or the smartest,' Kamran said finally, as the dazzling peach burst forth. Abimelech said nothing, but the shapes behind Kamran's head began to swim and blur together. Kamran continued, 'That was very dangerous.'

'Why did you protect me, Hazrat-e Aghdass-e Vaalaa?'

'It was the honourable thing to do.'

'But the note you sent me...'

'We are not allies anymore, Abimelech. I do not trust you. Today does not change anything.'

'Then why not remain silent?'

'I was falsely accused.'

'You were protecting your honour.'

Kamran looked at him. 'I was certain the perpetrator was in the room. I was happy to hold him accountable.'

'Thank you, Hazrat-e Aghdass-e Vaalaa.'

'You are on your own, eunuch.'

'I understand.'

'You understand?' Kamran snapped. 'Well, I do not. You betrayed me, and why? Out of bitterness? Greed?'

Abimelech paused, trying to halt the frown that was stretching over his face. 'The decision felt too big to fall upon my shoulders. I did not want to make the wrong choice. I abstained.'

'You thought Mozaffar should rule?'

'I did not say that.'

'It is what would happen if you kept silent, and you knew it.'

'I also knew what the Shāh had told me of his wife whose quarters we used to talk in – Jayran.'

Kamran's eyes flickered. 'He never talks about her. He has never told us anything.'

'She died because he broke the rules.'

'He thinks she was murdered?'

'He asserts it.'

Kamran's brow was furrowed, but he said nothing. Abimelech watched him in nervous silence. Hostility quivered in the air. 'I am not a fool, Abimelech. You are very smart, but I am no fool. You chose your ambition. I could not promise you the role you wanted, so you relinquished your support.' He sighed, his eyes narrowing. 'I am not sure which is more disappointing – your ambition or your lies. Maybe it is your naivety. You would not have started in such a position, but Abimelech, you knew I held you in high regard. You knew there would be a place for you, and you would have become an advisor in the end.'

'I was just supposed to wait, was I?' Abimelech called to Kamran's retreating back.

'Yes.'

'Have you ever lived your life based on somebody's whim?'

Kamran stopped. 'I am a prince. You are a slave. That is not my fault, nor my responsibility. I cannot make your life a fairer one, or a better one, for that matter.'

'Can you not?'

The words drifted on the air. They looked at each other.

'Not anymore.' Kamran walked away.

45

She was sitting in a teashop in the bāzār, waiting for Shapur to arrive. Unless she was running an errand for Chehra, she usually made sure she was wearing a niqāb. Today, however, she felt indifferent. She had stepped out – marched out even – wearing her niqāb, but now, seated in this quiet teashop in a discreet part of the timcheh, she unhooked the veil covering her face and placed it on her lap. She stretched her fingers and pressed them against her tea glass. She wanted to feel the pain of the heat swell against her skin. She held her fingers there, waiting for the weals to form. She lifted her hands and looked at them. The welts were visible for a moment before disappearing.

She tried to forget her earlier meeting and imagine instead what Shapur had been up to. Another demonstration, at least, or something more subtle. She was hoping for the latter. She was hoping to join. She welcomed an opportunity to do something unthinkable – break into a government office and steal Qājār secrets. She was no longer fearful of getting caught, in fact, part of her longed for it. The last time a man would touch her without her consent would be to arrest her for treason against the Shāh. She would be shackled and then shot or dragged to the gallows and then hanged. She might be remembered, only for a moment, in the minds of the Persians as an errant African slave, but perhaps amongst her own people, her fellow slaves, other radicals, her sacrifice would mean more: a revolt against futility, a rejection of the eventuality that was supposed to be her life. Despite her best efforts to hold on to this fleeting fantasy of defiance, her mind kept returning to the discussion she had

had with Chehra earlier that day before she had marched out of the palace.

Chehra, who had taken to wandering when she rose before dawn, had entered the slaves' room and asked Jamīla to accompany her to her own. The walk across had been strained; Chehra's voice was cheery yet brisk. She had asked Jamīla questions, as though the latter were a stranger she was entertaining for the day. *Did Jamīla have plans for tomorrow? The new mosque in the bāzār had been completed – had she seen it?* Jamīla tried to conjure answers that might suit this line of questioning, but she could not match Chehra's careless breathy tone. She felt anxious; she suspected Chehra might have found out about her plans to visit Shapur. With the door closed behind them, Chehra instructed Jamīla to sit down. Jamīla sat on the bed, noting how clean the room now was.

'I am to marry the physician!' Chehra burst out and clapped her hands together. Jamīla felt a dull sense of dread. 'The move will not happen for a few weeks, but I thought you should know that you will not be following me. I will be taking Gul and Laleh instead.'

'Not unlike Sanaa advised. An older slave to teach the younger. I understand.'

'No,' Chehra interrupted, her voice hard. 'You do not understand. I did not want you to accompany me. This has little to do with Sanaa or Laleh and Gul. Your service as a slave has been poor. You have been shoddy: neglecting your duties to chase after a prince when you were not at court to be a concubine – you were here to be my slave. You have been disobedient: domestics have caught you stealing food from the kitchen; the chief eunuch saw you leaving here at night. You have been treacherous: you encouraged me to meet with radicals at a time when the Shāh's life is at risk. You are rebellious and dangerous. I cannot risk angering my future husband by bringing him an arrogant slave.'

Jamīla did not speak.

'I suggest you speak to Sanaa about finding a new wife to serve.'

'Yes, Shahzadeh Khaanoum.'

'I think it would be prudent for you to move out of this apartment. There is more than enough room in the harem to house an additional slave, and Laleh needs to acquaint herself with your duties.'

'I could teach her.' Jamīla could not recognise her own voice, desperate, dry and pleading.

'No. You would probably corrupt her. Gul will teach her.' Chehra rose. 'Please return to your room.'

Jamīla was still caught in her thoughts when Shapur arrived, the appearance of his gleaming black turban jerking her out of her reverie. There was a faint, polite smile on his face as he took a seat, slowly. He looked different. He eschewed his usual discreet greeting. Instead his eyes fixed on hers for a moment, without blinking.

Then he began. 'I was surprised when the gatekeeper gave me your note,' He paused. 'Is something wrong, Jamīla?'

'We shall be forgotten,' she said, staring up at him with empty eyes.

He leaned closer to her, darting a quick glance around the quiet tearoom. 'What has happened?'

'Everything has happened…and nothing at all.'

He gritted his teeth for a moment, then relaxed his jaw. Adopting a softer tone, he said, 'Jamīla?'

'My mistress, Chehra Khaanoum, is leaving the court.'

'You are leaving?'

'No. I am being left behind. She does not want me to follow

her.' She stared into her glass. She could not put her thoughts into words Shapur would understand. She sipped her tea.

'You did not want to follow her.'

'No.'

'But you wanted to be wanted.'

'I...wanted—' She stopped and shook her head. 'It cannot be explained.'

Shapur watched her without speaking.

'There are no words...Everything is finished.'

'What do you want, Jamīla?'

'I want...' She sat up straight. 'Give me an assignment. Make it dangerous. That is what I want.'

Shapur's expression changed. For a moment, there was a dark flicker of amusement. He looked around the tearoom once more. 'Your enthusiasm is noted,' he replied. 'There is a plan in motion.'

She glanced down at her tea glass waiting for him to continue. He did not.

In the silence that followed, she returned to her former daydream and envisioned herself being dragged towards the gallows. Her legs refused to either walk or buckle, and she was pulled along, her skin scraping against the concrete. It was a public execution, and people gathered in a local square, raising arms, shaking fists. They hurled epithets and ethnic slurs. She soaked in it; she shared their rage. At the centre of the crowd stood a tall, brown man with an angular face but the soft chin of a boy. He wasn't moving, neither shouting nor sobbing. He watched with an almost neutral curiosity as she was led to the stoop, a noose pressed snugly to her throat. Abimelech's was the last face she saw, and when they pulled the trapdoor open, she felt certain that he had smiled.

Taking a deep breath, Jamīla looked back up at Shapur. 'What is the plan?'

'You cannot be part of it, Jamīla.'

Jamīla smiled, trying to keep her voice calm. 'Why not? I am keen, I am available...'

'Zainab Pasha recruited you to retrieve some information from the palace, did she not?'

'Yes...'

'I understand that you failed to complete this request.'

'Well I-'

'You delivered something immaterial and you were caught by the chief eunuch and your mistress, to whom you confessed something of your activities whilst under duress. Is this correct?'

Jamīla felt her face grow warm. She closed her eyes for a moment. 'Sanaa gave me the impression you would want to hear from me.'

'I would say Sanaa was mistaken but she rarely is. I have wanted to address your disruptive and arrogant ineptitude for some time. I am able, in most cases, to put my personal feelings aside for the sake of the movement. In this case however, I cannot as it endangers our very existence. Why are you seeking details of our plans? *What is your agenda?*'

'I am following Sanaa's instruction –'

'Sanaa, like myself, has no use for you. You are indiscreet. You have been caught once already. Even if you were sincere, you would be a liability.' He rose from his seat.

Jamīla felt too stunned to speak. Before she could gather her thoughts, he was gone.

She returned, deflated, to Chehra's rooms to find Gul standing at the entrance. It took Jamīla a moment to realise Gul was not letting her in. Gul stared at her, her face a mixture of frustration and pity. Jamīla didn't move. She had no interest in making this easy for Gul. If Gul was to ban her from entering the apartment, then Jamīla would compel her to say it aloud. They stood in this stalemate for what felt like an hour. Finally, Gul, her hand over her face, began to sob. 'Oh, Jamīla. What did you do?'

Jamīla struggled to remain defiant as Gul broke down. 'Gul,' she sighed. 'What have I ever done?'

Gul glared at her, snapping through her tears, 'Take responsibility, Jamīla! You are *always* doing something. Never what is expected. You are a slave. You have a mistress. All you should be doing is making her happy and remaining invisible.'

'And if I find that unsatisfactory?'

'We do not get to be satisfied. For all your rebellions, are you satisfied now?'

Jamīla tried to speak but kept stammering.

'You cannot collect your things. Chehra Khaanoum insisted. You are to sleep with the domestics in the harem until you can find a new mistress.'

'I have...gifts from Prince Nosrat.'

'Chehra Khaanoum is keeping them.'

'She cannot!'

'What did you expect?'

'I will tell Prince Nosrat.'

'Do not do that!' Gul snapped.

'Why not?'

'If you tell the prince and he complains to the Shāh, he might call the wedding off.'

'Good!'

Gul shook her head. 'Do you know an 'aqdi wife died years ago, murdered by other women in the harem? The Shāh's cat was killed when he was deemed to have shown it more affection than his wives. Do you think that if you anger Chehra Khaanoum and thwart her plans you will not face punishment? This is a wrathful place, Jamīla, and whilst I might not carry out an order to take your life, there are *hundreds* of slaves in this palace. Do you not think one of them would?'

Jamīla laughed, a broken, hollow sound.

'Go to Abimelech.'

'You just told me not to seek help from the Qājārs.'

Gul ignored her. 'He has a room next to the prince's. I can delay telling the chief eunuch of your dismissal, and perhaps you can stay there whilst he helps you find another mistress.'

Jamīla felt too numb to thank her. She walked towards the kalwat, unable to shake the suspicion that with each step she took she was melting away.

<u>46</u>

He stood watching the waters from under an alcove. He appeared oblivious to how the shimmering stillness refracted the light – his gaze transcended that which the eye could see. She wondered why hovering here gave him so much peace. It had never occurred to her to ask. She tapped him on the shoulder, and he nodded; he knew she had been standing there for some time. 'The Shāh is at the cemetery. He prefers to go alone,' he said. His tone was cool, but he was justifying his apparent idleness. Jamīla, who made a habit of trying to cultivate idleness, frowned but said nothing.

'You received my note?'

'Yes. You have caused yourself some trouble.'

'I?' she faltered. 'Well...Gul suggested you might let me sleep in your quarters, since I have nowhere to stay.' Jamīla added, 'She thought you might speak to the chief eunuch on my behalf.'

'You cannot stay in the harem?'

'No...the chief eunuch said they have no need for an additional slave. He offered to help me be resold.'

Abimelech scoffed. 'Nobody would trust a slave who leaves the Qājār court.'

'I know that. I need your help, Abimelech.'

'My position is precarious. I am unsure that I can be of much use.'

Jamīla looked at his handsome clothes. 'You could speak to the chief eunuch.'

'If I spoke to him, you would be out this evening.'

Jamīla frowned.

'He loathes me.'

'Right.' Jamīla sighed. 'Allow me to stay in your room for a few nights. I need time to form a plan.'

'A plan?' Abimelech's laugh was bleak. 'A plan? What plan has ever worked but giving them what they want?'

'What who wants?'

Abimelech did not reply. 'You cannot stay in my room, Jamīla–'

'Wonderful.'

'It was set on fire.'

'What?'

'Do you recall I said my place here is precarious?'

'Are you saying you cannot help me?' she demanded, stung.

Abimelech did not reply.

'Worry not – not that you are worried. I shall ask Sanaa–'

Abimelech spluttered. 'Ask Sanaa? Ask Sanaa?'

'Well I am out of options! I even tried to ask Shapur...'

'You returned to your radical cohort? Jamīla...?'

She bristled at his evident disdain. 'It was Sanaa's suggestion.'

'How unsurprising. I trust it proved useful?'

Jamīla could not speak.

'Why do you keep trusting her?'

'Why?' Jamīla frowned, 'She helped Chehra leave the court. With a husband. She has been helpful.'

'To you?'

'Yes!'

'Chehra is leaving court without you. Presumably the radical Sanaa recommended has no use for you?' Jamīla tried to interrupt but Abimelech continued. 'Be smart, Jamīla. Be smarter. Take Sanaa, she who slips through life unscathed. Her help could grant you a handful of days. Her treason would grant you a lifetime.'

'You expect me to betray Sanaa to the court? Have her executed in exchange for somewhere to sleep?'

'Do you think she held you back at court to keep you safe and well?'

'That was Chehra's choice!'

'And this Shapur...?'

Jamīla shook her head. 'He... he disagrees with her. He does not trust me.' She faltered. She could not tell Abimelech why.

'Jamīla, this is not hard. Chehra and the mullah distrusting you is unlikely to be an accident. You are who Sanaa will sacrifice. She must be worried. And you are more vulnerable than you realise. It would be wise to use her first.'

'This would not be mere "using",' Jamīla insisted. She could not take his accusations seriously. The bitterness in his voice was laden with bias. But she felt a prick of discomfort... The fantasy of a defiant death swam like a nightmare to the front of her mind.

Abimelech rolled his eyes. 'If you cannot use Sanaa, pick a different name. You should at least try to protect yourself. How many were in those meetings? Name three or five, suggest you overheard something about a plot. Tell the chief eunuch, then having proved yourself valuable, he might reconsider.'

'You are asking me to betray people, put their lives at risk, for a possibility?'

Abimelech walked away. 'Everyone is betrayed in the end.'

47

Jamīla spent an uneasy hour staring into the pool, at the crimson daisy-and-diamond tiles, trying to decide what to do next, when the chief eunuch himself happened to walk across the garden. Chasing after him, she recalled the time he had punched her repeatedly in the face. He turned to her, a smile playing on his lips. She wondered if he was reliving the same moment.

'Jamīla – I have somewhere important to be.'

'You need to listen.' She kept her voice neutral as his eyes widened. 'I have information.'

She had struggled with her list of names. *How does one select who to single out for untold punishment?*

She could not decide who to list. Not Shapur, which would surely prove his point. Not Sanaa, even as Abimelech's sober 'sacrifice' pronouncement ran through her mind. Not those she admired, Zainab Pasha or the women she had spied for. She also had to be prudent – suppose they were questioned and revealed the extent of her efforts and involvement? But then, how was she to select people? She would have changed her mind about choosing any at all had the chief eunuch not been seated opposite her, staring at her hard. In that moment, she was a loyal slave revealing a dark faction of court and society. If she kept silent, he would beat her until she spoke and treat her like all the others for trying to protect them.

Whom could she choose? *Who was safe?* Noblemen, mullahs? Religious men publicly condemning the Shāh was not an uncommon practice. They might not be punished at all. Royal wives? Their slaves? She could not imagine women being executed. Slaves would just be expelled.

The chief eunuch watched her closely as she scribbled down the names she could remember. She thought back to that first night, to the first time she saw Zainab Pasha, who stood proud as she gave a speech, sneering at 'a Qājār who bows to a purse'. Jamīla had called it a farce. Full of self-righteousness, she had seen through them. And now she was here. Bowing.

He made her sit in his office and locked the door. He didn't return until the following afternoon, when he slapped her awake, pulled her up from the cushion she was curled on and dragged her to the ḵalwat. He pushed her against the wall, a hand slipping onto her breast. He jerked his hand away, wincing in disgust before pushing her again, this time in the stomach, and stepping past her into an anonymous room.

'Senior people in the ḵalwat need to hear this,' he hissed when she demanded to know what was happening. It didn't explain, of course, why he had to twist her arm. She stood outside, rubbing her wrist.

As Jamīla listened to the chief eunuch sneer about her in the room, she wondered if he knew how thin the walls were.

'Did her information prove useful?' a voice she did not recognise asked.

'Perhaps,' came the snappish tones of the chief eunuch. Jamīla strained to hear as he dropped his voice. 'We have rounded up the Abyssinian slaves in..., from...They are being questioned. A few people are...She mentioned some wives too. I have to think about who could question them. Fatali, perhaps? They like Fatali.'

'No!' a heavy voice, slow and commanding, interrupted. 'You cannot investigate the Shāh's wives. If the information is faulty, you will be killed for treason.'

'Yes, but...'

'What did this girl want anyway?' the first voice enquired.

The chief eunuch chuckled. 'Not what I expected.'

'Oh? Not a house, maids, an allowance?' the first voice sneered. 'She does not wish to be a sigheh of the Shāh?'

'She asked for a room.'

'A room?' the heavy voice repeated.

'She did not ask for freedom?'

'Yes, a single room, writing paper and,' Jamīla heard the clattering of items; she told herself the chief eunuch had emptied his pockets, 'a list of books.'

'These are not Persian writers,' the heavy voice cautioned.

'The authors are as violent as Persian kings!' the chief eunuch said, chuckling.

'Imran!' the first voice snapped. 'Let me not catch your tongue so loose again.'

There was a silence. Jamīla tried to imagine the chief eunuch's face. *Was he bowing? Was he nodding?*

'What else did she want?' the first voice asked.

'An allowance.'

'Of course.' The heavy voice sighed.

'Her request is small.'

'She is a slave – she does not know how much money there is.' The first voice sounded dismissive. 'How long is the list?'

'I counted 40 names.'

'40 names? Within Tehran?' the first voice yelped.

'There were more. These are just the names we did not collect last night. Many are slaves.'

'Do not count the wives,' the heavy one instructed. Jamīla heard a scraping sound. Was someone pushing back a chair?

'I had not – but there are other nobles.'

'Men?' the first voice asked.

'Mullahs.'

'Find them,' the heavy voice ordered.

The door opened. Jamīla jumped back, but only the chief eunuch exited the room.

'What will happen to them?' Jamīla asked as he led her back to the harem and locked her once more in his office. The chief eunuch left without replying, and she could not decide whether or not he had heard her question.

What will happen to them?

She stared in silence at the locked door.

She tried taking a deep breath.

What will happen to them?

'They will not kill so many slaves!' Sanaa's voice, contemptuous and confident, pierced her inner self-dialogue.

They will be expelled from the court. All of them, banished from their home.

Is that all?

Is that not enough? It would have been her fate.

Should it be theirs?

They will be fine.

Assuming that is all. Is that all?

The voice grew louder in her head, demanding to escape. *What else will happen to them?*

Nothing else. They have not done anything.

They have gathered, grumbled and disagreed. These are not crimes. These are not real crimes. They shall not face extreme penalties.

They will be expelled from the court.

Is that all?

That is all.

***

'I am going to do you a favour,' the chief eunuch said when he returned. 'Sit there and say nothing.'

Jamīla had not eaten since the previous afternoon. She sat, trying not to fall asleep, wondering whether she should ask for more money. She thought about Shapur. *What would he say?* He would hear that they had rounded up his friends. Would he know who was behind it? Would he guess? She could not face him again. She could never see any of them, ever again. He had called the act of tutoring her 'futile, dangerous and self-indulgent', and she had not proved him wrong.

She put her face in her hands. What had she done? What had she done?

The chief eunuch pulled a chair from a far wall and placed it behind a spotless bureau. He tugged at one of the drawers and withdrew a qalam and some paper and began writing. Jamīla watched as he crumpled many of these papers and threw them onto the floor.

'This is not easy,' he hissed and threw one of the papers at her. It didn't fly, but she crawled off the cushion to pick it up. She stretched it out and read the heading, surprised to see her own name included.

'What is this?'

'Wait,' he snapped, looking over the paper in his hand. He blew on the ink and sighed. He walked over to her, snatched the crumpled page and handed her the new one. 'Be careful,' he insisted.

She glanced at it. It said the same things as the previous one, although she counted fewer splotches and spelling errors. She still didn't understand. 'This is an official document...with my name on it. What – Why? You have to explain.'

The chief eunuch looked at her face, a sneer resuming its place on his own. 'Chehra used to call you intelligent. But then, what would she know?' He leaned closer and snickered into her face and then stepped back. 'Listen. The men I spoke to – they want this to disappear. They are going to find the names you mentioned and search for any others. They will also want you to disappear – you were with these people, after all. You say you attended one meeting with your mistress. For them, that is one meeting too many. Without this document, they will kill you, and I cannot stop them.'

Jamīla stared at him. 'You are trying to *save* me?' *Does this mean they will kill the others?*

They will not die, Jamīla. You chose carefully. They will be fine.

The chief eunuch frowned. 'I am trying to save the court. You have done a good thing. You have revealed a dangerous faction of rebels operating within and beyond the palace. If you are killed for that, then nobody will speak out in the face of treason. We cannot reward loyalty with disloyalty. I do this for the good of the court.'

Jamīla nodded. 'Fine. This paper?'

'This is how.'

'It is a contract.'

'Yes. I will give this to one of the court lawyers. He will make amends, I am sure, but then I will produce copies, deliver them to the men I mentioned and have them sign it. It enshrines all your requests and thus ensures they will honour your life.'

'They will obey the contract?'

The chief eunuch shrugged. 'They would not be punished if they did not – you are just a slave. However, it would be a hassle. There might be a little trouble, and it is just simpler for them to adhere. All you want is a room, some books and some money

– you are not inconveniencing them.'

Jamīla's eyes were fearful.

'They may not have killed you otherwise. This just makes it much less likely.'

48

The chief eunuch told her to be discreet. He would deliver her monthly allowance to her room; she was discouraged from entering the harem. She would buy her own food and cook it in one of the disused pantries. Late at night, nobody noticed if she used one of the old libraries, ignored by most of the court. She would wake to the smell of wildflowers rising below her window. She didn't know all their names yet, but she could feel their scent rushing through her nose, pressed against her throat. She would wander over to the open window and stare out into the garden. May had arrived, and the tulips were in full bloom. Their vivid crimson reminded Jamīla of Chehra Khaanoum's blood orange-stained room. She looked up at the cerulean sky, where hesitant clouds were starting to form. Perhaps this was what it meant to be carefree. She closed her eyes and smiled.

It was not until the floorboard creaked beside her bed that she realised somebody else was in the room. She snapped round and saw none other than Sanaa, her mouth pinched, her eyes brimming with disdain. She stared so pointedly around the room that Jamīla could read her thoughts. She took it in: a ceiling so high she had to tilt her neck up at it; an ornate chandelier hanging long and low; shimmering curtains that fell to the ground, pushed to one side, allowing the burning light of a vibrant sun to thrust the mirror work into sharp relief.

'You disappeared,' Sanaa said, the corners of her mouth twitching. Jamīla did not answer. 'I thought...perhaps you had left the court. Now, I wonder, have you become a concubine?'

Silence.

'I would know, were there a new concubine. So when I find you sequestered in so palatial a room, *outside* of the harem, I think, how did she attain such luxury and why has she chosen to hide?'

Silence.

'Shapur was arrested with some of his men. Some of our men, from the movement.' Her voice sounded further away when she added, 'They will be executed tomorrow.'

Jamīla's eyes flew open. Sanaa was not even looking at her, she was walking towards the door. 'I have been summoned for questioning.' As she placed her hand on the door, she turned back to Jamīla. 'You have a really beautiful place here,' and she smiled her brilliant smile, flooding the room with inescapable light.

49

It wasn't until the screams that Abimelech began to suspect that something had gone very wrong. The Shāh had been visiting the shrine of Shāh-Abdol-Azim; when he returned, they would prepare the celebrations for his golden jubilee. He insisted on going alone; Abimelech had been ordered to wait in his office. It was becoming a common occurrence. Despite their continued talks, late into the night, the Shāh was seen out with Abimelech less and less often. Abimelech knew things had changed since he accused Kamran, even with the prince speaking to the Shāh on his behalf.

Abimelech never felt appropriate sitting in the Shāh's private offices, and he stood now behind the desk, flicking through a volume of the Shāh's own poetry, his eyes returning to the more morose. He paused at the sound of the screams, and, placing the book down, began to walk to the door. It burst open before him, and a crowd of men all but rushed in, speaking at once. A number of voices shouted words at him, turned to each other and pulled items off the desk. Abimelech did not know what to do. He stood, confused, as people rushed past him, collecting things and hurrying out. Nobody was interested in answering his questions.

He hurried out after them, but they were already gone, running towards the Divan Khana. To Abimelech, the palace began to resemble the bāzār; men and women were rushing in all directions, screaming at the top of their lungs. Abimelech had never seen women at court outside of the harem, but today, sigheh wives joined slaves and entertainers rushing to exit the palace, screaming as they went. Abimelech, trying to follow a small group of running eunuchs, was buffeted by a slew of armed men in military uniform. He was thrown to the ground, and as he struggled to his feet, he caught sight of Kamran Mirza looking harried. He ran past, followed by another troop of men, one of whom shouted an order to seal the harem. Abimelech hurried into the Divan Khana. Men were rushing out of offices; he bumped into Fatali. 'Have you seen Mozaffar Mirza?' the latter asked him.

'No, I...' Abimelech didn't finish his sentence; Fatali appeared to be crying. The latter nodded and hurried away, a cluster of slaves behind him. People continued to speed past, running in all directions. The soldiers were dispersed, some leaving the palace, others rushing into it, securing different buildings. Abimelech grabbed the first person who moved slowly past him. It was a British advisor, his face flushed with wonder. He looked askance at Abimelech's hand. 'My apologies, Lord...'

'Mister Sheringham. Second son, so not a lord,' he said with a grimace.

'Please, Mr. Sheringham, what has happened?'

'You cannot be serious?' Sheringham shook his head in wonder. 'You Africans are inept! Your shāh has been shot, boy. He is dead.'

'Dead?'

'Yes! Very dead. There are soldiers going to collect him now. Let me tell you something,' he pulled Abimelech close, his voice jolly, 'I did not want this posting at first. Not at all. Nobody wants to come to Persia and wrangle with the Russians! The boys at home said it would be frightfully dull. I would not see a moment of action! They mocked me and the daily telegrams I would send. But *did* I! There have been marches and protests. It has been marvellous fun. But they were right, of course. I missed the most exciting moment of all. Now I have to send a telegram to the British government. But I have nothing to say! Do you think you could find me some information, boy? So I have something to tell them? I could give you some money. I know your kind is not to expect it, but it can be our little secret.' He took something of a step back and looked more thoroughly at Abimelech. His eyes lingered on Abimelech's mouth before he straightened up. 'Visit me this evening, in my chambers,' he said, with a pointed smile. He began to give Abimelech directions, but the latter could not hear him. He nodded until the Briton had finished and stood there for an hour longer, unable to move.

***

He couldn't remember their last conversation. *What were the last things that the Shāh had said?*

He would have been afraid. Abimelech kept thinking of the attack he had witnessed, when the Shāh was almost crushed by his own horse. But he had been with him. They had been together. He didn't know who had accompanied the Shāh to the Shāh-Abdol-Azim. *Was he alone when he was shot? Had he felt alone? Was he with anyone who loved him in his final moments? Was anyone?*

Abimelech stood staring at the scorch marks on the floor of his room.

This is not panic. I do not panic.

He tried to think practically. He had to contemplate his next steps.

And he would. *Without panicking. Except*—

It was the morning after the Shāh's death.

Abimelech was fine.

I am fine, he told the scorch marks on the floor.

He had spent the night in Nosrat's room.

Absolutely fine, he insisted, to the tears that splashed onto the scorched wood.

He had not slept, listening for the men who might come to take him away.

But that, too, was fine.

He was now on his knees. Though not deliberate, that was fine.

He was making *noise.* Also not deliberate and definitely not fine.

He could not make himself stop.

He could not recognise the sound.

An unending sound.

A wordless sound.

An angry sound.

A bitter sound.

A panicked, frightened, desperate sound.

But I do not get frightened, Abimelech insisted, when he was able to rise to his feet. And there were practical things to consider.

***

The prince's room was cleaned out; a sealed letter on the mantelpiece was addressed to his brothers. Abimelech could not fathom how Nosrat had chosen such a tragic day to leave. It occurred to him that Nosrat might have left before the assassination and failed to realise that his father had been killed. On any other day, Abimelech might pity him, but Abimelech was too busy feeling fearful for himself.

He had returned to his own room at dawn and listened out for the domestic who would clean the floors outside. He had pulled the domestic in, given him some coins and insisted he find Abimelech's most trusted eunuch and return him here, speaking to no one else. When the young boy arrived, Abimelech sent him out to find one of the Shāh's European lawyers; he did not trust the Persian ones not to report back to the Grand Vizier and the new shāh. He sought an update on the climate outside, but the eunuch knew nothing. It was chaotic; the killer had been captured at the shrine; Mozaffar Mirza was now the shāh, but he was somewhere out of sight with the Grand Vizier, and nobody could find him. The eunuch returned a second time, before he found the Shāh's lawyer, to warn Abimelech that Kamran's eunuchs were looking for him. They were on their way to his room. Abimelech, trying to breathe, thanked the eunuch and asked him not to return in person but send him a note detailing his progress.

Abimelech jumped as his door was flung open. Adult men with thick necks and broad chests crowded against the frame. He slid off the bed and took a careful step back, wondering whether it would be his last. He thought for a moment of everything he had wanted to say but hadn't - to the Shāh, to Jamīla, to his siblings. His eyes were wet. One of the men stepped forward, and Abimelech willed himself to be brave, but he couldn't stop backing away, moving further towards the window.

The man watched him shrink away and snickered. 'Kamran Mirza has summoned you to his office. You can walk but, if necessary, we can drag you.'

Abimelech was not dragged, but he was walked. Each of the men held on to his arms and led him from the ḳalwat to the Divan Khana. They had chosen the most visible route, for Abimelech encountered almost everyone he knew. Eunuchs, slaves and playmates of the princes all gathered and gawped as he was marched like a traitor through the palace. He was deposited in Kamran's office, a room he had, until that point, yet to enter. The man himself sat in a stiff chair behind a small desk. He looked as confident and comfortable as he ever did, although dark shadows ringed his reddened eyes, the lone evidence that it might have been a difficult few days.

Kamran gestured to the men, and they left the room. Abimelech bowed his head and then shook it. When he rose, his face was marred with the effort of holding back his tears. 'My sincere condolences, Hazrat-e Aghdass-e Vaalaa.'

The prince nodded. 'I appreciate that you loved him too. You must be grieving.'

'Yes!' Abimelech said with a burst of relief.

'Nevertheless, you have a day to leave the palace for good.'

'A day?'

'Yes.'

'Can I see him first?'

'Father?'

Abimelech nodded.

'He has been moved to the Tekyeh Dowlat.'

'Can I...'

Kamran's expression flickered for a moment. 'No. You must leave at once.'

'Please, Hazrat-e Aghdass-e Vaalaa, please! I have no documentation. I would be deemed an errant slave and resold.'

Kamran was unfazed. 'This is where disloyalty leaves you.'

'Please—'

'It may even be safer for you, if you are resold. I cannot say when the Grand Vizier's men will come for you, but I can promise you they shall.'

Abimelech straightened up. 'The Shāh had left me some... property. If I were to go there, could I trust I would be undisturbed?'

Kamran looked unconcerned. 'The Grand Vizier has already been through his finances. Father did not have the funds to grant you anything – and if he had, the Grand Vizier would know of it now, and you would not last there either.'

'Wh-wh...' Abimelech was gibbering.

'He probably assumed he had more time.' Kamran leaned back in his chair. 'You can leave now, Abimelech.'

As Abimelech walked to the door, Kamran called out to him once more. He didn't turn, but stood and waited.

'He has been placed in the Tekyeh Dowlat,' Kamran repeated, 'but he won't be there for too long. He will be buried beside Jayran...moved to the Shāh-Abdol-Azim. I thought you would like to know, should you one day choose to visit.'

As Abimelech left, it occurred to him that it might be less dangerous for him to be surrounded with people. He sought his army of eunuchs and had them accompany him to his appointment with the Shāh's European lawyer. The eunuchs waited outside as the lawyer, with horn-rimmed spectacles and a thin smile, informed Abimelech that not only had the Shāh failed to make any provisions for him, he had not intimated at any point that he intended to. He asked, speaking very slowly, where Abimelech might have heard this information, and when Abimelech told him it was from the Shāh himself, his eyebrows flew into his greying hair and his nostrils fluttered. 'I can only repeat what I have told you,' he said in his slow voice. Abimelech left and tried to reassure his eunuchs, who were staring into his fearful face.

'Can you ask anyone from the British consulate?' one of them asked, and Abimelech felt ashamed that they could see how desperate his situation had become.

The British diplomat seated opposite Abimelech had a voice so clipped and brisk it was difficult to understand. He spoke Farsi but with a heavy English accent, and Abimelech, his patience dulled by a creeping sense of foreboding, struggled to sit through it. 'I understand that you were a very prominent figure in the former shāh's court. The problem we have is two-fold: you are a slave of the court, not an independent man, and as such, you are beholden to their orders. You could hypothetically be freed, but that could also leave you in a vulnerable position. The other problem is your unpopularity. If you had come to us whilst the Shāh was still alive, we might have been able to assist. A eunuch is only as powerful as his master. Your master is dead, and you are...ah...resented by the new shāh, his brothers and the Grand Vizier. We understand that the fourth son has left for Paris – rather...ah...unorthodox timing for a European jaunt – and his absence in particular leaves you without hope of patronage. I would consult with the Shāh's lawyers. Given your closeness to him, it seems he might have left you some estates to reside in. For your own safety, I would suggest you sell such estates and leave Tehran. If you decide you wish to be freed, then you could become a wealthy landowner. Provided you exercise discretion...'

Abimelech stopped listening.

50

He did not own a travelling bag. He had never thought he would need one; even if he had suspected, he could not have asked. It was through the offhand gestures of Nosrat and the Shāh that he had acquired all that he owned. They had treated him not unlike a vacuum, a void that would absorb those things they no longer needed, be it scarves or frock coats, rooms or rubies. Carelessness passing as generosity. He entered Nosrat's room, to see if he might have left one, wondering if there was anything else he could take along with him. The letter still sat atop the mantelpiece, addressed to Nosrat's brothers. Abimelech fingered the letter with disbelief. Not a word for Sanaa, Jamīla or himself. Not a whisper for him. They were so similar, those men, he snickered with disdain. Wealth made them forgetful, indifferent, vengeful – from this distance, those different attitudes looked exactly the same.

He thought back to the years he had spent cradling Nosrat's head as the latter insisted that he cuddle him in bed. Nosrat cried often and easily, and Abimelech had played every role required of him – lover, comforter, mother. He thought back to those hours with the Shāh, nervous whispers at daybreak, doleful confessions at dark. He sighed. There was nothing in Nosrat's room.

He returned to his own. One of his eunuchs had been and gone, for there was a travelling bag, some cloth, some string, accompanied by a note. Abimelech couldn't bring himself to look at it. Words from the wrong person. He propped it on the mantelpiece, in the same spot that Nosrat's sat, in the other room.

He wanted to take the letter Nosrat had left for his brothers. He wondered if Nosrat knew how much they mocked him in his absence; he wondered if Nosrat knew they would never care that he had left. Abimelech gritted his teeth. The words flickered like a nightmare, printed on his lids. *Could he live this life once more and innumerable times?*

He sat amongst his scant possessions as another of his eunuchs entered.

'You cannot leave,' the boy squeaked as he blinked his wide eyes at Abimelech.

'It would not have been my choice.'

'What will happen to the rest of us?'

'You? Little will change.'

'This is very selfish of you,' the boy squeaked again, this time bowing as he spoke.

Abimelech frowned. 'I have not chosen to leave.'

'You have not tried to stay—'

'How could I—'

'For us.'

Abimelech wished he was the kind of man who shouted when he was angry. He watched the small eunuch, his dovelike face twisted in fear, and felt something curdle in his stomach. 'Go,' he said.

The boy whimpered.

Abimelech paused for a moment and took a deep breath. 'Take the travelling bag with you.'

He pushed the door closed, ignoring the boy's hopeful gaze. Then he went to the window, opened it, and stared out. He wanted to see the sky, one last time.

51

He would rise with the sun. It was a particular habit of his to wake and watch the dawn and one he grew to relish as they travelled towards the ports. As a child he had loved to watch the clouds unfurl, slow gossamer shadows descending on the saffron sky. His brother had insisted on being woken with him so they might sit and gaze together, but even when he did this, Abimelech considered himself to be alone. In the public markets, he was disabused of that notion. As they travelled between cities, walking in pairs, people chained together, bodies pushed against bodies, the sweat, saliva and waste of strangers was impossible to avoid. On those rare occasions he was walked at the front, without the sunken spirit of another striding before him, he still couldn't pretend to be alone. His shoulders, carrying the merchant's produce, bore the weight of his purpose there, a constant reminder of others and of his life relative to theirs. Once they arrived in the towns, isolation grew ever more remote: the slaves were allowed to roam the markets, and his mysterious magnetism again attracted attention when he hoped to remain unseen. Rising at dawn proved his one reprieve. He held a few unguarded moments where he might dream with his eyes open, watching the sky.

He would pile the crates high, sometimes snatching those from another seller. Then he would climb atop the unsteady mound and envision himself on a mountain. From there, his view was unencumbered: the burnt papaya glow sprawled itself across the fading lilac sky, and Abimelech allowed himself to exhale.

'Am I interrupting?' A voice appeared below him.

Abimelech jerked round, struggling to maintain his balance. The 'alīm, a Muslim scholar who had been travelling with the slaves, was far beneath him and yet already too close. He tried to ignore him, returning his gaze to the sky, but it looked different now. The papaya glow cannibalised the lilac night, the sunrise chasing out the previous day.

Abimelech sighed.

'Perhaps you could come down?' The 'alīm was shouting. It occurred to Abimelech that the 'alīm's voice would soon rouse the others. His mental sojourn was over.

'Do you understand the concept of privacy?' Having climbed down and dismantled the crates, he turned to face the 'alīm.

'I do. I apologise.'

'Do not approach me again.'

'Are you so unused to having a friend?'

'I have no need for friends.'

'Just a master to your slave?'

Abimelech snapped, 'It is not my choice.'

'Perhaps, perhaps not.' The 'alīm looked back at the saffron sky. 'There are masters and then there are masters. Those you obey and those you revere. We are all slaves to something, we all serve something – an idea, a purpose, a person. I serve Islam; I serve Allah. What would you say you serve?'

Abimelech frowned at him. 'Why do you care?'

'I have seen you every morning when you wake. You watch the sky. You meditate before it. Is this an Oromo tradition?'

'No.'

'Well, you should cultivate it, nevertheless. The master you serve – the one you revere, not the one you obey – is what will help you in your life in Persia.'

Abimelech said nothing.

'What did you want for your life?'

People were starting to rise. The merchant and his men were dragging sleepy slaves out into the main square, loading their arms with boxes of goods. The 'alīm was watching for the girl with the bruised face. He and Abimelech had been pacing slowly, but once the 'alīm spotted her, he stopped, and with a theatrical turn, gestured towards her with one hand, imploring her to join them. She moved tiredly, with soft steps, but her eyes were frowning as she spotted the 'alīm. She turned and walked in a different direction, and Abimelech wanted to laugh; he felt sure her expression mirrored his.

'She has suffered,' the 'alīm said to Abimelech in a sombre tone.

'We have all suffered,' Abimelech replied, his tone obstinate. The man's sanctimony irked him for reasons he couldn't explain.

'She is female.'

'Yes.'

'So, whilst life will get better for you, it shan't for her.'

Abimelech thought of Abeba. 'Because she is a slave?'

'Well...' The 'alīm paused. 'There are many reasons. In Persia, there are many Abyssinians. Abyssinian eunuchs find senior positions in noble houses, and their masters provide for them when they die. Female slaves do not have that luxury.'

'The luxury of becoming rich?'

'You may mock me now, but you will be grateful when you arrive.' The 'alīm sighed. 'I asked about the master you revere earlier. I am here to spread Islam, to teach men about the master I revere. The difference between you and the girl is the absence of reverence. She has nothing of value. As long as you continue to seek reverence in...whatever I interrupted, you can transcend the transience of a life in chains. And then, yes, you can become old and rich. Would that really be so bad?' He was laughing now.

Soon they were both laughing, and the girl in question was watching them.

'I wanted to understand the universe.'

The 'alīm looked confused, 'What?'

'You asked, what did I want, before I was enslaved? I wanted to understand the universe. My mother was a devout Christian, a defiant one. She would tell me about her God.' Abimelech took a deep breath. 'P-perhaps, perhaps you can tell me about yours.'

'It is the same God, the same Allah, understood in different ways.' The merchant began calling, shouting for the 'alīm. The market was awakening; all the merchants had arrived and were setting up their stalls. The first few buyers had begun to flock in. The 'alīm turned to look back at Abimelech, but he had turned his glance upwards. A vivid blue had overtaken the saffron, a move so seamless it had passed unnoticed. A heavy drop of honey hung low in the sky, and the 'alīm broke into a smile. 'You have your God – you do not need mine. But the peace you seek you shall not find outside. Not even at dawn. You must learn to conjure it, at all times, in the dark, within yourself.

52

ای هـ.ب دای راد حـ.بان بادپ.ی ام ار

Remember old companions who travel upon the breeze – Hafiz

She was gaunt. Jamīla staggered back as the door burst open and stared at her, stunned. Sanaa, shuddering in oversized clothes that were not her own, hurried past her, gibbering and unsteady on her feet. She nodded as though Jamīla had grasped her previous words.

'I know,' Jamīla said with some irritation. 'I know that he is dead.'

'How...how could you know?'

Jamīla sighed. 'Everybody knows.'

'Why did you not stop him?' Sanaa's voice was menacing.

Jamīla looked confused. 'Stop who?'

'Abimelech!'

'Abimelech killed the Shāh?'

Sanaa stared at her for a moment, her bloodshot eyes filled with pity, and let out a laugh that was at once sharp and hard, like a bark. 'Abimelech killed himself.'

***

The slaves had planted fresh flowers in the garden. They covered the expanse of the green, but the flowerbed she could smell lay under her window. Jamīla had watched the blooms spring forth, slowly at first and then almost overnight. Roses blushed a rich vermillion, nestled beside a shrub of amber chrysanthemums. The white orchids were hidden by the sprawling flower bush; though their dazzling ivory was diminished, their subtle presence belied a powerful scent. Abimelech had thought white orchids smelled like freesias, and they all agreed. At Jamīla's insistence, Gul had made domestic slaves plant them in his memory.

She didn't linger by her window often anymore; months had passed since the Shāh's assassination, but the gardens were still flooded with ambitious men paying their respects and patrolled by military soldiers. She used to stand by the tall windows, mesmerised by how they opened outwards and left almost nothing between her and the world outside. She would step as close to the edge as she dared, the wind pushing the curtains out, shimmering against her limbs to call her back in. It was different now. To watch a swathe of large, anonymous bodies amble around, currying favour, their glances darting askance at the soldiers, was more than Jamīla could bear. She could not watch their oblivious saunter, hear faint echoes of their indulgent laughter. It was still too soon. She would gaze down at the flowers from her vantage point before returning to her chair, her chest pressed against the bureau, her hand trembling as she tried to write. The smell of freesias would inevitably rise up, inhibiting her progress.

Her mind would return to Abimelech. Several months had passed since his death, but the harem was in mourning, two sets of women grieving on parallel lines. The Shāh's wives were despondent; they grieved the loss of their Shāh and the loss of their lives. The new shāh, Mozaffar al-Dīn, had issued a formal expulsion of his father's women, and the harem was emptying day by day. Wives and concubines were made homeless overnight, and the new shāh seemed in no hurry to repopulate the harem. The palace grew quieter. The slaves were floundering. Their mistresses were pushed out whilst they were left behind. The former wives could not afford to take them, and the current shāh made no plans to sell or keep them. Abimelech's death compounded the generalised anxiety in the harem. That the death of the kindest eunuch – who was also arguably the most powerful eunuch, allied to three Qājār men, including the former shāh – was by his own hand led to all kinds of rumours that chilled the palace walls.

It soon became common to see slaves sobbing in the harem. The women who served in the coffeehouse were said to have cried into tea glasses, several female slaves collapsed and eunuchs became morose. Work became sloppy; emotions hitherto repressed were now unguarded. Slaves were not just sad, they were fearful, and the ambience in the harem and the kalwat grew tense. Jamīla did not know how the kalwat resolved it, but Gul had informed her of a women's meeting. The debate had been relentless – *Do we punish the slaves? Do we question them?* Nobody knew how to respond. Yasmin Khaanoum suggested a warning shot, and that was grudgingly accepted. The next slave to grieve was killed; everybody else fell in line. The killed slave was not popular; few even knew his name, but, as Yasmin had predicted, it did not matter; his death had the required effect.

Jamīla kept reliving that cluster of days. On the day of the assassination, she had been in her room, her back pressed against the door. She could hear screams and cries echoing through the palace as people ran from building to building, seeming to enter or exit with no clear agenda. A eunuch had pounded on her door as he marched past. She opened it and called after him, but he did not stop. Another rushing eunuch slowed as he saw her standing. His eyes took in the elegance of the room with a curiosity that could go unfed. He picked up his pace, and Jamīla shouted after him, asking what had happened. He all but skidded to a stop and turned towards her in disbelief. People of all backgrounds ran past at full tilt, forcing Jamīla back into her room and forcing the eunuch to flatten himself against the wall. He told her of the Shāh's assassination; she was unsurprised.

He glanced into the room again, his eyes on the French windows that were flung apart. 'It might have been a coup,' he said, his voice low. 'If you want to live, you would do well to leave this room.' He attempted to take her by the hand and haul her into the hallway. She shook him off, an instinctive yet unexpected response that unsettled them both. He rolled his eyes and hurried off, and she pressed her door closed again.

She could not think of what might happen next, but her mind turned to Abimelech. She wondered what this would mean for him, whether he would be demoted now to a common eunuch from his unspecified role that granted him unfettered power. Sanaa's comments had perturbed her. It seemed absurd that the Shapur and his men had been executed. She had not said anything *definite* about them. She wanted to know from Abimelech whether he had expected such a punishment. She could not help but hold him accountable. This was not her fault; she needed to convey that to him, to everyone. She needed to see Abimelech. Part of her welcomed this regime change. If Abimelech could not count on the Shāh's constant acquiescence, perhaps that might give him pause. He had ignored her messages filled with questions. She suspected he might see her now.

A few days passed like this. Jamīla, fearful of the turmoil, had hidden in the room, eating the remnants of dishes she hadn't removed, growing increasingly nauseous. The hallway outside was silent; whenever she heard footsteps, she would press herself against the door, her eyes closed, little though it would do. It was close to midnight when she felt the handle twist against her back; she felt cold marble on her skin. The handle didn't hesitate. It forcefully continued its clockwise progression until Jamīla stepped away, sickened with fear.

It was Sanaa. Jamīla staggered back.

Sanaa remained. She spoke those words.

As Jamīla sat at her writing desk, she remembered Sanaa's explanation. Without waiting for Jamīla to process the words, she had proceeded to explain that Abimelech had formed a noose in his room, wrapping a piece of silk fabric around his neck.

They had stood apart, isolated in their grief, Jamīla gasping at the window, Sanaa motionless by the door. They entered the new day like this, wholly oblivious but for the sound of the hallway flooded again with people. A eunuch informed them the Shāh's funeral was about to commence, beginning with a public procession.

The following days swept by in a perpetual state of flurry. Prince Nosrat was returned; shortly after paying respects to his father, he left. In the whirl of activity, Jamīla was invisible. Her room was untouched, her presence unnoticed and, beyond brief trips to the bāzār to meet Gul, she remained inside with her books. Abimelech's room had been cleared. His scant property was returned to the ḳalwat or otherwise disappeared. She had tried to visit his room one last time but found the chief eunuch guarding it with enthusiastic zeal.

'Will you help me?' Jamīla had asked Gul as they sat together in a tearoom one late afternoon.

Gul had looked at her with trying eyes. Her voice dropped to a whisper. 'What would you need it for?'

'His address?'

'Shhh.'

The tearoom was almost empty.

'He loved Abimelech.'

Gul's smile was heavy and fleeting. Her face sagged long after the smile left, carrying an oppressive weight. 'As did y–'

'–others?' Jamīla interjected hurriedly, but her eyes were wet. 'Certainly, they did. But do they recall him? He is never talked about anymore. His name is not even breathed.'

'Do you remember Aabir?'

'Hardly.'

'Jamīla, this is just what happens. Slaves are–'

'Please.' Jamīla almost gasped. 'This is why I need Nosrat's address.'

'How can I find it, Jamīla? I do not live at Golestan Palace anymore.'

'You must have friends in the harem! Can you not ask Elaheh Khaanoum?'

'What harem? Jamīla, do not be naive. Elaheh Khaanoum has been expelled. I do not know where she is. I will never see her again. Besides, I cannot visit the palace with ease. I have far fewer girls in Chehra Khaanoum's new house and an abundance of work. I rarely visit the bāzār. It would be impossible–'

'Please,' Jamīla's voice cracked, 'he cannot be forgotten.'

'I understand that,' Gul snapped. 'Jamīla, you still live in the palace. Is there nobody you could ask?'

'I do not...I am kept away from the harem. I...' Gul was staring at her with an impenetrable expression, and the words burst through in a tearful rush. 'You were there when Chehra pushed me out, when I had nowhere to sleep. I did not have a choice. Abimelech gave me a choice. I am not...I am not...proud of my choices, but I gave him information which h-he gave to the chief eunuch.'

'I know what you did, Jamīla. Sanaa told everyone in the harem.'

'How...how...yes, well.' Jamīla sighed.

'You received everything you wanted.' Gul's smile was tight.

'I did not know—!'

'That people would die? Your peers? Abyssinians? Domestics?'

'I did not think—!'

'Do you know what happened? Men came to the harem, armed men. They rounded people up – they dragged slaves from their beds. They were tortured; they talked. Slaves from other noble houses were gathered. You are fortunate, Jamīla. It is of great fortune to you that the Shāh died when he did. People were distracted; people left. Do you know what would have happened, had they not? You would have been found. Not by the Shāh's men. By slaves. You would have been punished for your betrayal.'

Jamīla stared at her in silence.

'What do you actually want, Jamīla? Was this it? To be sequestered in secret quarters in the court, with nobody to talk to, living out an invisible life?'

'You are wondering what this is, Gul?' Jamīla snapped back, but she was trembling. 'This is what desperation looks like. Where were you when Chehra was forcing me out? You were right there, barring the door. You accuse me of selling my peers? Did you support me? Did you tell Chehra you needed me? Did you insist that I join you?'

Gul looked sharply around the tearoom.

Jamīla leaned closer to her, pressing her hand on Gul's. 'A handful of words from you would have saved all of those lives. You are not blameless – neither of us are.'

Gul looked drained. She gazed at their hands, speechless.

'So help me. Find Nosrat's address.'

Gul produced the address at their next meeting. She left immediately after; Jamīla had not seen her since. Jamīla, her skin aflame, returned with haste to her room and brought out the letter.

Each time she looked at it, the smooth, blank sheet so bright with purpose, a surge of duty would suppress the slither of guilt. Yet she would sink too easily into the reservoir of her mind where, unchained from the crush of memories, a single realisation would arise.

Theirs was a moment that had been forgotten by time.

For she had been waiting. Waiting for him to return to her. For him to remember her. To remember himself. The Abimelech who slipped her works of his favourite literature. The Abimelech who made clumsy, wistful plans to leave Tehran together.

It was not their moment yet. Not now. Not while their lives still resembled the refracted needs of others. He had deemed her foolish. Pretended to see a child. It irked her, but she knew the truth. Faint and flickering like the hazy edges of an old unburied dream.

They would have the time.

Their time.

It would be hours before she noticed her hand still hovered over an empty page and many more until the cycle began again.

She would try to approach the task, but the words would fail to form. Her fingers would clench around her qalam as she sought a compulsion to propel her to write. Having thrown all her efforts into finding Nosrat, she froze at the prospect of contact. It was not him to whom she had anything to say. Nor by whom she wanted to be read.

She was to live with the promise that she would forever be unheard.

Shackled to her grief, the sentiment carried rage. Able at last to sift through their shared history, in Nosrat, she found someone she could blame. The impetus to accuse brought the return of her drive. Once more, she sat before the smooth sheet and readied herself to write. Her qalam was shaped like a scorpion's tail; she hoped her words might carry its sting. She would inform him of their tragic loss, recount the legacy of their cherished friend and implore him to return to them, to honour his memory. She looked at the name written across the top: Prince Nosrat al-Din Mirza Salar es-Saltaneh. She wondered how he would receive a letter from her, how he saw their little triad of competing affections and where she sat in his. Would he seek to honour her wishes, or did he see her as she saw him, always somewhere in between herself and Abimelech?

She put the qalam down. She would tell herself, *Perhaps tomorrow.*

The words remain unwritten.

Postscript

In her own words, the real Jamīla Habashī, the inspiration for this novel, recounts her story:

> My name is Jamīla Habashī, my father is Lulā'd-Dīn from Sāho, my mother Loshābah, and from the Omrānīah tribe. I was enslaved when I was a child then was brought to Mecca where I was sold to a broker; the broker took me to Basra from the Jabal, and sold me to an Iranian broker named Mullā 'Alī, who shipped me from Basra to Muhammara and from there he took me to the Bushihr port and there he sold me to a merchant called Hājī Mīrzā Ahmad Kázirunī who is in Shīrāz now, I was his concubine for four years in Bushihr then Hājī took me to Shīrāz and kept me there for five years; in total, I was with him for nine years and then he sold me to Nasir Nizām the son of 'Atāu'llāh. After one year, Nasír sold me to Hājī Muhammad 'Alī Khān. Now it has been five years that I have been with him.'

The letter, dated 1905, is the only existing first-person account of an African slave in Iran, written in their own hand.

Acknowledgments

This limited space and my limited words could not come close to reflecting the extent of my gratitude. *In the Palace of Flowers* has been a long labour of love. No novel is a solo effort and this was no different.

To Anna, for seeing the potential in me – thank you for not giving up and reaching out a second time! I'm enamoured with the boldness of your vision. To Maria, for having the patience to endure the intensity of who I am. For being in the trenches with me. Ellie, too, for understanding me! Agents are kept in the shadows of literary careers and yet said careers cease to exist without them.

Bibi, my North Star, you are everything I could have ever wanted in a publisher, a mentor and a friend. You remain an ideal to strive towards. I'm always humbled to be in your presence. *In the Palace of Flowers* flourished under your guidance. As did I! To my editor, Layla, your mastery, your deft yet delicate touch cannot be quantified. Emma, thank you for your warmth and open-heartedness, for being a strong advocate for the book.

Max Millard, my trusted first reader; you'll never know how far your words propelled me. To the readers: the two JKs, Chris K, Alex B and more. James, your efforts deserve a second mention. To Sunny, for the assistance.

Alex Bryant, Selena Wisnom, James Harding and Catherine Menon – you inspired me with your preternatural talent.

Pedram Khosronejad.

Without your visual scholarship these lives would have been forgotten. Thank you for everything.

To Anthony A. Lee: I still marvel at your generosity.

And finally,
To the late great Oscar Pearce-Higgins who couldn't let a conversation slip without asserting that I must become a writer; your needling words were the seeds that grew my little Palace of Flowers.

To my mother, a pragmatic woman, where I am an idealistic young dolt: you have been the engine fuelling my creative ambitions. Filling me with inner confidence and affirmation. I wouldn't be a writer without you.

And to Jamila—
From a sliver of your voice
I crafted a construct of a self
Precocious, wilful, soft
In her tender years

Thank you

Support *In the Palace of Flowers*

We hope you enjoyed reading this book. It was brought to you by Cassava Republic Press, an award-winning independent publisher based in Abuja and London. If you think more people should read this book, here's how you can support:

1. Recommend it. Don't keep the enjoyment of this book to yourself; tell everyone you know. Spread the word to your friends and family.

2. Review, review, review. Your opinion is powerful and a positive review from you can generate new sales. Spare a minute to leave a short review on Amazon, GoodReads, Wordery, our website and other book buying sites.

3. Join the conversation. Hearing somebody you trust talk about a book with passion and excitement is one of the most powerful ways to get people to engage with it. If you like this book, talk about it, Facebook it, Tweet it, Blog it, Instagram it. Take pictures of the book and quote or highlight from your favourite passage. You could even add a link so others know where to purchase the book from.

4. Buy the book as gifts for others. Buying a gift is a regular activity for most of us – birthdays, anniversaries, holidays, special days or just a nice present for a loved one for no reason... If you love this book and you think it might resonate with others, then please buy extra copies!

5. Get your local bookshop or library to stock it. Sometimes bookshops and libraries only order books that they have heard about. If you loved this book, why not ask your librarian or bookshop to order it in. If enough people request a title, the bookshop or library will take note and will order a few copies for their shelves.

6. Recommend a book to your book club. Persuade your book club to read this book and discuss what you enjoy about the book in the company of others. This is a wonderful way to share what you like and help to boost the sales and popularity of this book. You can also join our online book club on Facebook at Afri-Lit Club to discuss books by other African writers.

7. Attend a book reading. There are lots of opportunities to hear writers talk about their work. Support them by attending their book events. Get your friends, colleagues and families to a reading and show an author your support.